A W.
HEAT.

## ALSO BY JULIE HOUSTON

# A WEDDING AT HEATHERLY HALL

## Julie Houston

HEAD of ZEUS

*An Aria Book*

First published in the UK in 2024 by Head of Zeus Ltd,
part of Bloomsbury Publishing Plc

9 7 5 3 1 2 4 6 8

A catalogue record for this book is available from the British Library.

ISBN (PB): 9781803280080
ISBN (E): 9781803280066

Cover design: Jessie Price/HoZ

Typeset by Siliconchips Services Ltd UK

Printed and bound in Great Britain by
CPI Group (UK) Ltd, Croydon CR0 4YY

Head of Zeus Ltd
First Floor East
5–8 Hardwick Street
London EC1R 4RG

WWW.HEADOFZEUS.COM

*For my big sister, Valerie.*

# Prologue

The *Midhope Examiner* – Saturday October 15th 2022

*On this day*

For our ON THIS DAY feature this week, we are heading back eighty-six years to 1936 to resurrect a mystery that continues to fascinate and yet remains unresolved.

It was the evening of October 15th 1936, and the newly crowned Edward VIII, together with Mrs Wallis Simpson, was the honoured guest of Henry Astley, eleventh Marquess of Stratton, and his wife, at Heatherly Hall on the outskirts of the village of Westenbury. The Marquess of Stratton, allegedly wanting to show his allegiance to Edward when so many disapproved of the new king's relationship with his divorced American lover, Mrs Simpson, is known to have commissioned a fabulous and priceless jewellery set of necklace and matching earrings for the American divorcee. The future Duchess of Windsor's jewels were unique, not only due to the record price they would eventually fetch, but also because these pieces immortalised one of the most controversial love stories of modern times. The set, made from the famous Yorkshire Whitby jet, was to be presented to Mrs Simpson (whose fabulous collection would, in time, reach the highest world record for a single owner jewellery sale ever conducted) at a celebratory dinner to be held at Heatherly Hall in honour of the royal couple's visit to the area.

While the black Whitby jet is very beautiful, it is not, in itself, the most valuable or expensive of stones. However, this particular Jet Set, to be presented to Mrs Simpson by the then Marquess of Stratton, was reputed to have been studded with diamonds excavated from the Kollur mine in India, with one particularly ravishing stone seemingly hewn at the same time as the world-famous Koh-I-Noor diamond given to Queen Victoria in the 1840s. Named the Sah-I-Noor diamond, the Heatherly Hall stone was allegedly won in an evening of intense gambling in 1860 during the early days of the British raj in India by George Astley, ninth Marquess of Stratton, and had remained in the vaults of the Astley family bank in London. Until, that is, Henry, George's grandson, made the decision to honour Edward VIII's lover by having the diamond set into the Whitby jet necklace.

But here's the rub: on the evening of the gala dinner at Heatherly Hall, when Henry Astley went to fetch the Jet Set from his locked bedroom drawer ready to present to Wallis Simpson, he found the leather jewellery box empty. According to the story passed down through the decades, the Jet Set was never seen again. One would have imagined that, over the years, with the Sah-I-Noor diamond being so celebrated, it would eventually have reappeared in some form or other, whether in its original state or broken up. However, its disappearance remains a mystery...

# I

## Heatherly Hall, Westenbury, Yorkshire

*January*

'Do you not think it looks a bit, you know, *meaty*?' Hannah Quinn pulled a face as she poked suspiciously at the contents of the dish on the table in front of her with a knife.

'Don't worry, nothing in there's had even a sniff of an animal; it's a totally vegan haggis.' Rosa Rosavina smiled in her sister's direction. 'Lentils, mushrooms and oats and that's it. Stop poking at it like that; I'm not convinced it's going to stay in one piece before I get it to the table.'

'And stop complaining as well, Hannah,' Eva Malik, the third of the Quinn triplets added, moving Hannah to one side before shooting a dish of glazed carrots towards the haggis. 'Hell, that's hot.' She shook her fingers and reached for a bottle of wine. 'It's about time you learned to cook, Hans, especially if you insist on inviting hordes of people for Sunday lunch.'

'I just *had* to have a big lunch here at the hall for everyone, since it was Burns Night this week as well as Lachlan's birthday.' Hannah smiled.

'How's it going then?' Eva raised an eyebrow. 'You know, you and Lachlan?' She and Rosa glanced at each other before redirecting their eyes simultaneously towards Hannah. When an answer, re Hannah's six-month relationship with Lachlan, the hall's estate manager, was not forthcoming, Eva turned back to the bottle of wine in her hand.

'So, Eva,' Hannah eventually said, obviously not wanting to pursue the subject of her relationship with Lachlan, 'we're leaving it up to *you* to address the haggis.'

'Address it?' Eva stared. 'As in: "Sorry, Haggis, we welcome you here to Heatherly Hall, but I'm afraid we're moving with the times and you're vegan now?" Something along those lines? Blimey...' Eva broke off as Lachlan Buchanan strode through the ornate double doors of what had previously been the hall's ballroom.

'Blimey,' Eva said again, taking in Lachlan's kilt and sporran. Descending into a strong Yorkshire accent, she added, 'You've a grand pair o' legs on you there, love. There really is something about a man in a skirt.'

'*Kilt* please.' Lachlan threw Eva a pained look as he picked up a carving knife, waving it in her direction, and Eva stepped back in alarm. 'So, you Sassenachs...' he grinned '...this is what *should* happen: a previously designated reciter...' Lachlan raised an eyebrow at the triplets and waited '...ah, you want me to do it? I thought you'd never ask. So, a previously designated reciter,' he repeated, 'reads a poem over the haggis. A *guid whisky gill* is then offered to the piper, chef and reciter...'

'Hang on,' Eva interrupted, 'Rosa's the chef and you're the reciter. Who's the piper? Anyone here play the bagpipes?'

'Again, I thought you'd never ask.' Lachlan grinned, stretching his whole six foot over the back of an ancestral sofa – so that Rosa, Hannah and Eva automatically bent their heads in unison for a sneaky upskirt – before retrieving a set of pipes from behind it.

'Blimey.' Eva grinned for the third time in as many minutes as Lachlan attempted a few wailing notes. 'You kept that to yourself. And actually...' she winced as the whining lament reached some sort of climax '...maybe not a bad thing.'

'And then,' Lachlan continued, obviously enjoying himself,

'with some *alacrity*, the haggis is sliced open with a ceremonial dirk…' Lachlan put down his bagpipes and waved the knife once more '…though, to be fair, any old knife will do. The meal is then served with all its many courses, as well as copious helpings of *guid ale and whisky.*'

'Right. All its courses, Rosa?' Hannah and the other two turned expectantly to their village vicar.

'Soup, main and pud.' Rosa raised an eyebrow. 'And lucky to get that. I was so tired this morning, it was all I could do to drag myself out of bed, wash my face and take the ten o'clock Sunday service. Lucky there were no christenings or I might have ended up dropping the baby in the font.' Rosa yawned loudly.

'You're OK, aren't you?' Eva was concerned. Ever since Rosa had become ill with Hodgkin's lymphoma eight years previously, there'd always been the fear that her sister might fall ill once again. 'You've a new husband, new stepdaughter and you're racing around attending to everyone in the village, dashing about looking after your parishioners as well as cooking for Hannah. And you're surprised you're feeling tired?' Eva's eyes narrowed as she looked across at Rosa, sizing her up. 'Any nausea…?'

'Eva,' Rosa snapped. 'I'm *not* pregnant. You do know, you constantly eye me up like I'm some sort of prize breeding heifer every time I see you, don't you? You *know* I can't get pregnant the conventional way after the treatment for my cancer.'

'I'm sorry, I'm sorry.' Eva pulled a face of contrition as Hannah elbowed her crossly. 'It's just I know it's what you want, so badly. I promise I won't say another word. Or ever, ever ask you again. So,' she went on, 'I bet you've already been over to administer to Mum again as well, before you came on up here?'

'Well, you know Mum never misses church normally…' Rosa frowned '…but she wasn't there today, sitting in her normal pew with Virginia. Actually, Virginia wasn't there either.'

'Really?' Eva frowned. 'Never known that big sister of ours

miss the chance to prostrate herself in front of God and his judgement.'

'Bit bitchy that, Eva. Virginia *is* our sister...'

'Only by adoption,' Eva said curtly. 'I've never felt the same bond with Virginia I have with you two.' She scowled. 'In fact, she drives me mad.' She shook her head. 'Ever since it became common knowledge Bill wasn't actually my father, and Yves Dufort *was*, she's never missed an opportunity to try and get one over on me.'

'That's Virginia for you.' Hannah put down the Scotland-flag-decorated napkin she was attempting to origami into a thistle and drained her glass before reaching for the bottle of wine once more.

'I thought you were cutting down on the booze again, Hannah?' Eva raised an eyebrow.

'I have done,' Hannah said, cheerfully refilling her glass. 'I only drink at the weekend now.'

'Really?' Rosa frowned, glancing at Hannah's full glass. 'You had a couple of glasses...'

'Oh, don't go all vicarly on me, Rosa.' Hannah scowled. 'Anyway, back to Virginia... She's so envious, isn't she? Bitter even. She can't bear it that we three have been handed this place...'

'*On a plate*, were her words.' Eva grinned. '"You three have been handed Heatherly Hall *on a plate*." It's really getting to her, especially now the new art retreat here looks like it's going to be a success.'

'So how *was* Mum?' Hannah asked. 'Is she feeling any better?'

'Actually, she's a lot better.' Rosa smiled. 'It's Virginia who I find really hard work at the moment. I really don't know how Tim puts up with her.'

'Well, poor old Timothy's always done as he's told. That brother-in-law of ours really is incredibly wet.' Eva started laughing. 'Actually, probably just terrified of Virginia. I'll never understand how it wasn't Virginia who followed Grandpa Cecil into the church, rather than you, Rosa.'

'She once told me she'd seriously thought about it – she'd seen it as her calling, but didn't believe God or the parishioners would *ever* approve of female vicars.' Rosa grinned. 'Her way of telling me she doesn't think I'm any good at the helm of All Hallows.'

'Cheeky mare,' Eva sniffed. 'She doesn't improve with age, does she? Not like this bottle of wine.' Eva swirled the ruby red liquid around her glass, before placing the glass under her nose and inhaling deeply. 'Jolly glad Bill laid down all this wonderful stuff and left the lot to us.'

'Well, if it was up to Our Virginia, you'd be relinquishing your share of everything here, wine and all, Eva.' Hannah raised an eyebrow. 'She doesn't think it at all Christian that you're still hanging on in here now the DNA test proved you weren't actually Bill's natural daughter.'

'I don't profess, and never *have* professed, to be guided by any Christian values,' Eva snapped. 'Having once had a grandfather – and now a sister – running the village church, I long ago distanced myself from any religious dogma telling me how to live my life.' Eva, in the process of bringing the glass of wine to her mouth, placed it, instead, on the kitchen table while pulling herself up straight in the chair. 'Shall I pour it back in the bottle then? You know, if I'm taking what isn't now considered to be mine?'

'Oh, don't be so bloody sensitive.' Hannah laughed and shook her head in Eva's direction.

'Even if he *had* known you weren't his, Bill would have included you in his will,' Rosa soothed. 'He loved you just as much as he did me and Hannah.'

'You know,' Eva said, picking up her wine and taking a sip, clearly mollified. 'I've really hardly told *anyone* the truth about my being Yves Dufort's natural daughter rather than Bill's. Even when Yves came over from France to officially open the art retreat last month, he made no mention of who I was to the guests and journalists. And yet half the village appears to know.' She scowled and tutted. '*You* two haven't been telling everyone, have you?'

'Well, it's not a great secret, is it?' Hannah looked slightly guilty. 'And I'd have thought it's something to be proud of, to be the natural daughter of France's greatest living artist, rather than something to hide?'

'I'm not ashamed of being Yves Dufort's daughter – far from it – but I'd still rather Bill had been my biological dad, as we always thought he was. Especially as he left a third of his shares in this place to me.'

'It'll be Virginia mouthing off about it in the co-op or at Young Wives' meeting – anywhere she can get an audience,' Hannah said sagely.

'You know,' Rosa now said, 'Mum's hypochondria really is her hobby these days. And Dad just listens and sympathises.'

'He adores her, doesn't he?' Hannah said, almost wistfully, glancing across at Lachlan.

'Always has,' Eva agreed, 'despite her landing him with her sister's new-born triplets. Not many men would have adopted us the way he did.'

'I've been called up to her bedroom to say a final prayer over her more times than I can remember.' Rosa grinned. 'She always says she wants to go to her maker absolved of her sins...' Rosa broke off quickly to attend to the huge vat of Cullen skink simmering on the stove.

'Absolved of her sins?' Eva said, as she and Hannah stared at Rosa's back. 'You're not a Catholic priest, Rosa. And since when has Mum done anything sinful? Susan was always the good girl – a teacher, married lovely Dad, went to church regularly before she did the noble thing adopting us three new-borns when naughty little sister Alice got herself pregnant, even though they already had three-year-old Virginia and not enough money to go round.'

'Oh, I don't know.' Rosa, still stirring, shrugged nonchalantly.

'Actually, you *do* know,' Hannah interjected. 'Remember when she had "*a touch of HIV and was going to end up like Freddie Mercury*"? She told me she'd written letters to all four of us girls and we weren't to judge her too harshly. So, there is *something* there, you know.'

Rosa carried on determinedly with her careful soup-stirring. 'Mum's always had a bit of the drama queen about her. Anyway, she's absolutely fine now.'

'And you, Reverend Rosa Rosavina, need to sit down and take it easy.' Eva took the wooden spoon from Rosa's hand and stirred enthusiastically, slopping some of the contents of the pan onto the hotplate as she did so. 'So, Rosa, you're feeling tired? Any, you know? Sore…?'

'Eva, I'm *not* pregnant.' Rosa cut Eva off once more. 'You've *just* promised you would never, ever ask again…'

'OK, OK, sorry.' Eva wiped at the spilt soup with a dishcloth, silenced for a good ten seconds. 'But your frozen eggs in the clinic in Wimbledon, Rosa? Shouldn't you and Joe be making some decision about those…?'

She broke off as her two daughters, eight-year-old Laila and four-year-old Nora ran in, together with Chiara, Rosa's stepdaughter.

'I've been showing Chiara the rudie-nudies,' Laila boasted.

'Ladies with *no clothes* on.' Four-year-old Nora appeared scandalised. 'I don't know *why* they haven't not got their vests and pants on…' She turned. 'And why's Uncle Lachlan got a dress on?' Nora stared in fascination both at the kilt, Lachlan's hairy legs and the man himself as he stood over by the window overlooking Heatherly Hall's acres of park and farmland while endeavouring to get an actual tune out of the bagpipes.

'*Uncle* Lachlan?' Eva mouthed in Hannah's direction as the man in question turned away from them, put down the sulking bagpipes and bent to pull out a bottle of whisky from his bag. '*He's* getting his feet under the table,' she mouthed, amused. 'And, Chiara,' Eva went on, turning to Rosa's seven-year-old stepdaughter, 'what Laila has been showing you up in the long gallery is art. Beautiful artwork created by Bill Astley, the previous Marquess of Heatherly Hall.'

'Where is he now?' Chiara asked, eyes big as saucers.

'He died,' Laila interrupted importantly. 'And now my mummy and my Aunty Rosa and Aunty Hannah are a bit like King Charles and are in charge round here. And people have to do what they say.'

Chiara giggled at that but looked a bit nervous. 'And which one is the queen?' she asked looking at each of the triplets in turn. 'Is there a Queen of Heatherly Hall?'

Laila shook her head. 'No, of course not. But there *is* another marquess now,' Laila said knowingly. 'He's the *fourteenth* marquess...'

'Thirteenth,' Eva corrected her daughter.

'And where is *he*?' Chiara turned her blonde head in all directions apparently in the hope of manifesting some aspect of royalty.

'Nobody likes him,' Laila sniffed. 'He's called Jonny Astley and his wife is an awful loud American lady called Billy-Jo and Mummy says...'

'Enough, Laila. That's enough.' Eva raised an eye in her elder daughter's direction.

'But Mummy, you *said* so,' Laila argued, unwilling to let it go. 'Chiara, Jonny Astley was Bill's *real* son and because he was the leg... leg... hit... image... leghitimage... he was the *real* son and a man as well... he became the next marquess. But Bill left Heatherly Hall to Mummy and my Aunty Rosa and my Aunty Hannah because he loved them best and didn't like his real son, Jonny, and Jonny was very cross and slammed the door and he and Billy-Jo went back to America where they belonged.'

'Laila, enough. Take Chiara and Nora and go and wash your hands for lunch.' Eva gave Laila one of her looks.

'*My* real mummy's in Australia,' Chiara suddenly announced. 'And I'm going to see her soon.'

Eva looked across at Rosa who appeared to flinch at her stepdaughter's words, but then stood and smiled before bending to kiss Chiara's blonde head. 'Chiara, sweetheart,' Rosa was now saying, 'I'll explain all about Bill Astley and the hall to you properly when we get back to the vicarage this evening.' Rosa replaited Chiara's hair before tying the narrow pink ribbon around its end.

'Right,' Hannah said, returning from the far end of the room where the huge oak dining table was laid for the ceremonial Burns' supper feast. 'I know it's lunch rather than supper, but we're about ready to eat. Where are Joe and Andrea?'

'Joe's helping Andrea with the kiln in the outhouse,' Eva said. 'Apparently, it's not heating up as it should. And Daisy and Jude are coming too, you say? That's great, Hannah; I know how friendly you've become with her.'

Hannah nodded. 'Ever since Daisy's been working with her dad, Graham, she's the one who turns up to deal with the hall's livestock. We've really become quite good mates.' Graham was the village vet.

Eva glanced at her watch. 'What time did you tell them to come, Hannah?'

'Quarter of an hour ago. Daisy's probably got her hand up some cow and Jude will have been commandeered by one of his constituents complaining about the potholes in the road or machete-wielding thirteen-year-olds causing mayhem down on the council estate. God, I wouldn't be either a vet or an MP for any money.' Hannah glanced out of the tall window and down on to the formal gardens where, despite the cold wind, dark clouds and threat of rain, visitors to the café – Tea and

Cake – were still queuing for the hall's famous ginger flapjack and a welcome cup of tea.

'Oh,' she said, 'they're coming now. With Joe and Andrea. Right, is that it? Another glass of something and then food? I'm starving.'

## 2

'Sorry we're late!' Daisy Maddison walked into the room bringing with her a blast of cold air. 'Hell, it's not half cold out there; it's starting to rain too.'

'Where's Jude?'

'He's just helping Andrea and Joe with the kiln. I think they've finally got it working again. So...' Daisy turned to Eva. 'How's it all going with the lovely Andrea then? All good?' She lowered her voice as the three little girls came back into the room, pouring and spilling juice for themselves and bagging their seats at the table. 'He's bloody gorgeous. What is he again?'

'What *is he*?' Eva laughed.

'Where's he from?'

'His mum's Italian and dad's Russian. He was born in Moscow, but lived most of his adult life in Milan.'

'Blimey – Moscow to Milan to Midhope. How exotic is that?'

'Being a village vet not exotic enough for you?' Hannah laughed and held up the bottle of wine in Daisy's direction.

'Please.' Daisy removed her coat, threw it over the sofa and held out her hand for the glass of wine. 'Exotic? Standing in cow shit all day? Oh, I just seem to have been training *for ever*.' Daisy broke off to kiss Lachlan. 'Wow, you're looking very... very...'

'Very?' Lachlan raised an eyebrow.

'Scottish. Yeah, that's it, Scottish. And very lovely too.'

Daisy, though she'd spent hours alongside Lachlan helping with the estate livestock, had obviously only ever seen him in his work clothes. 'So, what *do* you wear under—?' She broke off as Joe Rosavina, Andrea Zaitsev and Jude Mansell made an appearance, followed by a tall, dark-haired man. The four women turned expectantly, none of them having any idea who the stranger might be.

'I'm afraid these are the hall's private quarters,' Hannah started. 'What were you looking for?'

'He's looking for Lachlan,' Joe said, glancing to where Lachlan was still contemplating his bagpipes.

'For me?'

'Sorry, Lachlan, we met last spring... I'm a day early...' The man's accent was heavily North American.

'Oh, apologies, didn't recognise you.' Lachlan moved over to the man, extending a hand. 'And yes, we were expecting you tomorrow. Zachary, isn't it?'

'I can go and come back tomorrow.' The man was clearly embarrassed. 'I don't want to intrude on your lunch. I've booked a room for the week at The Jolly Sailor down in Westenbury.' He hesitated, eyeing Lachlan's traditional national costume. 'Is it fancy dress?'

'Burns Night.' Lachlan smiled. 'Even though it's lunchtime and a few days late.'

'Look, I'll leave you.' The man made to retreat through the still-open door.

'No, no, come in. At least have a drink with us and get warm.' Lachlan turned to the others. 'This is Zachary Anderson...'

'Zac, please.'

'Zac's from... Maine, isn't it?'

Zac nodded.

'He was here at the hall for a day last spring. He's researching a book about old English ancestral homes. And,' Lachlan went on, 'I said you three would help him all you can with what you know of Heatherly's history.'

'Not much I'm afraid.' Rosa frowned. 'There are various books in the town's library, I believe, but, to my shame, I have to admit to knowing very little. What about you two?' Rosa turned to her sisters.

'A bit embarrassing really,' Hannah admitted. 'You know, to be running the place and not know much of its history. Bill never really appeared to know much either, did he? He was always far more interested in the present than the hall's past.'

'I'll come back tomorrow.' Zac again made to turn to leave.

'Have a drink,' Lachlan insisted.

'Stay for lunch,' Rosa insisted in turn. 'There's tons. Really. You're more than welcome. I'll lay another place for you.'

'No, absolutely not...'

'Absolutely, yes.' Hannah grinned across at the man. 'The more the merrier. And you'll get to hear Lachlan torturing the pipes.'

'Well, if you're sure?'

'Totally.' Rosa, Hannah and Eva spoke as one.

'Come on, have a drink,' Hannah said. 'Numb your senses before Lachlan assaults our ears with that bag of wind.'


'So, Zac,' Jude Mansell said, helping himself to bread and lifting his spoon, 'have you written many other books? Besides this one you're researching?'

'Several, actually. I'm based at the University of Maine – it's the state's only public research university – where I'm an associate professor of history.'

'Oh, you're not teaching at the moment?'

'I'm on a one-semester sabbatical: English history fascinates me – particularly pre- and post-industrial eighteenth-century history – and I just decided to bite the bullet and get the book I've always wanted to write actually researched.'

'Fabulous soup, Rosa,' Daisy enthused. 'What is it exactly?'

'Cullen skink.' Rosa smiled.

'Cullen stink?' Four-year-old Nora sniffed suspiciously at the contents of her bowl. 'Don't like this, Mummy.'

'It's fish,' Laila said knowingly. Showing off in front of the others that she knew the correct way to eat soup, as once taught her by Bill, Laila manoeuvred the monogrammed silver spoon across the bowl and away from her.

Obediently, Nora picked up her own spoon, copying Laila, but pulled a face as she sucked tentatively at its contents.

'So, which other ancestral homes are you researching, Zac?' Hannah asked, heading off Laila's incessant determination to be the centre of attention.

'Oh, the usual.' Zac smiled across at Hannah, while Rosa and Eva – noting the frisson of interest between their sister and this exceptionally handsome newcomer – exchanged glances.

'The usual?' Lachlan had obviously been aware of the longer-than-necessary glances between Hannah and Zac but smiled back pleasantly at the American.

'Oh, erm, Castle Howard, Harewood House, Chatsworth House. I intend working my way through Yorkshire over the next few months.'

'I think you'll find Chatsworth is actually in Derbyshire.' Lachlan smiled.

'I bow to your superior knowledge,' Zac replied, lowering his head slightly in the other man's direction as Hannah frowned across at Lachlan.

'Funnily enough,' Daisy said, 'I've been looking after Dad's dog, Malvolio, while Dad's away for the week. He's become incontinent...'

'Your dad has?' Rosa asked sympathetically. 'Become incontinent? Oh, the dog? Sorry!'

'What's in continent?' Nora, struggling with her soup, laid down the heavy spoon and took a large bite from her bread roll.

'Incontinent means he's going to live in France or Germany or Spain,' Laila said sagely.

'Is he? Why?' Nora frowned through her mouthful. 'Doesn't he like living with Daisy?'

'He's weeing a lot.' Daisy smiled. 'Where he shouldn't, Nora. So, I have to put a load of newspapers down for him. Anyway, going through the pile of old newspapers I found in Mum and Dad's utility, I came across an article about Heatherly Hall. It was in the *Midhope Examiner* – the "On This Day" article they run every weekend – and from last October. Did you know Edward VIII and Mrs Simpson actually stayed here?'

'Really? Here at Heatherly Hall? Gosh, how exciting is that?' Hannah gazed, almost reverentially, around the room. 'Mind you, the layout has been altered so much in the past forty years we can't be sure which were the original sitting rooms and bedrooms: probably what's now the conference centre and wedding venue, over in the west wing of the hall. I didn't even know Edward was actually crowned king?' she added. 'I thought he fell in love with Mrs Simpson and, when they wouldn't let him marry an American divorcee, he resigned?'

'Abdicated.' Jude laughed. 'He was king for just 325 days. He didn't manage even a year before he abdicated for the woman he loved.'

'So, this article,' Daisy said, spooning the last of her soup and wiping her mouth on her napkin, 'was about some mystery involving a piece of jewellery.'

'A jet set?' Hannah nodded. 'Jewellery made from Whitby jet? Yes, I remember Bill telling us the story when we were just little girls and Mum and Dad let us stay up here at the hall for Sunday lunch. Don't you remember?'

Rosa and Eva both shook their heads.

'You were always the one most interested in this place, Hannah,' Rosa said. 'You loved Heatherly Hall from the minute you set foot in it. Always nagging Mum and Dad to let us come up to see Bill.'

Eva nodded. 'Dad thought we should get to know our natural father, but Mum didn't want us to. She never came with us when

Dad brought us up to see Bill, did she? The thing is,' Eva went on, turning to the others in explanation, 'our mum's always been a bit jealous of Alice, because Alice was our birth mum, and, I guess, Mum was relieved that, most of the time we were growing up, Alice lived in the States and we had very little to do with her.'

'This all very confusing.' Andrea frowned. 'Pass the wine over, Eva – let's see if alcohol helps it make more sense.' He grinned at Eva and she took the bottle over to him, planting a kiss on his cheek as she poured the wine.

'Actually, you know…' Eva stood, the bottle at half-mast '…it is coming back a bit now. In fact, don't you remember, you two, Bill told us the story of the missing Jet Set and we went off all around the place, treasure hunting. Tapping at the oak panelling and desperately hoping to find a secret passageway. We never did.' Eva laughed, and lowered her voice. 'But we did end up in the attics where we'd been told we mustn't go. *And* came across Bill's artwork: the rudie-nudies that the girls have just discovered for themselves.'

Rosa frowned, trying to recall the stories Bill had tried to tell them. 'I have to say, I do seem to remember Bill mentioning something about it when we were teens. But, to be honest…' here Rosa actually laughed and glanced across at Joe, loving the fact that he was hers, that she'd adored him since she was sixteen '…I reckon we were more into boys and music than history at the time, and probably far too impatient to sit and take it all in.'

'You should have listened to Bill Astley.' Jude smiled. 'It really is quite a fascinating tale. One of the guys in the village, who's always helped with leafletting and so on, has talked to me about it in the past. When I told him I was coming round here for lunch, he insisted on telling it all again. I'm not convinced he knows as much as he thinks he does, but his name's Roy Newsome. Lives just behind The Jolly Sailor. He's always in the pub, having a pint. If you're interested in the whole story – perhaps you could hold an evening of local history or something here – he might be able to shed a bit more light on what actually happened.'

'If it happened back in 1936, this Roy bloke must be getting on a bit now?' Eva frowned.

'No, no,' Jude went on, 'Roy's well into his seventies. I think it was his dad who was around at the time, and was involved somehow.'

'*Involved?*' Hannah leaned forward. 'You mean this Roy reckons his dad had something to do with its disappearance?'

'I doubt it.' Jude laughed. 'If his dad had nicked a priceless set of jewellery intended for the king's mistress, I wouldn't have thought he'd have been singing from the treetops about it. I get the impression his dad was perhaps working up here at the hall when the Jet Set just disappeared into thin air.'

'To be quite honest,' Rosa went on, standing to help Joe clear the soup plates, 'I'm not convinced Bill knew a great deal about it either. I seem to remember him saying that there was a story about a necklace and earrings – I've never heard of it being referred to as the Jet Set, but I guess that's what you're talking about – that his father had commissioned in order to impress someone visiting the hall. Apparently, before he could present it to whoever, it disappeared and was never seen again. Bill was convinced that, knowing the little he did about his father, there probably never *was* such a jewellery set and Sir Henry Astley, the eleventh marquess, made up the story of it being stolen to get out of not actually having had the money to commission it in the first place.'

'Bill didn't get on with his father then?'

'He didn't really know him. Bill was a bit of an afterthought, I believe, and, by the time he was growing up, his parents – Henry and Winifred – were divorced and he was living in London with his mother who was originally from there. The war took off his two very much older brothers and he suddenly found himself inheriting both the title of the Marquess of Stratton as well as, at the time, a badly-in-need-of-repair Heatherly Hall. Quite a shock after his London life.'

'And now it's in your hands.' Jude's eyes gleamed with interest and excitement. 'You three actually own a historic hall.'

'Sorry, Jude.' Rosa laughed. 'That probably doesn't sit comfortably with your socialist principles? And, in truth, we certainly don't *own* Heatherly Hall – we're just looking after it for the trust. Deciding the best way forward to have it continue to pay for itself.'

Daisy nodded. 'It's a local legend, apparently, although I'm local and I'd never heard about it until I came across the old newspaper in Mum's utility. I was across at one of the farms up by Norman's Meadow yesterday and ended up asking the cowman there about it. Apparently, the legend of the Jet Set at Heatherly Hall rears its head every few years or so. You know, a bit like the Loch Ness monster?'

'*I* know, we could do a sort of murder mystery evening here and tell the story,' Hannah said excitedly.

'Someone was murdered?' Andrea asked, still confused by the discussion.

'No.' Eva laughed. 'Well at least I don't think so.'

'Alright – a mystery evening, then. Without the murder.' Hannah's enthusiasm wasn't to be diminished by the absence of a corpse.

'The problem is, Hans,' Eva said, 'no one is really sure what *did* happen. It *is* over eighty years ago. If you were planning on holding a sort of Agatha Christie mystery evening, with everyone dressed up, you'd have to use quite a bit of poetic licence.'

'We could get the local Amateur Dramatic Society in to act it out, then plant some cheap jewellery and let the audience have a treasure hunt round the hall and then supper, for £30 a head…'

'My dad's big into am-dram,' Daisy said enthusiastically.

'I'm still lost,' Andrea said plaintively. 'You Brits are bit strange. The men dress up in skirt, stab a pudding while reciting poetry over it and then want to get dressed up and act out some murder that happened a century ago.'

'No, no one was murdered.' Joe laughed. 'Have another glass of wine,' he offered, grinning as he passed over the bottle to Andrea.

'And my Granny Vivienne is too.'

'Is too, what?'

'Big into am-dram,' Daisy said proudly. 'In fact, she was a famous actress, on TV, in her day.' Daisy's eyes gleamed with pride. 'An evening dressed up, and acting out the mystery of the disappearing Jet Set in this fantastic hall would be right up her and my dad's street. And mine too, actually. Let's do it.'

'OK!' Hannah was just as excited. 'What do you think, Lachlan?'

'Well, it will need a lot of thought – a lot of planning...' Lachlan shook his head. 'We'll be bang in the middle of lambing season.'

'Hang on...' Hannah started feverishly scrolling through her phone '...right, one hundred years ago this March, Agatha Christie published her third book – *Murder on the Links* – and the second featuring Hercule Poirot. That's it,' she added in some triumph, 'we'll have a week in March celebrating the centenary of the life and works of Agatha Christie, culminating in our own production of *The Jet Set of Heatherly Hall* – in the style of Christie – followed by a treasure hunt – maybe a facsimile of the original Jet Set if we can find out more about it – topped off with a fabulous dinner. Forget £30 – we can charge £50 a head at least.'

'*I've* actually done quite a bit of community theatre.' Zac Anderson spoke for perhaps only the second time since sitting down for lunch.

'Is that the equivalent of our amateur dramatics?' Hannah asked, dimpling at the man.

'Sure.' He smiled back.

'Don't take too much on, Hannah,' Lachlan warned.

'Oh, it'll be *fine*.' Daisy, usually in league with Lachlan where the stock and the land were concerned, was now very much rooting for Hannah. 'In fact, it'll be wonderful.' She turned to Zac, patting his arm. 'And will you be around for the next couple of months to join us in rehearsal?'

'I fully intend being in the UK until the Easter break,' Zac said, holding Hannah's eye once again. 'It would be an honour to join you for weekly rehearsals if I'm near enough and if you think I can make a contribution.'

'Great stuff.' Hannah beamed at everyone around the table.

'OK,' Rosa said, as Joe and Eva jumped up to help her bring dishes and plates to the dining table. 'Crispy neeps and tatties cake as well as the glazed carrots. Lachlan? Drum roll for Lachlan please as he gives us a rendition on the bagpipes and then addresses the haggis…'

She broke off in surprise as the huge oak-panelled door leading to the outside long red-carpeted corridor was flung back on itself to reveal Virginia, the fourth of the Quinn sisters, standing in the doorway. Coatless, she was exceptionally wet – it had obviously been raining heavily – and her fair bob, usually so neat and without a hair out of place, was dripping.

'Virginia?' Rosa stepped towards her.

'You *knew*,' Virginia spat at her and, with a sinking heart, Rosa closed her eyes. 'Did you two know as well?' She swung round wildly, searching out first Hannah and then Eva. 'You all knew, didn't you? You effing bitches…'

## 3

'Virginia, what on *earth's* the matter?' Hannah spoke first as Rosa ushered their big sister from the dining room, and the other two followed on behind. Eva appeared stunned into silence, not only by the state their sister was in, but by the words she'd never before heard pass the usually straitlaced Virginia's lips.

'*She* knows.' Virginia glared at Rosa, before actually approaching her and jabbing one finger with its short, unvarnished nail at her sister's dog collar. 'And her a vicar too. You should be ashamed of yourself, *Reverend* Rosa.'

'Is this something to do with the missing Jet Set?' Hannah ventured. 'Have you known all along what happened to it, Rosa?'

'What?' Virginia wheeled round angrily to face Hannah and Eva. 'Jet Set? What *Jet Set*? And don't tell me you didn't know, you two. You three have never been able to keep anything from each other. But you kept it from *me*, didn't you?'

'Virginia,' Eva started, moving towards her, one hand held out in a gesture of comfort, 'is it Tim?'

'Is *what* my husband?' Virginia snarled.

'Well, that's just it. We don't *know* what.' Eva looked helplessly from Hannah to Rosa who was standing, her face totally ashen, her hands clutching the edge of a rather lovely Queen Anne polished table, white with the effort of doing so.

'So, Rosa, are you going to tell them? Or shall I?'

When Rosa appeared unable to speak, Virginia ran a hand through her rain-soaked hair and said, almost softly, 'Eva, do you remember the shock you had when that DNA test revealed you weren't Bill Astley's biological daughter, after all?'

'Well, yes, of course...' Eva frowned. 'Are you trying to tell me, Virginia, that it was wrong? That I *am* Bill's daughter, after all? Is that what this is all about?' Eva's face was hopeful.

'No, I'm NOT telling you that, Eva,' Virginia said coldly. 'The DNA was proof enough Alice Parkes was a total and utter tart, sleeping with Yves Dufort in France before having sex with Bill Astley up amongst those nudes in the attic twelve hours later. Isn't that the story?'

'Hang on, are you trying to tell me it *was* a story?' Eva leaned forwards, her face set.

'Not at all.' Virginia paused for effect. 'I've just found out... Dad is *not* actually my dad.' There was a gleam of triumph in Virginia's eye.

*Oh, hell*, Rosa thought. *She's enjoying every single minute of this.*

'He's *not*?' Eva flinched. 'So, who the hell is then?'

'The Marquess of Stratton.' Virginia's tone was imperious.

'Hang on. Bill was *our* dad. Well,' Hannah amended, 'mine and Rosa's dad anyhow. Obviously, the DNA test proved he wasn't *Eva's* dad.'

'Alright, alright, don't rub it in, Hannah.' Eva, always unhappy at being reminded that Yves Dufort's Usain Bolt of a sperm had snuck in before Bill's and she, herself, the result of that winning race to one of Alice's three eggs, scowled across at her sister. 'Virginia, what the hell are you talking about? Have you been drinking? Are you on something? Are you trying to tell us we're quads, not triplets...? What? *What...?*'

'*What* Virginia is trying to tell you...' All four sisters wheeled round as Richard Quinn, the triplets' adoptive father, walked quietly into the room, his hands in his mac pocket, his thinning hair as wet as Virginia's. He broke off, unable to go on, and then attempted a smile, rubbing at his face and went on. 'What Virginia is trying to tell you, girls, is that I'm not her biological father.'

'Hang on, Dad,' Eva snapped, 'you're definitely not *our* – me, Rosa and Hannah's – biological father. Why suddenly are you saying you're not Virginia's dad either? And who's told you?' Eva turned to Virginia crossly. 'Have *you* just told him this for some reason? Just look at him. Look what you've done to him.' Richard had lowered himself into one of the ancient but comfortable settees, head in hands.

'*Told* him?' Virginia sneered. 'Dad didn't need *telling*. And I think that's the worst thing about all this. Dad knew all along...'

'No, Virginia,' Richard said tiredly. 'I didn't *know* all along. I just sort of *guessed* all along. You know, I never had any proof Bill Astley was your biological father as well as the others here... well, Rosa and Hannah anyway. I never challenged your mother with it.'

Eva turned to Rosa. 'So, Rosa, are you telling us you knew this? You've kept it from us?'

'It wasn't my secret to tell,' Rosa replied. 'Mum made me swear I'd never tell anyone about it.'

'And when was this?' Hannah asked. 'How long have you known?'

'The day the DNA test came back, just over a year ago, and it showed Eva wasn't Bill's biological daughter after all, Mum came round that night. Dad, here, was ill in bed and she came round, said she needed to get something off her chest at last and she told me what had happened.'

'And what had?' Eva's face was white. 'Had Mum been having an affair with Bill? While she was married to Dad? Before Bill met Alice?'

Rosa shook her head. 'Not an affair. No, absolutely not.'

'What then?' Eva asked.

'This was three years or so before Alice was having the

weekend back home in Westenbury when she met Bill and… well you know the story: Alice had a one-night stand with Bill here at the hall, and we were conceived.' Rosa exhaled and continued. 'Three years *before* this happened, Alice was living abroad, desperately trying to carve a name for herself in Paris and Mum was in a bit of a bad way…' She glanced across at Richard who gave an imperceptible nod in agreement. 'Mum knew, after seven years of trying for a baby with Dad, nothing was happening. Nothing was *going* to happen. She was teaching at Little Acorns in the village and apparently there was a baby shower after school for a member of staff and she was beside herself with the distress of not being able to get pregnant herself, when it was all she'd ever wanted.

'She escaped, crying, from the baby celebrations in the staffroom, up to her classroom, to find Bill waiting for her to discuss how she wanted him to go about some history talk he was going to give her class before they were up at the hall on a visit the following week. They were doing knights and castles apparently. Anyway, Mum was terribly upset about her failure to get pregnant, and totally broke down. Bill comforted her, and one thing led to another.'

'In Mum's classroom?' Hannah asked as she and Eva stared in disbelief.

'In her stockroom, apparently.'

'Mum, herself a vicar's daughter, had sex with the Marquess of Stratton in her stockroom while she was married to Dad? Bloody hell, I don't believe it!'

'Well, I suggest you do believe it…' Virginia smiled coldly, breaking off as Laila, with Chiara in tow, opened the sitting room door and made to join them.

'Mummy…' Laila started, her brown eyes wide as she took in her mother, aunts and now her grandfather, jump apart and become suddenly silent. 'What's the matter? Has somebody died? Has my daddy died?' Ever the drama queen, Laila appeared genuinely frightened.

'It's fine,' Eva soothed. 'Daddy's fine. He's at home with Yasmin and Farhan and absolutely fine. Look, go back in to the others in the kitchen and, if you've all finished Aunty Rosa's lovely haggis, ask Daisy or Uncle Joe...' Eva attempted a smile '...or both of them to sort the pudding. Is there pudding, Rosa?'

'A pudding?' Virginia hissed, in the manner of Lady Bracknell. 'You're able to discuss *pudding* after what I've just told you?'

'Virginia, for heaven's sake.' Eva glared at her elder sister before clapping her hands firmly round Laila's ears and bundling both her daughter and Chiara back towards the dining room.

'Cranachan.' Rosa pulled a hand through her long dark hair, before turning to face Virginia.

'I *beg* your pardon.' Virginia whirled round once more towards Rosa who took a step back. 'Don't you dare swear at me, Rosa.'

'What?' Rosa put out a hand to Virginia before shaking her head and then speaking as if reading from a recipe book. 'Cranachan is a classic Scottish dessert. It's a beautiful medley of double cream, toasted oats, raspberries, honey and a great big slosh of whisky. It's the perfect ending to a Burns Night feast.' She gave a huge sigh. 'Apparently.'

'What's going on?' Joe appeared in the doorway. 'Rosa?' He made his way across the room. 'What is it? What's happened? Is it your mum?'

'Oh, Joe Rosavina.' Virginia sneered, folding her arms and looking hard at Rosa's husband. 'Yes, well *you'd* understand all this, wouldn't you? One-night stands resulting in unwanted pregnancies!'

'I think you'll find, Virginia,' Richard interrupted quietly from his settee, 'that what your mum did all those years ago resulted in a very much *wanted* pregnancy. She wanted *you*, Virginia. Wanted a baby so much, she was prepared to... you know...' Richard faltered, unable to go on. 'Put it this way, sweetheart, if your mum hadn't seen an opportunity...'

'Seen an opportunity? Oh, for heaven's sake, Dad.' Virginia shook her head.

'Yes, seen and seized an opportunity, Virginia, or *you* wouldn't be here.'

'Part of me wishes I wasn't.' Virginia put up a trembling hand to her forehead.

'Oh, don't be so bloody dramatic, Virginia,' Eva snapped. 'What you're miffed about is that Rosa knew Bill was your biological father and you didn't.'

'What? Bill was *your* father as well?' Joe stared across at Virginia before turning to Rosa. 'And you knew this, Rosa?'

'Oh, don't come the innocent with me, Joe Rosavina. Rosa must have told you.' Virginia actually prodded rudely at Joe's arm.

'I most certainly did not,' Rosa said gently. 'I repeat, it wasn't my secret to tell...' She trailed off as the door from the corridor opened once more and Timothy, Barty and Bethany, Virginia's husband and adolescent offspring, trooped into the room.

'Hell,' Hannah muttered in an aside to Eva, 'it's getting more like an Agatha Christie novel every second.'

'No one's been murdered...'

'Give it time.' Hannah felt the start of a hysterical titter trying to make its escape and she swallowed.

'I'd have said *EastEnders* myself.' Eva nodded.

'I told you not to come over to the hall,' Timothy was saying now to Virginia. 'Not until you'd got over the initial shock of all this and could discuss it calmly and logically.'

'Since when has Virginia ever done anything Timothy's suggested?' Hannah whispered to Eva and then, remembering all her guests in the next room, presumably trying to work out just what was going on as they ate Rosa's Cranachan, she turned to Virginia. 'Look, Virginia, we can see what a terrible shock you've had. I can't begin to imagine what you're feeling now, knowing what you've just been told, but, really, it's Mum and Dad you should be talking to, not us three.' She glanced across at

Rosa, still deathly pale and now holding Joe's hand. Of the three of them it had always been Rosa who'd hated confrontation of any sort, while Eva had never been averse to – welcomed in fact – a jolly good, in-your-face showdown. Hannah, as always, was somewhere in the middle.

'Hannah's right,' Timothy almost pleaded. 'Come on, Virginia, I've got your coat. And look, they've got guests here...'

'Well, they would have, wouldn't they? All three playing the *big I am* up here at Heatherly Hall and *entertaining*. I see *we* weren't on the guest list.' Virginia wheeled round to face Eva. 'And when *she* has absolutely no right to inherit anything from *my* father – and *she*...' Virginia turned round, almost comically, to glare at Rosa '...the oh so virtuous woman of God, has been determined to deny me my rightful inheritance.' Virginia shook off both Tim's arm and her best navy Jacques Vert winter coat. 'I think you'll find, Eva,' she continued, turning once more to Eva, 'that any share of the rights to Heatherly Hall, now legally belong to me and not you.'

'Virginia, come on. Enough now.' Richard Quinn patted his eldest daughter's arm, but his voice was firm. 'I think you need to come back home with me and apologise for the things you said to your mother.'

'Apologise to Mum? After she's kept this from me all my life? I'm never speaking to her again.'

'Well, to be fair, Virginia, if you hadn't been snooping around in her bedside table...' Richard started.

'Snooping? I wasn't *snooping*. I was tidying up the packets of pills and bottles of medicines to try and make her feel a bit better. When I found the letter addressed to me, there was no way I wasn't going to open it.'

'Virginia,' Richard said tiredly, 'those four letters – one for each of you girls – specifically say, on the front of the envelopes, to be opened only on your mother's death.'

'Well, Mum said she was on death's door.' Virginia had the grace to look slightly embarrassed.

'Mum's been saying she's off to meet her maker on a regular basis ever since we were kids,' Hannah pointed out. 'She's always been a total hypochondriac. You know that. We've teased her for years about it.'

'You just couldn't resist it, could you, Virginia?' Eva said crossly. 'You were dying to know what was in those letters – the four of us have always known she'd written letters to us to be opened when she was no longer with us – and you were just dying to know if she was leaving her string of pearls to you, instead of one of us three.'

'Well, as the eldest of the four of us, as well as being the only *real* daughter, I would hope that...' Virginia broke off as the door from the dining room opened once more.

'Mummy?' Four-year-old Nora's voice was accusing. 'Are you coming back in? Uncle Lachlan and Andrea and the... the other man have drunk a lot of whiksy and they're singing songs. And I need a wee and Laila won't come with me to the toilet because she says there are ghosts down the long red corridor.'

# 4

'Hello?' Hannah tapped the shoulder of the man sitting alone at the table in the far corner of The Jolly Sailor, the main pub in Westenbury village. 'Is it Roy?'

The man turned, draining his pint as he did so and looking with some suspicion at the attractive dark-haired girl who was smiling down at him. 'Might be. Who's asking?'

'Jude Mansell – you know, our local MP? – said I'd more than likely find you in here, sitting at this table in the corner.'

'Oh aye? And is that a problem then?'

'Not at all.' Hannah laughed at the thought. 'In fact, I'll join you if I may?'

'Depends what you're after, love. Collecting for charity or summat, are you?' Roy Newsome patted his jacket pocket. 'Not much in here, if it's money you're after.'

'Jude said you're the person to talk to about any goings-on in the village.'

'Goings-on? Nowadays?' Roy sniffed. 'Depends what you want.'

'Look, can I get you a drink?' Hannah asked, waving to get the attention of the landlord as she moved to stand at the bar. 'I'm going to have one.'

'I'll have a half with you, love, if you're paying.' The man proffered his glass and Hannah ordered Tetley's for Roy and a large glass of white wine for herself before turning back as he carried on talking. 'So, if you're not collecting for the poor, or the RSPCA, what *are* you after?' He frowned. 'You're not from the *Midhope Examiner*, are you? Or the Inland Revenue?'

'No, not at all.' Hannah paid for the drinks, took a sip of the slightly warm, very acidic wine and, wincing slightly, perched herself on the leatherette-topped stool at Roy's side, taking in the slight grey-haired man who, she reckoned, must be in his late seventies. 'Sorry.' She thrust a hand in the man's direction. 'Hannah Quinn. Jude said you might know something about some missing jewellery?'

'I beg your pardon?' Roy glared in Hannah's direction. 'You accusing me of pinching some jewellery?' He pronounced the word joo-ler-y.

'No, no! Gosh no, course not.' Hannah felt herself go slightly pink. 'I'm chair of the management committee up at Heatherly Hall. Jude's a friend of mine – he said I should come and talk to you.'

'That's alright then.' Roy sniffed again but didn't expand further.

'So...' Hannah was eager to explain her business to the man sitting in front of her. 'Jude said you were the best person to talk to about the missing Jet Set up at Heatherly Hall? About ninety years ago? When Edward VIII was staying at the hall? The king who abdicated?'

'You don't have to explain who's who in history, love. I know who Edward VIII was. And that American divorcee wife of his an' all.'

'The thing is, Roy,' Hannah said, warming to her theme, 'we – the management committee at the hall – know very little really about its history, and, I'm afraid, absolutely *nothing* about this missing Jet Set. We're planning on having an Agatha Christie type mystery evening up at the hall around Easter time. We're going to get the local am-dram society in to act it out. But before we can do that, you know, before we can actually *write* the script for the production, we need to know what really happened. I mean, did it ever even exist? Or is it just one of those stories that's been passed down the generations until no one's sure what's true and what's legend? You know, a bit like Robin Hood?'

'Robin Hood?' Roy frowned. 'Where does *he* come into this?'

'No, no, I'm not saying it was Robin Hood pinched the Jet Set...'

'Well, I'm glad to hear that, love, because, as far as I know, there were no outlaws stealing from the rich to give to the poor up on yon moors around the hall. Robin Hood was around way afore Edward VIII was on the throne...' Roy took a good long drink of his full glass '...although Edward wasn't on it long enough to warm his arse, never mind make a difference as to what was going on in the world at the time.'

'Right.' Hannah tried once again. 'So, Roy, what do you know about this Jet Set then?' She leaned forward, holding Roy's eye. Roy simply eyed her back for a good few seconds before relenting.

'My dad – Frank – knew a lot more than he ever let on.'

'Did Frank work up at Heatherly Hall then? Was he employed there?'

'My dad? Work for the toffs up at the hall?' Roy gave a bark of laughter. 'Not he.'

'Oh?'

'Listen, love, let me tell you, right now, what my dad was like. What he believed to be right and proper. As I do myself. That's why I like young Jude Mansell: good socialist principles, has the lad.'

'So, your dad was a bit of a political animal, was he?' Hannah smiled in Roy's direction.

'Aye, I suppose you could call him that. Not that it did him much good. It wasn't easy standing up for what you believed was right, back in the twenties and thirties, you know.'

'Are you able to tell me what happened?'

'Well, as much as I know. If you're thinking I can tell you exactly what happened to that Jet Set, love, then you're going to be disappointed. There was only one person who knew exactly where it ended up – as far as my dad was concerned, anyroad – and she came to a sticky end.'

'*She?* Blimey.' Hannah leaned forward.

'Thirsty work all this talking.' Ron raised an eye as well as his glass.

'Let me get you another.' Hannah jumped up.

'It's alright. My round.' Roy smiled across at her and reached for his jacket. 'I always pay my way. Another of them wines, is it? Hang on and I'll tell you all about my dad.'

'Oh, wait two minutes, Roy. My sisters've just come in. I did ask them to meet me here – I hope that's OK?' Hannah turned, beckoning the other two over.

'Your sisters?' Roy looked up in surprise as Rosa and Eva made their way across the bar once they'd spotted Hannah. 'How many are there of you?'

'There's the three of us – we're triplets, all of us are on the management committee of Heatherly Hall. And, there's our big sister Virginia as well. But she's not.'

'Not what?' Roy looked puzzled.

'Well, she's not a triplet. And she doesn't have anything to do with the hall. Well, not at the moment, anyway...' Hannah trailed off.

'Right.'

'But Rosa – she's the village vicar...'

'Aye, I can see that for myself,' Roy said, taking in Rosa's dog collar.

'...and Eva, who is still working part time at Malik and Malik – you know the village dentist? Well, we're triplets.'

'Fancy.' Roy stared across at the newcomers before shifting his glance back again to Hannah.

Once Rosa and Eva had bought drinks at the bar, introductions were made and coats and scarves abandoned, Eva jumped in straight away with: 'So, what did your dad have to do with the Jet Set, Roy?'

All three girls stared in anticipation as Roy started talking. 'I was just explaining to Hannah here, it was October, 1936, and my dad, Frank, had taken himself off to London.'

'Oh?' Hannah interrupted. 'For a holiday?'

'A holiday?' Roy gave Hannah such a look she had to bury her face in her glass of wine. 'People round here, working in the mills, didn't usually get as far as London. Blackpool for a week if you were lucky. Anyhow, my dad had gone down to London – first time he'd ever been to the capital – because they knew Oswald Mosley's cronies were marching.'

'Right.' Hannah frowned. 'But, what's any of this to do with the Heatherly Hall Jet Set?'

'I'm just getting to it. Have a bit of patience: if you want a proper tale, you have to understand the background and you have to understand the effect all this had on my dad. So, that were...' Roy frowned, thinking '...Sunday, October 4th, 1936 and, as soon as my dad was back in Westenbury, he was at it again.'

'At it?'

'The Jarrow Marchers? You must have heard of them?'

Rosa and Hannah nodded somewhat dubiously but Eva said, 'Funnily enough, I've just been reading a biography of Ellen Wilkinson, the MP for Middlesbrough – only one of four women Labour MPs at the time – who walked some of the way with the men. I didn't realise the marchers actually made their way through Leeds and Barnsley.'

'Well, that's the whole thing I'm saying,' Roy went on proudly. 'My dad joined them.'

'How did your dad manage to get time off from work to go to London and then to Barnsley?' Hannah asked.

'The mill workers had all been put on short time, as it were called in them days. No work, no money coming in. Anyway, my dad was a young lad – only twenty year old or so – and he was boiling mad at the injustice being done to working men. When he saw these two hundred men, decent men, mind, marching on their tired feet with still nearly two hundred miles or so to go before London, he said something in his head sort of exploded. Probably, if he'd been born a lot later and had had an education, he'd've ended up standing for the Labour Party. He'd have made a good MP, an' all.' Roy's eyes filled briefly with unshed tears. 'He was a right decent man.'

'That's why you get on so well with Jude Mansell?' Rosa asked gently, patting his arm.

'Suppose.' Roy nodded briefly. 'He was a nice-looking lad, my dad, too, in his day. Had all the lasses after him, apparently. You know, not just full of fire and passion, but a right handsome lad into the bargain. Anyhow, one of these lasses worked up at Heatherly Hall.'

'Oh?' All three triplets moved in towards Ron as he continued his story.

'Aye. Jeanie Haigh. Poor lass. She was, as far as I can make out, in love with my dad. She'd have done anything for him, apparently… And, I reckon she did…'

# 5

## Heatherly Hall, Westenbury, Yorkshire

### *Wednesday October 14th 1936, 7.30am*

The heart-shaped leaves on the avenue of tall lime trees she was hurrying through were already turned from their summer acid green to the warm autumnal hues of sepia, russet and amber. Winter often came early to the outskirts of the village of Westenbury, but especially to Heatherly Hall, standing steadfast in its acres of grounds, the cold northern winds sweeping down from the Pennines to the west, and across from the North Sea to the east. There'd already been miserably cold rain, early frosts and even a slight smattering of snow, long before any was seen in the neighbouring cities of Manchester and Leeds or even the nearby town of Midhope. Out here, away from the hub of the village, the rural, unsheltered acres of moorland and agricultural land stretched for miles, broken only by the occasional farmstead, hamlets of cottages, enough sheep to keep the woollen mills in business seemingly for ever and the long metallic scar of the main railway line from Manchester to Leeds.

Jeanie Haigh was late for work. She'd only been employed up here at the hall since leaving Goodners' woollen mill at the end of August – to the fury of her dad who'd got her a job in the weaving shed, working alongside girls she'd left school with, two years earlier. She'd hated every minute of mill life: the deafening clattering of the great looms, the all-day standing and the stifling atmosphere of exposed shafting and belt-driven pulleys. She'd tried to learn how to lip-read – without this skill, you were totally isolated – but had never managed it, maybe because she wasn't overly interested in the other weavers' conversations, which appeared to revolve around the coming Saturday night dances or which of the *tattler* lads, apprenticed to solve the looms' mechanical problems, they fancied the most. Worst of all was the pernicious reek of oil, greasy wool and sweat attacking her every sense until she could stand it no longer and she had walked out.

Before she'd gone home to face her dad's wrath, she'd walked the three miles from Goodners' up to Heatherly Hall on the off chance there might be work for her either in the kitchens or as a cleaner. She knew Vera and Nancy, who'd both been in her class, had worked up at the hall since leaving school. At least the hall was only half a mile or so from where she lived down on Railway Terrace; it would only take a fifteen-minute walk across the fields to get to her new job each day.

The very next morning she'd started work in the hall's kitchens; the girl whose place she'd been given had, according to the gloomy cook ruling her downstairs domain with the tight rod of a European dictator, gone down with pneumonia and not been seen since. Finding herself working at Heatherly Hall had gone only a little way to mollify her father who'd said she was barmy leaving a bloody good job to pander to the idle upper classes who wouldn't know a day's hard labour if it came up and bit them on their soft, white, feckless arses.

And, now, not even six weeks later, she knew she couldn't stand *this life* much longer either, and was wondering what working in one of the large department stores in Leeds – Schofields or the newly opened Lewis's, both on the Headrow – would be like. At least she wouldn't have to be putting on her pinny and scrubbing sinks and peeling mountains of potatoes and cleaning slug-filled cabbages from the hall's kitchen gardens.

She didn't mind the hard work – it wasn't that. It was just the whole injustice and inequality of the English class system where, depending on the luck of the draw, you were either lording it up at the top, or cleaning up the mess left casually and carelessly by the toffs *lording it at the top*.

Jeanie picked up speed as she ran along the avenue of trees. She'd always been the best runner at school whenever they'd been taken up to the Jubilee Fields for what amounted to little more than a quick sprint round, their dresses tucked into their pants, while the boys at least played football. Bit different from the girls who'd passed their eleven plus (and whose parents could afford the uniform) and went to Midhope Grammar School for Girls. On the way up to the municipal playing fields, Jeanie's class had had to walk the gauntlet of acres of manicured green, where the daughters of local solicitors, doctors and accountants played hockey, lacrosse and tennis.

Life hadn't been fair then – Jeanie knew she'd have been a whizz with a lacrosse stick – and, as she walked round to the back of the hall and in through the kitchen door, glad, at least, to leave the drizzle and unseasonably chilly October morning behind her, she knew it was certainly no better now.

'Jeanie, you've to get yourself upstairs to madam's bedroom.' Mrs Walters, the lugubrious cook pounded the huge lump of dough on the cold marble as though it were madam's head. 'Mrs Prescott says to get up there this minute. She came down while you were in the lav.'

'Upstairs?' Jeanie frowned. 'I don't *do* upstairs.' Four hours into her morning's work, she was actually quite enjoying making pear and ginger chutney, under the cook's directions, from the glut of fruit in the hall's orchards.

'Don't you be under any daft impression you're about to be promoted to upstairs lady's maid. You've to take a bucket and soap up with you. She's seemingly spilt the pot of chocolate I sent up ten minutes ago. All over that ridiculously expensive cream carpet – silk apparently – she only had fitted last week.

More money than sense, that one. She's in a right tizz, what with the visitors coming tomorrow.'

'I don't believe the king and Mrs Simpson are actually coming here.' Jeanie pulled a face. 'Why would they come out to a bloody cold place like this when they could be swanning off to the South of France? I'd love to go to France,' she added wistfully.

'Wouldn't we all.' For once, Mrs Walters was in agreement with her. 'Mind you, they eat funny foreign stuff over there.'

'What are you cooking up for them tomorrow then?' Jeanie asked, looking round. Mrs Walters didn't appear to be in the throes of a huge amount of culinary creativity.

'Not me, love. The marquess has hired some fancy chef from Leeds. He's arriving later this afternoon and you and me and the others'll have to get out of his way, into the little kitchen across the corridor. Mind you, I've to prepare food for all the king's hangers-on: you know, his bodyguards, his chauffeur, Wallis Simpson's maids and the like. They'll be eating in here with us, and Mrs Prescott will be looking after them all. She's getting herself into a right panic about it an' all. You know, all of the king's retinue...' she pronounced it retinoo '...with their London ways, thinking they're better than any of us up here. And it's not even as if they're staying the night.'

'Doesn't this Leeds cook...'

'Chef,' Mrs Walters corrected.

'...want us to help then?'

'Apparently not,' Mrs Walters sniffed. 'At least not with the upstairs' food. He's bringing six of his minions to look after the preparations.'

'Six? Blimey. To make a meal for just twelve of them? Bit of a cheek that, isn't it?' Jeanie felt a bit sorry for the cook. 'Aren't you a bit offended? I mean, you've cooked for more than that before now, haven't you?'

'Me? Offended? Not in the least.' Jeanie could see, by the way she was manhandling the dough, and the grim expression on her face, that the cook most certainly *was* offended, her long sharp nose utterly put out of joint. 'Last thing *I'm* wanting to do is get myself into a panic cooking for the king.' Mrs Walters gave the dough a final thump before dumping it unceremoniously into a large oiled mixing bowl, covering it with a clean tea towel and parking it near the stove. 'Anyhow, it's not like it used to be years ago when I was one of the kitchen maids here. We had some right grand dinners then, I can tell you. King George stayed here for a couple of days with his lordship, but it was always his younger brother, the new King Edward, who the marquess was right friendly with. His lordship and the new king were born in the same year apparently, and then met when they were at Oxford. And then they both ended up in the Grenadier Guards together. Oh yes, right mates, pair of 'em. Eh, never mind gassing here with me. Get that bucket and get yourself upstairs to madam's bedroom.'

'Can't Edith or Mary do it? I'm in the middle of this chutney.'

'Mary's in the silver room with Mr Baxter, polishing everything in sight for tomorrow. And Edith? She's as daft as a brush, that one,' the cook said unkindly. 'Anyhow, I've got her trying to unblock the sink in the pantry. She's wet through – got more muck on herself than she's got out from the plughole. And madam's got company up there – her sister Mrs Casterton's come up from London for the occasion, wanting to hobnob with the king along with the rest of them. Mrs Prescott says it's you who's to go up there. So get a move on, or Mrs P'll be after you as well. You know your way?'

Jeanie found the large galvanised bucket she always used to mop the kitchen floor, filled it with hot water and found a new cake of green soap. She'd no idea if it was going to be the right stuff to use, but neither Vera nor Nancy, the housemaids who she'd been at school with, appeared to be around to either ask, or to help, and she didn't know any of the other staff. Mrs Prescott – the housekeeper – and Mr Parkin – the marquess's valet – were obviously up to their ears with preparations for the forthcoming royal visit the following day and wouldn't want disturbing to ask the best way to get chocolate out of a new cream silk carpet.

Jeanie climbed the stone stairs from the kitchens to the main body of the hall where a crowd had gathered around temporary scaffolding erected with the intention of cleaning the hall's renowned and celebrated giant chandelier. Instructions and suggestions were being sent skywards towards the fixture whose mammoth girth, awash with sparkling crystal, appeared beyond reach. She stopped to watch Nancy, below, intent on beating the living daylights out of the hand-knotted Persian and Turkish rugs, while Vera went round with the Goblin vacuum cleaner.

She climbed the marble stairs from the hall, and then another flight, and saw she was now above the chandelier and able to look down into its scintillating, shimmering radiance. Jeanie realised the whole enormous structure was fixed to an ornate mezzanine ceiling and she stopped to gaze in wonder at this amazing feat of engineering. How clever men were – she'd bet anything it was a man – to design and hang such a beautiful structure, and she wished, not for the first time, she'd paid more attention in the maths and science lessons – inadequate as they were – at school.

Sighing, she continued her ascent. No one took any notice of her as she climbed the next set of steps – carpeted in red this time – swearing under her breath as the sharply edged bucket cut into her shin and hot water slopped over and down her black-stockinged legs. Sweating slightly now, she made her way along the corridor where she knew Winifred Astley – Lady Stratton – had her bedroom and private sitting room. But which one was hers?

Jeanie gazed round in wonder at the tapestry chairs and oil paintings, at the frescoed ceiling and at the – she counted them under her breath – ten closed doors ahead of her. Which bloody one was she supposed to be going to? She put down the heavy bucket, straining to hear any voices that might indicate exactly which was Lady Stratton's bedroom with the now-chocolate- stained carpet in need of a good scrub.

'Oh, there you are. Have you come to clean the carpet?' A door to Jeanie's left opened just a few inches and a woman she'd never seen before beckoned her in. This must be Lady Stratton's sister, Mrs Casterton. 'Come on, before the marquess sees what a mess we've made.' She laughed slightly, pulled a face and, looking down the corridor both ways, opened the door further to allow Jeanie and her bucket entry.

Blimey, Jeanie thought. How the other half live. Their house down on Railway Street could have fitted twice into Lady Stratton's bedroom itself. Did she share it with the marquess? she wondered, as the woman led her forward. Or did he have his own bedroom as well? But came a-visiting whenever he wanted his marital rights? Marital rights: *conjugal* rights, apparently. That's what they were called. Jeanie knew all the proper terminology because she'd been reading a book called *Married Love* – in secret. Her mum, Janet – a straight-talking Glaswegian who'd come south to find work in the West Yorkshire woollen mills and met and married her dad then had Jeanie and brother and sister – would have called the book, written by some woman called Marie Stopes, mucky. It was a bit old-fashioned now, but its tattered pages had done the round of the weaving shed along with the rhyme, very pertinent to herself:

*Jeanie, Jeanie, full of hopes,*
*Read a book by Marie Stopes,*
*But, to judge from her condition,*
*She must have read the wrong edition.*

Not that she, Jeanie, was going to end up with any unwanted kid. She'd read her Marie Stopes; knew all about rubbers. So many of the mill girls were married and pregnant (or pregnant and then married) by the time they were eighteen, but if *she* ever did it with Frank Newsome – and she was pretty sure it wouldn't be long before she *did* do it – she'd make sure he had a packet on him once they were behind the bandstand in Greenstreet Park on a Sunday evening.

'The carpet?' Lady Stratton asked, bringing Jeanie back to the present while pointing both her and the bucket in the direction of what was apparently her sitting room, which Jeanie could now see through the open bedroom door. 'Bit of an accident I'm afraid. We're all in something of a doodah today what with *the king...*' she emphasised the two words so that Jeanie would be under no misconception just who was the lauded guest of honour '...and Mrs Simpson invited here to dine tomorrow evening.' Lady Stratton swept a ring-laden hand across imaginary sweat on her brow, before pretending to fan herself with both hands and giggling girlishly. While youthful she most certainly wasn't, the Marchioness of Stratton appeared to be behaving almost like a child, twittering with excitement, patting somewhere in the direction of her heart under the teal silk dress with its puff sleeves, belted waist, and – to Jeanie's eye – ridiculously large yoke and collar.

'Now, I don't want my husband to know that we've spilt chocolate on the carpet. He's got so much on at the moment and the carpet was only laid last week. At ridiculous expense,' she added confidentially. 'Do you know the best way to get chocolate out of silk?' she asked hopefully. 'Because I'm afraid we don't.' She giggled again, pulled a scary face in Jeanie's direction without actually looking at her, and pointed once again to the sitting room adjoining the bedroom they were all three now standing in. 'Do take your time over it. Dabbing, I would imagine, rather than scrubbing, do you think?'

Jeanie took the bucket and followed Lady Stratton's directions to an area in front of a cream silk Knole sofa, its sides tied back with gold-tasselled rope. Oh, for heaven's sake, Jeanie thought. Had she been dragged up here – she rubbed at her wet and sore shin through her black stocking – just to dab at a bit of spilled cocoa the size of a half-crown? She'd been expecting a big brown puddle of chocolate to administer to. She got down on both knees at the side of the stain, glad, at least, to be able to take the weight off her legs after standing at the kitchen worktop for the last few hours and, reaching for the cloth in the bucket, tentatively set to.

'Come on, Win, let's have a look at it. You can't tell me about it and then not let me see it.' Excited, halting whispers were drifting in Jeanie's direction as she began to carefully work at the brown stain on the beautifully soft silk carpet.

'Henry'd kill me.'

'Henry won't know. Come on.'

'It's locked up in the drawer.'

'I'm amazed he's not left it in the safe.'

'He keeps forgetting the combination,' Lady Stratton tutted. 'He keeps forgetting *everything* at the moment. And then he has to ring the bank to get the safe combination. And then the bank has to send someone out here to reset it. He was terrified that, when he comes to take it out of the safe tomorrow, he might have forgotten the combination once more. Better to keep it here, locked in the drawer in my bedroom. He's in such a bally tizz about the visit – well we all are – I mean, he so wants *David*...' here, Lady Stratton paused grandly, eager to remind her sister of the intimate terms on which her husband and the new king were on '...he so wants *David* to know we approve of Mrs Simpson. Even though...' Winifred lowered her voice and Jeanie, from her place in front of the huge sofa, had to strain to hear '...of course, *we don't.*'

'Maude Greenford-Smythe reckons Mrs Simpson is an absolute sexual dynamo, who was trained to give, you know...' Mrs Casterton lowered her voice '...*pleasure*, in an oriental brothel.'

'Really?' Jeanie could hear, rather than see, the delicious shock on Lady Stratton's face.

'Oh absolutely. Bessie Wallis Warfield is just a jumped-up, American divorcée *parvenu* – for heaven's sake. The tart just wants to be Queen of England.'

'Shh. Shh.'

'She's not queen yet,' Lady Stratton's sister said scornfully. 'We're not going to be carted off to the tower. So, come on, show me the set.'

'Henry will kill me if I do,' Lady Stratton repeated.

'And I'll kill you if you don't,' her sister tittered.

Silence, followed by the opening and shutting of drawers and then an audible gasp from Mrs Casterton. 'Oh, Winifred, that is utterly magnificent. Goodness me. But I thought Henry was on his uppers? You keep telling me so,' she added almost accusingly. 'Took all your persuasion to get that new carpet out of him. How many nights did you have to put up with him in your bed to get him to agree to that?'

Jeanie heard a succession of sniggers and ribald laughter and then more shuffling and whispering coming from the adjacent bedroom. 'Oh, Win, that is just out of this world. Whitby jet, you say?'

'Well, Henry wanted the Yorkshire connection, obviously.'

'But the diamonds, Win? Where the hell did *they* come from? This central one is as big as a Brazil nut.'

'Bit of a story to it actually, Margaux.' Winifred lowered her voice and, again, Jeanie strained to hear. 'Given to George Astley, Henry's grandfather, by the son of some Indian Mughal to pay off a gambling debt in Bombay apparently. He was an absolute rogue, was George Astley. *His* father, fed up with him drinking, gambling and seducing every young deb in London and Yorkshire – as well as spending too much time with… you know…' Winifred lowered her voice '…ladies of the night, shipped him out to India to look after the Astley family interests in the East India Company. Apparently, all he was bothered about were his *own* interests: women, drink and gambling – at which he was particularly successful.'

'Goodness, Winifred.' Margaux was obviously scandalised that her sister's husband was descended from such a black sheep.

'Apparently, this diamond was hewn at the same time as the Koh-I-Noor diamond. You know, the absolutely priceless one given to Queen Victoria when she was on the throne? Anyway, this one you've got round your neck at the moment – come on, Margaux, take it off; Henry will have an absolute dicky fit if he walks in – was brought back to this country and deposited in the vaults of Coutts on The Strand years ago. Not convinced it was all above board – you know what I'm saying, Margaux? – he kept it hidden away in a vault in the bank in London.'

'Win, I cannot *believe* Henry is being so, so stupid, so *desperate* as to ingratiate himself with Edward and the American whore...'

'Shhh, Margaux... for God's sake... Get it off... Give it to me *now*... Put it back with the earrings...' Jeanie could hear panic in Lady Stratton's high-pitched whisper.

'Utterly unbelievable...' Margaux was in full flow '...that Henry has commissioned this Jet Set, Winifred, using the Astley family jewels, to present to *that woman*. When this place is crumbling around your ears. What's he after? A dukedom? Are you going to be promoted to the Duchess of Westenbury?' Margaux started to laugh and Winifred joined in, tittering nervously.

'Right,' Winifred uttered an audible sigh of relief, 'all safely locked away in my drawer.'

Jeanie, standing to cast a critical eye over her cleaning, quietly picked up the bucket and moved towards the door.

'Put the drawer key on that chain round your neck, Winifred,' Mrs Casterton advised. 'Keep it safe, for heaven's sake.'

'Oh, don't be ridiculous, Margaux. It's far too big to have dangling around my neck all day.' Lady Stratton tutted. 'And who knows who might knock me out? *Murder* me even, to get their hands on it? Hang on, I know. No one would ever think about looking for it here. Safe and sound until Henry comes to bring it down tomorrow evening.'

The pair of them laughed conspiratorially and Jeanie watched through the open door as they placed the key to the drawer in its hiding place and, obviously totally forgetting her presence in the adjoining room, made preparations to leave as the luncheon bell sounded down below.

# 6

## January 31st

'Dad?' Rosa let herself through the vicarage gate, looking forward to the huge mug of tea and big piece of ginger flapjack she'd promised herself all the way back from the funeral she'd been conducting. 'You OK?'

'Where've you been?' Richard attempted a smile, but Rosa could see he was upset. 'Been administering to the parish poor and needy?'

'Funeral over in Dewsbury. You look as if you're in need of a bit of TLC, Dad. Come on, let's get you inside – you look frozen – and put the kettle on. You seem pretty much done in. Are you not sleeping?'

'Not sleeping. Not speaking...'

'Not speaking? Who's not speaking to you?'

'Well Virginia, obviously. And now Mum as well.'

'What? Mum's not speaking to *you?* It's Mum's little indiscretion – actually, bloody big indiscretion – that's led to all this daggers at dawn stuff. I'd have thought she'd be on her knees begging forgiveness, not sending *you* to Coventry.'

'Oh, you know what your mum's like: she's wearing her hair shirt; taken a vow of silence like a damned nun. Says she's too embarrassed and ashamed of what she did with Bill Astley all those years ago to have me look at her over the toast and marmalade. When I try and tell her it's all alright, that if she

hadn't done what she'd done we'd never have had Virginia...'
Richard paused '...who, by the way, has changed her name.'

'Changed her name?' Rosa, in the process of handing a
steaming mug of tea to her dad, stopped and actually stared.
'Oh, please don't tell me she's become Virginia Astley – *Lady*
Virginia Astley?'

Richard attempted a smile. 'Wouldn't surprise me if eventually
she decides on that. But no.' Richard took a long grateful drink
of the hot liquid, warming his hands on the mug as he did so.
'No, apparently we have to call her Ginny now.'

'*Ginny?*'

Richard shrugged and Rosa saw again how her father had
aged recently. Only in his mid-seventies, he looked a lot older.

Rosa started to laugh. 'If Virginia's looking to bear the mark
of aristocracy she now believes is rightfully hers, then I'd have
thought the name Virginia superseded *Ginny?* Don't you think,
Dad? Or maybe not?' Rosa laughed again. 'I suppose she thinks
Ginny's a bit finishing school, a bit, you know, Lady Di, a bit
horsey and county set. That's it!' Rosa started to laugh. 'Virginia's
decided, two days after being given the news she's the Marquess
of Stratton's daughter that she's part of the county set. She'll
be up on horseback now, hunting and calling everyone "gels".'
Rosa was really chortling now. 'She'll be calling you and Mum
*Mummy and Daddy* next...'

'I doubt it,' Richard replied, his Scouse humour never far
away. 'She's not actually *speaking* to your mum. And, I'm *no
longer* her daddy.'

'I know, I know.' Rosa paused. 'Oh blimey. But actually, Dad,
there *is* a sort of black humour to it all.'

'Try telling your mother that now she's taken to her bed with
a nervous breakdown.'

'Hasn't she surfaced yet? Do you want me to come over and
see her again? I spent a good hour with her yesterday morning
after the showdown at the hall. I prayed with her and tried to
tell her it had all worked out for the best. That you and she had

Virginia. And that *no one*, including the Lord above, is cross with her.'

'Virginia is. Furious in fact. Leave it for a while, would you, Rosa? The thing with Virginia is not that she's upset I'm not her biological father and Bill is. I think she actually quite approves of that.' Richard ran a tired hand through his thinning grey hair. 'Obviously loves the idea of having aristocratic blood, that her new father is some distant cousin of King Charles. Very distant, to be honest: I did some googling last night.'

'So, what's her problem then?'

'That Mum and you – and I suppose me – kept it from her. That your mother never let on, especially when you three triplets inherited the hall. You can see her point? She *is* the Marquess of Stratton's biological daughter and yet it's Eva – who we now know is absolutely no relation to Bill Astley – who's inherited a third of the hall, while Virginia's been left nothing. I think she's particularly wild Mum told you and not Virginia herself. That Mum had planned it so that Virginia would know the truth only when she read the damned letter once Mum was, you know, *no more*. I should keep out of Virginia's way for the time being – it's you she's at war with.'

'So, Dad, you've always known then?' Rosa put down her own mug and went to sit at the table with Richard, holding his hand as he hesitated.

'I knew there was only a very *very* slim chance I could be Virginia's actual biological father.' Richard sighed. 'Your mum and I tried for seven years to have a baby and then, suddenly, halleluiah, she's pregnant.' Richard sighed again. 'What Mum didn't know was that, six months or so before she fell pregnant, I'd taken myself off to the doctor for some, you know, *advice*. He said I had to come back with Mum, that it was a joint problem...'

'A joint problem?' Rosa frowned. 'Something wrong with your joints? I thought it was a getting pregnant problem?'

'Joint. *Together*, you daft thing. And you with a degree from Durham?' Richard gave Rosa a look. 'It's hard enough, Rosa, talking about, you know, a lack of the readies as it were, without you trying to make fun of it.'

'I wasn't, honestly,' Rosa protested. 'I thought that's what you meant.'

'Anyway, I found the name of a clinic back in Liverpool. Told your mum I had a meeting over at Liverpool Poly on Tithebarn Street and, instead, spent an hour or so doing the – you know – the thing with magazines...' Richard trailed off, embarrassed. 'Anyway, the upshot was, I was told that basically I'd never be able to father a child.'

'And you didn't tell Mum this?'

'How could I, love? Tell her that, married to me, she'd never have a baby? Never be a mum?'

Rosa had a sudden insight into what Susan must have gone through. After seven years of desperately trying for a baby, the crimson proof of failure arriving with monotonous monthly regularity, Susan must have been bereft of all hope. And wasn't she, Rosa, herself going through something the same at the moment, knowing that those ten frozen eggs she'd left in the clinic in Wimbledon eight years previously, now waiting patiently for her and Joe, were her last chance to become a mum herself? If the IVF route she and Joe were about to go down – starting with the coming clinic appointment – didn't work, she'd never hold a baby of her own in her arms. Rosa felt both total empathy for her mum, as well as a sense of panic for herself. But she was brought swiftly back to the moment by the banging of the vicarage front door.

'Oh, you're here are you, Richard?' Susan Quinn marched into the kitchen, head held high, defiance in her voice. 'I assumed this is where you'd be.'

'Mum? You OK? You're looking a lot better than when I saw you yesterday.' Rosa went forward to hug her mother.

'I'm fine,' she said tartly, and Rosa saw, in her stance, just a little of Susan's father – Rosa's own grandfather – the curmudgeonly Reverend Cecil Parkes, who had ruled both his daughters – good girl Susan and the feckless Alice – as well as his flock here in Westenbury with a most unchristian rod of iron. 'I've come to tell you, Richard, that if you want to divorce me, I'll understand. As you know, I'm totally against divorce – when God joined us together, it was to be for ever – but you have good grounds for obtaining one when considering my... my *adultery*. Having said that...' Susan pulled a face and brought both hands to her stomach '...I'm not convinced I'm long for this life. I've just been on the bathroom scales and I appear to have lost a lot of weight and you know what that's a sign of: poor Karen Lucas – you'll know her, Rosa, she's on the church flower rota – has just been given the awful news that her insides are riddled, absolutely riddled...'

'Mum,' Rosa snapped irritably, her mind still on her frozen eggs in Wimbledon, 'you've lost weight because you've locked yourself in your bedroom in your hair shirt for the last three days, refusing to talk and eating absolutely nothing. Now stop being a martyr, be thankful your secret's out and that we all now know, and life can go on as before.'

'Don't think that's going to happen.' Hannah, followed by Eva, had walked in and, hearing the tail end of the conversation, folded her arms and faced the others. 'Looks like *Ginny* – oh you knew about the change of name, did you? – well, looks like *Ginny* has got a top Leeds law firm on board and is contesting Bill's will. She wants herself in it. And Eva here, well and truly out.'

'I thought it best to catch you and Eva down here at the vicarage,' Hannah said, once Richard had persuaded Susan there would be no imminent divorce, that he loved her, would always love her and why didn't they go off for a coffee and a bun at the Merry England Café – on neutral ground as it were – to really talk things over?

'Oh?' said Rosa.

'Well, I knew Eva would have some time once she'd finished her shift at the surgery.' Hannah lowered her voice almost conspiratorially. 'And I need to talk to you both.'

'About Virginia?'

'Well yes, there's that as well, obviously, but I've only just found out, an hour ago, what she intends doing re Bill's will. I appear to be the only one of us three she's speaking to: she's not speaking to you, Rosa, because of keeping Mum's secret from her and, as she's about to do the dirty on you, Eva, I doubt she'll be ringing you anytime now for cosy sisterly chats.'

'She can't just contest the will,' Eva said scornfully. 'It doesn't work like that. Does it? I mean, look at Jonny and Henrietta Astley – Bill's legitimate heirs – they got very little apart from Jonny being handed the title of marquess. Chuck Virginia a pair of candlesticks or something. That'll shut her up.'

'Eva! She's your sister.' Rosa was cross. 'Have a little compassion for what she's going through. Remember how *you* felt when you suddenly found out you weren't Bill's daughter after all. That you were Yves Dufort's.'

'Well, I didn't decide to change my name to something French and demand his family jewels.'

'Does he have any?' Hannah laughed.

'Alright, Yves' art *masterpieces*. There's one worth an absolute fortune hanging up, on loan from Yves himself, in the National Portrait Gallery in New York. He never sold it because it's of Arlette, his twin sister who died. He says he's leaving it to me.' Eva looked slightly embarrassed.

'Really?' Rosa asked, as she and Hannah stared.

'You kept that to yourself,' Hannah sniffed. 'You'll never be able to afford the insurance to actually keep it and hang it up in your front room.'

'Well don't let on to Virginia what I've just told you. She'll double her effort to get what she reckons is her supposed fair due if she knows I'm in line for a Dufort painting. And, by the way, Virginia is *not* my sister…'

'Stop it, Eva, bitchiness doesn't become you,' Rosa snapped, feeling tired and fed up with all her family. She just wanted Joe home from London where he'd gone with work for the day, and Chiara back from school for her tea.

'Since when?' Eva laughed and Hannah joined in. 'Alright, alright, I'm sorry. Virginia may be my adoptive sister, and I know we're actually cousins, but I don't feel the blood tie between us is all that strong. It may have now been proven that she's your two's actual half-sister rather than merely your adoptive sister, but Virginia and I have different fathers as well as different mothers and, as such, there's very little familial loyalty between us. She's never liked me. You know that…'

'So,' Hannah interrupted, standing up as a knock came on the front door, 'that'll be Tara and Felicity.'

'Felicity the wedding planner?' Rosa frowned. 'How come?'

'Hang on, Rosa, stick the kettle on and I'll let them in.' Hannah moved quickly down the hall.

'Is she getting married?' Eva hissed towards Rosa who was retrieving more mugs from the kitchen cupboard.

Rosa paused. 'Do you reckon Lachlan's proposed and it's all a big secret? Oh, I do hope so.'

'Why would it be a secret? And the way she was batting her eyelids at Zac, that American researcher who turned up out of the blue at the hall on Sunday, I wouldn't have thought so. Poor Lachlan looked pretty put out at Hannah's flirting with Zac, but then, I suppose, she's not committed to Lachlan, even though I reckon he's pretty much in love with her. I don't know what's wrong with Hannah, Rosa: she lands herself a gorgeous, loyal man like Lachlan Buchanan after her affair with that waste of space Ben Pennington, and yet she still appears to be looking over her shoulder for her next conquest.'

'Well, she's only been with Lachlan six months,' Rosa said. 'Same as you and Andrea I suppose, and I can't see…'

'Right, take a seat, you two.' Hannah indicated the kitchen table upon which Felicity, who'd taken charge of Heatherly Hall's wedding venue after Hannah had promoted Tara to be her own deputy the previous summer, had laid her laptop and notebook. 'I bet you've got cake somewhere, Rosa?' Hannah turned to the newcomers. 'Rosa always has cake.'

Once the five of them were settled with coffee and an array of Rosa's traybakes, Hannah launched into it. 'OK, I've only told Tara this so far...'

'You *are* getting married?' Eva said, almost accusingly. 'And you've got us all down here at the vicarage because you want Rosa to marry you?' No matter how much one loved one's sibling, one didn't want them having the upper hand in their love life.

'Married? Me?' Hannah shook back her dark hair and frowned. 'Who to?'

'Who to?' Rosa stared. 'I thought you were serious about Lachlan. You know, after the disaster that philandering Ben Pennington turned out to be?'

Ignoring the reference to the married man on whom she'd wasted over a year of her life, Hannah said, '*I'm* not getting married, but...' Hannah lowered her voice for dramatic effect '...but guess who is? And wants *us* to arrange the wedding at the hall?'

'Boris Johnson? Oh, hang on, no, he's married.' Eva visibly shuddered. 'How anyone could have consensual sex with Bo...'

'Cliff Richard?' Rosa asked hopefully. 'I've always liked Cliff Richard. Mum really likes him, you know...'

'Oh, for heaven's sake,' Hannah breathed. 'Will you all just *listen* to what Tara and I are about to tell you...?'

'Drew Livingston?' Rosa said, laughing at the very thought.

'Yes.'

'Sorry?' Everyone turned and gaped. 'Come off it, Hannah. Who is it really?'

'Drew Livingston and Aditi Sharma.' Hannah hit the air with a triumphant clasped fist.

'Well yes, everyone knows, they're the most "loved-up" couple around.' Eva air-quoted the words. 'You only have to read the tabloids to know that.' Eva frowned. 'But they're getting married up at some huge, in-your-face castle in Scotland, aren't they? It was in the *Express* yesterday.' She paused. 'Not that I read the *Express*,' she added hurriedly.

'Nope. Not anymore they're not. Aditi's fallen out with the venue and, I think, from what he said, not on the best terms with her wedding planner at the moment.'

'Who said?' Felicity, Rosa and Hannah leaned in.

'Aditi's PA.'

'Aditi Sharma – the greatest Bollywood actress on the planet? Her personal assistant called *you?*' Eva sat back and slowly let out her breath.

'Better than that.' Tara grinned. 'He arrived in person, yesterday, out of the blue – roaring up in the most divine shiny black Alfa Romeo – actually, he was pretty divine himself – and then spent the next three hours, once we'd taken him on a conducted tour asking – nay demanding – that we put Heatherly Hall wedding venue at their disposal.'

'What do you mean?' Rosa asked. 'At their disposal?'

'What do you think we mean?' Hannah grinned excitedly. 'They want us to arrange the wedding for Drew and Aditi.'

'Bloody hell.' Felicity dropped her pen in her excitement.

'And it's suddenly *Drew and Aditi*, is it?' Eva laughed in delight, Hannah's excitement contagious. 'Drew Livingston, the biggest solo artist ever. Until Ed Sheeran came along.'

'Right,' Rosa eventually said once they'd calmed down slightly. 'So, what did you say?'

'Well, *yes*, of course.' Hannah was ecstatic.

'But, it's a huge commitment, Hannah.' Rosa frowned. 'Think of all the security you'll need.'

'They'll bring their own, Vikram said. That's not a problem.'

'Vikram?'

'The PA.' Tara's eyes were shining.

'Right. So, when then?' Rosa glanced across at the Little Acorns School academic year calendar, which was still – because

Chiara was featured in the nativity scene – resolutely open at December.

'End of March.' Hannah glanced across at Tara who nodded in agreement.

'March? March next year?' Felicity's eyes were wide with alarm.

'This.'

'*This* March? In less than two months' time?' Felicity shook her head, blanching slightly. 'Six weeks? But, Hannah, the wedding venue diary is full. You know it is – we were only saying the other day how every weekend is accounted for.'

'And it is. But they want a Thursday – rather more upmarket to *not* actually marry on a Saturday. You only have to look at the royal family to know they never lower themselves to marry on a Saturday. And don't worry, Felicity – Tara and I will be with you on this until most of the planning is done. I mean, the guest list is done, the menu they want is already planned. But it'll be all hands on deck nonetheless. And...' Hannah turned to Eva and Rosa '...you two will have to pitch in as well. I'm afraid, Eva, if you've guests in for the art retreat that week, you're going to have to cancel them...'

'Hannah,' Eva squawked, 'no way...'

'Sorry, Eva, absolutely way. This takes precedence. Just think of the free marketing and advertising we'll get from this. We'll be in every newspaper and magazine. *HeyHo* and *Yes!* are apparently already on board. In fact,' she went on excitedly, 'when I told Vikram that you, Rosa, not only own the hall...'

'Hannah,' Rosa pointed out for what seemed the umpteenth time, 'we don't *own* it – we three have a shared responsibility for the running of the place.'

'As I said to Vikram,' Hannah went on, ignoring Rosa's words, '"my sister is the village vicar and will be more than happy to come and perform the marriage ceremony up here at the hall for you."'

'Up at the hall?' Rosa frowned. 'I'm not sure I'm able to conduct a wedding other than in...'

'Yes, you are,' Hannah interrupted, laying a soothing hand on Rosa's arm. 'I looked it all up and can quote verbatim: "For some religions, the ability to officiate at any wedding ceremony is automatic. Church of England, Catholic, Jewish, Anglican and Quaker leaders, such as priests, vicars and rabbis, can all officiate at weddings outside of a church." You're a vicar – QED – you're good to go.'

'Right,' Rosa said faintly.

'Yay,' Eva whooped. 'We're going to put Heatherly Hall right on the map!'

# 7

*February*

Several weeks later, Lachlan Buchanan made his way down the stone stairway from Hannah's apartment at the top of the hall to the estate office.

'Come on.' Lachlan, intent on taking Hannah away from the office computer, stroked her arm. 'Come and take a break. In fact, you really have to finish for the day now; it's getting close to nine and you've not eaten since breakfast. And,' he added persuasively, when Hannah didn't seem to be listening, resolutely attached to her screen while making notes before feverishly googling another query on her list, 'I've filched Eccles cakes from Tea and Cake for pudding.'

'Can't,' Hannah muttered without looking up. 'I've told Felicity I'll hunt down Bollywood-style decorations.'

'Why? I thought it was an English-country-house-style wedding the bride was after?'

'Aditi's now decided she wants the bathrooms and rest rooms done out Bollywood style.'

'Since when?'

'Since an hour ago.' Hannah closed her eyes before turning to Lachlan.

'Hannah, you're doing it again, taking on too much as usual. Look what happened with the pigs last summer.'

'What *did* happen?' Hannah snapped irritably. 'We ended

up with fifty healthy piglets, which we managed to send off to market.' She winced slightly, remembering how it had in fact been touch and go: how Lachlan had managed to find a buyer only at the last minute, when the piglets were five months old and their sale and future becoming almost untenable. They'd made little profit on them and Hannah had had to promise Lachlan never again to put the randy old boar, Napoleon, in with the sows in the petting zoo when he appeared 'to be looking a little lonely'. Had had to promise to keep to the management of *her* side of Heatherly Hall: the wedding venue, the new art retreat, Tea and Cake and Astley's – the new wine bar on the estate – and leave the running of the stock, the children's zoo and the surrounding approximately four thousand acres of farmland, woodland, moorland and parkland acres to him and his team in the future.

'Come on, Hannah,' Lachlan said once again, 'I'm going to make us both some pasta. You've got twenty minutes and then we're eating.'

'OK, OK.' Hannah turned back to her screen, immediately forgetting Lachlan's presence and returning once more into the world of planning The Wedding of the Year. She, Felicity and Tara could not afford to mess this one up: Heatherly Hall's future as the upmarket go-to place to get married was dependent on getting everything right, everything perfect, everything just as the bride demanded for this – their first, in-the-media wedding. Hannah leaned back, rubbed at her eyes, gritty with tiredness, stretched her stiff limbs, feeling once more the panic she'd started to feel the moment she'd assured Vikram Bakshi that yes, absolutely, they'd accept the booking for Drew Livingston and Aditi Sharma's nuptials, and yes, of course they'd done weddings on such a scale prior to this one.

Hannah scratched at her unwashed hair and knew she'd have to be up early the following morning to tart herself up. She and the wedding team – and that, she'd instructed both Rosa and Eva, included both of *them* – had their first meeting with Drew and Aditi themselves at eleven the following morning. All meetings and arrangements up until now had been with Vikram Bakshi and Blake Woodfield, the pair's personal assistants. Was her black pinstriped business suit clean? she wondered, closing her eyes again. Wasn't there a greasy stain on the sleeve where she'd devoured a bulging vanilla slice from Tea and Cake, the filling shooting out at speed as she'd taken an overenthusiastic bite? Hell, something else to worry about.

And she knew Rosa wasn't happy. Rosa had stated firmly, from the very beginning when Bill had left his majority shares to the three of them, that her priority was her church and her parishioners and, while she was happy to be a sort of consultant sleeping partner, attending board meetings, she didn't intend to get involved in the day-to-day running of the hall, particularly now she and Joe were married and she was stepmother to Chiara. But *especially* since she and Joe were about to go down the IVF route in order that Rosa might have a chance to have a much-wanted baby of her own.

Hannah had rung Rosa that morning, informing her that, as the person in charge of actually marrying the pair of them, she *had* to be there at the hall to meet Drew and Aditi and their entourage who were flying up from London in some private jet to Manchester before helicoptering (was that a word?) the thirty miles or so from the airport to the hall. (Oh Jesus, where were they going to land? She needed to make sure Lachlan's recently acquired and much-prized highland cattle were well out of the way. Hell, what if Aditi stepped into a steaming cowpat in her Bollywood slippers?)

Rosa had informed her fairly calmly that no, she wouldn't be there, *couldn't* be there, that Joe and she had an appointment at the Wimbledon fertility clinic the following afternoon. And there was no way she was missing that, even for the UK's most celebrated musician and his equally famous bride-to-be. Hannah, she was ashamed to recall, had had a bit of a hissy fit and told Rosa she *had* to be there. Rosa had repeated that she really *didn't*, and most certainly *wasn't* going to be, and perhaps it would be better if the wedding team found another vicar to perform the nuptials and – very unusual for Rosa – had calmly, but deliberately, ended the call.

With so much to think about, so much to do, how could Lachlan think she had time for *him* as well? Hannah added the suit and helicopter queries to her list, saved and closed the computer files and made her way back up the stairs to Lachlan.

'Oh, Daisy? I didn't realise you were here. Sorry.' Hannah headed immediately for the fridge and poured herself an exceptionally large glass of wine, before turning back to Daisy Maddison. 'Is there a problem with the stock? Has Lachlan had to call you out?'

'No, no, not at all. I've just been ten minutes away, helping my dad over at Jack Sykes' place – one of his cows has gone down with a particularly bad mastitis; I tell you now, Hannah, this job doesn't half put you off having kids yourself – and Jude's in London as usual, so I thought I'd come over and deliver the good news myself.'

'The good news?' Hannah's head shot up. 'What, you *are* pregnant?'

'Pregnant?' Daisy pulled a face. 'Jude is so often away, there's not much chance of that happening.'

'So, good news?'

'Yes, brilliant news.' Daisy accepted a small glass of wine, looked at the contents and sighed. 'God, I could drink the whole bottle, I'm so stressed with having my arms up so many cows' fanjoes. Anyway, yes, *brilliant* news.'

'What?'

'Dad's am-dram group are totally up for it.' Daisy beamed.

'Up for it?' For a second, Hannah couldn't think what Daisy was talking about. 'Oh, the Agatha Christie thing?'

'Duh! Yes! What else?'

Hannah hesitated. 'The thing is, Daisy, I've – we've – just accepted a major wedding do for March. I'm not sure…'

'You're *joking*? Hannah, I've spent the last couple of weeks with Dad rounding up his troops, holding meetings down at the church hall – where they're now having to meet because the village hall has a hole in the roof – and they're totally up for it. They love the idea of acting out the missing Jet Set. *The Jet Set of Heatherly Hall*: it's got such a ring to it. And I bumped into your sister…'

'Which one?' Hannah asked tiredly, draining her glass and reaching for the bottle, despite Lachlan's frowning at her. 'I've three.'

'Ginny, is it? You know, the one who turned up in such a strop the other Sunday when we were all here? She was just leaving Hilary Makepiece's new yoga class.'

'Virginia was doing a yoga class?' Hannah stared. 'She's always sworn yoga's the work of the devil, and grandpa Reverend Cecil would *turn over in his grave* – she does have a tendency to speak in clichés does Virginia – would turn over in his grave at scantily clad women in exotic…' Hannah thought for a minute '…or was it erotic…? poses – in his church hall.'

'Yes, certainly your sister Ginny. Dressed from head to toe in the latest *Lululemon* tights and crop top. I know it was the latest stuff because I was coveting it in Harrogate when I was there last week. Bloody expensive gear, and I'm not convinced it helps you fart any less – you know when your leg and bum are in that dangerously embarrassing position above your head? – than if you were wearing *Primark*.'

'Virginia? In a crop top? She never goes without a vest and liberty bodice over her bra.'

'You do exaggerate.' Daisy laughed. 'Have to say, she did look different. Has she done something to her hair? She looked a lot blonder than usual.' Daisy paused. 'And I thought her name was Ginny? She gave me her phone number and wrote *Ginny* on it.' Daisy drained her glass but shook her head as Hannah proffered the wine bottle. 'Anyway, she appears to have calmed down a bit from when I saw her – heard her – last and, when I told her what we were planning, she said she'd be delighted to be part of it, absolutely *insisted* on being part of it as – how did she put it? – "the subject matter is particularly relevant to myself knowing that the whole mystery of the Jet Set is pertinent to my father and my family's ancestry."'

'Blimey.' Hannah felt a headache starting. So, not only was Virginia thinking she could contest Bill's will in her favour, she was obviously dressing, and in training, for the event too. As well as seemingly being in on the whole Jet Set thing that Hannah was now totally regretting getting involved in. She turned to Daisy. 'I didn't know Virginia was actually aware of the missing Jet Set. I've certainly never discussed it with her.'

'Well, she's got it from somewhere.' Daisy smiled. 'She couldn't stop talking about it to me. And, she also said she has great experience in putting on productions and would very much like to be involved in this one.'

'Putting on productions?' Hannah started to laugh. 'She taught Reception for years until Barty and Bethany came along and she gave it all up to be a "proper stay-at-home mummy – in the kitchen where mummies belong." Or some such twaddle. The only productions she's had experience of is Reception's annual nativity at Little Acorns.'

'Supper!' Lachlan called. 'Are you staying, Daisy?'

'Me? Oh no, I couldn't…' She gazed hopefully in the direction of the table where Lachlan had laid three places.

'You could.' Lachlan laughed. 'Come on.'

'Look, Hannah,' Daisy said through a mouthful of the most superb prawn linguine, 'I know you said you'd write a script for the Jet Set yourself but, if it helps, we'll all pitch in. My Granny Vivienne – once a professional actress, I'll have you know – has actually written a couple of plays. Sent one off to Script Yorkshire and they acted it out at one of their open evening dos. I think we know the story: the priceless diamond-studded Whitby Jet Set, commissioned for Wallis Simpson to curry favour with the new king, goes missing from Lady Stratton's bedroom and basically is never seen again. What we don't know is where it ended up; so, we'll just have to use poetic licence. We can write a script, but the Westenbury Players are pretty good at ad-libbing too: they can just make it up as they go along. Have you any idea what the Jet Set looked like?'

Hannah shook her head. 'No. You know, Bill wasn't convinced it ever even existed. There was certainly a huge Astley family diamond that had been brought from India decades earlier and that diamond was, apparently, removed from the vaults of Coutts, the bank in London, by Bill's father, Henry. But, according to Bill, Henry was pretty canny, as well as pretty broke; it's quite possible it was all a scam, that Henry took the diamond and flogged it and had a facsimile made with glass instead of the diamond. Bill reckons he then panicked – I mean a bit of a cheek giving the king's mistress a glass bauble he bought at Woolies – and pinched and hid it himself so the scam wouldn't come to light.'

'Well, we can discuss this. Would you be OK with the Westenbury Players coming up to the hall at some point and getting a feel for the place? They need to get on with it: if the evening is to coincide with Agatha Christie's centenary of the publication of *The Murder on the Links* it needs to be put on around mid-March. A Saturday, preferably.'

'I'd prefer to get this wedding out of the way first,' Hannah started. 'Then I can relax and give my whole attention to any Agatha Christie evening.'

'I thought the wedding was towards the end of March, Hannah?' Lachlan raised an eye.

'It is.'

'Whose wedding is it? Anyone I know?'

Hannah hesitated. Pride and excitement that they were hosting the wedding of Drew Livingston and Aditi Sharma at the hall was tempered by knowing it was still a secret and the couple might still look elsewhere if they weren't won over by what Hannah and the team were going to put in front of them the following day.

'Sorry, bit of a secret.' Hannah smiled.

'Ah, another mystery. Go on, tell all.' Daisy's eyes were wide.

'Nope. So, look, the wedding's Thursday March 23rd. How about the following Saturday? Oh, hang on, no.' Hannah frowned. 'We've other weddings. We just can't do a Saturday, Daisy. Friday? Maybe in April?'

'Friday March 24th would be better. In fact, spot on.' Daisy beamed. 'Right, leave it with me.'

'You're giving yourself a lot of work, Hannah.' Lachlan looked at her as he cleared plates. 'That's the next day.'

'It'll be fine,' Daisy said. 'Honestly. Now we have a date and venue. The Great Hall will be ideal, Hannah. There's obviously not a stage, but we can bring makeshift blocks and do a sort of theatre in the round.'

'You wouldn't be better actually acting it out in the church hall?' Lachlan was still looking concerned.

'No, absolutely not. It's far too small and Hilary and her damned yoga classes are always in there. We need the atmosphere of *this* place – it'll get the punters in.' Daisy was brimming with enthusiasm. 'It'll be all alright on the night,' Daisy went on. 'Trust me – I'm a vet.'

# 8

## Wimbledon, London

### *Late February*

'You OK, Rosa?' Joe Rosavina took Rosa's hand in his own, placing both in the pocket of his navy Crombie winter coat. 'You're cold.'

'I'm frightened.' Rosa breathed out, clenching the hand in Joe's pocket before removing it. 'I don't know where to put myself.' She exhaled loudly once more. 'Maybe a walk round?' She made to stand.

'Do you want coffee?'

'Joe, we've had a bucketload since we set off at five this morning. I'm totally coffeed out. Jittery as hell. Look.' Rosa held out her hand with the plain gold wedding band Joe had placed on her finger just three months earlier.

'Nerves.'

'Of course, nerves,' Rosa snapped. 'I'm sorry, I'm sorry.' Rosa exhaled again and twirled a strand of her long dark hair – something she'd done since she was a little girl when anxiety got the better of her – and tried to smile. 'You get one. Something to do.'

'I should lay off caffeine, I think.' Joe, Rosa could see, was just as nervous as she was. 'Might affect the condition of my, you know...'

'Joe, we're here for consultation. I don't think you're going to be asked to get your willy out this morning. And you don't think coffee might be a *good* thing? You know, make your little swimmers supercharged? All up for it and raring to go. I can almost hear the Stud of the Scrotum shouting: "Hey up, you lot,"' Rosa went on in her best Yorkshire vernacular, '"had my double espresso and BABY, I AM ON FIRE and I'll..."' Rosa started to giggle – always a sign she was nervous – and Joe took her hand once more and smiled.

'The thing is, Joe...' Rosa giggled and hiccupped, unable to calm down. 'What if my eggs have accidentally defrosted and then been frozen again? I've lain awake so often over the last eight years thinking of them, terrified that some minion in the lab's turned the electricity off – you know because the electricity bill was too high – and then, realising what she's done, turned it back on, hoping no one will know? I mean, the last thing you should ever do is refreeze defrosted food...'

'Rosa Rosavina?' The white-coated woman in front of them smiled. 'Whoa, what a fabulous name. You couldn't make that up: I bet you hooked up with this guy just to match his name to your own?' She laughed and held out a hand. 'I'm Dr Shevchenko. I'm going to be with you through every stage.' She turned to Joe. 'And Joe, is it? Do come with me and we can get started.'

'I thought I'd be under Mary Cooper?' Rosa blurted out, disappointed at not seeing the consultant who had taken her through the cycle of her egg harvesting and their freezing eight years previously.

'Miss Cooper retired a couple of years ago.' Dr Shevchenko smiled. 'But I'm here to work with you and I'll do everything in my power to get that baby – or babies – into your arms.'

'Thank you so much.' Joe gave Rosa a warning look. 'We're so grateful for this chance.'

'So,' Dr Shevchenko went on briskly, 'you need to know there are several hurdles a frozen egg has to get over to result in a healthy pregnancy...'

'Hurdles?' Rosa had a sudden vision of her ten eggs competing at Westenbury Comp's annual sports day. 'Oh, right, sorry...'

'First the eggs must be successfully thawed. Typically, 85–95 per cent of frozen eggs survive the thawing process. Then just one has to be fertilised with sperm in the lab and develop into a healthy embryo. *This* step has a 71–79 per cent success rate. *That* embryo then has to implant in the uterus. The success rates go down at this point – a 17–41 per cent success rate – before continuing to the development of a healthy and viable pregnancy.'

'Oh.' Rosa felt her heart plummet. 'The odds are stacked against us then?' She reached for Joe's hand as tears threatened.

'Not at all, Rosa, but I do have to give you the facts as I see them.' The doctor gave a brief, hard stare in both their directions. 'Otherwise, we'd all be living in cloud-cuckoo land. On the positive side, our success rates here in this clinic are comparable whether you use fresh or frozen eggs. And,' she went on, warming to her theme, 'one great plus point is that you are now...' the doctor glanced across at her screen '...almost thirty-nine and yet your eggs are just thirty years old.' She smiled. 'And, Rosa, you've already done most of the hard work – the actual harvesting of your eggs is the sometimes painful, quite arduous part of IVF.'

Rosa nodded in agreement. 'It was. So, when can we do it? When can I try and get pregnant?'

Dr Shevchenko smiled again. 'So, as part of today's consultation process, we need to discuss the recommended number of eggs to thaw and consequently the fertilised embryos to transfer, and how the uterine lining needs to be prepared to accept the embryos.'

'Oh,' Rosa said. '*My* uterus is *so prepared* to accept embryos. It's been on tenterhooks, waiting for the right moment, and the right man...' Rosa searched for Joe's hand once more '...for the last eight years.'

The doctor laughed. 'I'm sure you have a very hospitable uterus, Rosa, but it's a bit more complicated – rather more biological – than just opening your uterus's door and saying:

"Do come on in, little embryos."' She laughed again, obviously amused at the vision. 'Rosa, we have to have the best endometrial preparation for embryo transfer.'

'Right, so how do you do that?' Joe leaned forward.

'The development of an optimal uterine lining in which a newly fertilised embryo can implant is a crucial step in all this.' She turned back to Rosa. 'So, Rosa, you'll be required to take birth control pills for two to four weeks to quiet the ovaries.'

'I don't think they're very noisy at the moment,' Rosa protested. 'I think chemo put paid to them partying for Britain.'

'Just listen, Rosa,' Joe said calmly.

'When you're instructed, Rosa, you'll stop taking the pills and, instead, begin a daily oral tablet to stimulate the growth of the uterine lining. After two weeks of this we'll do a blood test and also an ultrasound of the uterine lining to make sure an adequate endometrial thickness is developing. Then...' Doctor Shevchenko patted Rosa's hand '...*then* your eggs will be thawed, Joe here will do his stuff – we'll have to test your semen for quantity, mobility and shape, Joe – and hopefully we'll have lovely embryos created in the lab. And then, five days prior to the embryo transfer, progesterone is started to make your womb lining receptive to the embryo. Or embryos.'

'So, and I know I'm being impatient, Doctor, what's the time scale?' Rosa leaned forward eagerly.

'Well, we'll get started now by giving you the usual health check-up, Rosa: you know blood pressure, a couple of blood tests and the like. If everything's good to go, we'll get you started on the birth control pills immediately.' Doctor Shevchenko glanced at the calendar on her desk. 'So, it's the end of February now, and... erm... let's say the end of March to have had you on the contraceptive pills, then another two weeks on the tablet to get your uterine lining the best it can be... With a bit of luck, if everything goes to plan, we'll possibly be able to transfer embryos at some point towards the end of April. If that's the case – and I have to remind you both, it so often *isn't* – then we could be looking towards May or June in order to know if we've been successful.'

Rosa found she was crying. Hell, if this was all it took to make her want to howl with gratitude, what on earth would she be like if she and Joe did manage to actually make this work? To have a baby?

'What I would say to you, Joe, is keep yourself and your sperm as healthy as they can be. Increased scrotal temperature can hamper sperm production. Although the benefits have not been fully proved, wearing loose-fitting underwear, reducing sitting, avoiding saunas and hot tubs, and limiting scrotum exposure to warm objects, such as a laptop, might enhance sperm quality. So, you know the rules: no hot baths, no tight boxers.' The doctor smiled across at both of them. 'Rosa, I know, given the circumstances, it might be difficult but you must try to be as stress-free as is humanly possible. Don't go taking on more work than you can cope with; don't put yourself in stressful situations. Try some yoga – keep calm.'

'Just one question, Doctor?' Rosa brushed away a tear.

'Only one, Rosa? I'm sure you've got loads.'

'Can I just ask if the clinic has ever had problems with the electricity? Any power cuts during the last eight years?'

While the Wimbledon clinic's good doctor was laughing and reassuring Rosa that her eggs were snugly ensconced in antifreeze rather than on a freezer's shelf amongst the staff's frozen peas, beans and dinner-for-ones, Hannah was at a meeting in Heatherly Hall, giving it all *she'd* got in the reassurance stakes.

'I can assure you both,' Hannah was saying, desperately trying to remain calm and professional although, in the presence of such a megastar as Drew Livingston, she could feel sweat trickling down the cleavage of her best white shirt, 'Heatherly Hall has been the wedding venue of choice for many years. The previous Marquess of Stratton, Bill Astley, started the venue with

Tara here.' Hannah extended a hand towards her deputy. 'And we also have Felicity, who has been with us for years also, now at the helm.' When neither Drew nor Aditi Sharma deigned to respond, appearing bored if not actually disbelieving, Hannah pushed on. 'As this is obviously such a high-profile wedding, and we certainly don't have a surfeit of time to play about with...'

'Are you saying, Ms Quinn, that this is beyond your professional capability?' Aditi turned her exquisite face to the window overlooking the parkland where, unfortunately, it was blowing a gale from across the Pennines, the February morning sullen under the unbroken blanket of granite-grey West Yorkshire, sky.

'Not at all.' Hannah beamed in what she hoped was a persuasively convincing manner. 'What I *was* going on to say was that, because of the limited time we have, myself and Tara will be joining Felicity here at the helm to ensure everything goes to plan. As well, my sister here...' all faces turned to Eva who, finding herself under the blatant inspection of Drew Livingston flushed an uncharacteristic pink (hell he was bloody gorgeous) '...will be putting the Heatherly Hall Art Retreat, of which she is in charge, on hold for the week beforehand in order to...'

'Of course. Of course.' Drew Livingston sat back in his chair while continuing to stare at Eva.

'Of course?' Eva found herself reddening even more as Drew continued to scrutinise her face at length: it was like being weighed up by a gorgeous but predatory tiger and Eva felt her heart miss a beat. And then, in true Eva Malik style, she came out fighting. '*Of course*, Mr Livingston? Of course, *what?*'

'You are the daughter – the daughters of Dame Alice Parkes – while you, Eva, I believe, are also the biological daughter of Yves Dufort?' Drew Livingston's eyes gleamed as he finally sat back in the chair, folded his heavily tattooed arms and crossed his long black leather-clad legs.

'I'm sorry, I don't see what that's got to do with anything...' Eva started.

'My fiancé, Ms Malik, loves art almost as much as he does his music.' Aditi flapped her hands dismissively before turning to her personal assistant, Vikram, who was making notes on his laptop. 'What do you think, Vikram? It's all a bit… a bit… oppressive, don't you think? Somewhat grey and colourless?'

'Ms Sharma…' Hannah was back in the throes of persuasion before Aditi's PA could venture an opinion '…I can assure you that by the middle of March, the daffodils – for which Heatherly Hall is famous – will be an utter riot of colour, a… a… yawn of yellow to greet your guests.'

Eva and Tara exchanged glances: what the fuck was a *yawn of yellow*?

Hannah went slightly pink herself, but soldiered on. 'May I ask what made you change your mind about Falkness Castle at such a late date in the proceedings?'

'We were promised James McDonald Ballantine would be inhouse to sketch the guests.' Aditi pouted. 'Now, that has fallen through.'

'Blimey,' Eva exhaled. 'James McDonald Ballantine? Wow.'

'Many of our guests, like myself, are huge art connoisseurs,' Drew went on. 'Great art *collectors*. Aditi decided – I was away touring in America – that she'd go with Falkness Castle when she was told Ballantine was willing, and would be there to meet our guests and sketch some of them. Apparently, he's not.'

'Not what?'

'Available,' Aditi explained, somewhat irritably. 'He was to be my surprise wedding present to Drew. And that has now fallen through. Anyone who lets me down in such a cavalier manner doesn't get a second bite of the cherry.'

'Tell you what, Eva…' Drew sat forward, his attention concentrated only on her while starting to sound a bit like Simon Cowell. 'It's a definite yes from me to hold the wedding here at Heatherly Hall if you can get either Dame Alice Parkes or Yves Dufort to join us as our guest.' He put up a hand as Eva started to protest. 'I'm not saying they have to *work* for their supper

74

– I'm not suggesting they sketch; as far as I know, neither of them is a portraitist – but one or the other being here among the guests would just be wonderful. We'll pay them to be here of course.'

'Oh, I'm sure they'd be delighted to accept,' Hannah gushed. 'I know Dame Alice Parkes, is a big Bollywood fan...'

Eva shook her head imperceptibly at Hannah and mouthed: '*Nope*' but the latter roared on like an out-of-control steamroller.

'...and both Alice and Yves were over just before Christmas to actually open Eva's fabulous new art retreat.'

'The thing is, Ms Quinn...' Aditi was obviously bored with artists and wanting to nail what she was now referring to as *the serious stuff* '...most of the planning is done: the menus, the guest lists, the entertainment. It really is just a matter of transferring everything here – if we *do* confirm we're going ahead with this place. Mind you, I'm not convinced we have much choice now. Obviously, new invitations will have to go out, but we'll supply you with all of that – I'll send over the designer ASAP. My friend, the chef Jasper Solomon, is doing most of the food along with Safe Rao.'

'Blimey.' Felicity gawped, dropping her cool as well as her pencil. 'Two of the most feted chefs in the world?'

'Absolutely.' Aditi preened. 'With their respective teams of course. And they'll both have to come and check out your kitchens. Again, ASAP. See if they're up to scratch, and they will actually be able to cook in them.'

Hannah had a sudden terrifying vision of the celebrity chef, the infamously bad-tempered Jasper Solomon, jack-booting about Heatherly Hall, blaming her when it all started to go wrong, of having to prostrate herself over the kitchen's stainless-steel worktops shouting, 'Yes, Chef,' in the bastard's direction. She couldn't do this...

'I've seen the kitchens, Aditi.' Vikram pulled a tired hand through his hair. 'When I was here last week. They're as good as, if not better than, the kitchens up at the Scottish place. There really isn't a problem with moving the wedding here.' He turned to the girls who were busily jotting down notes of their own. 'The entertainment will be Drew himself and friends...'

'Friends?' Eva asked, wide-eyed, as Hannah, Felicity and Tara's heads shot up in unison.

'Paul of course – although he'll be disappointed he's not back in Scotland.' Aditi counted on her fingers. 'Elton possibly, and Harry and Madonna...'

'Right.' Hannah felt a frisson of excitement ripple through her, followed by another surge of utter panic. She was going to have to tell these three she'd made a mistake: she was an absolute imposter. She was a youth worker, not the organiser of the wedding of the year. 'The thing is...' Hannah started, panic threatening to overwhelm her. She desperately needed the bathroom; knew she shouldn't have had those prunes for breakfast.

'The thing is,' Eva interrupted, giving Hannah a warning look before smiling and turning to the others, 'we can *absolutely* do all of this. Whatever you want, we can do. And I'll get straight on to my parents this morning.'

*My parents?* Hannah's eyes opened wide at Eva's sudden volte-face re Alice and Yves Dufort, before smiling beatifically, first at Eva and then at the three guests in front of them. Tara and Felicity, she saw, were both wearing the same rictus of a smile she knew was on her own face. Since when had Dame Alice Parkes and Yves Dufort kicked Susan and Richard into touch re Eva's parentage? The former pair had certainly supplied the sperm and the womb, with Eva the result (oh hell, in all this, Hannah suddenly remembered Rosa who was at present in London trying to get pregnant, and her heart gave another little lurch) but since when had Alice and – admittedly – the very charming and charismatic Yves Dufort, suddenly become Eva's Mummy and Daddy?

'So, are we on then?' Vikram asked.

'I'm not sure we have a choice,' Aditi sniffed, giving each of the four girls a hard stare in turn.

'We've only just over three weeks now,' Tara said pointedly.

'And we'll work every hour God sends. It'll be a bit like that TV programme – you know – DIY SOS.' Felicity beamed.

'I most sincerely hope not.' Aditi shot a withering look towards a now obviously embarrassed Felicity before turning once more in Hannah's direction. 'Vikram, you *have* explained to Miss Quinn that I shall be leading the Bharatnatyam and Kathak?'

'Erm…?' Hannah, feeling her insides protest at something else she didn't know about, looked desperately towards the office door and the lavatory.

'Bhangra-style dancing, Hannah,' Eva put in cheerfully. 'How fabulous. Bags I first up on the dance floor…' Eva stopped in her tracks as the door to the office opened and Virginia strode into the room.

'Thought I'd find you all in here…' Virginia trailed off as she took in the guests around the office table, her head bobbing almost comically from one to the other as she tried to work out just who these people were. Hadn't they been in last week's *HeyHo* magazine, the rag she publicly decried as the devil's work but privately hoovered up once she got hold of Hilary the church warden's abandoned copy?

'Hello, am I too late for the meeting?' Virginia simpered. She thrust a hand in Drew Livingston's direction. 'I'm Ginny Forester-Astley, the late Marquess of Stratton's daughter. And you are?'

# 9

'Virginia!' Eva turned on the eldest of the four Quinn sisters once Hannah had led Drew, Aditi and Vikram out of the office and back down to the waiting helicopter which, despite Hannah's earlier concern, the pilot had managed to land and park (did one *park* a helicopter?) without recourse to the hall's highland cattle.

'Yes?' Virginia had moved to the office window, apparently surveying the acres of parkland in front of her, as well as the retreating backs of those making their return journey to the helicopter, before now turning to face her sister. 'What can I do for you?'

'What can you do for *me*?' Eva stared. 'What are you playing at, Virginia?'

'It's *Ginny*,' Virginia replied, a slight smirk on her pretty face. 'And I think you'll find that very soon there will be no *me*.'

'What? What *are* you talking about?'

'I think I made it abundantly clear to Hannah that I intend contesting my father's will, Eva. You have absolutely no right, no claim whatsoever to Heatherly Hall. You're not Bill's daughter and, as such, you should do the right thing and hand over your share of what he left you, to me.'

'Hand over my share?' Eva actually laughed out loud at that. 'Oh, for heaven's sake, Virginia, stop it. Just stop it. What do you think Rosa, Hannah and I were actually handed in Bill's will?'

'Well, this place of course.'

'Virginia, we were handed 51 per cent of the shares in a company. Heatherly Hall PLC is a company just like any other, owned and run by the trust. We three girls hold the majority share, that's all. We don't actually own the bricks and mortar – we don't own all *this*...' Eva flung a hand in the direction of the Queen Anne table, the exquisite Chippendale chairs and then to the somewhat tired-looking office curtains. 'The drapes are Laura Ashley, circa 1990. Do you want to own *those* as well?'

'He left you his wine collection,' Virginia said sullenly.

'Then go down into the cellars and help yourself to a few bottles,' Eva snapped. 'You don't even like wine. In fact, I've never seen you with a drink.'

'Well don't tell me Bill didn't leave you any money. Some jewellery maybe? I've just been hearing about this Jet Set...'

'Oh, not you as well? It probably never existed, Virginia. It's a modern myth that's rearing its head again because...'

'Vivienne Maddison was absolutely full of it at yoga class yesterday.'

'Well, I suggest you concentrate on your *Dog's Got Worms Again* or your *Burning Thighs of Hell* poses instead of listening to idle village gossip.' Eva laughed out loud as she pictured Virginia attempting just that.

'I want my share,' Virginia continued softly. 'I want acknowledgement that I am the Marquess of Stratton's legitimate daughter.'

'Actually, *Ginny*, I hate to remind you of this...' Eva gave a little hoot of derisive laughter '...but you're NOT. In basic terms you're Bill's *illegitimate* daughter – a bastard no less. Just as we three are.'

'Excuse *me*! Do you mind keeping such language to yourself?' Virginia glared across at Eva. 'You always did have a foul mouth on you.'

'Virginia, come on.' Eva held out a placating hand, which Virginia ignored. 'I don't want to fall out with you: that would really upset Mum and Dad.'

'I have grounds.'

'Grounds? What grounds?' Eva felt impatience mount.

'The grounds of an individual who *is* or *was* related to the deceased, or who was dependent upon the deceased.' Virginia's tone was triumphant as she quoted legal speak verbatim. 'I *was* related to the deceased – to William Astley, twelfth Marquess of Stratton of Heatherly Hall. As well as all the... all the... *marquessesses*—' Virginia added far too many plurals '—that have gone down in history. I *am* his daughter. I am of his line.' (Now she was sounding like something from the Old Testament.) 'While you, Eva, quite plainly are not.'

'What's up, Virginia?' Hannah had walked back into the office. 'Bloody hell, I need gin, Eva. Or class-A drugs. Is it too early for either, do you think?' When neither Eva nor Virginia spoke, Hannah folded her arms, leaning against the long office table over which the management committee regularly thrashed out ideas, before raising a questioning eye at both her sisters. 'Well?'

'Virginia here wants my share of Heatherly Hall.'

'Well, she can't have it,' Hannah replied drily. 'Next?'

'I have *every* right...'

'You have *no* right, Virginia,' Hannah snapped, pointing a finger in her direction. 'Bill didn't even know you very well.'

'You three all made sure I didn't get to know my father.'

'We didn't know he *was* your father, Virginia. And as far as I recall, I don't remember you even liking him when you did have anything to do with him. Which wasn't very often. *A scruffy, philandering individual*, I seem to remember you calling him.' Hannah picked up and drained the remains of her abandoned cup of coffee, grimacing at its cold contents but needing the caffeine hit. 'Oh, for heaven's sake. I've enough on my plate without all this.'

'I've already started proceedings,' Virginia hissed as Hannah started to pick up her laptop and notebooks.

'Good for you,' Hannah snapped back. 'Now, if Eva and I can get on...?'

'Jonny and Henrietta Astley are on their way over from the States. It's going to be a joint contesting of Bill's will and, as the legitimate offspring...'

'Offspring?' Hannah and Eva spoke as one.

'As the legitimate heirs...'

'Heirs? Virginia, Jonny and Henrietta inherited *nothing* from Bill apart from Jonny being given the title of the thirteenth Marquess of Stratton. For what that's worth.'

'The lawyers will match my DNA to theirs to prove I'm their half-sister as much as you and Rosa are, Hannah. And that you, Eva, have no rights whatsoever.'

'OK, OK, have it your own way,' Eva said tiredly. 'I need to get back home to Andrea. He's just texted me.'

'Isn't he up in the art retreat or welding down in the outbuildings?' Hannah asked. 'The kiln's working again down there, isn't it?'

'As far as I know, but he's back at the house for some reason.' Eva looked at her watch and made to pick up her own things. 'Look, Virginia, you must do what you have to do. And probably, you know, in your position I might just do the same. All I would say is, that if you're going to get into bed with Jonny Astley...'

'Into *bed* with him?' Virginia was obviously quite horrified. 'He's my *brother.*'

'It's a phrase, Virginia,' Eva said tiredly. 'Into *cahoots* with him. That better? If you're going to get into cahoots with Jonny, just take care. He's a slippery character: he'll only be out for himself.'

'As you appear to be, Eva.' Virginia raised an eye, determined to have the last word.

'Whatever,' Eva sniffed, equally determined that Virginia should not.

\*

Eva made her way back through the village of Westenbury before taking the country road to drive the five miles or so out towards the house in Heath Green, the large modern box of a house she'd shared for the last fifteen years with Rayan, her husband, before the breakdown of her marriage. As she drove along country lanes, the overhanging branches of large oaks and sycamores showing no signs of waking from their winter sleep, Eva ran through every bit of the conversation she and Hannah had just had with Virginia, knowing that, when she'd told Virginia that, in her place, she'd more than likely be as miffed as her big sister was and wanting her rightful place at the helm of Heatherly Hall, she'd been telling the truth. Maybe it was best if she did relinquish her share in the place; she wasn't really entitled to it, after all. Oh, but she loved her new life so much. So loved being one of the Girls of Heatherly Hall, running the art retreat, being at the helm. She wasn't prepared, she knew, to give it up without a fight.

Andrea's Harley-Davidson was parked up at the top of the drive as well as, most unexpectedly, an extremely large white transit van out of which Andrea was now exiting. So large, Eva saw with irritation as she manoeuvred her Evoque through the narrow gate at the bottom, it had obviously taken a huge lump out of part of the wooden structure.

'What are you *doing*?' Eva asked, surveying what she now realised was a type of removal van. 'You moving in?' Andrea spent many nights in Eva's bed – particularly when Laila and Nora were at Rayan's place – which, since Yasmin, Rayan's new partner, had given birth to their son, Farhan, a couple of months previously, seemed to be more and more, eager as they both were to see and help with their new baby brother. In reality, since coming to find Eva here in Yorkshire at the end of the summer, Andrea had rented the beautiful cottage next door to Daisy and Jude over at Holly Close Farm. Eva felt slight panic mount: she might be in love with Andrea – had fancied him and lusted after him ever since meeting the Russian-Italian sculptor on an art retreat in The Lakes back in June – but she didn't think she was ready for the whole moving in together bit. Separating from Rayan after so many years of marriage had knocked her sideways at the time, but she knew she was beginning to relish her independence, the ability to grow and develop as a single woman – as well as an artist – and she wasn't convinced living her life *totally* with another man was what she wanted.

'Moving out.' Andrea appeared stressed.

'Oh.' Well that totally floored her: she'd believed and trusted Andrea when he said he was in love with her, that he'd left his home in Milan to be with her.

'Eva.' Andrea jumped down from the cab and came towards her, wrapping his leather-jacketed arms firmly around her. 'The project I work on, it speed along much quicker than I anticipate.' He moved her away from him slightly, looking down into her face.

'The commission for the city hall in Milan?'

'Yes of course, the commission. What else?'

The weekend in Cumbria had involved Eva sitting for Andrea while he made simple preparatory sketches, telling her she was the influence, his muse even, for a sculpture for Autumn. Since then, he had demanded she sat often for him, and sometimes she'd felt impatient, knowing she had other things to be getting on with: her two days a week work as a dentist at her and Rayan's surgery; her insistent aim of making the Dame Alice Parkes' Art Retreat at Heatherly Hall the very best in the north, if not in the whole UK.

Eva certainly accepted that this commission of Andrea's was everything a sculptor could dream of. The hall in Milan was, Andrea had informed her, originally a beautiful palace designed by Galeazzo Alessi and built in the sixteenth century for a very wealthy Genoan trader called Tommaso Marino but, since the nineteenth century, this original Palazzo Marino had been used as a city hall, its *Sala Alessi* made over as a reception hall for special guests of the city. Each corner of the ceiling of the *Sala Alessi* was apparently decorated with paintings by Aurelio Busso representing the four seasons, as well as frescos and bas-reliefs showing the story of Perseus. The sculptures Andrea had been working on in the outbuildings at Heatherly Hall for the past six months were structures to complement Busso's paintings and would be erected in the courtyard of the hall bordering the *Piazza della Scala*. Andrea had spent several sessions already over in Milan, flying from Leeds Bradford airport, but returning to Eva, either animated or slumped in despondency over the progress of his work.

'I have done as much preparatory work as is possible here in Yorkshire,' Andrea was now saying. 'But I have to go – I have meetings and I need to be there. This cold Yorkshire air not conducive to my art...' Andrea stretched his fingers and wiggled them in her direction before weaving them lovingly through her long dark hair and kissing her with such passion she thought she might just fall over on the drive. She was glad Steve and Annie, her next-door neighbours, were out at work.

'Why the big van? The removal van?' Eva indicated the white vehicle in front of her.

'I take my bike. And the sculpture pieces already done: I have to drive back to hall for them before driving down to Kent and Eurotunnel. Need to see how they will fit in with ambiance of courtyard there.'

'Driving all that way?'

'It nothing. I drive down through Strasbourg, Basle and then on to Milan; I cannot take bike and pieces of metal and pottery on EasyJet.' Andrea frowned, impatient, Eva could tell, to be off.

'So, you'll be away long enough to need your bike with you?' Eva had a sudden fear she wouldn't ever see him again. Was this his way of leaving her? Letting her down lightly? Had he had enough of her? Rayan's rejection still made her smart; feel unsure of herself. 'I thought Milan was just as cold as here, in February?' Eva went on, feeling totally bereft at his going. 'So how long will you be away?' she repeated.

Andrea shrugged. 'Depend on how much I have to do. It's a lot I have to do, Eva. I behind with it all. Come with me, Eva,' Andrea now whispered into her neck. 'Please come with me. I don't want to be without you. I need you there.'

Eva couldn't help a surge of elation at the proposition. But she knew it was impossible. 'Andrea, I have two little girls who need me more. As well as this wretched wedding of the year and some farcical Agatha Christie... *farce*... to get underway in just three weeks or so.' Eva ran her hands over his taut buttocks, loving the feel of his denim-clad backside under her hands.

'Well, come inside with me then before I go?'

'What are you after? A ham sandwich and a cup of Yorkshire tea to see you on your way?' Eva grinned, reaching up to run the tip of her tongue experimentally along his beautiful full top lip.

The experiment obviously worked. Andrea groaned slightly, adjusting the belt on his Levi's before taking Eva's hand, propelling her through the front door and upstairs, discarding both their clothes on the bedroom floor in a way their respective mammas had never condoned, before making love to her in the way only an Italian lover can.

Feeling somewhat at a loss once Andrea had quickly reversed the van down the drive where, despite her yells to be careful, he'd succeeded in knocking yet another piece of wood from the garden gate, Eva set to and made Bolognese for the girls. She saw she had a good hour before driving down to Little Acorns to pick up her daughters: not enough time to go back to the hall and check the itinerary and preparations for the group of ten booked into the art retreat for the coming weekend; nor start on the apologies and postponements for the week that had now been given over to the Livingston/Sharma extravaganza.

Blimey, that Drew Livingston was something. She'd always had a bit of a thing about him – what woman hadn't – and, if truth be told, not only was he even more charismatic in person, she could also understand why she still had. A thing about him, that is. With his dark curls, and brilliant blue eyes, he was a much younger version of that guy from INXS. Hadn't people always got Michael Hutchence and Drew Livingston mixed up? Eva glanced at her reflection in the hall mirror – she looked slightly out of it all. Which, seeing she fancied she'd momentarily lost consciousness at the point of orgasm, so strong had been her climax at the conclusion of Andrea's expert lovemaking, was perhaps understandable.

Eva decided she'd perhaps better calm down a bit before she did the mummy thing at the school gate, and what better way than to go and see her own personal vicar? She'd call in at the vicarage and see how Rosa and Joe had got on at the fertility clinic in Wimbledon.

Eva drove the reverse journey back down to the village she'd motored up only three hours or so earlier, taking the corner rather too quickly before driving through the rusting gates and up the drive to the vicarage kitchen door. She jumped out, but could see Joe's car wasn't in its usual place behind Rosa's little Corsa. She was surprised Rosa didn't treat herself to something a little bit more upmarket – she must have plenty of money squirrelled away somewhere after selling her business in London but then, she supposed, never being hugely materialistic, it wouldn't be on Rosa's list of must-haves. Joe had obviously driven the pair of them to Wakefield Station and left his own car there before taking the train down to London.

'Not back yet, love.' Denis Butterworth, the verger, appeared at her side, a bunch of turnips and a stick of Brussel sprouts in his right hand. 'I've brought the vicar these from my allotment...' Denis lowered his voice '...you know to help...'

'To help?' Eva stared. 'With what? Her sermon on Sunday?' She started to laugh at that.

'Her sermon?' Denis gave her a look. 'What's turnip greens and a few sprouts got to do with praise of the Lord? No, you know, it's them there fo-lates the vicar'll be needing. If she gets lucky.'

'Gets lucky?'

'Well, our Sandra reckons it's right. Been talking to Hilary Makepiece – who knows these things – and our Sandra says, Hilary says... you know...'

'What?' Eva couldn't decide if she wanted to laugh or bang her head against the wall. Banging Denis's head might be the better option.

Denis lowered his voice theatrically. 'For having babies. *Folates* it's called. Or summat like that. Because that's where she's gone, you know, to defrost them eggs of hers. After she'd had that cancer treatment she had to go through...'

'Denis, I do *know*,' Eva said impatiently. Blimey, was nothing sacred round here? 'Thing is, Denis, how do *you* know?' Eva lowered her own voice. 'About Rosa's... you know...?'

'Oh, we all know all about it, love. I think it was your mum who told that big sister of yours, who told Hilary at yoga, who let on to our Sandra. And we're all praying for the vicar. In fact, we had a special prayer for her at Evensong on Sunday – you know, when I lead the congregation, to give the vicar a bit of a break, like.'

Congregation? Eva wanted to laugh at that: Denis was lucky if three people turned up on a Sunday evening at the church and Sandra, his wife, was always one of them.

'Well, Denis, I'd ask you to keep it to yourself if you don't mind,' Eva advised. 'This is a very personal thing Rosa's going through. Personal and sensitive. Best not to share it with the world and his wife.'

Denis thrust the turnip tops and sprouts in Eva's direction before tapping the side of his nose discreetly. '*Mum's* the word, love.' He turned to go back down the path. 'Well, we hope so, anyhow.' Denis paused before turning once again in Eva's direction. 'Just one other thing we're not sure of?'

'Oh?'

'Chiara – you know, the little lass that's come to live at the vicarage?'

'What about her?'

'She's a grand little lass, isn't she? Our Sandra's fair taken with her.' Denis paused. 'So, she's Joe's daughter?'

'That's right.'

'So, who was he married to then? Who's Chiara's real mum?'

'Long story, Denis. And not one Rosa wants bringing up, to be honest.' Eva relented slightly. 'Chiara's mum, Carys, used to work for Rosa when Rosa was running her financial company in London.'

'Oh, fancy.' Denis's eyes widened. 'And?'

'And what?'

'So where is she now? This Carys?'

'Safely in Sydney, Australia. A good ten thousand miles or so, away. Right, that's enough gossip for one day, I think, don't you? Hell, it's raining.' Eva gave Denis what she hoped was a firm cutting-off to the conversation before pulling up the collar of her mac, fishing for her keys in its left-hand pocket and heading back to the car.

Eva made her way back down the path. Blimey, what a day this had been: meeting the rocker Drew Livingston; Virginia's threat to knock her out of Bill's inheritance; Andrea's sudden and very unexpected return to Milan and the subsequent lovemaking that had *literally* knocked her out.

Eva paused at the vicarage gate, narrowing her eyes as she stared across to the entrance of The Jolly Sailor pub through the now heavy rain where a couple was just leaving. She recognised immediately the tall, dark-haired Zac Anderson, the American researching the UK's historic halls who had shared their Burns' lunch a couple of weeks earlier. Eva frowned, wiping at her wet face while squinting furiously once again as she tried to get a handle on the tiny, blonde-haired woman accompanying him. Her heart gave a lurch, her pulse racing as she saw the pair separate and, before Eva could race across the road to confirm her suspicions, jump into their respective cars and take off in the opposite direction.

Eva's heart continued to race. Was that who she'd thought it was? She knew she'd not seen Carys Powell, Rosa's best friend and PA in London, for almost eight years, but the woman who'd just walked out of the pub with Zac Anderson looked remarkably like her. Eva shook her head slightly; it must have been because she'd just been chatting to Denis Butterworth about Carys that she'd sort of manifested her presence when, in reality, she was across the other side of the world in Australia.

Eva unlocked the back door of the Evoque, reaching in for her umbrella before heading along the pavement through the village towards Little Acorns primary school in order to pick up Laila and Nora. What time were Rosa and Joe due back from London? She knew Roberto and Michelle, Joe's parents, were looking after Chiara while Rosa and Joe kept their appointment in Wimbledon.

Should she say something to the Rosavina grandparents? Something to the school? Should she ring Rosa herself? Michelle Rosavina had obviously picked Chiara up on time – Eva herself, she now saw, was ten minutes late – and Joe's mum gave her a friendly hoot as she drove herself and the little girl in the direction of her own house at the other side of town.

Admonishing herself for being fanciful, Eva turned to her own girls who now showered her with book bags, swimming bags and, from Nora, a somewhat phallic-looking snake made from paper cups, before hurrying them through the pouring rain back to the Evoque and the vicarage.

# 10

*March*

'OK, let's brainstorm what we already know about this Jet Set, mythical or otherwise.' Daisy, seated in the middle of Hannah and Eva in the boardroom of Heatherly Hall, looked somewhat expectantly – and then hopefully – across and along the table. When no one amongst the five Westenbury Players, and less so amongst the four from Heatherly Hall itself, appeared willing – or able – to contribute to getting the ball rolling, Daisy looked at her watch. 'We've only just over three weeks, to write, rehearse and actually put on this little scenario to celebrate both the centenary of one of Agatha Christie's novels – *Murder on the Links* – as well as telling the story of the missing jewellery commissioned for Mrs Simpson, Edward the Eighth's mistress, here at Heatherly Hall.' Daisy turned to Hannah who was furiously scribbling notes.

'Hannah?'

'Sorry?' Hannah attempted to cover what she'd been writing, with her arm. 'Sorry,' she said again.

'Everyone's wanting a little background to the story, Hannah.' Eva nudged her sister sharply. 'And how you see the evening panning out?'

'Right, yes, so we're looking at three weeks...' Hannah volunteered.

'Hannah, we *know* that.' Eva appeared as stressed as Hannah.

'What we don't know, is what the hell we're supposed to be *doing*. Look...' she turned apologetically to the others '...since first mooting this idea of the missing Jet Set a couple of weeks ago, we've now taken on a major wedding the same week, actually the day before – I mean a really big, hugely important event, and Hannah and I are not convinced we can do both.'

'Ditch the wedding then.' Graham Maddison, local vet and Daisy's father, grinned before turning to face Hannah and Eva. 'Come on, girls, we've been looking forward to this, ever since our Daisy asked us. We were supposed to be putting on Alan Bennett's *Office Suite* in the village hall in March, but there's a bloody great hole in the roof and we've had to postpone it until the summer. This Jet Set idea will tide us over nicely until then.'

'You don't fancy just having the winter off?' Eva ventured. 'We *are* extremely busy here.'

'*No*, we've got the bit between our teeth now,' Daisy said, crossly. 'It's a brilliant idea: a murder mystery evening...'

'I keep telling you, no one *died*, Daisy.' Hannah exhaled deeply, turning over the sheet of paper to which she'd surreptitiously been adding notes and reminders for the Livingston/Sharma wedding, before attempting to give her full attention to the gathered group. 'Well, as far as we know, anyway.'

'That's the absolute beauty of this, Hannah. No one knows what actually *did* happen.' Daisy's eagerness was infectious. 'We can totally make it up as we go along.'

'Daisy's right, Hannah,' Tara, Hannah's deputy, enthused. 'The main thing is to tempt people up here with an hour or so's drama à la Agatha Christie, and then set them off on a treasure hunt to find the facsimile of the Jet Set – there'll be a jet necklace with a glass stone somewhere on eBay – before feeding them a 1930s-style buffet...'

'Which is?' Eva interrupted doubtfully.

Tara frowned. 'I'll google it.' She turned to the laptop in front of her.

'So,' Daisy went on, 'once we've put on our little play, the audience will be given envelopes containing messages to decode, and clues to decipher, in order to reveal the whereabouts in the hall of this facsimile Jet Set…'

'I'm hopeless at crosswords.' Eva frowned.

'Well, luckily for you, Dad and I are absolutely brilliant.' Daisy preened a little. 'Dad here, as well as administering to the village's cows and sheep, compiles the weekly crossword in the *Midhope Examiner*…'

'Oh,' Eva stared. '*The Gem?* Is that you, Graham?'

'Graham Edmund Maddison.' Vivienne Maddison, Graham's very glamorous mother – and Daisy's granny – who, up until now had been unusually quiet, announced proudly, 'He's all there, is my son, you know,' she went on in her affected actress voice. 'Compiling crosswords is his way of relaxing after having his arms up cows' wotsits or amputating a heifer's toe, as he was doing today.' Vivienne stroked Graham's arm. 'I always wanted Graham to follow me on to the stage, you know; he really is very good at taking on a variety of parts…'

'Cows have toes?' Eva pulled a puzzled face at Hannah and Tara, before turning back to Graham. 'Well, Graham, I hope any clues you set the audience to lead them to this Jet Set – which we need to get on with and actually buy if the evening is going ahead – will be a lot easier than that clue from the one in Saturday night's *Examiner*.' Eva screwed up her face to remember: '*Damp fog hides nothing?* One word, five letters? What was all that about?'

'Moist,' Graham said proudly. 'One of my better clues.'

'So,' Tara went on, looking up from her laptop. 'I'm really up for this now: there'll be plenty of chills, thrills and, of course, delicious cocktails and canapés to help the investigation. The audience will be told to dress in their best detective clobber, or 1930s frocks, and they'll have the run of the hall to start searching for those clues!'

'Not the whole of the hall,' Hannah demurred, once again

engrossed in the list in front of her. 'We'll still be clearing up from the Livingston wedding, Tara, don't forget.'

'The *Livingston* wedding?' Five Westenbury Players turned as one. 'You haven't gone and got Drew Livingston's marriage to Aditi Sharma?' Hilary Makepiece, church warden – and latterly, newly trained Yoga Goddess – stared.

'Hannah, for heaven's sake,' Eva warned crossly.

'It was all over the papers at the weekend that they've sacked that castle in Scotland,' Hilary went on excitedly. 'But all a big secret where they were planning to actually get married now.'

'It *was* a big secret, Hilary.' Eva shook her head in Hannah's direction once more. 'And still is! If this gets out…'

'You *have*, haven't you?' Daisy leaned back in her chair, exhaling. 'You've bagged Drew Livingston! Whoa, no wonder you want to cancel us and concentrate on the wedding of the century here at the hall.'

'Absolutely, Daisy.' Hannah, mortified that she'd let slip about the coming wedding, now breathed a sigh of relief as she saw a chance to postpone this Agatha Christie do. 'So, you can see our difficulty, Daisy. Let's postpone this farce until the summer.'

'Hannah,' Daisy snapped. 'This was all *your* idea to begin with. Dad, Vivienne and I have already done a load of work on this.' She frowned. 'When I *should* have been revising for my module on Zoo Animal and Management Welfare Study.'

'Zoo animals? I didn't know you were thinking of going into zoo work, Daisy?' Tara's eyes lit up. 'If you're planning on staying round here, that would be good. We could think about snakes and tarantulas for the petting zoo. Hannah? What do you think?'

'Sorry?' Hannah didn't appear to be concentrating. 'No, they'd scare the pigs and the llamas. And Lachlan as well,' she added. 'He's a total arachnophobe.'

'I do hope, Hannah,' Vivienne interrupted crossly, 'that when you're bandying about the word *farce*, you're referring *literally* to a comedy that seeks to entertain an audience through situations that are highly exaggerated, extravagant, ridiculous, absurd, and improbable…'

'Don't forget,' Graham put in, 'the mockery of real-life situations, people, events, and interactions; unlikely and humorous instances of miscommunication; ludicrous, improbable, and exaggerated characters; and broadly stylised performances.'

'As opposed to *your* patently obvious meaning, Hannah, that what the Westenbury Players want to put on here is *farcical*?' Daisy had joined her grandmother and father in dissing Hannah.

'I'm so sorry,' Hannah started to say, embarrassed at being told off.

'That's alright then,' Daisy said cheerfully. 'Let's continue. And…' she started to laugh '…the reason Dad and Vivienne can spout verbatim as to what a farce actually is, is that they were both interviewed the other week on Radio Midhope about the Westenbury Players – and gave this place a plug into the bargain – and had done their homework and been practising for days. Right, let's get on.'

'So,' Tara said, obviously pleased that her googling had borne fruit, 'then we'll finish with an afternoon-tea-type buffet: you know, cucumber sandwiches and the rest. It's what they always ate in the olden days apparently.'

'Afternoon tea? In the evening?' Hannah exhaled again.

'Well, I'm sure you can come up with a different menu.' Daisy flapped a hand impatiently.

'But, Daisy, people will need to know if they're just having nibbly bits or a full-blown meal,' Hannah said anxiously. 'Should they have had their tea before they set off? You know what folk round here are like – they don't like to miss their tea.'

'I'll sort the food aspect,' Tara said cheerfully. 'Simon downstairs in marketing will sort the advertising – he's got good contacts with the *Midhope Examiner* as well as with local radio.'

'Bit more than good contact,' Hilary Makepiece snorted. 'He was snogging the life out of that Trixie Turner – you know the blonde who runs Radio Midhope's teatime slot every day? – in The Jolly Sailor car park last week...'

'Really?' Tara and Hannah's eyes opened wide as they spoke as one.

'I thought Simon was engaged to...' continued Tara.

'Can we just get on?' Eva interrupted, looking at her watch. 'I've a ton of stuff I need to check up on at the art retreat before the new visitors arrive in the morning.' Laila and Nora were staying the night with Rayan and Yasmin and new baby Farhan and, rather than go back alone to the house at Heath Green, she'd planned to spend a couple of hours sorting the materials needed for the next day's art classes. Eva turned her gaze on Graham, Daisy, Vivienne, Hilary and Pandora Boothroyd who apparently made up the main body of the Westenbury Players. 'Aren't you a bit short of players?' she asked. 'Particularly men? You appear to be the only male, Graham?'

'Am-dram has always had a dearth of men,' Graham agreed somewhat gloomily. 'Or at least *young* men. We men do have a tendency to die in our sixties – you know heart attacks, prostate cancer and the like – and you merry widows get together to sing in choirs and join am-dram societies, go on Tinder and have girly weekends away to Marbella and, all in all, have a whale of a time once you...'

'What about Lachlan, Hannah?' Daisy deliberately interrupted her father's apparent envy of the sybaritic lifestyle of what he considered to be out-on-the-pull, let-loose middle-aged widows.

'Lachlan? I wouldn't have thought so.'

'Well, we know he's not a *player*...' Daisy laughed at the ambiguous meaning of the handle as she patted Hannah's arm, but you can't say he's not a bit of an entertainer.' Daisy grinned. 'He addressed that haggis very *theatrically* at the Burns' do that Sunday lunchtime.'

'He'd put away quite a bit of Scotch beforehand,' Hannah said doubtfully.

'Well, we can always make sure he's had a couple of drinks before he goes up on stage,' Daisy reassured the others.

'I thought it was going to be theatre in the round, not *up on* stage?' Hannah's head shot up. 'We won't have time to assemble a big stage just the day after the wedding.'

'In the round, Hannah,' Daisy soothed. 'Definitely *In the Round*. We can have audience participation that way.'

'It's not *Live at the Apollo*, you know, Daisy,' Eva warned.

'And,' Daisy went on, deliberately ignoring Eva, 'the absolutely brilliant thing is that we'll all be around and on tap to help you with this coming wedding.'

'Absolutely *not*,' Eva snapped. 'There will be a very apparent dividing line between the two events, and extra staff will be taken on for the former.' Eva turned to Tara. 'Make sure Felicity and HR get straight on with that this morning, will you? The wedding will be over, and the guests well on their way by the time you all arrive to perform, Daisy.' Eva mentally crossed her fingers.

'So, we won't be able to rehearse the day before the performance?' Daisy asked. 'That's when we always have a full-dress rehearsal – you know, *always* the day before.'

'Not this time, you won't,' Eva said irritably. 'There'll be a big wedding going on the day before and *every* part of the hall will be accommodated.'

'Honestly, we don't mind coming up to help…' Daisy grinned '…as well as getting a good gawp at Drew Livingston.' She sighed. 'Hell, there'll be so many famous people. He's big mates with David Beckham, you know; always had a thing about David Beckham…'

'Oh,' Hilary tutted, examining her nails. 'Been there, done that, worn the tattoo.'

'What? You've had David Beckham?' Tara glanced across at the church warden before moving her gaze for confirmation to Hannah, who shrugged back in her direction.

'In your dreams, Hilary.' Daisy frowned but, glancing across at Hilary who was now sat back in her chair with folded arms, a little smile playing mischievously on her still very pretty face, it was obvious there was a seed of doubt in Daisy's mind. Hadn't Hilary, in the sixth form, famously knocked about with the Manchester United youth team?

'Right,' Hannah said, shuffling papers importantly in the manner of a BBC newsreader. She was eager to leave this farce – and yes, she did mean farce – and meet up with Felicity to get on with the real work of planning the wedding. She stood up, but sat down again as she remembered Lachlan. 'Oh, and Eva's right,' Hannah went on, 'it's definitely not Lachlan's thing at all – you know, acting. Anyway, he'll be far too busy with the lambing next month…' She trailed off as the office door opened. 'Oh, Zac, you made it?' Hannah stood again to welcome the American researcher, going slightly pink as she did so.

'The security guy said to find you up here, Hannah. I hope I'm not too late?'

'No, no, not at all. I've…' Hannah flushed a deeper shade of pink '…*we've* been waiting for you. You're just the *very person*.' Hannah almost fell over her words as she continued to gaze at the man.

'Oh?'

'We're going ahead with putting on *The Jet Set of Heatherly Hall* and you did volunteer your services as an actor, if I recall?' Hannah smiled beguilingly in the newcomer's direction, and Eva shot her sister a look. What on earth was the matter with her? Eva inwardly tutted, recognising the look on Hannah's face: she'd been exactly the same when Hannah'd been in love – in lust – with married man Ben Pennington, the adulterous tosser. Ben Pennington and this man Zac appeared somewhat similar – tall, dark-haired and blue-eyed and with that air of confidence, that veneer, which had women falling at their feet in a mushy heap. Eva didn't recall her sister ever swooning over her partner, Lachlan, the lovely, steady red-haired Lachlan, who'd probably been in love with Hannah ever since his arrival from the Balmoral estate to take over as estate manager at the hall, just before Bill's death the previous summer.

'Not a problem, Hannah,' Zac was now saying, his eyes never once leaving her face. 'Happy to oblige. In fact, I've been staying the past couple of nights down at The Jolly Sailor while spending my days in the local library as I research Heatherly Hall and, as luck would have it, I've spent a couple of evenings chatting with some old guy who's always in there over a pint. He certainly knows some background to the story you're going to be acting out.'

'Roy?' Eva asked. 'Roy Newsome?'

'Yes, that's the guy.'

'Beat you to it,' Eva said bluntly. 'The three of us had a long chat with him just after Jude told us about the Jet Set.'

'Where *is* Rosa?' Pandora Boothroyd asked. 'I think it's my turn for the church flowers next week. I was hoping she'd be here to confirm.'

'Yes, where is our village vicar?' Daisy smiled. 'I thought she'd want to be in on this meeting? She *is* part of the Heatherly Hall management committee, after all.'

'Rosa had an important meeting in London yesterday...' Eva started.

'Oh? With Justin?' Pandora Boothroyd asked.

'Justin?'

'Welby. The Archbishop of Canterbury.' Pandora turned to Hilary. 'I met Justin once you know.'

'Yes, Pandora,' Hilary responded with a derisory sniff. 'You said.' Hilary turned back to Eva, lowering her voice. 'It's Rosa's eggs, isn't it?'

'Shhh,' Eva retorted crossly. 'Don't tell *everyone*, Hilary.'

'Oh, we all *know*,' Hilary said, poking Eva in the arm. 'And we're all with Rosa, Eva. We're her family; her family in God. We're going to be urging her on to be a mummy every bit of the way: praying for her, keeping our fingers crossed.'

'Just don't broadcast it, Hilary,' Eva snapped again crossly before turning back to Hannah who, she saw, was twiddling her hair around her finger, red-lipsticked mouth slightly open as she continued to listen to Zac. And she was leaning in to him as well, Eva saw. 'You made notes, Hannah? Hannah! As we chatted to Roy the other week?' The spell was obviously broken and Hannah turned. 'Hell, don't know what I've done with them.' Hannah flicked through her notebook. 'Back in the flat I think.'

Eva turned back to Zac. 'So, you've been staying at The Jolly Sailor then, have you?'

'I have. Quaint little place. Bed's rather too narrow for my liking, but folks are friendly.'

'I'm amazed,' Eva said. 'It usually takes a lot of sizing you up and finding out who you are, as well as *why* you're here, before the locals will deign to include you in their conversation.'

'As I say, all very friendly and ready to give me what I'm looking for.'

'Which is what?'

'Eva!' Hannah was obviously annoyed by her sister's sharpness. 'Zac, do you want to follow me and I'll begin to give you a bit of a guided tour round some parts of the hall and point out some of the history as I know it? There are several books and pamphlets that do give a fairly brief outline of the hall in the souvenir shop on the ground floor, but it'll be all locked up at this time of evening. If you want to follow me, I'll get my keys and see what we can find for you.'

Hannah turned to the rest of the people in the room. 'OK, all. Thank you so much for coming this evening. It appears we're definitely going ahead with *The Jet Set of Heatherly Hall* then? Fine. I'm going to have to leave a lot of its planning to you, Eva, and to you, Daisy, and your players. I'm sure you can all work together? Just keep me in the loop, would you?' She paused before turning to her deputy. 'Tara, I want an early breakfast meeting back up here in the boardroom to get on with the *important* business pertaining to Heatherly Hall. Would you inform Felicity – 7am?'

'Bloody hell.' Daisy laughed as Hannah left the office, Zac in tow. '*She's* suddenly come back to life after spending most of the meeting trying to get out of us doing this Jet Set evening. She's suddenly become Miranda Priestly.'

'Who?' Eva frowned. 'Who's Miranda Priestly?'

'*The Devil Wears Prada* boss. Hannah's turning into her: as she left just now, I thought she was going to come out with: "Truth is, no one can do what I do…"' Daisy turned to Eva. 'Who's lit *her* fire?'

'I'll give you two guesses.' Eva sighed. And then, realising she was beginning to miss Andrea terribly, and not relishing the idea of making her way back alone to a cold, quiet house, addressed Daisy and Tara. 'Do you two fancy a pint down at The Jolly Sailor?'

## II

'I certainly get what Hannah sees in that American,' Tara was saying as the three of them moved to find a seat at the back of the pub. The pub was surprisingly full for a March school night and they had to quickly bag a table when the couple in front of them stood to leave.

'Really?' Daisy frowned. 'I can't. Compared to Lachlan who I've always had a bit of a thing for, Zac seems very smooth: not a hair out of place, designer gear. I bet he uses moisturiser.'

'And has a manicure,' Tara suggested, laughing. She glanced round the room as Daisy took off her jacket before starting in the direction of the bar. 'How come it's so busy in here? On a Wednesday night?'

'Quiz night,' Eva confirmed as she pointed to the quiz master gearing up with microphone and sheets. 'And also, people are fed up of dry January and February, as well as the bloody heating bills at home. Probably cheaper to turn off the gas fire and come down here to get warm – as long as they can spin out one drink all evening – and be entertained into the bargain.'

'Actually,' Daisy ventured, 'while that guy's got his microphone to hand, I'm going to ask if I can tell the punters about the Jet Set evening.'

'Are you? Just like that? A bit of free advertising?' Eva was doubtful.

'With only three weeks to go, we really need to get the information out there. If he says I can't...' Daisy grinned determinedly '...I'll remind him he owes the surgery a couple of hundred quid for the removal of various socks and a thong from the gullet of his black Lab. And, looking at the size of his wife, I can tell you now, that red lacy thong could not *possibly* have belonged to her.'

Ten minutes later, Daisy was back with three glasses of wine. 'He says I can have the mic at the break in the quiz.'

'So, Daisy,' Tara said, sitting back on the black faux-leather banquette, 'you were saying you don't think much of Zac Anderson?'

'No, I *didn't* say that. He's exceptionally good-looking, I can see that. It's just that I love Lachlan to bits and I just don't get it if Hannah's going to mess him around with Zac.'

'What makes you think she is?' Eva frowned.

'Oh, come on, Eva, Hannah's eyes were out on starry cartoon stalks as soon as Zac walked into the office. And she went all pink and started twirling her hair round her fingers when she was talking to him. You must have seen her. And taking him on a sightseeing trip of the hall? In the dark?'

'She can switch the lights on.' Eva relented. 'OK, I know what you mean. I'll have a word with her. We all love Lachlan. I mean, he's gorgeous: all that lovely auburn hair, and that wonderful Highland accent. And did you get a load of him in that kilt the other Sunday? Blimey!'

'Well,' Tara said, blushing as she downed her wine. 'I'll tell you now, *I've* fancied Lachlan Buchanan ever since he arrived at Heatherly Hall. If Hannah's going to throw him over for that American chap, I'm ready to catch him. What *does* your sister see in these smooth characters? Look how she fell for Ben Pennington's charm. Tosser that he was.'

'Well, if it's confession time...' Daisy grinned, downing the contents of her own glass '...if something were to happen to Jude...'

'Something happen to him? What like?' Eva was concerned. 'He's not ill or anything, is he?'

'No, no, but let's just say he was seduced by a blue-rinsed Tory matron.'

'What? Jude with a modern-day Margaret Thatcher?' Eva started to laugh. 'That's never going to happen.'

'Well, alright then, a bolshie left-wing twenty-year-old pushing her way upwards through the political glass ceiling...'

'Much more like it.' Tara and Eva nodded sagely.

'I mean, I know he won't, because I trust him and I love him. Blimey, don't think I've ever said that about a man before.' Daisy appeared slightly embarrassed. 'Goodness, am I allowed another glass? It's nearly Thursday and Thursday is the weekend after all.'

'So, you were saying?' Tara elbowed Daisy.

'All I'm trying to say is that if Jude were to go off the rails when he's far away from me and being seduced by all that political rhetoric down in London, then I might find myself looking Lachlan's way. What I'm also trying to say is, if your sister plays around with the American, and Lachlan ends up a free agent, then he *won't be* for long.'

'He certainly won't.' Tara paused. 'There's another one who's got the hots for him.' Daisy and Eva turned to where Tara was nodding her head. Lachlan's assistant up at Heatherly Hall, Geraldine ('call me Ger') McBain, a fiery-haired young Glaswegian who, the previous summer, had graduated from the local agricultural college, was standing at the bar waiting to be served.

'Who's she with?' Eva hissed, craning her neck. 'Not Lachlan?'

'Don't think so,' Tara said thankfully. 'I'd hate to think of Lachlan with the fiery one. She's quite terrifying, isn't she?' The three of them silently admired Ger's voluptuous leather-clad figure, undisguised even when at work in her dungarees, overalls and toe-capped boots. Ger, Eva knew, strode the perimeter of the parkland like a modern-day Valkyrie. Daisy squinted across at the man who was standing with Ger. 'No, not Lachlan.'

'Some biker, I reckon,' Tara sniffed.

Ger turned, a mass of red wavy hair framing her beautiful pale face. She raised a hand when she saw the three of them pointedly staring and Eva hissed, 'Don't look. She'll think we're talking about her.'

'We *are* talking about her.' Daisy laughed. 'God, to be twenty-five again and with a figure like that. She and Lachlan would have divine red-haired babies,' she added almost wistfully.

'She and Lachlan are not going to be even *thinking* about having babies together,' Eva snapped crossly. 'He's with Hannah.'

'Ah,' said Daisy, standing as the mic man waved his microphone in their direction. 'But is Hannah with Lachlan?'

At the very moment Daisy was posing the question as to whether Hannah was *with* Lachlan, it would appear she most certainly was not. Lachlan Buchanan, having cut his hand rather badly while removing, and then replacing, a section of rusty barbed wire as the lengthening March daylight began to fade, had realised the injury needed more attention than he could give it. Unable to find Hannah, or anyone else who might oblige, he'd made his way to his Land Rover, his hand wrapped in a tea towel and dripping blood, ready to take himself over to A and E.

'Lachlan? You OK? Goodness me, what have you done?' Rosa, on a post-London high, had driven up to the hall from the vicarage, bursting with the news that she and Joe had taken their first steps to having a baby. OK, they *were* the first steps, ridiculously tiny steps on the long journey ahead. But Joe, holding her tight once they were back at the hotel in Kensington and in bed, had whispered: '*The journey of a thousand miles begins with one step.*'

'Bit of a cliché that, Joe,' she'd said, recalling the wise words of Martin Luther King and smiling into her pillow. 'How about: *Faith is taking the first step when you can't yet see the whole staircase?*'

Drunk on love, hope and expectation, Joe had wrapped his arms tightly round her and, while he'd immediately fallen into a deep sleep, exhausted by the travel and events of the day, Rosa had stayed awake giving thanks to God for giving Joe back to her, and the opportunity to have their baby.

Now, having travelled back up from the capital, she just wanted to share the anticipation and excitement with Hannah and Eva because, otherwise, it was a bit like having a good feel of and then opening exciting presents on Christmas morning, but all by yourself.

'Shall I go and find Hannah?' Rosa blanched slightly as she saw blood start to seep through the Heatherly Hall tea towel wrapped round Lachlan's hand.

'It's fine – just remembered they're all in a meeting. I'm taking myself off to A and E.'

'You can't drive, dripping blood like that. Joe's over at his mum's fetching Chiara. Come on, I'll take you.' Rosa shook her car keys in Lachlan's direction.

'No, really…' Lachlan broke off, his face white. He steadied himself on the bonnet of the Land Rover. 'I'm not very good with blood,' he apologised.

'I'm even worse,' Rosa said, 'but you can't drive with it like that. Come on, my car's round the back.'

Two hours later they were still waiting in an exceptionally busy A and E department in Midhope General, the triage nurse having assured Lachlan he wasn't going anywhere without stitches and a tetanus shot.

'You go back home, Rosa. I can get a taxi back.'

'It's OK. I'm not going to leave you. Waiting in A and E is bad enough when you're with someone but, by yourself, pretty damned boring. I bet you've not brought a book with you, have you?'

Lachlan laughed at that. 'Going back to my apartment to hunt for Dickens wasn't uppermost in my mind at the time. Was enough that I messaged Ger to take MacDuff out for a pee if I wasn't back in time.'

Rosa looked round at a plethora of crying babies, whining toddlers intent on going AWOL from harassed mothers who, to Rosa, appeared not much older than kids themselves (perhaps they weren't) as well as several bewildered elderly, bearing the marks of both falls and fear. She smiled sympathetically at the adjacent young girl as she made another unsuccessful attempt to insert a dummy into her child's mouth. But the girl only glared back in response before tutting and moving to reception to ask, yet again, how much longer she was going to be kept waiting.

'You're still pretty pale, Lachlan.' Rosa broke off from conversing with a just-mobile one-year-old clutching precariously at her pink cassock who, now he'd found his feet, was obviously on a mission to explore his newly accessible universe. The baby advanced in Lachlan's direction and he smiled down at him, reaching down to steady the child with his one good hand as the infant began to totter.

'I never thought of you liking children,' Rosa said as Lachlan, obviously amused, continued to watch the child's progress along the line of waiting clients.

'Oh?' Lachlan gave her a searching look.

Slightly embarrassed at his reaction, she backtracked. 'Sorry, I've just got babies on my mind at the moment...' She trailed off. She really had to stop thinking about babies and the idea that one day soon she and Joe were hopefully going to make one together. Hadn't Doctor Shevchenko advised her to just get on with her normal life? But without any added stress?

'Oh of course,' Lachlan was now saying. 'I'm sorry, Rosa, how did it go in London?'

'Yes, good, I think. But, you know, I really must stop talking about it; thinking about it all the time. I'm becoming obsessed.' Rosa laughed, still embarrassed. 'There's a danger I'm going to become a baby bore: going to have to stop myself writing my Sunday sermons about babies.'

Lachlan turned back to her. 'Understandable. You'll make a great mum, Rosa.'

'Well, I'm asking the man above for as much help as possible. So,' she ventured, 'you and Hannah seem to be getting on pretty well.'

'Do we?' Lachlan ran his one remaining good hand through his thick auburn hair. He hesitated and then, obviously wanting to talk, went on, 'You know, when I left the Balmoral estate last summer, I was actually running away.'

'I think we all run away from something or someone at some point in our lives. I certainly ran back up here to Yorkshire from London when Joe ended up with Carys.'

'But you'd just been diagnosed with cancer, Rosa. I'm not surprised you ran away: ran back to your mum and dad and Eva and Hannah.'

'So, what were you running from, Lachlan?'

He hesitated, wincing slightly as he moved his hand. 'The thing is, Rosa, I can understand what Hannah was going through last summer. You know, with that married surgeon bloke? I knew that *my* relationship up in Scotland was well and truly over. I mean…' Lachlan broke off, trying to smile '…let's face it, you can't get much more *over* than the woman you're in love with – and who you thought was in love with *you* – going back to her husband.' Lachlan looked away. 'The thing is,' he said once again, 'I never for one minute thought I'd fall in love again.' Then he smiled and Rosa thought, not for the first time, what a thoroughly decent, lovely – and bloody attractive – man Lachlan Buchanan was. 'I remember seeing Hannah for the first time. I'd no idea who she was – didn't realise she was one of Bill Astley's daughters – and telling her off for not having your dad's dog – Brian is it? – on a lead when there were sheep in the next field.'

'It takes Brian all his time to get off his bed.' Rosa laughed. 'He certainly wouldn't have the energy to sniff at sheep, never mind chase them.'

'I know all that now. I was just in a foul temper – didn't want to be down here in Yorkshire. I was missing Scotland.'

'And Bridget?'

'You know her name?' Lachlan's head came up in surprise.

'Hannah told me. We weren't gossiping... well, I suppose we were.' Rosa laughed and Lachlan smiled.

'As I say, I never thought I'd fall in love again, but seeing Hannah at Bill's funeral, so devastated at losing her dad...'

'*Richard's* our dad,' Rosa reminded him gently. 'But yes,' she relented, 'we all loved Bill as our second dad. But I think, of the three of us, it was always Hannah who adored Bill and Heatherly Hall. And I don't think she's allowed herself to grieve him properly. She turned even more to Ben Pennington for love and comfort when Bill died. And Ben just wasn't there for her.'

'He was no good for her.' Lachlan raised an eyebrow.

'He wasn't,' Rosa agreed. 'He's a serial womaniser as far as I can see.' She hesitated. 'Eva and I are so glad she saw the light eventually and threw him out of her life. And you, Lachlan...' Rosa patted his arm '...are so good for her. You're just what she needs.'

'Rosa, I'm not a prescription to be taken to tide Hannah over during a difficult time in her life.' Lachlan frowned crossly before obviously relenting. 'I'm there for her as she – as always – continues to take far too much on at the hall. She's constantly trying to prove something. Trouble is, I'm not sure what.'

'She just wants the hall to be a success.'

'It's more than that.'

'Is it?' Rosa turned in surprise.

'I don't know what she wants.'

'I don't think Hannah does.' Rosa smiled. 'I think, as I've got older and can see more of a way through my own life – oh hell, sorry, that came out a bit sanctimonious, a bit *vicarly* – I'm realising Hannah's always had a bit of Middle Child Syndrome.'

'Middle Triplet Syndrome?' Lachlan grinned.

'Well yes, but don't forget we had Virginia as well as our big sister. Eva was always – and I mean *always* – the naughty one of the three of us. Mum was constantly being called in to school because of Eva. And then there was me: the good girl. Fell in love with Joe at sixteen and ended up as a vicar for heaven's sake.' Rosa fingered her dog collar and laughed slightly self-consciously. 'I actually did some research on Middle Child Syndrome,' she added. 'A few years ago, when I needed a break from all the religious stuff I was having to cram in at vicar college.'

'Oh?'

'Apparently, it can leave some adults with an inferiority complex due to a perceived lack of attention as well as a constant need to grab from those around them. Being a middle child – maybe feeling they're not one thing or the other – can lead to feelings of inadequacy and not being worthy of love and affection. And – and I think this might apply particularly to Hannah – there's always this sense that they don't deserve someone who really loves them.'

'Right.' Lachlan scratched at his head.

'But for God's sake – sorry God – don't *ever* let on to Hannah that I've discussed her with *anyone* – but particularly you. She'd go absolutely ape.'

'Cross my heart.' Lachlan smiled.

'The thing is…' Rosa smiled '…and I'll shut up after I say this, I think you're very special and just what Hannah needs right now in her life.'

'I love her, Rosa,' Lachlan said bleakly. 'I'm just not convinced she feels the same…' He broke off as his name was called. 'Right, that's me. Shit, I'm as bad with needles as I am with blood.'

Back at The Jolly Sailor, at the precise moment Lachlan Buchanan caught sight of both the needle and the jagged, deep cut about to be stitched and, having assured the young doctor he'd never once fainted in his life, proceeded to crumple in a heap on the floor of the A and E side room, Eva stood to pull on her coat. As she did so, she looked across at the four arrivals who'd just walked through the heavy wooden entrance to the pub, before disappearing, en masse, into the back room.

Her heart pounding with disbelief, Eva wrapped her scarf firmly round her neck before turning to Daisy and Tara. 'You two get off,' she said quietly. 'Looks like I've a bit of unfinished business over there.' And, without looking back, she set off determinedly in the direction of the snug to where the four newcomers had made their way.

# 12

'It *was* you,' Eva almost snarled at the petite blonde now unwinding her scarf from around her slender neck as she stood with the others towards the back of the snug, behind the main bar of The Jolly Sailor.

'It *is* me,' Carys Powell corrected as she turned, two pinpricks of red in her otherwise tanned face the only indication she might be feeling any sense of nervousness at facing Eva after all these years. 'Bloody cold in the UK,' she said in her sing-song Welsh accent, pointedly pulling up the collar of her beautiful navy woollen coat. 'Don't know how you stand it, Eva.' She shivered dramatically, rubbing her hands together before turning to Jonny Astley who stood to one side of her. 'I'd love a glass of white.' She smiled. 'Just a very small one, I think, and, if at all possible, in this godforsaken backwater, an Australian one? Sauvignon Blanc?' She smiled coquettishly at Jonny who moved to the bar.

Eva turned furiously on Virginia who was trying to stand her ground, knowing she was next in line to face her sister's wrath. 'What the hell are *you* doing here with *her*, Virginia?' she hissed quietly, grabbing at Virginia's arm and pulling her away from the others. 'And with these two as well?' Eva turned to Jonny Astley, Bill's legitimate son and, since his father's death, the new Marquess of Stratton of Heatherly Hall, who offered up a little wave of acknowledgement from his stance at the bar.

'Eva, I can't say it's a pleasure to see you again,' he drawled, 'but we've come all the way from California, so will you join us in a drink?'

Ignoring him, Eva glanced at Billy-Jo, Jonny's wife, giving her the advantage of the best withering look she could muster, before turning back to Virginia. 'Well?' she hissed. 'Virginia? Don't you care that you seem to be… seem to be… *in league* with someone who has hurt Rosa so badly?'

'Do I look as if I'm someone who gives a shit?' Virginia gave a little smirk.

'Sorry?' Eva felt totally and utterly floored. This was Virginia, her big sister, who up until this moment had thought uttering 'damn' blasphemous.

'And,' Virginia went on, obviously relishing a sense of pride and victory at her bravery in facing up to Eva, as well as basking in the safety of her new-found mates, 'I've told you, I prefer to go by the name of Ginny now, if you don't mind.'

'I don't believe this.' Eva ran a hand through her hair, unsure who to face next. The obvious choice, being the most dangerous, was Carys. 'Does Joe know you're here?'

'Not yet. But he will. I got the impression he was in London with Rosa?'

'You got the impression?' Eva stared. 'How dare you, Carys? How dare you come here, telling me you know what's going on in Joe's life? And Rosa's life?'

'Of course I know.' Carys smiled and Eva wanted to slap her. 'And I think it pretty obvious what I want. I want my daughter, Eva. I want Chiara and I'm going to have her.'

'Well, I'm telling you now, you can't. You're *not* having her. There's not a court in this land will allow a seven-year-old little girl to be taken from her father and handed over to the woman who abandoned her to go and live in Australia with another man.'

'Oh, I think you'll find there's a way,' Carys said softly.

'Joe has *parental responsibility* for Chiara,' Eva snapped. 'You can't take her to live in Sydney without his permission, and there's no way on this planet that he will give it.'

'I've done my homework, Eva; I wouldn't have travelled all this way if I didn't feel fairly confident the courts would work in my favour. I shall point out my son, left in Joe's care here in Westenbury, almost ended up in prison. How he turned into a burglar? I believe he broke into Rosa's vicarage one night?' Carys gave an affected little laugh. 'I still can't get over that high-flying Rosa Quinn of London ended back up here in the sticks as a village vicar. That really does take some believing.' She laughed and then paused. 'And, Eva, you only have to look at Rhys's exemplary school records, when my son was living with me in London, to see that living with Joe was detrimental to his welfare.'

'What?' Eva almost laughed. 'Rhys went off the rails because *you* left him. Left him and Chiara to run off with some loaded fancy man who, I'm assuming, didn't want *them* as well?'

'I think you'll find, Eva, I left Joe for my own mental – and physical – wellbeing. I could no longer live with a man who had such coercive control over me. Who beat me...'

'*Beat* you? Joe?' Eva actually laughed out loud at that. 'And controlled you? No one has ever been able to control you, Carys Powell.'

'Carys Carter now,' Carys corrected smugly.

'It's true, Eva.' Virginia took the proffered glass of wine from Jonny Astley who was taking in the conversation, a little smile playing on his thin lips. 'Carys has told me how Joe constantly manipulated her, threatened what he'd do to her if she tried to leave him; how she had to, in the end, *run* for her life.' Virginia's eyes were saucers.

'Ran all the way to Australia?' Eva snorted disparagingly. 'Ran ten thousand miles with an exceptionally rich and good-looking man?' She turned back to Carys. 'Yes, Carys,' she went on, nodding her head, 'I've googled him: Spencer Carter, one of the wealthiest men in the southern hemisphere. I bet you had your running gear and Nikes on when you set your cap at *him*.'

Carys flushed slightly, but came out fighting. 'Spencer's wealth had absolutely nothing whatsoever to do with my having to flee for my life.'

'What?' Eva really did laugh then. 'Joe is the gentlest man I think I've ever met. Alright,' Eva demurred, nodding slightly as she recalled how she, herself, had refused to have anything to do with Joe Rosavina after his one-night stand with the woman now standing in front of her, 'I had no time for the man myself, at one point but...'

'Oh,' Carys purred, stroking at Eva's arm almost flirtatiously, 'you'll be a character witness then, Eva? Tell the courts how he treated Rosa when he got me pregnant?'

'I think you got *yourself* pregnant, Carys,' Eva snapped, removing her arm from Carys's hand. 'Don't tell me that wasn't your plan all along – get Joe drunk, seduce him and take him off Rosa, knowing he wanted children at a time when Rosa most certainly didn't? Oh, we knew *exactly* what you were up to.'

'I'm asking you to speak the truth, Eva.' Carys was suddenly looking directly at her, reaching for her hand once more, and Eva was instantly taken back ten years or so when she, Hannah and particularly Rosa had all fallen under this woman's spell. 'The courts have to know, Eva, what a thoroughly dangerous man Joe Rosavina can be. That my daughter isn't safe with him.'

'*What?*' Eva said once again. 'Of course he isn't *dangerous*. Of course I won't give evidence...'

'He broke her arm, Eva.' Virginia, obviously loving the drama of the whole situation, was almost gleeful. 'Look.' She grabbed at Carys's arm, pushing up her coat sleeve in her eagerness to have something on Joe.

'What am I looking at, *Ginny*?'

'Carys broke her wrist. Well, *Joe* broke it.'

'What am I supposed to be looking at?' Eva said once more, glaring at her elder sister before turning back to Carys. 'So, Joe broke your arm, did he?' Eva asked softly. 'And why was that?'

'He most certainly did.' Carys was vehement. 'I was trying to escape the house, and he grabbed me and pushed me down so I wouldn't leave. I landed awkwardly.'

For the first time that evening, Eva felt a flicker of doubt with regards to Joe Rosavina. She'd known and loved her brother-in-law since the triplets had first met him at Heatherly Hall's Petting Farm, when they were all just sixteen and about to start A levels. All three of them had fancied him like mad, been determined to be the one, once they saw he was at sixth-form college with them, to get off with him. But he'd had eyes for no one but Rosa.

Until Carys Powell, the tiny, charismatically beautiful, organised firecracker of a woman, had appeared on the scene in London, taken on by Rosa to be her PA and constantly at her side, as Rosa's financial company, *Rosa Quinn Investments*, took off and then soared. Carys Powell, on whom Rosa had come to rely and whom, she'd often said, she just could not be without.

While Eva had always accepted Carys's manipulation of Joe Rosavina had been to blame for Joe leaving Rosa once he knew Carys was pregnant with his child, Eva had never been able to forgive Joe himself. Even when he'd returned to Westenbury, a divorced man, together with Rhys Johnson, Carys's son from a previous relationship and Chiara, his own daughter with Carys. Until eventually Eva had seen how he still loved – adored – Rosa. Eva had forgiven him, not only because to not do so would go against what Rosa wanted, but because she genuinely saw that one drunken night of being seduced for sex was nothing, absolutely *nothing*, compared to his total love for Rosa.

But could Carys be telling the truth here? Had Joe been

so determined to keep her, once they were married, that he'd actually physically hurt her in his efforts to stop her leaving? Had she been so terrified of Joe, she'd fled leaving her children behind? Eva shook her head, unsure where to go next. She turned to Jonny Astley.

'And how have *you* got yourself embroiled with all this? What has Carys Powell go to do with you?'

'Absolutely nothing.' Billy-Jo, Jonny Astley's Californian wife, spoke for the first time. 'Never met this charming woman before until Ginny introduced us earlier this evening. Although,' Billy-Jo sniffed, 'we hear she's suffered at the hands of you three Quinn girls, as has poor Ginny here as well as Jonny and myself. We're here because Ginny contacted us.'

'Quick work, Virginia.' Eva gave her sister another of her looks before turning back to Jonny Astley's wife.

'And why wouldn't she want to get the will sorted?' Billy-Jo snapped. 'Ginny here was on the phone to us as soon as she was told the truth about her parentage. She's Bill's daughter for heaven's sake – Jonny's sister.'

'Oh, spare me the familial connection,' Eva said crossly.

'She *is* family.'

'As are Rosa and Hannah,' Eva said tiredly. It had been a long day: she had a headache, she hadn't eaten since the bowl of cornflakes at breakfast, and she knew she had to get round to the vicarage before she returned home in order to warn Rosa and Joe of Carys's arrival and intention. She wasn't looking forward to being the bearer of such awful tidings.

'Well, we certainly know *you're* not,' Billy-Jo went on rudely.

'Not what?'

'Family,' Billy-Jo said crossly. 'I don't know how you live with yourself, Evelyn...'

'It's Eva,' Eva snapped.

'How you *live* with yourself,' Billy-Jo went on unperturbed, 'knowing that Bill left you a third of Heatherly Hall under the misconception you were his biological daughter.'

'Absolutely,' Virginia now put in, tossing back what Eva realised was newly extended hair. 'You should hand over everything my father left *you*, to *me*. It's my entitlement.' When Eva didn't reply, when part of her thought *Ginny* was actually correct, she had no moral right to Heatherly Hall, her sister went on, excitedly, 'And now that Jonny is on the trail of Edward VIII's Jet Set…'

'Sorry?' Eva turned back to her sister. 'Oh, you've got yourself involved in *this* as well now, have you, Virginia?'

'The whole village is buzzing with it,' Virginia said almost sulkily. 'After the article in the *Examiner* there was a big piece both in *The Yorkshire Post* and even *The Sun* – didn't you know? And now the Westenbury Players are going to be acting it out up at Heatherly, there's even more interest. Oh yes,' she went on, smirking, 'the interest over Heatherly Hall is national and international now.'

'International interest?' Eva actually laughed out loud at that. 'Another little fairy story to add to your being the long-lost princess in the castle tale? You'll be growing your hair next – oops, sorry, already been there, done that, I see – and letting it down to Prince Jonny here once he shouts "Rapunzel" up at you from the roof of Tea and Cake.' Eva tutted, shaking her head at her big sister.

'Actually yes, *international*, Eva.' Jonny Astley smiled a little smile of triumph. '*The New York Times* got hold of the story a few months or so ago. Anything to do with Wallis Simpson is big news over the pond.'

'I've had enough,' Eva snapped, pulling on her woollen gloves and turning back to Carys. 'I'm off over to the vicarage to break the news to my sister that you're here to take back her daughter.'

'*Her* daughter? *Hers?*' Carys's face flushed red with anger. 'Rosa, I believe, is unable to bear children?' Carys turned before slowly and deliberately unbuttoning the navy coat and facing Eva. The well-rounded little bump was unmistakable through

Carys's sky-blue cashmere fitted dress. She removed the coat and placed it over the back of a chair before rubbing at the small of her back in the manner of all pregnant women and smiled up at Eva. 'You wouldn't deny Chiara the right to be with her new little sister, would you, Eva?'

'Eva?' Joe came to the vicarage door in his stockinged feet. He glanced at his watch. 'What's up? You OK?'

'Where's Rosa?'

'She's up at A and E with Lachlan.'

'Is she? Why? What's wrong?' Eva felt the usual frisson of panic that always took hold of her whenever Rosa's health was at stake.

Joe smiled. 'No, it's OK. *She*'s OK. It's Lachlan who's cut his hand very badly. Rosa drove him up to A and E and stayed with him. Good job she did, I think.' Joe grinned. 'Apparently, he went over like a ton of bricks when he caught sight of the needle. Cracked his head on the edge of a table as he went down.'

'Oh goodness. But Rosa's OK?'

'She's fine. I've told her to come home now and let Lachlan get himself a taxi once he's had his head seen to.' Joe laughed again. 'You don't expect a big strapping bloke like Lachlan to go funny at the sight of a needle, do you?'

'Where's Hannah? Why isn't *she* with him?'

'Oh, I don't know.' Joe shook his head. 'At a meeting or something, I think Rosa said. Come in, come in.' Joe made to open the door wider. 'Are Laila and Nora with Rayan?'

Eva nodded and followed Joe down the passageway. A fire was burning in the log burner and the sitting room was warm and cosy, a sharp and welcome contrast to the cold damp evening outside.

'Where's Chiara?' Eva felt anxiety rise once more.

'She's in bed.' Joe sounded surprised. 'It's almost ten. She's fast asleep.'

'Joe, Carys is here.' There was no other way to say it – to soften the blow.

Joe's handsome face drained of colour and he stared at Eva. 'What do you mean? Here? In the UK?'

'Across the road, Joe. She's staying at The Jolly Sailor. And she wants Chiara.'

Joe sat down heavily on the sofa, his face anguished.

'Look, Joe, can I ask you something?' Eva sat down beside him. 'The thing is, I told Carys there was no way any court would give her custody of Chiara.' Eva hesitated. 'She says she'll get her back because you... What's the words they use all the time now...? Because you exercised *coercive control* over her...'

Joe actually laughed out loud at that. 'I did *what?*'

'Carys says she ran away because she was frightened of you. Joe, she said you *broke her arm.*'

Joe stared. '*I* broke her arm? Eva, she'd been off with Spencer Carter all weekend. He's the Australian bloke she's ended up with,' he went on by way of explanation. 'She came back home, wanting to take Chiara off to meet him. She'd been drinking: champagne very probably. And driving. There was no way I was letting Chiara go anywhere in the car with her in that state. In any state, drink or no. Chiara wanted to go with her; Carys tried to take her and I had to intervene. She fell over my briefcase and broke *her wrist* when she put her hand out to save herself. It wasn't her arm and it certainly wasn't my doing.'

'Really?'

'You don't believe me?' Joe stared. 'You think I'm capable of violence against a woman?'

Eva shook her head. 'I just don't know anymore, Joe.'

'Eva, I *wanted* her to go. I can't tell you how awful it was, being married to her. But there was no way I was letting Carys take my daughter once she finally left for good.'

'Right.'

Joe shook his head in turn. 'I don't know what to say, Eva, I can't believe you think I'm capable of what Carys is saying. It's her way of getting Chiara back, you know, making up stuff like this.'

'OK.' Eva turned, placing a hand on Joe's arm. 'I suggest you pour yourself a stiff drink, Joe. And then, are you going to tell Rosa? Or shall I?'

# 13

'U p here, watch your step.' Hannah, behind and guiding Zac
Anderson up the flight of marble steps leading from the
cavernous body of the Great Hall towards what had been Bill's
apartment, and into which she'd moved after his death, admired
the American's firm denim-clad backside as he climbed upwards
in front of her.

'This is so amazing, Hannah. Thank you so much for taking
time to give me a guided tour of the place.' He smiled a perfectly
white smile over his navy sweater and Hannah felt her insides
melt. She was getting exactly the same feelings with this man as
when she'd first met her ex, married man Ben Pennington. But
one big difference: this man didn't have a wife he was cheating
on, wouldn't have to start glancing at his watch knowing he
needed to be back at home with her and two children. Except
then again, this was a massive presumption: Zac Anderson could
have a whole tribe of wives and offspring back in the States. Or
was that just Mormons? And living in Salt Lake City?'

'Where are you from actually, Zac?' Hannah asked casually
as they came to a halt on the mezzanine floor overlooking the
Great Hall. 'Was it Salt Lake City?'

Zac turned, frowning. 'Salt Lake City? Where've you got that
from?' He grinned down at her. 'Maine. A good two and a half
thousand miles from Utah.'

'That's good.' Hannah breathed a sigh of relief and went over to join Zac where he was gazing in wonder down over the great oak banisters and across to his left where one could look down on the famous Heatherly Hall chandelier.

'Wow,' Zac said. 'That is some lighting. Even when it's not switched on.'

'Certainly is,' Hannah said proudly, basking in his admiration. 'We don't actually turn it on much these days. Too expensive – you know, the electricity bill for this place is horrendous, and rocketing at the moment with the energy crisis. The management committee holds the purse strings and are pretty stingy with funds.'

'Do you mind if I take a couple of photos?' Zac reached for his phone and, when Hannah nodded her consent, snapped at the surrounding architecture. 'So,' he eventually asked, turning back to face her, 'when we put on this Agatha Christie evening, where will it be actually performed? Over in the wedding venue?'

'Oh, you really want to have a part in it?' Hannah asked, trying hard not to appear too eager.

'Of course, if Daisy will have me.'

'Have you?' For a split second, Hannah nearly said: *I'll have you; I'm more than willing.*

'Have me in this production.' Zac nodded. 'It sounds a blast – it would be a total honour to be allowed to be part of such a historic story. So, across at the wedding venue?' he asked once again. 'In the west wing?'

'Yes, that was the plan.' Hannah nodded. 'But, with the huge society wedding and all the security and media presence that that will entail just the day before, I've said we have to move it and perform it here, in the round. The Great Hall itself is so big we should be able to seat the audience comfortably. I'm leaving it to Daisy and her dad to sort out. I really don't have the time.'

'I can understand that.' Zac stroked her arm, giving her the benefit of his smile once more. 'Daisy's already been in touch and invited me to help with the script. I'm meeting up with the rest of the Westenbury Players in The Jolly Sailor one evening next week.'

'Oh?' Hannah felt a little stab at being left out.

'Daisy says not to bother you. You've enough on.'

'Well, I'm sure I can take an evening off to come down to the pub. How are you finding it, staying down there?'

'Quaint.' Zac laughed. 'Little old England at its best, I guess: the bed's pretty narrow and the shower's just a dribble. But I'm not here for the comfort of staying in a five-star hotel. I'm up and out and about early, straight after breakfast. I've been up to Castle Howard for a look around today. That is one amazing pile. Then Wentworth the day after tomorrow.'

'So why the interest in English historic houses?' Hannah asked, turning and leading Zac up the final flight of stairs – stone now – wanting to show him the fabulous art retreat Eva had project-managed and now spent time in charge of, as well as actually teaching some classes there. 'Are your family originally from England? You know, leaving on the *Mayflower* with the first settlers?'

'I wish.' Zac laughed. 'That really would be something to write about. No, no British ancestors as far as I know, although I've dug deep in the hope that there may be. All Americans like to think of England as home. No, I studied English history at university and then went on to teach it at Maine. I'm an associate professor of history there and, I think I said, it's the state's only public research university.'

'Maine?' Hannah said almost dreamily. 'I've been to New York and Las Vegas but never to your part of the States. I know absolutely nothing about it.'

'You'll have to come and visit me there,' Zac said softly. 'Maine is most famous for its lobster – it has 3,478 miles of coastline,' he went on proudly. 'And, a couple of facts for you, Hannah: Maine's coastline has so many deep harbours that it could provide anchorage for all the naval fleets in the world.'

'Wow!'

'And, the first naval battle of the Revolutionary War was fought off Machias Maine in 1775...'

'Goodness.' Hannah's eyes were saucers, although she had no idea what the hell the Revolutionary War was. 'You really do love all things history, don't you?'

'It's my job...' Zac broke off as he made his way through the heavy wooden door Hannah opened to his left, and he caught his first glimpse of Bill Astley's nude murals painted a good fifty years before. 'Whoa, now that *is* something.' Zac whistled as, obviously entranced, he made his way slowly along the beautifully painted walls.

'My nieces call these the rudie-nudies,' Hannah explained, embarrassed at being with this exceptionally attractive and fanciable man while surrounded by pornography. Alright, eroticism. Was there a difference? Was one art, while the other smacked of sleaze? She followed Zac as he took in every aspect of the artwork – every wall, from floor to ceiling, as well as the actual ceiling itself in what was a long gallery, stretching seemingly for ever, covered in exquisite figures. Huge, vibrant oil paintings alive with exotic flowers, flying and swooping tropical birds; trees whose limbs became entangled with those of naked men and sultry wanton women, their heads thrown back in abandonment.

'My mother – my birth mother – once said this gallery was like being where Paradise met with Sodom and Gomorrah: a benign deity crossing swords with the devil.' Hannah laughed slightly in an effort to break the ensuing silence as Zac stood and stared, spellbound.

'Your birth mother?' Zac asked, without turning, his gaze fixated on a semi-naked man whose legs, muscled and rippling, were wrapped possessively around a woman dressed only in a thin, transparent shift.

'Hmm.' Hannah laughed self-consciously but carried on regardless. 'My birth mother, Alice, had just met Bill Astley, the twelfth Marquess of Stratton.' She paused. 'My sister and I were, apparently, conceived on this very spot.' Hannah felt herself flush scarlet and was glad she'd not turned on all the art retreat's lights.

'Your *sister*?' Zac finally turned in Hannah's direction. 'I thought you had *sisters*? I thought you were triplets?'

'We are. Long story. Eva has a different biological father to Rosa and me.'

'Right. You'll have to explain that to me one day – obviously one hell of a story to be told. Oh, I'm sorry.' Zac now gave Hannah his full attention, smiling down at her, his beautiful blue eyes concerned. 'I've embarrassed you, asking you to show me this place. I'm sorry,' he said again. He moved towards her and for one awful – wonderful? – moment Hannah thought he was going to kiss her. How ironic it would be if she was overtaken by lust as Alice had been on that fateful evening with Bill, and history repeated itself. Wonderful if he'd kiss her because... *Come on, Hannah*, she censured herself, *you've thought and fantasised about nothing else ever since Zac Anderson walked in on Lachlan's Burns' supper birthday lunch*. But awful if he *had* come on to her because she was with Lachlan. She was *with* Lachlan, she reminded herself: she was his girlfriend, his partner, his mate. Mate in the sense of being his pal as well as, you know, mating...

All these thoughts crashing through her mind like some out-of-control juggernaut disappeared as Zac took her hand, turned her to him and, reaching a hand into her long dark hair, kissed her lightly but obviously very meaningfully on her open mouth.

Abruptly Zac pulled away as footsteps sounded up the stone steps and along the corridor, leaving Hannah flushed and confused, but wanting more.

'Oh, it's you.' Geraldine (call me Ger) McBain, Lachlan's deputy, stood at the entrance to the art retreat, dressed from head to toe in black leather, hands very pointedly on her hips. Behind her, Brian and Charlie, two of the hall's night security staff were ogling both the rudie-nudies and Hannah's obvious discomfiture. 'We thought there'd been a break-in,' Geraldine sniffed, eyes narrowing as she took in first Hannah and then a totally composed Zac.

Hannah came out fighting. 'Why on earth would you think that?' she asked crossly. 'I'm just showing Mr Anderson, here, around the hall.'

'At ten o'clock at night?' Ger retorted.

'I didn't know there was a rule about only showing people round before 6pm?' Hannah said archly. 'Mr Anderson is a professor of history, researching British stately homes.' She fought to get the upper hand with Ger who'd always terrified her. 'So, what were *you* doing hanging around the hall at ten o'clock at night?'

'I do live on site, Hannah,' Geraldine said as though she were talking to a recalcitrant child. 'And wasn't it you yourself who only a couple of days ago suggested security be upped in light of this coming great big fuck-off wedding?'

Wincing at the profanity, (for some reason Hannah didn't want Zac to think her staff thought themselves able to cuss and swear in front of her) Hannah said tartly, 'I doubt anyone's going to be hiding up here ready to take photographs of the bride and groom, three weeks before the actual do.'

'I came up from my flat to help Lachlan,' Geraldine now said with just a modicum of triumph.

'Help him?' Hannah frowned. 'Help him do what? Have the ewes finally started to lamb?'

'Lachlan cut his hand very badly this afternoon,' Geraldine said loftily, obviously delighted that she knew something Hannah didn't. 'Rosa's been with him up at A and E all evening.'

'My Rosa?'

'Do you know any other? Rosa's been trying to message you, but when she couldn't get hold of you, she asked me to come up and meet her and Lachlan at the gates. I've just helped him to bed as well as seen to MacDuff. He's back in his own flat,' she added meaningfully.

'My phone's off,' Hannah said. 'I never put it back on after this afternoon's meeting.'

'Other things on your mind?' Geraldine suggested, glancing across at Zac. 'Anyway, I saw the lights were on up here in the art retreat and called security.'

'Thing is, Ms Quinn,' Charlie now put in, obviously eager to have a say, 'since that there article about the Jet Set jewellery keeps appearing in all the newspapers – it were even in *The Sun* a couple of weeks back – we've had all sorts of strange characters hanging around with metal detectors. We're only doing our job you know.'

'Of course you are,' Hannah soothed. 'And thank you so much for being so on the ball, both of you.' Hannah smiled winningly at the security guys while making a big thing about not including Ger. She turned to Zac. 'I'll see you out, Mr Anderson. And then,' turning to Ger with a saccharine smile, added, 'go and see what I can do for Lachlan.'

'I think you'll find, Hannah, he's fast asleep.' Ger obviously wasn't having her rival thinking she could take over as Florence Nightingale. 'Rosa said the hospital gave him a couple of heavy-duty painkillers and said to let him sleep it off.'

'Sounds like he's been out on the tiles,' Hannah said, immediately regretting it.

'Hardly,' Geraldine snapped crossly and somewhat pointedly. 'Not *everyone* round here needs a drink to get through. My rooms are just across from Lachlan's – I'll be there if he needs anything.'

While Hannah and Ger were squaring up to each other, Rosa was pulling up into the vicarage drive. While she felt bone-weary after four long hours sitting on an uncomfortable seat with only a disgusting coffee to relieve the ennui, she was also feeling the satisfaction of a job well done. She'd really got to know Lachlan, and was so pleased that there appeared to be no side to him; that what you saw was what you got. Hannah would be an absolute fool to let this lovely man slip from her grasp while she pursued the American, even if Zac Anderson was personable and friendly as well as exceptionally good-looking and, it was pretty obvious, had been captivated by Hannah. Oh well, she thought, locking the car door and making her way up the drive, eager to be sliding under the duvet with Joe, as long as Hannah was happy...

Rosa came to a sudden stop, aware there was something not quite right: a sense of something – or someone – watching her. She glanced across to the wall and lychgate separating the vicarage garden from the church graveyard. She'd never, even when living here by herself before Joe and Chiara moved in with her, been afraid of the dead – it was the living who often unnerved her – but Denis had warned her, only that evening, of a shady-looking bloke hanging around both the vicarage and in the church itself.

'The thing is, Vicar,' Denis had said, 'since the world and his wife seem to have got hold of this blooming Jet Set story, and knowing your... your 'eritage, your *descending* from the marquess up at the 'all... as well as the *assumption* that the village vicar probably knows more about the missing joolery than she's letting on...' here Denis had paused hopefully '...then we're going to have every bounty hunter from every county traipsing round the village, leaving their litter and trampling on the daffs once they're up. You need to keep a lookout, Rosa. You know.' Denis had made a big thing of peering round suspiciously. 'We don't want you being abducted and held to ransom for them there jewels.' Denis's eyes had hovered somewhere around Rosa's middle. 'Especially in your condition.'

'My condition?' Rosa had tutted. Did the verger really think that one visit to a fertility clinic in Wimbledon and she was instantly pregnant? Maybe he did.

The conversation came back to Rosa now as she peered into the darkness, trying to work out what exactly had spooked her. Maybe it was Eva's car, parked further up the drive. Why was her sister here at ten at night? She shook her head at herself and set off once more towards the porch and the heavy front door, key to hand.

'Hello, Rosa.'

Rosa's head shot up in fright as a slight figure slipped, wraith-like from the shelter of the porch and moved towards her.

'I was just coming to see you both.' Carys smiled. 'Well, to see you *all*,' she went on, a defiant little smile on her pretty face. She took both hands from their resting place in the deep pockets of her navy coat and, laying one briefly on Rosa's arm said, 'Shall we go in?'

'There's nothing for you here, Carys,' Rosa managed to get out, her heart thumping.

'Not very Christian of you, that, Rosa.' Carys almost purred the words and then, changing tack said, 'Rosa, I've come all the way from Sydney for my daughter, and I'm not going back without her.'

Rosa stood stock-still, not knowing what to do. 'Chiara's not here,' she lied. 'She's with Joe's parents.'

'And here was I thinking women of God don't lie. Rosa, you know and I know that's not true; I watched as Joe brought her home in the car. She's grown,' she added almost proudly. 'And so pretty.'

'You didn't speak to her?' Rosa said, frightened. 'She doesn't know you're here?'

'No.' Carys smiled. 'But, Rosa, if you don't let me in right now so I can talk to both you and Joe, then I'm going to shout out her name at the top of my voice until...'

'No, no, don't do that. You'll waken her and frighten her.'

'How on earth can a little girl who has been deprived of being with her mother for the last two years be frightened? Of her own mother? How, Rosa? How?' Carys appeared genuinely puzzled.

'This will kill Joe, Carys,' Rosa pleaded. And me, she added silently into the darkness of the chilly March night. She found her hands were shaking and she shoved them deep into her jacket pockets.

'Surely not,' Carys said. 'I hear you're trying for a child of your own, Rosa?'

'You hear...?' Rosa almost gasped.

'A new child is such a gift from God, don't you think? And I'm sure God will be on your side in this. You know, after giving up your high-flying London investment company to serve him and look after the spiritual needs of the villagers? And, from what I've seen...' she tinkled merrily '...these country bumpkins appear to be in need of *something*.'

Rosa stared. 'I really don't think...' she started, but was cut off mid-sentence as the door opened and a white-faced Joe stood illuminated in the light of the hallway.

'You'd better come in,' Joe said dully, moving aside to allow Carys entry, followed by a still-trembling Rosa.

'It's almost as though you were expecting her,' Rosa hissed into the back of Joe's black fleece as, almost regally, Carys led the way into the sitting room.

'I was,' Joe said, not even turning to take Rosa in a brief, empathetic embrace that would have shown some solidarity, some nuance as to how she was feeling. 'Eva's here. She came round to warn me...'

He broke off as the start of a furious riposte between Eva and Carys came from the direction of the sitting room, and both he and Rosa ran towards it. But then turned as a hand appeared over the banister, only to disappear and be replaced by two bare feet on the top step. And then a nightie-attired Chiara, long fair hair framing her beautiful little face, made her way slowly down each step, her arms clutched around a cuddly toy koala bear.

Joe stepped towards her. 'Go back to bed, Chiara,' he whispered. 'You've been having a dream.'

But Carys was suddenly at his side, her coat now open to reveal her full, round bump. Rosa gave a silent gasp of envy, and then a more audible gasp of hurt as Chiara flung herself into Carys's arms with a 'Mummy, Mummy. You came for me.'

# 14

Eva was missing Andrea terribly.

She knew she'd held back from giving herself fully to this new relationship after the breakup of her marriage to Rayan. Wary of jumping from one commitment straight into another when her aim, after being with her husband since meeting Rayan at dental school, had been to spend some time on her own to find herself and not fall immediately into another permanent one. She knew Andrea had, himself, withdrawn slightly in order to give her space. Bloody silly phrase: *finding herself*, she tutted as she caught the toast with one hand as it popped up while scrambling eggs with the other and simultaneously calling for Laila and Nora to get a move on or they'd be late once again for school.

Finding herself? As though she were lost. Maybe, she conceded, as she placed the breakfast eggs in front of her girls, she *had* been lost. *Oh, for heaven's sake, you daft bint*, she chastised herself once more – how could she be lost when she lived in this lovely house with her two adored girls and was in a relationship with the very gorgeous Andrea. In a relationship? Eva glanced at the Malik and Malik Dental Surgery calendar hanging on the kitchen wall and realised Andrea had been gone a couple of weeks and, apart from a text in reply to her own to say he'd arrived safely in Milan with his sculptures, she'd heard nothing since.

For the first time since he'd left, Eva began to wonder whether

Andrea had, in reality, gone for good. Her heart gave a little dip as she contemplated the awful possibility. Had she kept him at arm's length during their six months' relationship, happy to have him in her bed, but not willing to share her whole life with him? She'd insisted Andrea rent the cottage next to Daisy's down at Holly Close Farm once it came free, and he'd demurred but eventually acquiesced. Had this led him to think Eva wasn't fully committed to the relationship?

Eva picked up her phone and messaged Andrea:

Hope all well?

Before immediately erasing the words – realising it sounded like a granny's message on a postcard from Bridlington – and replacing with:

Missing you. Give me a call when you can!

Feeling slightly better, she chivvied the girls into coats and scarves, handed over book bags, Tupperware boxes of carrots and grapes for snack time and hunted under the sofa for Laila's lost set of Jacks.

'Mummy,' Laila said from the back seat, once they were almost at Little Acorns, 'Miss Stuart was asking me about the jewels yesterday.'

'Which jewels?' Eva turned slightly. 'And who's Miss Stuart?'

'The Jet Set jewels, silly,' Laila tutted, as though Eva was a halfwit. There were times, Eva conceded as she braked for Deimante the lollipop lady's non-negotiable instructions to STOP that, compared to this precocious eight-year-old of hers, she was just that.

'And Miss Stuart?'

'She was a guest.'

'A guest?'

Laila tutted once more. 'Mrs Beaumont said she was a guest

in our school. She'd come from somewhere very important to give us a talk about the Tudors.'

'Oh, you're doing the Tudors now, are you?' Thank God Laila had moved on from the bloody Victorians at last.

'What's a *Chew Der*?' four-year-old Nora asked, her little face, as Eva glanced at her through the rear-view mirror, so like Rayan's that, for a moment, Eva's heart lurched as she remembered, once again, she'd lost her husband to Yasmin. *You didn't lose him, Eva*, she chided herself, *you gave him away because you no longer required him.*

'A Tudor man chops off his wife's head when he's fed up with being married to her,' Laila explained patiently. 'Mummy was very lucky Daddy didn't chop her head off. But now Daddy loves Yasmin, and they have a boy which is what all Tudor men *aimed for*, Miss Stuart said. Daddy and Yasmin now have an heir to the throne.' Laila paused, considering. 'Well, an heir to Malik and Malik anyway.'

'Girls are just as important as boys,' Eva protested. 'You two girls can take over Malik and Malik if that's what you want to do.'

'*I* know that,' Laila pouted. 'We do it in PHSE. And, if I want to be a boy, and wear boys' clothes that's fine too...'

'I don't want to be a boy.' Nora frowned. 'I want to be a princess.'

The pernicious guilt at depriving her girls from living with their father full-time flooded Eva's whole being once again; it was a relief to pull up into Rosa's drive at the vicarage where she always parked on the school run, before chivvying the girls along the pavement to cross the road. 'So, what did you tell this Miss Stuart?' Eva asked Laila as they trotted across the road once Deimante had given them the go-ahead (you didn't cross Deimante – or her road without permission – and live).

'What do you mean?' Laila asked, glancing up at her mother. 'I told her and the class all about Henry's six wives because I'd researched it all on Daddy's laptop last week.'

'I mean when she asked about the Jet Set?'

'I told her that the jewels belong to you, Mummy. And Aunty Rosa and Aunty Hannah and not that bad man, the American Jonny and his trollop of a wife, Billy-Jo…'

'What? You didn't? Oh, for heaven's sake…'

'…and when we find them, we'll be rich and have a swimming pool in the garden.'

'Right.' Where on earth had Laila got this from?

'And she asked if you'd already found them?' Laila frowned. 'And I said I didn't know. Have you, Mummy? Have you found them? Can we have a swimming pool? With a hot tub?'

'*I* want a swimming pool in the garden,' Nora piped up.

'You can't swim as well as me,' Laila crowed. 'You'd drown and die.'

'I don't want to drown and die and Mummy have no head.' Nora's bottom lip started to tremble. 'And I don't want to go to school. Don't like it.'

'You love Nursery class, Nora,' Eva protested. 'You love Miss Baker and Mrs Daunton.' Oh heavens, this was all she needed.

'No, I don't. Don't like Nathan. He smells funny. And he pushed me off the mat.'

'Wait until you're in year three, Nora,' Laila taunted. 'You'll have to learn all your tables right up to twelve times table.'

'I can't do tables,' Nora sobbed. 'Want to go to Daddy's to see Yasmin and Farhan.'

'You know you don't do up to twelve times tables in year three,' Eva admonished Laila crossly, stung at Nora's request to be with her new stepmother and baby brother.

'*I* do,' Laila boasted. 'Mrs Beaumont says *I* need to be pushed.'

Yes, right off a sodding great cliff, Eva thought irritably, and then felt immediate guilt. 'Look, Nora, let's go and have a little chat with Miss Baker.'

Ten minutes later, relieved that Nora, once in Nursery, had immediately donned the princess outfit and was sat laughing with a gaggle of similarly dressed little girls, Eva left school.

She'd aimed to pop along the corridor to the year three classroom to ask why this Miss Stuart woman had been questioning Laila about the Jet Set but, looking at her watch she knew she was well behind with her work up at the Heatherly Hall Art Retreat. Ten guests were arriving that afternoon for a two-night ceramics residential and she wanted to be sure all the materials Kate Maddison, Daisy's mother – an award-winning potter – would need were to hand. She also checked with Tara that the bedrooms and meals were booked and ready for the guests. Although not really a ceramicist herself, Eva had thrown, decorated and fired enough pots to be another pair of teaching hands among the guests, who were all novices to the art, so she'd be needed on that front too.

'Oh, Joe?' As Eva let herself out of the Victorian school building, Joe Rosavina was just making his way in, Chiara in tow. 'You're late? You OK?'

'Not really. Hang on.' Through the open door, Eva watched Joe quickly admit Chiara for registration at the reception window before hugging his daughter goodbye – almost fiercely, Eva saw – and return to the playground where Eva was waiting for him.

'Chiara wants to go to Australia with Carys, Eva. I don't know what to do,' he blurted as soon as he'd reached her.

'You don't know what *to do*?' Eva felt the survival instinct of a mother tiger immediately gird her loins. 'You get a bloody good lawyer, Joe, and you absolutely refuse to let Chiara go. *And* you don't let Chiara out of your and Rosa's sight. *And*,' Eva went on vehemently, 'you don't let that woman have *any* access to Chiara, even if you or Rosa are with her. I hope you've informed the head...' Eva nodded back towards the school door '...that Chiara must not, under any circumstances, be allowed to go with her mother?'

'Of course I have,' Joe snapped crossly. 'Do credit me with some common sense, Eva. I rang this morning at eight. Mrs Beresford is already aware of the situation, but I needed to warn her Carys was actually here. In Westenbury. And means business. *And*,' he went on, 'I've already got a lawyer.' Joe's face was thunderous. 'When Chiara, Rhys and I moved back to Westenbury over a year ago, I got straight down to Blackwell and Brown in town – James Blackwell's my brief. With Rhys being sixteen and my stepson, there was little I could do to prevent *him* going off to Sydney to be with Carys once she decided she wanted him with her, after all. He appears to have settled and is doing well in school in Sydney. He FaceTimes Chiara – and me and Rosa, to be fair – and is full of his life out there. He's big into surfing – goes out on Spencer Carter's speed boat in Manly harbour. It's got him away from the toxic crowd he was mixed up with here in Midhope, and he's living the life. So I haven't any complaints on that front, to be fair.'

'And what does this James Blackwell say?' Eva was impatient, eager to know if Joe had put in place all that was available to him to stop Carys removing her daughter from Joe's guardianship. 'Surely you make Chiara a ward of court?'

'I've got to go, Eva.' Joe rubbed at his face tiredly. 'The business isn't doing as well as it should and I can't afford to miss meeting up with this client in Manchester.'

'Really?' Eva frowned. 'But your finance company was always doing so well, Joe. You and Rosa were flying high, years ago.'

'When I was still in London, yes. Listen, Eva, keep all this about my potential business problems to yourself – I don't want to worry Rosa when we're desperately trying to have a baby of our own.' He looked at his watch, frowning. 'And, the last thing a court needs to hear is that I'm out of work when it comes to deciding where Chiara should live. I can just see it.' He attempted a smile. '"What was it, Your Honour, that saw you make a judgement in favour of the billionaire lifestyle in the sunshine of Manly with the little girl's mother?"'

'You're not on the point of losing the business, are you?' Eva's eyes widened in shock.

Joe shook his head. 'Hopefully not, but things are tight and I have to follow up every lead. I'll have to spend some time in Scandinavia in the next week or so where there's a bit of a problem. I can't just bury my head and not attend to it.' He paused. 'You don't have ten minutes to go and see Rosa again, do you? She's pretty down, as you can imagine. All the excitement of being told to get on with trying for a baby feels to have gone now she might lose Chiara. She loves her, you know. Loves her as much as I do.'

'Rosa would love anything or anyone that was yours, Joe. You know that.'

'The thing is,' Joe said, pulling car keys from his coat pocket and starting to walk in the direction of the vicarage, 'we were told she needs to be as calm and stress-free as possible in preparation for the transference of any embryo...' He trailed off. 'That bloody, bloody woman...'

'Without her you wouldn't have Chiara,' Eva said, hugging him, something she'd not done for years. 'Just remember that. And don't let Chiara go. It's that simple, Joe. Surely?'


'Rosa?' Eva let herself into the vicarage where she found Rosa still in pyjamas and staring into space at the kitchen table, a cup of untouched cold coffee in front of her.

'She wants to go, Eva,' Rosa said bleakly. 'And why *wouldn't* she want to go with her Carys? To be with her mum and brother in Australia? And now there's a new little sister on the way too. Of course Chiara wants to go.'

'Never mind what Chiara *wants*,' Eva snapped crossly. 'It's what's *best* for her. Carys Powell is an absolute nightmare.'

'Carys is her mum, Eva, and don't they always say the best place for a child is with its mother? You can't deny that, Eva.'

'Rosa, stop it this minute. Carys Powell left her son and five-year-old daughter over two years ago. I'm surprised Chiara even recognised her last night.'

'Carys has been Zooming and FaceTiming Chiara for the last twelve months, showing her the house in Sydney, the bedroom she's prepared for her, the beach and the swimming pool in the garden. What little girl's head wouldn't be turned, especially when her brother's there as well. And you know, compare that to living here in bloody cold West Yorkshire. In a gloomy vicarage, her bedroom here overlooking the graveyard.'

'Well, put like that...' Eva said, frowning and thinking, given the same circumstances, Laila would be off like a shot, bags packed, at the airport, passport and swimming goggles in hand before you could utter g'day.

'Thanks for that, Eva.' Rosa glared at her sister.

'But there's no way a court will let her go if the pair of you put up a fight. You're a vicar for heaven's sake. A pillar of the community.'

'Carys said she'd tell a court how she used to score drugs for me.'

Eva laughed out loud at that. 'Oh, for the love of God, Rosa, she occasionally got some uppers for you when you were desperate to stay awake at night so you could do business in New York over the phone.'

'And she's certainly prepared to say Joe was controlling, Eva; that he broke her wrist, that she had to flee for her life.' Rosa appeared to not know Eva had heard all this the previous evening.

'Yeah, yeah, yeah,' Eva snapped. 'Heard all this before. It's bullshit.'

'Is it?'

'Oh, for heaven's sake, Rosa, don't say you believe what she's making out?' Eva stared.

'I don't know what to believe anymore.'

'Do not let Carys Powell come between you and Joe again. She did it once when she ran off with him. Do not let her worm her way between you again. The woman is a manipulative bitch.'

'Eva, Chiara *wants* to be with her mum.' Big fat tears rolled down Rosa's face and she made no attempt to stop them. 'How can we deny her that? How *can* we?'

\*

Eva made her way directly upstairs to the Heatherly Hall Art Retreat, not stopping to pick up a coffee and muffin at Tea and Cake as was her wont, nor calling in at the office for a quick chat with Hannah. She knew she needed to update her sister, tell her Carys Powell was back and what was happening with Rosa and Joe, but she was so behind with the art retreat arrangements – the guests would be arriving after lunch – and it was the little touches she needed to know were in place. The flowers and Heatherly Hall chocolates put out in the bedrooms; the gold-trimmed menus offering the lavish lunch and dinner menus over in the conference centre as well as the very best art materials ready for their use that she needed to make sure of.

These delegates, or guests as Eva preferred to call them, had paid a lot of money to spend two days at the hall, and her first job was to meet and greet them, give them a tour of all the main buildings while detailing their history, before leading them to the newly designed and decorated sitting room off the workrooms and overlooking the hall's parkland, where they'd reconvene for a full afternoon tea and their first session with Kate Maddison followed by drinks and dinner. This particular evening, Eva had organised a talk to be given by a professor of Indian art at the local university, Doctor Shweta Bhatia, who would be outlining the archetypal elements of Indian ceramics and their links with India's cultural past.

Eva had gone round with her checklist, saw she had a good half an hour to spare before her guests arrived, and was about to set off to find Hannah when there was a knock on the heavy oak-panelled door. Cursing silently to herself that someone appeared to have arrived early and been allowed by staff on reception to make their own way up, instead of being greeted by herself, she quickly whipped out her lipstick, ran a hand through her long dark hair and, plastering a smile on her face, went to the door.

'Oh. Hello.' For a split second Eva couldn't quite work out

why the world's most famous rock musician, Drew Livingston, was standing in front of her. One expected to see him on TV, being interviewed by Graham Norton, or splashed across the colour supplements of the Sunday papers. 'Can I help you?'

'I'm hoping you can. I snuck up here without permission I'm afraid.' He smiled down at her from his six-foot-two height and Eva felt the power of speech begin to desert her. How did one start to address an icon, a superstar?

'Erm, come in. Do come in,' she managed to finally get out. 'Would you like a drink? A cup of tea?' Did heavily tattooed rockers, dressed in denim and leather, drink tea? Surely it was bottles of Jack Daniel's downed while smashing up hotel bedrooms? Eva glanced round nervously at the new cream sofas, and the George Smith chairs she'd persuaded Hannah and the management committee to shell out for.

Drew smiled. 'No, really. I just wanted to see the famous Heatherly Hall murals for myself, if that's OK? And, more importantly, to ask if you'd got anywhere with asking Dame Alice Parkes and Yves Dufort to the wedding celebrations? We've only a couple of weeks to go you know, and it *was* part of the deal.'

'The deal?'

'That we'd hold the wedding here at the hall if you were able to arrange that, Eva? It is Eva, isn't it?'

'It is.' Shit, she'd totally forgotten she said she'd look into having Alice and Yves present. *Stop fibbing, Eva*, she censured herself: she hadn't forgotten at all. She just didn't think Drew had been serious about the request.

'You didn't think I was serious, did you?' Drew raised an eyebrow.

'Of course I did,' Eva protested and then, seeing Drew was actually trying to hide a smile, came clean. 'OK, OK, no, I didn't. But I *will* do it, I promise. Honestly. Hannah will kill me if I don't.'

'And I will be eternally grateful if you do. You know, Eva, I went to art college when I left school.' His tone was wistful. 'A lot of me wishes I'd followed my heart and spent my life painting.'

'You'd have probably ended up starving in an attic...'

'Hey, I wasn't that bad.'

'Oh, sorry.' Eva felt herself redden. 'Or teaching in the local comp, was what I was trying to say. I mean, how many artists actually make it?'

'Your natural parents appear to have done OK for themselves.'

'They're the exception to the rule, believe me. And they struggled for years before gaining recognition.'

'So, with such a pedigree, Eva, you must be an artist yourself?'

'Like you, I listened to my head, and my parents – my adoptive parents – rather than to my heart.'

'And?'

'And?' Eva smiled, and then relented. 'I became a dentist.'

'Man, that's tough.' Drew threw his head back and laughed, genuinely amused.

'I made a good living from it,' Eva said huffily. 'And I loved – love – being a dentist,' she lied. 'My husband and I have a very successful practice down in Westenbury village.'

'You're married, Eva?' Drew glanced down at Eva's fingers, devoid of any ring.

'On the point of my divorce coming through.' Why on earth was she explaining the wreck of her marriage to this superstar?

'I'm sorry.' He hesitated. 'I don't for one minute think *my* marriage will last. Do any marriages actually last these days, Eva?'

'Why on earth are you getting married if you think that?' Eva was genuinely shocked. 'For heaven's sake, don't tell Rosa that.'

'Rosa?'

'My sister, the vicar who's going to be performing the ceremony? She's a bit uppity about marrying couples who aren't genuinely marrying for love.'

Drew didn't respond, but continued to simply look down at her before raising a warm hand to her face.

Eva felt her heart race. Surely, the world's most famous rock star wasn't about to kiss her? 'An eyelash,' he explained, gently stroking the ball of his thumb across her cheek. 'I…' He broke off as the door opened and Hannah appeared, obviously in irritable mode.

'Eva, your art retreat people are downstairs waiting…' She broke off as she took in Drew and his proximity to Eva. 'Drew, how lovely to see you. I didn't know you were here? Did we have a meeting… I'm sorry…?' Hannah spoke quickly, flustered.

'Hello, Hannah. I just popped in from motoring down from seeing my mum up in Northallerton this morning. I was hoping to see Eva, here.'

'Is there anything *I* can do for you?' Hannah glared at Eva. 'I'm more than happy…'

'It's fine, Hannah, really. I'm on my way back down the M1 to London now and Eva and I have come to an arrangement. He turned back to Eva and this time bent and actually kissed her cheek. 'Thanks, Eva, another time maybe? And…' he paused '…I'll know where to come when I need filling.'

'He'll know where to come when he *needs filling*?' Hannah was cross. 'And an arrangement? What was all *that* about?'

'*A* filling.' Eva giggled, still reeling from the kiss, however innocent its intention.

'You told Drew Livingston you were a dentist?'

'Why wouldn't I?' Eva actually laughed out loud at Hannah's affronted face.

'Because we're supposed to be *professional* event organisers, not an amateurish gaggle of dentists, youth workers and… and… *vicars*. I wouldn't *dream* of telling our guests, especially bloody important ones like Drew Livingston and Aditi Sharma, that two minutes ago I was dealing with feral kids with machetes down their undercrackers, and you were pulling molars.'

'Oh, get over yourself, Hannah.' Eva was still laughing.

'And he kissed you! Why did he kiss you?'

'Maybe he fancied me?' Eva was suddenly fed up of Hannah's censure.

'You always thought everybody fancied *you*. Even Dean Sutcliffe when we were in Mrs Green's class when it was *me* he chose first to be his wife when we were playing Farmer Wants a Wife...'

'We were five years old, you pillock.' Eva laughed, linking her arm through Hannah's. 'Come on, come with me to do your Lady Manager Welcome bit with the new art people, and I can tell you what's happening with Joe and Rosa on the way down.'

## 15

Hannah had been up since 5am, working on the arrangements for one of the biggest weddings the county had ever, to her knowledge, seen, the date of which was galloping towards her at breakneck speed. Now Tara was Hannah's deputy, and Tara's previous assistant, Felicity, had been promoted to being in charge of the hall's wedding venue, Hannah and Tara had made the decision to let Felicity's two part-time assistants mop up the bulk of the already-booked weddings while they and Felicity put all their energy and expertise into this Big One. Hannah knew she needed Eva and Rosa on board too and, while Rosa had finally agreed, almost reluctantly, to marry the couple, Hannah still hadn't been able to set up an actual meeting with the three of them. She also knew she couldn't ask Rosa to clear her desk – her altar – of her every other commitment in order to concentrate on this one. She could, however, insist Eva be free for the remaining time leading up to the big day and warn her to rope in her part-time nanny, Jodie, to do some extra hours if Laila and Nora weren't with their father.

Hannah and Tara had arranged full-on meetings for the following week with Drew's security team; with the couple's quite separate PA and promotional teams who, allegedly, were not overly cooperative with each other, as well as the venue's chefs. Knowing the wedding planning business inside out, Tara had been adamant extra temporary staff would have to be taken on both in the kitchens and to serve the wedding breakfast as well as upping the number of security staff to man the place. Hannah had no idea how one kept the public and press away from the huge number of celebrities on the guest list (she'd actually gasped out loud when she saw who was on it) and she was, quite frankly, absolutely terrified at getting it all wrong: what if Amanda Holden were kidnapped or Piers Morgan photographed without his consent?

This then, had been her main priority all day, and her excuse for not going to see how Lachlan was when, in reality, it was the guilt she was now experiencing at kissing Zac the other evening. *Oh, for heaven's sake, Hannah*, she censured herself once she'd done her usual welcome spiel with Eva's art lot and was now walking back across the park. She was a grown woman – hell, forty next year – and *Kissing Zac* sounded like a boastful response to a request for details of how far she'd gone on a first date with one of the boys from the youth club when she was thirteen.

It was a drizzly, cold and miserable afternoon, almost dark at 5pm, and Hannah longed for the coming spring to get a move on. The daffodils, which would soon light up the parkland and surrounding woodland in a blaze of yellow, should, she calculated, be in full bloom for the wedding. She carried on past Tea and Cake, (which was gratifyingly full even on a weekday afternoon) censured a couple of waitresses for having a fag break in full view of visitors and headed down the main drive to the old coach house, which had been converted many years previously into accommodation for staff. Surely Lachlan had just a cut finger? Ger had made such a song and dance about his injuries, one would think he was at death's door.

'Hannah.' Lachlan opened his door on her second knock, stepping back to let her through.

'I've come to see the wounded soldier,' Hannah said gaily – too gaily – and then, catching sight of his heavily bandaged right hand as well as the huge angry-looking cut and bruise on the side of his face exclaimed, 'Blimey, Lachlan, what were you doing?'

When he didn't answer, but simply eyed her up and down before leaving her to follow him into the tiny sitting room, she went on, 'Why didn't you ring me? Why did you get Rosa to take you up to A and E?'

'Your phone was off, Hannah; I knew you were in a meeting. Rosa happened to be in the car park as I tried to drive myself there. I couldn't. She could. She was a godsend...'

'Well, yes, that's what she does: sent by God to do God's work.'

When Lachlan ignored this flippant comment, Hannah went on, 'How bad is it, Lachlan? And how come you've injured your face as well?'

'Possibly some tendon damage to this.' Lachlan held up his hand. 'And,' he obviously tried to make light of it, 'had a bit of a run-in with a table once I saw what I'd actually done, and the needle.'

'What? You fainted?' Hannah gave a little chortle. 'Lachlan Buchanan, the grrreeat Scottish Highlander,' Hannah affected a terrible Scottish accent, 'who once rescued me from wild boars and mad hole-digging badgers...'

'Hannah, it was a domestic sow and there wasn't a badger in sight, mad or otherwise, when you fell down that badger hole...'

'...was brought to his knees by the sight of a needle?'

When Lachlan didn't reply, but appeared genuinely embarrassed, Hannah went on hurriedly, 'You mustn't go to work, Lachlan. Well, outside, anyway; you can't be out helping with the ewes with your hand like that – it will get infected. I'm ringing the agency tomorrow re more staff for this great big wedding. Do we need to get some agricultural help in as well while I'm at it?'

'Don't fuss, Hannah. It will be fine,' Lachlan said irritably. 'Ger is more than capable of doing the stuff I can't do, and we've got two kids coming in on work experience from Askham Bryan agricultural college next week. Daisy's always on hand if needed, now most of her lectures at Liverpool are finished, and she's at home revising for her finals.'

'So why are you back down here, Lachlan?' Hannah finally asked, facing the elephant in the room. 'Why've you moved yourself out of the flat?'

'If you recall, Hannah, I hadn't moved myself *fully* into your apartment and, as such, I haven't moved myself *out* of it.' Lachlan turned away. 'I reckon I'll be having some sleepless nights over the coming week, and you've obviously a lot on. Taken on too much as usual. And...' he turned back towards her, holding her eye '...I think you need a bit of space. Need to work out exactly what it is you want.'

'What I want?' Hannah knew exactly what Lachlan meant but pretended she didn't. 'What I want, Lachlan, is to make Heatherly Hall the very best it can be; put it on the map as the go-to place to be.'

'I know, I know.' Lachlan kissed the top of her head. 'And you'll get there. Just be careful.'

'Careful?'

Lachlan smiled. 'Think I need my painkillers and a bit of a lie-down with a good book. I'll be up and running in a couple of days, Hannah.'

Feeling herself dismissed, Hannah asked, 'Look, Lachlan, can I get you anything? A cup of tea? Beans on toast? Anything?'

'Hannah, you always burn the toast and put the beans *on* the toast rather than on the side.' He smiled. 'Just ask Ger or Daisy if there's something you're not sure about as regards the estate.'

He turned away once more and Hannah *knew* herself dismissed.

Today 4.15 pm

Hannah, is it OK if the Westenbury Players meet at the hall this evening? We had been going to meet at The Jolly

Sailor to thrash out some ideas re the Jet Set evening, but the upstairs conference room at the pub is being used for the village brass band practice. Now that the village hall is out of bounds because of the hole in the roof, everyone is looking for alternative meeting places. We'll be up at 7.

Daisy

Already feeling a sense of being put in her place by Lachlan, Hannah now felt a stab of irritation reading Daisy's text as she walked back up to the office. This was something else she was going to have to sort. If Daisy and her am-dram lot had kept to the original plan of meeting down in the village pub to practise the Jet Set script, she could have just made an appearance down at The Jolly Sailor in her own time. If at all.

If at all? Hannah had already planned a hair wash and what she would be wearing when she saw Zac Anderson again. It would have all fitted in nicely with calling in to see Rosa at the vicarage before crossing the road to the pub. She pulled out her phone once more to ring Rosa and then put it back in her pocket: Rosa deserved more than a hurried phone call between jobs. Now, she was going to have to check which part of the hall was free for the Westenbury Players to meet up and practise. She mentally ticked off her options as she walked: there were a couple of largish groups booked into the conference centre, as well as Eva's art group who would more than likely all end up in the bar.

Hell, she suddenly remembered it was Brett Rogerson, the conference manager's, night off. Oh, bollocks squared: that meant she'd have to be duty manager herself tonight from seven o'clock until the night staff came on. Oh well, that worked then. She could combine her stint as duty manager while popping in – somewhat prettily with refreshments – for the players. Just a matter now of which room she could find free for them. She'd go up to the office, have a cup of tea – she'd not got round to lunch – ring Rosa and then work out the logistics of the players' rehearsal room. And – her heart gave that delicious little lurch to which she'd become so addicted when meeting up with her illicit lover, Ben Pennington, the previous year – she'd be seeing Zac Anderson again in just a few hours.

Hannah set off towards the office.

## 16

'Right, OK, let's see who we've got and who we need.' Daisy pushed back her chair, stood, and faced the small group of people sitting in front of her.

'Who you *need*?' Denis Butterworth, All Hallows' verger, appeared somewhat put out. 'Me and our Sandra thought there'd be a part for all of us in this concert. We've had to tape tonight's *One Show*, what with having to come all the way up here, rather than just walking across to the pub as was first *mooted*.' Denis uttered this last word proudly, sounding not unlike one of the hall's prize cattle.

'Ignore him, love,' Sandra Butterworth said comfortably, handing round a bag of Yorkshire Mixtures to the others present. 'He's just in a bad mood because he's had to fill up the car with petrol.'

'It's OK, Denis, there'll be a part for everyone who wants one.' Daisy frowned. 'And, I think it's actually really good that we're here tonight, that Hannah has let us use this room for rehearsals. She says, later on, if the actual Great Hall is free, she'll take us over there so we can see exactly where we're going to perform. Now, Vivienne, Dad and I have actually cobbled together a basic script, but I think all of us here are professionals – well, professional amateurs...' she corrected herself.

'I'm sure some of you are aware, I *was* a *professional* actress in my day,' Vivienne Maddison interrupted.

'Aye, we're well aware of that Viv,' Denis sniffed. 'You tell us often enough.'

'Vivi-enne, please,' the other answered. 'The emphasis is always on the second syllable.'

'...and,' Daisy went on, 'as professionals, we shouldn't be frightened of some ad-libbing, you know making it up as we go along, if the mood takes us.'

Nigel Cartwright, newly promoted choirmaster of All Hallows' church choir, raised a hand. 'Just go over the storyline once again, Daisy, would you?'

'It's all in your file, Nigel,' Daisy said, looking at her watch pointedly. 'Just a matter of reading it.'

Eva and Hannah, who had both just joined the group and were now standing at the entrance to the room, elbowed each other, wanting to laugh.

'Ah, Hannah. And Eva.' Catching sight of both of them, Daisy urged them forwards. 'Everyone, I'm sure you are all acquainted with Rosa, our village vicar, but you may not know her sisters, Eva Malik and Hannah Quinn, who, after the death of their father, the late Bill Astley, are now in charge up here at the hall. Do you want to say a few words, Hannah?'

Before Hannah could start on her prepared speech of welcome, (she'd hurriedly jotted down a few notes while drying her hair, an almost gymnastic feat of which she was inordinately proud) Virginia stood and made to join her sisters.

'Just to put you all in the picture, peeps...'

Peeps? Daisy exchanged glances with Hannah who dug Eva surreptitiously in the ribs.

'...it's now been revealed that I, myself, am also the late Bill Astley, twelfth Marquess of Stratton's, daughter, as well as Hannah here and, of course, Rosa.'

'What about t'other one...?' Denis started, peering round at Eva.

Hannah closed her eyes. This was not going to put Susan, their mum, in a good light. With Denis in the room, taking it all in, this meaty bit of gossip would be all over the village like a bad rash by tomorrow.

'As such,' Virginia went on, acknowledging Denis's question with a smile and nod of affirmation, 'it's been decided that I shall be known as Ginny Forester-Astley in acknowledgement of my ancestry.'

'Who's decided that, then, love?' Sandra Butterworth adored Rosa, but had little time for her uppity big sister. She moved her pear drop to one cheek and raised an eye in the interloper's direction.

Ignoring Sandra, who Hannah knew Virginia considered a blousy waste of space who didn't get her polish and duster into the very far corners of the church pews, Virginia continued holding forth. 'As a result, I'll be delighted to share what I know about my ancestral home with you all.' Virginia gestured a regal manicured hand (when had Virginia started painting her nails?) skywards towards the ceiling, but the overly dramatic overture was lost in translation when, as the others followed Virginia's waving hand, they realised the room they were rehearsing in was a 1980s-decorated storeroom, catering-sized boxes of coffee, washing powder and loo roll stacked haphazardly up the walls.

'And,' Virginia went on, 'probably most of you are *not* aware of this, but my sister, Eva, isn't ac...'

'Thank you for that Virginia,' Hannah interrupted, giving her big sister a non-negotiable warning stare. 'We need to get on. Now, I think the story of the Heatherly Hall Jet Set is, after the recent interest in it, well documented. I'm sorry all we could offer you this evening is this anteroom to practise in, but I'll be bringing in refreshments at some point, which I hope will compensate for that and, just before you leave, Eva and I should be able to take you all into the Great Hall so you can see for yourself where you'll be performing.'

'So, what do *you* think happened to the Jet Set, Hannah?'

Zac Anderson, his North American twang a stark contrast to the Yorkshire accents of the locals, smiled almost conspiratorially in her direction and, remembering the kiss of the previous evening, Hannah flushed. 'I mean,' he went on, 'do you think it actually ever existed?'

'Well, that's the thing, isn't it?' Eva took the lead and addressed the others present. 'We really have no idea whether this story is just one big fabrication and, to be honest, I don't think it matters. If the jewels haven't turned up after almost a hundred years, I'm sorry, but they're not going to be found now. But it makes a great story and an opportunity to put on an evening, here at the hall, to celebrate a centenary of Agatha Christie's *Murder on the Links*. And, in answer to your question, Zac, there was, at the time, according to Bill, obviously a huge search for the Jet Set, with the local bobbies and then detectives brought in from Leeds and eventually London to question everyone.

'However, I think Bill's assumption that his father, Henry, the eleventh Marquess of Stratton, who he knew to be a wily old devil, pretended it had been pinched is, perhaps, the correct one. Henry probably saw it as a way to raise badly needed funds for this place which, after the First World War, was apparently in a state of disrepair. He'd have saved face with Edward VIII and Mrs Simpson, claimed money from the insurance and, at some point, found a way to break up the set and get someone to move the diamonds overseas. Antwerp, maybe? Or South America?'

'Fascinating,' Daisy said, nodding her thanks in Eva's direction. 'Right, let's get on, shall we? Remember, we're going back in history to October 1936. So, the leading parts will be:

- Henry Astley, eleventh Marquess of Stratton;
- Winifred Astley, Lady Stratton;
- Edward VIII;
- Mrs Wallis Simpson;
- Lady Stratton's sister – Mrs Margaux Casterton;

With the lesser parts being: staff, maids, the butler – I think you'd be brilliant taking that part, Denis – guests and...'

Daisy broke off as the door to the room opened and two others were shown in by a member of the conference centre staff.

'Ah, may I introduce my brother and sister-in-law to you all?' Virginia gushed, standing once more to usher in the newcomers. 'The present Marquess of Stratton, everyone, Jon Astley and his charming wife – all the way from California to be with us tonight at our ancestral home – Billy-Jo Astley, the present Lady Stratton.'

'What the fucking hell are those two doing here?' Eva whispered furiously in an aside to Hannah as the others turned in their seats and stared. 'And bloody Virginia sounds like some sort of chat show host. Hannah, we've *got* to stop her.'

'Apart from gagging her and bundling her down the laundry chute, I don't see what else we can do,' Hannah whispered. 'Jesus, the woman's beyond belief. How can she be our sister?'

'Not mine,' Eva reminded Hannah.

'How lovely to see you both...' Hannah now took the lead, addressing the newcomers.

'Lovely?' Eva hissed.

'...but, as you can see, this is a private meeting. If you follow me, I'll make sure you have a drink at the bar.'

'I really don't think you can omit us from *anywhere*,' Billy-Jo said crossly. 'We are the Marquess and Marchioness of Heatherly Hall. This, as Ginny here reminded you, is our ancestral home.'

'Do stay and watch rehearsals, Jon and Billy-Jo. It will be of *such* interest to you both,' Virginia pleaded.

'I'd rather have a drink,' Jonny said, turning. 'Maybe, Hannah, if you show us to our quarters first?'

'Your quarters?' Hannah frowned.

'You don't think we're staying another night at that dump of a pub, do you?' Billy-Jo put in. 'It wouldn't surprise me if we've picked up bedbugs there.' She made a great show of scratching at her ankle.

'Let's see where we can accommodate you,' Hannah soothed. 'A drink first, I think, and then I'll get housekeeping to sort you a room. Let's leave these people to their meeting.' Hannah made for the door.

'Actually,' Virginia raised her hand skywards once more, this time in excitement. 'We could give Billy-Jo the part of Wallis Simpson. How authentic would that be?'

'These two are not going to be here in a couple of weeks' time,' Eva snapped.

'Oh, I think you'll find we're not going anywhere for a while, Eva.' Jonny smirked. 'Not until we've sorted what we came for, with my sister Ginny, here.'

Virginia preened, throwing Eva a triumphant look.

'Flippin'eck,' Denis Butterworth exhaled loudly. 'There's not half some goings-on up here, Our Sandra…'

Hannah had settled Jonny and Billy-Jo in the bar, made them a dinner reservation across at the conference centre and, with housekeeping not being available at this time of day, ended up back in her office in order to search for a room for them. How long they intended staying was anyone's guess, and Hannah had to work out where best to accommodate them, scrolling through housekeeping while looking at data she didn't really understand. There was a second tiny bedroom in her own flat – Eva had moved in there after she and Rayan split, staying up at the hall on the nights Rayan had the girls in the family home – but the last thing she wanted was Jonny Astley and his quite dreadful wife bunking down with her.

Eva had left the meeting at the same time as herself, telling Hannah that Jodie, the babysitter, was wondering where the hell she'd got to. The night staff were beginning to put in an appearance as Hannah made her way back down to see Lachlan in the staff quarters, but he was either ignoring her rap on his door or was asleep, knocked out, presumably with painkillers.

Was Ger in there with him? she wondered as she made her way back up to her flat. She was desperate for a glass of wine and, pouring a huge one, she kicked off her shoes with relief, undid the zip on the skirt of her smart business suit and lay on the sofa, closing her eyes and promising herself a ten-minute break while trying to work out just what she felt about Lachlan.

When he'd first arrived at Heatherly Hall, just before Bill died – would she ever stop missing and grieving her natural father? – she'd found Lachlan arrogant, quite obnoxious and seemingly determined to thwart her at every step in her new role as chair of the management committee. And now? Now she'd grown to really, *really* like him, enjoying the comfort of knowing that he was a good, dependable bloke. And bloody good-looking as well, she added to his list of attributes. So, why then, was she messing about with Zac Anderson when she had Lachlan? And she *did* have him. He might not be the most romantic of blokes, might not constantly be sending her flowers (had he ever?) but she'd felt so content with the relationship, felt wanted and loved which, after being with Ben Pennington and experiencing the ups and downs of *that* relationship, had been a bit of a revelation.

What was wrong with her that she felt the constant need to sabotage any good relationship? It had always been the same – she was fully aware of how she worked – and she felt shame that she appeared unable to function properly in a loving, stable relationship with a man who loved her, as she was sure Lachlan did. It was the chase, she knew: that glorious challenge – she thrived on challenge – and yet, with Lachlan, she'd felt in safe hands, out of danger, secure. Decent. While many of her relationships in the past – at university and during the past twenty years or so – had, after the initial elation of the chase and that first swooning kiss, left her feeling dishonourable and mendacious.

Indecent.

She was, she now admitted to herself, a junkie, chasing the drug of bad boys in order to get high, but afterwards left with a guilty, bad taste in her mouth and wanting only decency in her life.

Until the next time.

Ed Sheeran, she mused, certainly knew what he was talking about when he penned 'Bad Habits'.

Hannah sat up suddenly, wanting to see Lachlan, wanting him to *know*, to explain that she really did appreciate him. *Appreciate him, Hannah?* She tutted out loud at her choice of word: for heaven's sake, you appreciate the rain stopping so you can put the washing out; you appreciate someone opening the door for you when your hands are full; appreciate that no one's nicked the last of the milk when all you want is a big mug of tea. She was, she decided, going to be a decent human for once in her life, quash any ridiculous teenage-fantasy feelings she might be having for Zac Anderson; erase completely the image constantly dancing at the fore of her mind's eye of her actually kissing Zac back, once he'd made that first move and reached out for her up in the art retreat the previous evening.

And, instead take the right path. The decent path.

Hannah drained her glass of wine, swung her stockinged feet to the floor, zipped up her skirt and reached for her jacket. It was cold out there and she needed her warm coat but couldn't remember where she'd left it – somewhere in the conference centre probably – and, anyway, it would take her five minutes to run down to the coach house. She picked up a bread basket and started to fill it with all the fruit she'd bought earlier in the week in an attempt to make herself eat more healthily rather than grabbing a sandwich and bun on the go as she worked. She started with a huge spiky pineapple, an out-of-season melon, mangoes and kiwis, as well as the usual oranges and apples, topping it all off with a big bunch of black grapes. They were slightly manky and she pulled off the ones that were past their best, but was then left with a bunch of green stalks. Oh, sod it – she smiled, pleased with her attempts at an invalid fruit basket – Lachlan would find it amusing.

Hannah painted on fresh lipstick, squirted *Promise* by Jennifer Lopez and unlocked the apartment's main door.

'Oh? Zac?'

'Daisy sent me up to find you, to tell you we've probably done as much as we can for now, and not to worry about your taking us round and showing us the Great Hall.'

'What time is it?' Hannah glanced at her watch. 'Hell, it's going up to ten. How's it got to that time?'

'You look like Pomona.' Zac smiled, reaching into her basket for a grape, chewing on it rather sensuously, leaving yet another stalk for Lachlan to face.

'Pomona?' Hannah knew she should tell Zac she was busy, that she was on evening duty and needed to get on, but he was laughing down at her, those amazingly blue eyes of his never once leaving her face. 'Who's Pomona?'

'Who's Pomona? Pomona was the goddess of abundance in Roman mythology. She was a wood nymph, very beautiful, very seductive, and her name originates from the Latin word for orchard fruit.'

'Right.'

Neither of them moved and, in desperation, Hannah picked off a grape herself and popped it into her mouth for something to do with the hand that wasn't wrapped tightly round the fruit basket. It was actually getting quite heavy and, seeing her discomfiture, Zac asked, 'Shall I take that for you? Where were you headed?'

'Oh, just to see one of the staff who's not very well.' *For heaven's sake, Hannah. One of the staff? Lachlan's your partner.*

'Can it wait two minutes? If that's not taking up too much of your time? I've a couple of questions re this place? Daisy actually led us all out, making a detour through the Great Hall, so those who hadn't been down there, could see where they're going to be performing.'

'Did she?' Hannah frowned, feeling slight irritation. 'I didn't know she knew the way. And you'd have had to all go through the restaurant.' The last thing Heatherly Hall guests needed was a gaggle of villagers trooping past their table, gawping at their plates as the diners got stuck into their Artichoke Broth with Smoked Yolk and Winter Leaves or Pigeon Breast with Beet Puree.

'No, we didn't actually.' Zac smiled. 'I remembered the back way you showed me the other evening.'

'Right.' Hannah dithered, reaching for another grape. She didn't even like grapes, particularly these seeded ones she'd bought in error. Unable to spit out the offending objects as she'd have done if she'd been by herself, she swallowed the fruit wholesale, coughing slightly as it went down. 'What was it you wanted to ask?'

Zac nodded towards the door, producing a bottle of wine from the depths of the big research bag he always carried with him. 'I've brought you this as a thank you for showing me round the other evening...' he paused, smiling '...among other things. Shall we go in?'

# 17

## Heatherly Hall, Westenbury, Yorkshire

### Wednesday October 14th 1936

Jeanie made her way slowly back down the red-carpeted stairs from Lady Stratton's bedroom, taking in, now that the carpet cleaning job was complete (and not being in any great hurry to get back to Mrs Walters and the pile of potatoes waiting to be peeled) the magnificent surroundings of Upstairs at Heatherly Hall. So many pictures on the walls, so many pointless little polished tables and ornate, upholstered chairs. (Who the hell ever parked their backsides on them along *these* draughty corridors?)

Frank was right – as was her dad – when he talked about the idle rich having nothing better to do than sitting on chairs along draughty corridors, or swanning around while the workers in their mills, down their mines and sweating in their steelworks and foundries jumped to their bidding; danced to their tune to earn a few bob and keep their kids from the breadline.

What had Frank been telling her only the evening before as they'd sat in the village fleapit watching *Follow the Fleet* with Fred Astaire and Ginger Rogers? That the means of production should fall under the common ownership of the people living in a stateless society, through the establishment of a communist government. Frank told her that, 'only by protest and agitation, Jeanie, will the working-classes rise up and lead a revolution similar to the one in Russia'. She wasn't sure where Russia actually was – somewhere up past France and Germany she reckoned – and also wasn't totally convinced that the Russians murdering their king – the tsar – and his family was the right way to go about trying to change the world. She rather liked King George and Queen Mary – her granny had given her the coronation mug *she'd* been given in 1911 – and didn't like to think of them being shot or knifed or bludgeoned to death by a baying crowd, but she'd nodded in agreement with Frank's sentiment, taking his hand in her own and hoping he'd kiss her.

It was only when the two elderly women in front of them had turned, telling them to either shut up and watch the film or bugger off home or, better still, sling their hook to Russia, that Frank had eventually stopped talking and, within minutes, fallen asleep, his spent cigarette dropping its final collection of ash on to the floor of the picture house. Jeanie had removed the cigarette from his fingers and simply gazed down at him as his head fell onto her shoulder. She found herself stroking his dark hair, following the curve of his profile with her finger, admiring the length of his ridiculously long dark eyelashes as they moved slightly on his prominent cheekbones while wondering at, and loving, the smell of his skin as she moved her lips to his face.

And now, standing here, in the shadows above the Great Hall, having a bit of a rest, Jeanie wondered just what it was with these rich women that they had to send downstairs for help for a tiny bit of stained carpet? She supposed Lady Stratton and her sister had always had everything done for them, never had to put their soft white manicured hands into a bucket of hot soapy water. Jeanie set the bucket down, scratching at her hands which, already slightly cracked and weeping from the eczema she'd always suffered, felt inflamed from handling the green Sunlight laundry bar of soap. She alternated the blissful scratching of the raw skin between her fingers with rubbing crossly at the sore on her leg where the heavy metal bucket had not only put a hole in her stocking (she'd have to darn that this evening) but taken off a lump of skin, as she gazed down once more into the chandelier hanging below her.

As she continued to peer down into its vast and seemingly fathomless depths, watching below as those brought in to clean the chandelier appeared at a loss on how to do just that, she found herself unwilling to return to the work of the kitchen and an increasingly cantankerous Mrs Walters. Instead, Jeanie just stood, recalling how, as he'd walked her out of the village and to the tram, Frank had been unable to stop railing at the rotten state of British society.

'We need money,' he'd said. 'Harry Pollitt, General Secretary of the CPGB's urged all its members to find a way, by whatever means, of showing solidarity with our marching comrades as the Jarrow lot carry on with their journey to London. When I left them at Barnsley,' he went on, 'they were already having to put newspaper in their boots to stop up the holes. And when they get to Westminster,' he said crossly, 'once they finally arrive there, I can guarantee now, Jeanie, that nothing, absolutely nothing, will ever come of it. And *then*, the poor buggers'll have to walk all the way *back* up to the North East…'

'…an' all uphill on the way back, an'all,' Jeanie had sympathised, taking Frank's hand in her own, loving the feel of the rough skin combined with her own: two workers together, discussing the cause, but hoping against hope he'd stop in the darkness of the co-op doorway and they could do a bit of spooning. And more.

Bringing herself reluctantly back to the present, Jeanie picked up the heavy galvanised bucket again and made her way back down to the Great Hall and then through the green baize door in the corner and down a further flight of stairs to the kitchens.

'You've tekken your time, lass.' Mrs Walters frowned, turning as Jeanie emptied the bucket of water in the sluice and returned the bar of Sunlight to its shelf.

'If a job's worth doing an' all that,' Jeanie parroted, untying the grey housemaid's apron she'd donned to protect her dress and replacing it with her white kitchen pinny.

'Lovely up there, isn't it?' Mrs Walters now said, mollified slightly that Jeanie had gone straight to the pile of mud-clad potatoes with a knife and pan.

'If you like that sort of thing,' Jeanie replied airily. 'All a bit ostentatious for my liking – you know slightly vulgar and brash?'

'Aye, well, you *vulgarise and bash* them spuds, or there'll be hell to pay.'

And so it was, as the long afternoon wore on and Jeanie peeled, chopped and prepared the pile of potatoes; washed and chopped leeks, carrots and swede and stirred a vat of soup, it came to her. Of course: the necklace and earrings to be given to Wallis Simpson. *She'd* take them instead and give them to Frank; he'd be able to sell them somewhere. Hadn't his leader – Harry somebody – urged them all to get money by *whatever means?* She'd be part of the revolution Frank was always on about. Part of the group of brave women like Mrs Pankhurst and Mrs Stopes who weren't afraid of speaking out and getting what they wanted.

By any means.

A thrill of excited dread shot through every part of her body: there was no way she'd ever dare to do it. What would her mum say if she found out? But Frank would be over the moon; they'd get one over on the bosses, on his lordship Upstairs, on this Wallis Simpson woman who already had enough jewels (as well as, the papers said, enough former husbands). And Lady Stratton, at the end of the day, hadn't been very nice about the king's mistress, had she? Jeanie bet her ladyship would be quite pleased that the jewels her daft husband was giving away weren't going to end up round the neck of some jumped-up American.

And Frank would take her in his arms, tell her she was a revolutionary – tell her she'd go down in history as the young girl who'd dared to stand up to the toffs, dared to take from the rich to give to the poor. A bit like Robin Hood, she supposed. Hadn't Maid Marian done her bit for Robin Hood like she was going to do for Frank Newsome?

But the king was involved. *The king* for heaven's sake. But, then, she argued, as she stirred vegetables in the stockpot and lumps of carrot and turnip spun dizzily round, before shooting over the rim, just look how the Russian villagers had *killed* their king – their tsar – and his family. She wasn't planning on killing Edward VIII, just *redistributing* – wasn't that a word Frank often used – the wealth that was so unevenly shared out?

'Right, that's enough for today,' Mrs Walters said, eyeing the huge kitchen clock. 'You get off home, Jeanie. You've been here since eight and it's coming down dark.'

'Don't you want some help with dinner?' Jeanie looked round and was surprised not to see the cook up to her elbows in the usual, last-minute preparations for Upstairs.

'The whole lot of 'em are out: William's driven 'em all over to some do at Ilkley, apparently – they're already off. And Mrs Prescott's gone off with Mr Baxter to see the early showing of that new Fred Astaire and Ginger Rogers.'

'*Follow the Fleet?* I saw it last night.'

'Aye, that's the one. Any good? I'd have gone down with 'em meself, but they needed to get off so's they can get the nine o'clock bus back in time for when his lordship returns. Mind you, it's going to be after midnight when they're back, I reckon.' She grimaced, wiggling her toes in their broad flat lace-ups. 'Bunions playing up after being on me feet all day. Glad I don't have to prepare a big meal for upstairs on top of all the preparations for the king's retinoo tomorrow.'

'Are you getting a bit nervous?'

'Nervous? Me?' Mrs Walters laughed scornfully. 'I've been doing this job far too long to be nervous. All the preparations for tomorrow's Downstairs lunch and dinner are just about done – that soup's looking good, love, and Hilda and Mary'll be in tomorrow to help, as well as Hilda's mum as an extra. No, you get off...' the cook eyed the bottle of best sherry she'd used in the trifle '...and I'll have me shoes off and a plate of that chicken pie left from lunch, by the stove, and I'll be right as ninepence.'

'You sure?'

'You're a good girl, Jeanie; not afraid of hard work. Not like some round here. Mind you, get yourself here early, lass, in t'morning. We need to have this kitchen scrubbed and spotless and ready to go when them damned chefs from Leeds arrive to start their preparations.' She tutted. 'Chefs from Leeds, my backside,' she scoffed disdainfully.

Jeanie removed her apron, took her coat from its peg and, before she was even out of the door, Mrs Walters was pouring herself a large – a huge – glass of the Bristol Cream sherry and kicking off her shoes, settling herself with a whump of pleasure into the large battered armchair by the stove. Jeanie let herself out of the kitchen door, keeping to the cinder path around the back of the hall's periphery, staying within the shadows at the rear of the huge stone façade where the network of heavy lead pipes and guttering stretched upwards and outwards like a nest of black vipers.

It wasn't yet 7pm, but the unbroken grey cloud was efficiently blocking any last remnants of the sunset to the west, as well as any glints from an already rising moon to her right. Jeanie shivered, pulling her dark coat around her and reaching for the black woollen gloves in her pockets. The evening was incredibly quiet and dark, the velvet blackness disturbed only by the harsh shriek of tawny owls. Jeanie knew – because her dad kept pigeons and was wary of predatory owls – that, at this time of year, tawnies made more noise than all the other species put together. And all this extra shrieking, hooting and 'kee-wick'-ing was down to one thing: territory; young birds reaching maturity and looking for new homes while older ones fought to hold on to their patch.

She sniggered out loud to herself at the thought of gangster owls defending their patch a bit like Old Scarface himself, and the giggle brought her to her senses. *For heaven's sake, Jeanie Haigh*, she censured herself – she was being utterly, utterly stupid. What the hell was she even thinking about, hanging around with the intention of nicking the king's jewels like Al Capone? She stopped to think: *had* Al Capone ever been a jewel thief? Maybe just robbed banks? Maybe she and Frank could rob a bank together like Bonnie and Clyde?

Jeanie uttered a little snort of self-derision and set off in the direction of the fields down to her house on Railway Terrace.

# 18

*Two weeks before the wedding*

'I can't believe we've been roped in for this,' Eva snapped, examining the state of her backside in Rosa's bedroom mirror.

'Rosa needs to be doing something to help her destress and relax if she's going to be ready for the transference of her embryos in a few weeks' time; if it means pulling on our Lycra, and manhandling her bodily across to the church hall for Hilary's yoga class, then so be it.' Hannah joined Eva at the mirror, critically examining her own behind. 'Do you think my bum looks big in these?' she grinned, coming out with the tired old cliché of all women standing in Lycra tights in front of a mirror.

'Actually, I think you've lost weight, you know,' Eva said a little enviously. 'Mind you, your body never recovers after giving birth; you and Rosa do have an advantage in the bum stakes over me.' She patted at Hannah's tight buttocks. 'And in the boob department as well,' she added gloomily, lifting her chest under the white T-shirt and turning sideways to see the effect. 'Once you've had kids, they're never the same again, you know.'

'I bet Andrea's more than happy with your bosom.' Hannah grinned. 'Mind you, you don't want him going off with any perky-bosomed young Italian signorina. I bet they all look like Carla Bruni or a young Sophia Loren, over in Milan.'

'Do you think so?' Eva pulled a face. 'I am so missing him, Hannah, I really am.' She sighed heavily. 'Missing him a lot. I really should have told him what I was feeling for him when I had him to myself. I'm going to try and ring him again this evening, but I just don't seem to be able to get hold of him.' Eva lifted her chest once more and sucked in her cheekbones. 'There, that better?'

'Not massively. You know, I bet Rosa would rather have a baby than a pair of permanently perky tits.'

'I found her on her knees in the bedroom this morning,' Eva confided in a whisper.

'On her knees?' Hannah's eyes were saucers. 'With Joe, you mean?'

'What? Oh, for heaven's sake, Hans. Just because you seem to be up to no good – and no, don't tell me, I really *don't* want to know: the less Rosa and I know of what you've been up to this past couple of weeks, the easier it'll be to look Lachlan in the eye.'

'It's just…'

'Hannah, I really don't want *to know*,' Eva snapped again. 'It's your business, not mine and Rosa's, so just keep it to yourself, if you don't mind?' She glared at her sister through the mirror. 'I just hope you know what you're getting yourself into with Mr Smooth Man from Maine because, sure as hell, Lachlan will.'

'Eva, I need…'

'No, Hannah, I mean it.'

'You've always been up for gossip before,' Hannah retorted almost sulkily.

'Yes, when we were twenty and no one was getting hurt.'

'I don't know what to do.'

'And I'm in no position to advise you, apart from hoping you'll be honest and let Lachlan down gently, if that's your intention.' Eva sighed, relenting somewhat. 'The thing is, I'm missing Andrea like mad but, apart from a couple of texts, he's not really been in touch. I'm worried that's it, that leaving for Italy to work on his sculptures was his way of leaving me without having to actually tell me.'

'But meanwhile, you've got the hots for Drew Livingston and are cross with yourself for fancying another man who's about to get married when you're supposedly in a relationship with Andrea?'

'Is it that obvious?' Eva flushed slightly.

'Yep.'

'I think he's just being nice to me to make sure I invite Alice and Yves to the wedding.'

'And have you? Invited them?'

'Yes, I'm hoping they're both coming, although Yves hasn't totally confirmed he will be here. Alice particularly was delighted at the request for her company: says she's had a thing about Drew Livingston for years.'

'Heaven's sake. He's thirty years younger than her.'

'When has that ever stopped our dear mama from pursuing any man – or woman – she's got the hots for?' Eva paused, looking directly at Hannah through the mirror. 'Do you think you and I have inherited quite a bit of... you know... of *that* from Alice? I don't think it's a particularly good attribute to have, do you?'

Avoiding Eva's questioning look, and consequently the uncomfortable question itself, Hannah asked, 'So what was Rosa doing on her knees? Praying?'

'Yes, I was.' Rosa had come, unnoticed, into her bedroom and was now standing at the mirror, trying to see her own behind. 'Bloody hell,' she tutted crossly, but continued to suck in her stomach and stare at her reflection.

'Didn't think vicars were supposed to be vain.' Hannah raised an eyebrow.

'"*For the Lord sees not as woman sees: woman looks on the outward appearance, but the Lord looks on the heart.*" With apologies to Samuel 16 v7 – or somewhere around there.' Rosa pulled at the seat of the pink patterned Lycra tights Hannah had lent her. 'Really?' she tutted again. 'Really? Oh, I'm not doing this, you two. The last thing I want to do is a bloody yoga class with half my parishioners staring at my backside.'

'Stick your dog collar on as well,' Hannah advised. 'Then you'll feel more at home, especially when you're doing Downward Dog. And stop swearing,' she went on primly. 'That's two bloodies in as many seconds. You're supposed to be setting an example.'

'You're not in a good place, are you, Rosa?' Eva went over to hug her sister. 'Come on, tell us. Carys? The IVF?'

'I feel so... so hormonal,' Rosa wept. 'I've done the contraceptive pill for two weeks to "quiet" my ovaries and now I'm starting hormones to stimulate the growth of the uterine lining. Trouble is,' she went on, 'everything else's growing in sympathy: my bum, my tum and my boobs – bloody hell...'

'That's *three* now,' Hannah admonished, ticking the new profanity off on her fingers.

'...my boobs...' Rosa continued putting out both hands to cup each breast 'are coming out in sympathy too. I could compete with that Chesty Morgan woman...'

'How do *you* know about Chesty Morgan?' Hannah and Eva both started laughing.

'Well, when I couldn't get my bra to fasten...' Rosa laughed through her tears '...I needed to google just how big they might actually grow. Did you know Ms Morgan had a 73-inch chest?'

'No, but we do now.' Eva chortled. 'So, come on, Rosa, what is it really? Not the thought of doing Hilary's yoga class? Or ending up with a bosom like a porn star's?'

'I'm going to let Carys stay here.'

'What?' The other two immediately stopped laughing.

'For Chiara's sake. Carys is still staying across at the pub, but coming over here to see Chiara on a daily basis.'

'Why? Why on earth are you letting her anywhere near Chiara?'

'Because if we don't, Chiara cries, almost hysterical to be with Carys. She set off by herself to the pub the other day when I was in the loo. Crossed the road by herself and took herself through the bar and asked Neil, the landlord, for her mum.'

'Bit different from the two pints of lager and a packet of crisps Neil's normally asked for.' Eva frowned. 'Sorry, Rosa, that was crass of me. How long is she here in the UK for?'

'Well, she can't stay for ever,' Hannah said reasonably. 'Otherwise, she'll be giving birth in The Jolly Sailor. She'll soon get fed up of the pub's lumpy bed and greasy fry-ups and want to be back home in the lap of luxury in Oz.'

'I've not really spoken to her,' Rosa admitted, 'so I don't know what her plans are, if she has a return ticket booked. When she arrives, I just send Chiara to let her in and then remove myself across to the church to work, until she leaves.'

'What on earth does Joe think about your letting that woman stay?' Eva pulled a face.

'He's had to go over to Copenhagen for the week. Things aren't good with his business and he's had to fly off for a few days.' Rosa didn't meet Eva's eye.

'You've not told him, have you?'

'He wouldn't agree with me. But it's the decent thing to do.'

'It's the *daft* thing to do,' Hannah tutted. 'Get your God head off, Rosa, just for once, and put your fighting head on.'

'I'm not bloody Worzel Gummidge,' Rosa snapped. 'And I'm *not* coming over to this daft yoga session.'

'*Four* now,' Hannah rebuked and, with a nod towards Eva, both sisters proceeded to take hold of Rosa's arms, manhandling her with much hilarity down the stairs, out of the vicarage and across to the church hall.


'Come for a coffee with us, Rosa,' Hannah called as the class finally rolled mats and donned sweatshirts and jackets. 'We're going to try the new place behind Malik and Malik. It's only been open a week, but it got a great write-up in *The Yorkshire Post*; we need to suss out any competition for Tea and Cake.'

Rosa shook her head. 'Got too much to do.'

'So have I.' Hannah placed a hand on Rosa's arm as she headed for the church hall door. 'I can't tell you how much. But this is work – you know, marketing.'

'No, really.' Rosa was adamant.

'Well, don't forget we have a meeting – a really important one – with Drew and Aditi's people at six. You *have* to be there, Rosa; they need to see who's actually marrying them.'

Rosa turned. 'Yes, I do need to meet with them. Ask what their motives are for marrying.'

'Their motives? Rosa, they're not marrying in church, so there doesn't have to be a religious bent.'

'So why are you asking *me*? Just get in a wedding celebrant. That's all you need.'

'They've asked for *you*, Rosa.'

'How do they *know* about me? And that's why I *need to know* why they wish to marry.'

'Well, to amass their joint fortunes, I guess?' Hannah laughed.

'Hannah, marrying isn't a business matter. Or a laughing matter.'

'Rosa, you're being churchy and supercilious. In fact, you're beginning to sound like our grandfather.'

'Oh please, not the Reverend Cecil? I'm not, am I?'

'Just a little. But I know what you're going through at the moment.'

'Sorry. So, I'm assuming they've done all the paperwork? They're not just expecting to troll up on the day and go through checkout like at Aldi?'

Hannah laughed at that. 'Everything's in order and ready to go.' Hannah was proud of her and Tara's (well, Tara's as the professional, and very experienced, wedding planner) attention to detail.

'OK,' Rosa said almost tiredly. 'I'll get Joe's mum to come over to look after Chiara.'

*

This third week in March, winter appeared to have finally given up the uneven fight with the new season and Rosa's spirits began to lift as she let herself in through the vicarage gate and sniffed the air. Definitely a hint of spring there and, as she gazed in wonder at the stretch of yellow daffodils whose beauty – and bounty – she'd previously neglected to take in, her mind on overload with all the other goings-on in her life, she simply closed her eyes and breathed. Breathed in God's good air and the gift of nature.

This yoga lark obviously had something going for it. Rosa smiled to herself, deciding to simply sit now for ten minutes in contemplation, on her favourite bench, in her favourite sunny spot at the other side of the garden.

Unfortunately, there appeared to be someone already there.

'Hello, Rosa.' Carys moved her Mulberry, patting the now vacant space at her side. 'Will you come and sit and talk with me?'

'I don't think we have anything to talk about, Carys.'

'Oh, come on, Rosa, we have *everything* to discuss.' Carys shot her a look of disbelief.

'Actually, Carys, now we're face to face, you can start by telling me exactly why you went after Joe, eight years ago? Why, as my best friend as well as my PA, you decided you wanted to take my partner? *When* did you make that decision? Was it the minute you met him or was it just a whim? You know, Carys, the man I adored and had been with since I was sixteen; the only man I'd ever loved and ever wanted.' Rosa found her heart racing in the way it hadn't for years as she faced, once again, the awful knowledge that Joe had slept with this woman. Had had a child with her. Married her. 'Just tell me, would you, because I've sure as hell never understood it.'

Carys smirked slightly. 'I thought it was pretty obvious?'

'Not to me, it wasn't.'

'An exceptionally good-looking, rather wealthy man who had everything and yet had never once noticed me, never once flirted with me or made a ghost of a pass at me as most men I meet attempt to do?'

'Do they?'

'Don't they with you?' Carys raised an eyebrow. 'You are a very attractive woman, yourself, Rosa, although you've never realised it.' She smiled, glancing towards Rosa's pink-patterned, second-hand Lycra tights, ancient trainers and long dark hair, now damp with sweat and tied back with an old rubber band. 'And at the moment you're not making the most of yourself...'

'This isn't telling me why you did what you did,' Rosa said crossly.

'...but when I saw you the other night, I remembered just why it was I'd fallen in love with you.'

Rosa stared. 'Fallen in love with me? With *me?*'

'I loved you from the moment I came for interview. You were so gorgeous, so bright, so sassy and funny...' Carys paused '... about to take over the world with *Rosa Quinn Investments*. I wanted to work for you, wanted you to be my friend.'

'You *did* work for me, Carys,' Rosa said in exasperation. 'For two years. And you *were* my friend, my *best* friend; we did everything together.'

'No, we didn't. You went home to Joe every night.'

Rosa shook her head in disbelief. 'I'm lost here, Carys. Are you trying to say you wanted to live with me? Are you trying to say you're, you know...'

'Gay? A lesbian?' Carys paused, staring into space, as if the possibility had only just occurred to her. She smiled. 'No, I don't think so. I never wanted to get you into bed.'

'Well, thank the Lord for that.' Rosa glanced skywards.

'To be honest, Rosa, sex has never been high on my agenda.'

'You could have fooled me. From what I recall, you were

always relating your sexual conquests in the office. *And* you got Joe into bed.'

'Conquests – just that. There's a thrill in the conquest.'

'I'm sorry, I just don't understand any of this.'

'I wanted you to love me as much as I loved you.' Carys paused once more. 'Actually no, I think I wanted to *be* you.'

'This is weird, Carys.' Rosa made to stand.

'I thought part of your job was to hear confession?'

'I'm an Anglican vicar, Carys, not a Catholic priest.' Rosa sat down once more.

'And if I couldn't *be you*, then at least I could have your life.'

'You pinched my life? It was deliberate?'

'Oh, I don't know, Rosa. I was totally messed up…'

'And you want Joe and me to hand over a little seven-year-old girl to someone who is openly telling me they've got these issues? That they're totally messed up?'

'That's not fair, Rosa…'

'When were you and fairness ever in the same room?' Rosa snapped, feeling near to tears.

'I said I *was* totally messed up,' Carys countered. Her voice was quiet, calm. 'I've spent the last couple of years in rehab.'

'In rehab? In hospital?'

'No of course not.' Carys smiled. 'I knew – and Spencer was with me on this – I knew I needed some diagnosis as to why I behaved as I did.'

'You don't think it's possibly because you're a spoilt manipulative bitch who wants what the next person has, and she hasn't?'

'Harsh words from a woman of God,' Carys said.

'Just leave God out of this.' Rosa felt total anger.

'Rosa, I've spent two years in psychotherapy: facing my demons, finally facing up to what happened to me as a child…'

'And what did?'

'I'm still not able to talk about it.'

'You are such a fake, Carys Powell.' Rosa stood, made to leave.

'Rosa, I've come to say I'm sorry.' Carys took hold of Rosa's hand. 'Truly sorry for coming between you and Joe. It's taken two years of exceptionally expensive therapy and counselling for me to be able to say that.'

'I'd rather have listened to an apology years ago and without knowing how much it cost.' Rosa shook her head in despair.

'Rosa, I'm sorted. I hardly drink anymore...'

'You're pregnant.'

'...and I most certainly don't need any drugs to get me through the day. I *had* to leave Rhys and Chiara behind with Joe when I left to be with Spencer: Joe wouldn't let me take them; I was drinking, and an unfit mother.'

*You're a whore, a drunk and an unfit mother, Sue Ellen.* The line from *Dallas* (their Granny Glenys had been a huge fan) that always had herself, Hannah and Eva, convulsing with laughter, shot giddily through her head.

'Spencer is a good man.'

'As well as a billionaire?'

Ignoring the jibe, Carys continued: 'Spencer helped to sort me out; could see through the crap and saw I was worth saving. I'm fixed, Rosa. Rhys is back with me and so happy – a different boy from when he was here. I'm having another baby, and I want my little girl as well.'

'You want it all,' Rosa said bitterly.

'They're my children, Rosa. I can't be without them.'

'So what was all that about Joe coercing you? Breaking your arm?'

Carys had the grace to look embarrassed. 'I'm sorry. I made that up. Eva was winding me up in the pub. But if I have to, Rosa, I *will* use it in court. Joe never tried to control me; he tried to make the marriage work, but he was deeply unhappy. I did fall in love with him for a while, but I could never compete with you. Or with Chiara.'

'Compete with your own daughter, for heaven's sake?'

'For the love of your husband? It happens.'

'Carys, I don't think, despite all the psychotherapy you say you've had, I don't believe you've changed at all.'

'Oh, believe me, I have.'

'But Chiara is Joe's. You'll break his heart if you take her.' Rosa realised she was pleading.

'And it will break mine and Chiara's if I don't.'

# 19

Later that same day, Eva was in the schoolyard along with all the other parents and carers, waiting to pick up the girls before ferrying them over to Rayan's place. She and Rayan had come to an agreement about their staying with him every Wednesday during the school week, as well as every other weekend. She knew she was lucky – a lot of split families were just that: split between their parents on a one-week-on and one-week-off basis, but Rayan worked long hours at the surgery – he often had early evening appointments, and the last thing Yasmin wanted, Eva supposed, with a tiny new baby and the sleepless nights that went with the territory, was two stepdaughters to care and cater for, a week at a time.

'Ooh, Mrs Malik,' Grace Henderson, Little Acorns year four teacher was heading her way. 'We're very excited about this lost Jet Set evening up at the hall next week. I'm staff social secretary for my sins, and constantly thinking of new things we can do. This is great: I've just got our tickets from the library – they're on sale all over the village as well as online, so someone's being organised.'

'Well, we have Simon in marketing, but Hannah's also set up one of the students who usually helps out at Tea and Cake to do all the admin. He appears to be quite a whizz at it; we might have to give him a job with Simon once he graduates.'

'So, are *you* in it? Have you got a part?'

Eva laughed. 'Me? God, no, I couldn't act my way out of a paper bag. We're leaving that to the Westenbury Players. I'll be there in the background and probably get roped in to help with the 1930s-style afternoon tea we're laying on, as well as the treasure hunt to find the facsimile necklace and earrings. You have to think all things Agatha Christie, you know: leave behind today's world, your mobile phones et cetera, and come dressed in character. It's a celebration of her books as well as telling the story that's recently come to light up at the hall.'

One of the village childminders, gathering up the final of her brood of charges and overhearing the conversation, shouted in Eva and Grace's direction. 'Murder at the Vicarage, is it?'

'There's been a murder at the vicarage?' An elderly woman, obviously a child's granny, looked horrified. 'Not our vicar? Not Reverend Rosa?'

'Reverend Rosa's been murdered?' Mums and grannies were turning in fascinated horror as the rumour began to circulate.

'No, no!' Grace shouted, laughing and waving both hands to disperse any suggestion that their village vicar had come to an untimely end at the hands of foul play. 'We were just discussing the works of Agatha Christie. And, everyone,' she went on, 'it sounds like it's going to be one really brilliant evening's entertainment up at Heatherly Hall.' She turned back to Eva. 'Send Laila down with a couple of posters and a box of fliers, Mrs Malik, and I'll make sure they're put in a prominent place where parents can see them.'

'Should you be advertising in school for us like this?' Eva asked doubtfully. 'Isn't it against the teaching equivalent of the Hippocratic oath?' She looked round for Laila and Nora who had both headed off to play with respective friends, needing to get them to Rayan's place before driving herself up to the hall for two early evening meetings.

'No, of course not.' Grace Henderson laughed. 'Send them

down, really. Oh look.' Grace smiled. 'Reverend Rosa herself, alive and kicking and come to pick up Chiara.'

Eva and Grace turned as did several parents, relieved to see Rosa was still standing.

'Oh hell,' Eva swore. 'I told her not to talk to Carys.'

'Carys?'

'Chiara's mother.'

'Oh, of course. We've been told by her father not to let Chiara out into the playground at home time. Rosa will need to pick her up from the classroom.' Grace frowned. 'But that's her mother, is it? And Rosa's with her? Should she be?'

'No, she damned well shouldn't,' Eva snapped. 'Excuse me,' she said and, leaving the teacher to walk back into school, headed towards Rosa and Carys who were also making their way across the playground towards the main entrance.

'What are you *doing*?' Eva snarled, running to catch up with the other two. 'Rosa, what are you *doing*?'

When Rosa seemed unable to speak, Eva grabbed hold of Carys's arm. '*You're* not allowed to pick Chiara up from school – you know that. Joe said so. His solicitors say so.' Eva wasn't sure if this was fact, but anything to put the wind up Carys.

'It's fine, Eva, really.' Rosa attempted a smile. 'I'm going in with Carys to introduce her to Mrs Beresford and Chiara's teacher and giving her permission to pick Chiara up from school.'

'Joe will go ape…'

'Mummy, can we go now? Want to see Farhan.' Nora was hanging on to Eva's arm, pulling her back towards the main gate.

'Come on, Mummy.' Laila had joined them, obviously bored now that the remainder of the children had left.

'Hello, you must be Nora?' Carys bent down, smiling at Eva's younger daughter. 'And you, you must be Laila? Chiara's told me all about you. You're very clever, aren't you?'

Laila preened.

'And so pretty.'

'*I'm* pretty,' Nora lisped, eager to have her share of admiration, and immediately falling under Carys's spell just as Rosa, Hannah and Eva had themselves succumbed ten years or so earlier. Charismatic Carys. Wasn't that what they'd dubbed her when they'd all spent weekends away together? 'And I can read,' Nora was now boasting.

'I bet you can, you clever old thing.' Carys ruffled Nora's dark hair and the little girl leant into her.

'*And* I'm a princess. *And* I've got a new baby called Farhan.'

'How lovely.' Carys grinned. 'I've brought presents for you both,' she went on. 'I'm your... your aunty.'

'You are *not* my daughters' aunty!' Eva hissed furiously. 'We may have loved you once, Carys, and welcomed you as part of our family, but you are *not*, and never have been and never *will be*, my daughters' aunt.'

'Eva, leave it,' Rosa said tiredly. 'We have to think what's best for Chiara. And,' she went on, now glaring at her sister, 'I *don't* want to be airing my dirty laundry out here in the school playground, if you don't mind.' Several of the remaining parents and grandparents had turned in the direction of Eva's furious protestations and were openly staring. 'We've meetings at the hall, Eva; Hannah says I have to be there. I'll be up in an hour or so.' She turned, an almost desolate figure in her black vicar's togs, and Eva couldn't help but compare Rosa to Carys who, in the resplendence of pregnancy – as well as in the beautiful shocking-pink duster coat, artfully left open to reveal her bump – was blooming like a summer rose.

'So, Ms Quinn, can you take us through the security arrangements so far?' The large man – actually *amazingly* large – leaned back in his chair, his long, muscled legs finding a resting place a metre or so from Hannah and Eva who both, simultaneously, gawped in admiration. 'Just so you know,' he went on in a strong Bronx accent, 'I've spent the whole of today with your own security guys, who, I have to say, wouldn't appear to know how to secure a kid's hair ribbon, never mind a great pile like this. As such...'

'I'm sorry,' Eva interrupted, stung, 'Charlie and Jason have never had to deal with anything like this before.'

'I can see that,' Jefferson Garcia said bluntly. 'Your guys had absolutely *no idea* how to frisk a body.'

'Not much call for frisking in Westenbury,' Eva murmured while Hannah dug her crossly in the ribs.

'We're in your hands, Mr Garcia.' Hannah smiled encouragingly.

'Literally, by the sound of it.' Eva arched an eyebrow.

'Ms Quinn...' Jefferson went on, turning to Eva.

'It's Mrs Malik,' Eva shot back, still, she realised, cross and stressed after her confrontation with Carys Powell in the school playground.

'The two of you ladies don't seem to be taking this too seriously.' He paused, narrowing his eyes. 'You know, I was against Mr Livingston and Ms Sharma changing their wedding venue to this place from the start.' He gazed up and round at the boardroom as Hannah and Eva and the others present followed his gaze towards the ceiling where a dark brown damp patch was spreading after several recent days of rain. It resembled nothing more than a man's genitalia – a particularly well-endowed man at that – and Eva, finding herself the focus of Jefferson Garcia's hard stare once more, suppressed a nervous titter.

She swallowed her giggles and came out fighting. 'Sorry, Mr Garcia, I think you'll find my sisters and I are *women* – and professional women at that – as opposed to *ladies*. So, now that we've got *that* out of the way, can we get on? Here at Heatherly Hall, we're more than happy to adhere to extra security for the wedding. We'll leave all that with you. Just tell us the final cost and we'll add it to your bill. If you want to include Charlie and Jason's team in your own, then fine. If not, that's also fine: Charlie, particularly, might go off in a bit of a sulk, but we're happy for you to bring in a bigger security team if that's what you feel is needed.'

'It is. All the guests will need to be searched...'

'Even Aamir Khan and Akshay Kumar?' Eva went on, naming the current top two Bollywood actors. 'Well, good luck with that, mate.'

'They're used to it. You don't get to the top of your career without a whole host of security people on your tail. In fact, they'll be bringing their own.' He turned to his assistant, an equally huge and stacked black man. The pair of them, Eva surmised, most definitely downed weights for dinner. 'Horace...'

Horace? This glorious example of super-fit manhood was actually called Horace? Eva exchanged glances with Tara and Felicity who grinned back in her direction.

'...Horace, make sure you know what security, if any, each guest is bringing,' Jefferson barked. 'They'll have to be *catered* for as well,' he went on, addressing Hannah as well as both Aditi's chefs.

'Not happy with an egg sarni and a packet of crisps on the grass then?' Eva raised an eye in Garcia's direction.

'This is the sort of thing you don't seem to have thought of,' the man tutted. 'Are you sure you're capable of pulling it all off?'

'Mr Jefferson – sorry, Mr Garcia.' Tara suddenly stood, laptop to hand, two spots of red in her otherwise pale cheeks showing she was getting cross. 'I've been wedding planner here for years. And, while this may be the most famous we've ever catered for, it most certainly isn't the *biggest*. Now, if you'll just sit back in your chair once more and let Felicity, Hannah and myself take you through the presentation of what we've put in place, then you can ask any questions and make further suggestions at the end. Which, of course, will be noted and duly acted upon.'

Hmm, Eva thought, over an hour later as Tara brought the presentation to an end and the boardroom lights were put back on: very professional, very slick. Tara and Felicity had certainly done their homework, but Hannah had obviously had a huge input as well. 'Well done, Hans,' Eva whispered across the table to her sister. 'Fabbity fab!'

There was a protracted silence from the rest of the team sat around the conference table until Vikram Bakshi, Aditi's PA, started to clap and then, one by one, the rest joined in.

'Hannah.' Vikram stood. 'I can only say how impressed I am with the hard work you and your team have put into this already, and at such ridiculously short notice. I've yet another checklist here from Aditi – she's away at the moment in India – and, while the presentation was running, I've been able to tick off most of her demands... her queries,' he amended. 'I shall be speaking to her this evening, if I can get hold of her.'

'Is Aditi actually working in India?' Eva asked. 'Where is she? Delhi? Mumbai? Calcutta?'

She reeled off the only large cities she knew, and she thought, might have something to do with Bollywood.

Vikram shook his head. 'Andhra Pradesh, I think she said. To be honest...' he lowered his voice '...the woman's being an absolute nightmare at the moment. I just can't keep up with her, constantly kowtowing to her every need. Once all this lot's over, I'm off. Had a very good offer to PA for someone else.'

'Andhra Pradesh?' Eva pulled a face. 'Never heard of it.'

'Me neither. I think it's in the south-east somewhere, down towards the Bay of Bengal. To be honest...' he laughed '...I've never been to India. I was born in Luton.'

Once the presentation was over, Hannah felt able to relax, and relief that all had gone to plan was making her voluble. 'Before Jasper Solomon and Safe Rao here...' Hannah indicated and introduced Aditi's two chefs as though introducing celebrity chefs was commonplace – something she did every day '...go over the menus for the wedding breakfast, we'd like to take a little break and invite you to sample what *our* chefs here at Heatherly Hall come up with on a daily basis. If you'll excuse me...' She took her phone from the table, made a quick call and, five minutes later, three of the waiting staff from the conference centre made an appearance, followed by Greg, the young chef Bill and Tara had taken on two years previously after he'd started, straight from school, at Clementine's Restaurant down in the village. He was now making quite a name for himself at the hall. Hannah was constantly worried Greg was going to leave, on the next step up the career ladder but, a shy farmer's lad, living at home still with his mum and dad, engaged to Sally who worked in Tea and Cake, Greg appearing totally settled and happy where he was.

Today though, he looked terrified at being in the same room as the two celebrity chefs, never mind about to serve them the tiny taster dishes he'd concocted while, scarlet-faced and suffused with embarrassment, he also appeared unable to utter a word of explanation. Jenny, one of the waitresses, quite stunning in appearance and oozing a confidence rare in a nineteen-year-old, immediately came to his assistance.

'We have for you this evening, ladies and gentlemen, just a small example of what Greg here and his team daily create and cook in the Heatherly Hall kitchens. So, there's a baked scallop in a creamy coconut sauce; a sliver of chicken liver and hazelnut on a homemade pain perdu and a palm heart fettuccine carbonara. To finish we have Greg's speciality Yorkshire curd tart and, we'd very much like you to sample the local Yorkshire wine – yes, we do have some sunshine here, amongst the dark satanic hills...'

'Shouldn't that be *mills?*' Eva whispered to Hannah who shushed her, urging Jenny on with an encouraging look.

'...chosen carefully for you to complement the food. Our rosé is a medium-dry with candied fruit flavours and notes of bilberry picked in the Pennine foothills.'

The entourage of security and PAs, chefs and hangers-on immediately perked up, and then sat up, while Hannah, Eva, Tara and Felicity sprang forward to help distribute the food and glasses of wine.

'You've missed the presentation!' Blake Woodfield, Drew

Livingston's PA, shouted through a mouthful of baked scallop as Drew, himself, came in followed by Rosa.

'I'm sure it all went according to plan.' Drew smiled, ushering Rosa to the fore, while glancing round at the others in front of him around the table. His eyes met Eva's and he stopped searching. 'This lovely vicar,' he said, after holding Eva's gaze until she felt herself blush, 'is going to be marrying me. I've just spent the last half-hour being given the third degree with regards to my intentions.'

Hannah glared at Rosa who still appeared pale and not quite herself, despite an obvious attempt with a slash of lipstick and a pink ribbon tying back her long dark curly hair. Giving Drew Livingston, the most famous rocker in the world, the third degree, for heaven's sake? What the hell had Rosa been saying to Drew? Please don't say Rosa'd had him on his knees on the stone steps, reminding him of the Lord's Prayer and asking him to confess all his sins?

'I have to say, after sitting down and chatting with Reverend Rosa here over a coffee and flapjack in Tea and Cake, she's helped me iron out any last-minute doubts I might have been having about the actual state of marriage per se, as well as my reasons for finally giving up my single status after all these years. We appear, ladies and gentlemen, to be in safe hands here and, with just a couple of weeks to go, I'd like you to raise a glass...' he grinned at Jenny who rushed forward with a glass of rosé '...to the Girls of Heatherly Hall and their hard work so far. I think we've very much made the right decision in coming to this amazing place.' He walked over to Rosa and kissed her cheek before moving across to catch up with his PA and security guys.

Hannah exhaled, elbowed Eva none too gently in the ribs and moved over to Rosa who was nursing a glass of wine at the back of the boardroom, but refusing anything to eat.

'You OK, Rosie Posie?'

'I'm fine.'

'You don't look it. Eva told me about Carys at school. Was that a good idea?'

'I don't think I could have done anything else. Joe won't be happy, but Chiara was ecstatic, showing Carys off to the rest of the kids in after-school care. You know: "This is my mummy. I'm going back to Australia with my mummy, and to see my big brother."'

'*You've* been her mummy for the last six months or so.' Hannah was cross. 'Does that not mean *anything* to Chiara?'

'Chiara's seven, Hannah. She wants to be with her mum.'

'Shit… hang on.' Hannah suddenly took off in the direction of Greg who was deep in conversation with Jasper Solomon. 'If that jumped-up little cook is pinching my chef, I'll have him.'

## 20

'Eva?' Drew Livingston caught up with her as she helped collect used glasses and plates, taking her arm and manoeuvring her towards the back of the room and away from the others who were beginning to settle themselves for a short presentation from the two chefs, Jasper Solomon and Safe Rao.

Eva turned and faced Drew, her pulse racing at being so close to him. What was it about this man? His ability to ooze sex, his presence, his charisma? Or was it just because he was famous and Eva'd always loved watching him perform? One glance across at her sister told her Hannah was torn between separating Greg, Heatherly's young chef, and Jasper Solomon, celebrity chef and owner of Solomon's in London, who was taking the young chef to one side and handing over his card. And herself and Drew.

'Have you got five minutes?' Drew asked, smiling down at her.

'Ten if you want,' Eva replied, smiling back at him while deliberately turning away from Hannah. 'I saw you perform once, by the way.'

'Only once? I must be slipping.'

Eva laughed and she knew he was flirting with her, but didn't care. 'In London, years ago. An open-air concert in Hyde Park.

The three of us – actually four of us: Rosa was with Joe – we were all there, you know, travel rugs and inner bags of wine boxes hidden in cushions?' Eva smiled at the memory, wishing, just for a few seconds, that she was eighteen once again instead of thirty-eight.

'Joe?'

'Rosa's husband.'

'Right. Your sister talks a lot of sense.'

'In what way?'

'I'll be honest with you, Eva, I was having second thoughts about this whole shebang.'

'Oh? Goodness! Don't let Hannah know that!'

'When Aditi told me she was intent on pulling out of the Falkness Castle venue, part of me felt relieved.'

'At not having to troll all that way up to Scotland after all?' Eva smiled.

'No, more than that. Much more. I thought Aditi was having second thoughts herself, and I was really concerned that I'd felt a sense of relief that the marriage might not go ahead. At not being married to Aditi.' Drew paused. 'And then, I saw you, Eva, the natural daughter of both Dame Alice Parkes and Yves Dufort…'

'Ah…' Eva laughed '…nothing at all to do with my charm, good looks and irresistible personality, then?'

'All of those, Eva,' Drew said seriously. 'And then spending time with you up in your art retreat among those murals of Bill Astley's.'

'They do tend to have an effect on one.' Eva nodded. 'You're not the first. Probably won't be the last.'

'But I just wanted to be with you. Spend some more time with you. I wanted to get to know you; see your artwork. I felt a link with you – an affiliation if you like – through our joint love of art.' Drew paused, searching Eva's face. 'Aditi has no interest whatsoever in the art world.'

'Drew, I hear what you're saying, but I don't think what you were feeling up there had much to do with me. The art's sensuality clouded your judgement. Plus, I imagine you were hoping for a last-ditch attempt at freedom. A notorious commitment-phobe – I read all the papers, you know – seeking a way out of his marriage?'

'Rosa said the same.'

'Rosa did?'

'I bumped into her downstairs, saw the dog collar and resemblance to you and Hannah...'

'Oh of course, you'd not met her before.'

'...and persuaded her to come for a chat with me over in that little café of yours. Bloody good millionaire's shortbread – my mum used to make it for me. Must tell one of Aditi's chefs she's roped in to make some for the wedding.'

Eva laughed. 'We can always provide that ourselves, but I'm not convinced Aditi would be happy with it at her posh wedding.'

'She said she wanted to talk to me about it.'

'Who? Aditi?' Eva frowned. 'About millionaire's shortbread?'

'No, no, Aditi's over in India for a week for some reason. *Rosa* said she wanted to talk to me. It's what vicars have to do before they marry someone. She'll have to speak to Aditi and then both of us together as well.'

'No vicar talked to me and Rayan,' Eva mused and then laughed. 'Mind you, with neither of us being particularly religious – despite my grandfather being a vicar and Rayan's family all practising Muslims – we opted for a quiet registry office do in Sheffield. Didn't have to face any vicar at all who might put me through my paces and try to find out why I was marrying Rayan.'

'And why did you?'

'Why did I marry him? I fancied him hugely. And I loved him.'

'I'm sorry it didn't work out.'

'So am I.' Eva paused, feeling a little tearful. 'So, Rosa sorted you out, did she?'

'She did. What I really wanted to say, to you, Eva, was…'

He was interrupted by Hannah who had made her way over to herself and Drew, coming between the pair of them as effectively as any pre-planned chess move. 'Ah, Eva, I'm assuming you're assuring Drew that Alice and Yves will both be in attendance on the big day? I had confirmation from both of them a couple of days ago, Drew. All is in order. Lovely. OK? Eva, if you wouldn't mind just helping the waitresses with those final plates?'

Eva felt herself dismissed, which she knew was a good thing. There had definitely been something stirring between herself and Drew Livingston and she needed to step back from whatever it was, although Drew didn't appear to have any such scruples. She caught up with Rosa, who was clearly on her way out.

'Where are you going, Rosa? Hannah wants you to stay for the next bit of the meeting. And then we've got the Westenbury Players due here…' Eva looked at her watch '…in less than an hour.'

'I need to get back, Eva. I've left Chiara with Carys at the vicarage. Carys is making pasta for her.'

'Well, more fool you. What were you thinking? Joe will have a fit.'

'And what were *you* thinking,' Rosa shot back, 'flirting with a man who's about to get married?'

'I wasn't,' Eva protested hotly.

'Eva, you could cut the tension between the pair of you with a knife.'

'I don't think so…'

'As well as Drew telling me you'd turned his head, over in Tea and Cake.'

'I've never *been* with Drew in Tea and Cake.'

'Now you're being facetious. The result of a guilty conscience maybe? Anyway, you did. Turn his head. Made him rethink his whole engagement.'

'Oh, don't be ridiculous. I've only spent a couple of hours in his company, Rosa.'

'It only takes a couple of minutes, believe me. Just be careful, Eva!'

# 21

A week before the wedding, Hannah, who really didn't have the time, was meeting up with Daisy for yet another discussion about the Agatha Christie evening.

'I'm starving,' Daisy breathed, bringing out a bag of crisps from her bag and immediately opening it and diving in. 'Dad and I have come straight here from Fred Beaumont's place: lambing's well under way up there.' She paused. 'Sorry, do I smell?' Daisy sniffed at her arms. 'Need to get a move on with this meeting because Jude's on his way back up from London. I've not seen him for over a week; I need to give myself the works and change the dinner-for-one to a dinner-for-two at M and S.' She sniffed again, this time at her other arm, and frowned. 'Hmm, definitely need the works before I let Jude anywhere near this body of mine.'

'I can send down for some sandwiches?' Hannah said. 'There's only you and your dad and Vivienne tonight, isn't there?'

Daisy nodded. 'We've actually managed a couple of rehearsals down in the church hall this week. We're well on our way with it all. Know where we're going and who's playing who. Mind you, we had to work round Hilary's yoga class and the cubs. God, they were a noisy lot.'

'Who? The cubs?'

'No, Hilary's yoga lot: chanting and then falling over and

giggling as the occasional fart broke free. Not for me, I'm afraid. So, basically, we wanted to show you the Jet Set Vivienne found on eBay. See if you think it's OK. Vivienne should be here soon. And then go over the treasure hunt and the clues Dad's compiled.'

'How's he been able to do that without really knowing the hall layout?' Hannah frowned.

'Oh, we got a good look round the last time we were here. We didn't want to bother you, so we just wandered round making notes.'

'Right. Security didn't stop you then?'

'Who? Charlie's lot?' Daisy laughed. 'Dad's known Charlie for years. He used to be a farmhand before he changed career. If you can call wandering round with a dog and a mug of coffee a career. That Dobermann of his is as soft as he is.' Daisy glanced towards the door. 'Eva not coming? Or Rosa?'

Hannah shook her head. 'Eva *was* coming, but apparently Nora's thrown up and wants her mum. Eva's gone to fetch her from Rayan's place. And Rosa isn't either.'

'Oh?'

'Other things going on.' Hannah didn't elaborate; wasn't prepared to fuel any village gossip about Carys Powell turning up at the vicarage. 'Right.' Hannah looked at her watch. She could do with *the works* herself. She was feeling particularly sweaty and jaded after long and intense meetings all day with the different factions involved in the forthcoming wedding. And Zac had asked her out for a meal down at Clementine's in the village, said he wanted to go over a few things he'd researched about Heatherly Hall with her. She knew she shouldn't really be going – that she was on dangerous ground because of her relationship with Lachlan – but Lachlan had been away for over a week, something about going back up to Scotland to see his father who wasn't well. Hannah felt a stab of guilt and knew she must ring Lachlan once this meeting was over and she was back up at the apartment.

'Come on then,' Hannah said, slightly impatiently, 'let's get on with it. Is Vivienne on her way or what?'

'I'm here, darlings.' Vivienne had entered the office in a cloud of *Rive Gauche*, lilac silk and general bonhomie. 'Just stopped to chat with that glorious American of yours.' Vivienne glanced meaningfully at Hannah. 'Wooh.' She fanned herself theatrically with the package she was carrying. 'I bet you've your hands full with that one, darling.'

'Hands full? Of Zac?' Daisy's tone was sharp. 'Hannah is with Lachlan, Vivienne. And,' she added in an undertone, 'if you're *not*, Hannah, then for heaven's sake tell him and let him down gently.'

'I most certainly am not *with* Zac,' Hannah said, her pink face telling another story. 'Lachlan is away at the moment back in Scotland. He's not had a break for months. In fact,' she added, thinking, 'the only time I've known him take time off is for some wedding he went to in the summer.'

'Well, I hope he's back soon. Those ewes of yours are beginning to pop all over the place and, if he's away, I can guarantee you'll be ringing me or Dad in the middle of the night. And, Hannah, the last thing I'm wanting is to be out in the cold at midnight – it's still bloody freezing out there – when I have Jude in my bed for the next four days.'

'Ger is here to help,' Hannah said almost sulkily. She hated being told off, hated anyone thinking badly of her. At primary school it had always been her, out of Rosa, Eva and herself who'd sob if she was in trouble for anything: weep when she couldn't understand long division, cry if she forgot her PE kit and was made to wear the classroom's spare set of shorts and Aertex, which were always musty-smelling and far too big. Rosa never did anything wrong and Eva couldn't give a damn when she was given a dressing-down in front of the class and Susan called in yet again for a little chat re the latter's behaviour.

'Hang on, Viv…' Hannah started.

'*Viv-i-enne*, darling. The emphasis is always on the last syllable.'

Ignoring the correction, Hannah said, frowning, 'You've just been talking to Zac? Where?'

'He was up in the art retreat. Security brought me up via the other flight of stairs for some reason.'

'Some of the marble and brass on the main staircase is going to be looked at,' Hannah explained. It was just one more thing on Aditi Sharma's checklist. The bride-to-be had noticed that the very old marble steps needed work, and organised her own workmen to come in to put things right. Hannah had explained to Aditi that the hall's own maintenance people would see to it, but Aditi insisted on her own team coming in, in order to 'get the job done properly, Ms Quinn, and to my exacting standards'.

Despite Hannah insisting that the hall's maintenance people were pretty exacting, themselves, Aditi had got her own way and her *professional artisans* (Aditi speak) had arrived late that afternoon. 'She must have more money than sense,' Hannah had complained to Tara and Felicity, 'because, there'll be so many guests on that staircase on the day, a bit of chipped marble and tarnished brass won't be visible.' Capitulating to Aditi's demands, Hannah had specified only that the work be carried out in the evening when most of the visitors had left.

Hannah now frowned, turning to Vivienne. 'But you didn't need to go up as far as the art retreat, Vivienne?'

'I know, darling. I was being a bit naughty. Asked Charlie – or was it Jason? – to do a little detour so I could see the famous – or is it infamous? – murals. Goodness, they're quite something, aren't they?'

'And Zac was there?' As far as Hannah knew, he was still down at The Jolly Sailor.

'Oh yes. He's very thorough in his research, isn't he? I'm very much looking forward to reading this book of his when it's out. Now, do you want to see what I found on eBay?' Vivienne reached for the brown paper envelope. 'I think it's as near as we're going to get to the original.'

'But we don't know what the original was like,' Hannah frowned.

'From what we've read we know it was a necklace and earrings made from jet, and studded with diamonds. So...' Vivienne reached into the package '...what do you think?'

'Oh, that's fabulous.' Hannah was impressed. 'Well done.'

'It was £85,' Vivienne boasted. 'Nearly lost it to another bidder, but I kept my nerve.' She fastened the necklace and then added the earrings to her ears. 'I think they're very nice. Bit of tat, of course, and not something *I* personally would ever wear, but the jet is genuine Whitby jet with a date of... hang on... she reached once more into the envelope... 'circa 1930, so fairly authentic.'

'Look, can we get on?' Daisy was impatient. 'Jude will be back soon and...' she sniffed once more, this time at her hair '...I need to get home. Dad, come on, read what you've come up with so far for the treasure hunt.'

Clearing his throat, Graham Maddison took a file from his briefcase, shuffling papers importantly before starting:

*'I'm always running, though I never walk.*
*Sometimes, I sing, but never talk.*
*I've hands, I've a face,*
*I'll work out your pace.'*

Graham, Daisy and Vivienne turned expectantly to Hannah who screwed up her own face in anxiety. Hell, it felt like being back at junior school, doing those awful verbal reasoning tests she'd faced every Friday afternoon in Miss Hall's class. She could never do them then – had constantly tried to look over at Eva's paper, but Eva, on a roll, would have turned the page and be heading towards the finishing line – and had to wait until Rosa came to her rescue, discreetly sharing her answers, once Miss Hall wasn't looking.

'Erm...?'

'Come on, Hannah, this is an easy one to start.'

'Easy?'

'What's got hands? And a face?'

'Me?'

'Never talk, Hannah? You're always talking.' Daisy laughed in her direction.

'A clock, darling.' Vivienne finally took pity on her, just as Rosa had, almost thirty years earlier.

Graham laughed enthusiastically. 'So, this means we'll start the clues at the old grandfather clock in the Great Hall where the next clue will lead them to:

*'Pull me in the morning,*
*spread me out at night.*
*I might not keep you warm,*
*but my purpose is for sight.'*

All Hannah could think of was Ben Pennington, her ex. He'd always wanted an early morning session before going off to his work as a consultant neurosurgeon. Certainly, he hadn't been averse to most nights as well. Had he kept her warm? Not when he was off, in the early days of their relationship, back to his wife before he'd moved into the apartment with her. But he'd certainly been lovely to look at.

'A lover?' Hannah ventured.

'A lover?' The other three all stared.

'Whose lover?' Daisy started to laugh. 'We can't have the audience frisking anyone who they know is having an affair, looking for the next clue under their sweater.'

'Curtains,' Graham said almost crossly. 'Curtains! It's obvious. The audience will make their way up the Great Hall stairs, and up once more to those fabulous huge tapestry curtains on the mezzanine floor for the next clue and so on and so forth.'

'Right.' Hannah was beginning to feel stupid. 'If you say so. To be honest, Daisy, I'm already having sleepless nights about the Livingston wedding. This whole Agatha Christie Jet Set thing is only adding to my insomnia. I mean, I can just picture the audience all setting off and scrabbling about the place, desperate to win. Heatherly is an old historic hall, not a "free house"—' Hannah air-quoted the words '—that a teenaged kid finds himself in when his mum and dad go off for the weekend. If they've been on the champagne, which we're laying on for them, I believe…?'

'Co-op's best Prosecco actually.' Daisy grinned.

'How do we stop them going on the rampage?'

'The rampage?' Vivienne was affronted. 'The audience is mainly Westenbury villagers, not hooligans at a football match.'

'But, how do we stop them nicking a Victorian jug and bowl or… or going off with a Chippendale?' Hannah found herself beginning to panic, about to cancel the whole thing right there and then. She shook her head, panic rising – she just had to put a stop to this farce. 'I really don't think…'

'The Chippendales?' Vivienne's eyes lit up. 'Have you got *them* coming as well?'

'Oh, for heaven's sake, Viv.' Daisy looked at her watch. 'I'm off. Dad's done half the clues, but he needs another scout round to decide the next bit of the route to the prize. Have you got time now, Hannah, to show him and Vivienne round again? Or they could just wander?'

'We can just wander, Hannah,' Graham concurred. 'I get my best ideas when I'm just wandering.'

'Well, the world and his wife appear to be *just wandering* the hall this evening.' Hannah frowned once more before nodding her agreement. 'Look, I'm going to grab a shower and hair wash. I'll see you two out when you're finished. Oh, and if you spot Zac on your travels, tell him I'll be an hour and then I'll be with him.'

'Be careful,' Daisy warned, echoing Rosa's earlier words to Eva.

'Absolutely nothing to be careful about,' Hannah snapped. 'I'm going to ring Lachlan, see how his father's doing and then I'm off for a business meeting over dinner at Clementine's.'

'If you say so.' Daisy shot her a raised eyebrow. 'If you say so, Hannah.'

## 22

Hannah had always wanted to be taken out for dinner at Clementine's, the restaurant in the village for which Westenbury had become internationally famous. Ben Pennington had promised to take her there on several occasions, but the promise never seemed to have materialised. As she drank the triple gin and tonic she'd poured herself to ease the nervousness she was feeling at being taken out for dinner, and then shampooed and conditioned her long dark hair, she thought idly about Ben, wondering where he was and what he was up to now. She'd been so in love with him: in love with the idea of being in love, she supposed. But it hadn't taken him long to try his luck with Tara. And probably a whole raft of other women as well.

Hannah towelled her wet hair quickly. She wanted to find where Zac had got to and why he was strolling around here by himself when she hadn't even known he was on the premises. She was a bit miffed that he'd felt able to wander round the place without asking permission. While reception, the conference centre, hotel bedrooms, restaurant and kitchens in the west wing of the hall were all a hive of activity at this time of day, most of the hall's east wing, which housed the art retreat, the Great Hall, offices, boardroom and what had previously been Bill's private apartment, and into which she'd moved on his death, were most certainly not open to the public, or to guests at any time. Unless they were booked into the art retreat of course, but even that tended to be locked in the evening unless there was a late session, or a visiting artist in situ.

She put down the gin and carefully made up her face, outlining her large grey eyes with a soft kohl and adding another layer of mascara before painting her full lips with her favourite Red Poppy lipstick. Hannah wondered if Zac was spending as much time at other stately homes in the area as he appeared to be spending here at Heatherly Hall? He'd said Bramham Park at Wetherby and Wentworth Woodhouse near Barnsley, were next on his list, but, as far as she knew, he'd not been there yet.

Hannah revved up the hairdryer, raking fingers through her wet hair while deciding what to wear. Something a bit posh for Clementine's. She was, she realised, absolutely starving, and, as she pulled on underwear – white, lacy, her favourite Triumph bra and knickers – also realised she'd lost weight. She'd spent years on daft diets, trying constantly to compete with Eva to be the slimmest of the two of them and now, without trying, so engrossed was she at being in charge of Heatherly, the pounds appeared to be dropping off without any recourse to the gym or dieting.

She drained the glass of gin, wincing somewhat as the strong liquid went down, and then stood stock-still, pulse racing, as she realised someone was in the sitting room next to her bedroom. She was sure she'd locked the apartment's front door – she always did, whatever time of day she was up here by herself, but particularly in the evening. It wasn't unknown for a guest, especially after several drinks at the bar, to wander into the east wing despite the red ropes and 'private' signage prohibiting entry into this side of the hall. Feeling vulnerable in her half-naked state, she moved quietly to the open wardrobe and, quickly selecting a soft cream cashmere sweater dress, pulled it over her head.

Barefoot, she tiptoed to the bedroom door, straining to hear the noise again, every one of her senses on alert. Had she imagined it? Was she better staying where she was and ringing down for security? She looked round for her phone, remembered it was charging in the kitchen and swore silently under her breath. She dithered, hand on the bedroom door handle, ears straining once again.

Then someone sneezed. Surely mad axe murderers didn't sneeze like that? And sneezed again, more loudly this time. Bracing herself, Hannah opened the bedroom door slowly.

'Oh, there you are?' Zac turned from where he was sitting on the sofa. 'I knocked several times, but eventually let myself in. I hope you don't mind.' He sneezed again, pointing a hand in the direction of the bowl of lilac hyacinth in full bloom. 'I think I'm allergic to your flowers.' He paused, sneezed once more before saying, 'Are you ready? I came to find you because the restaurant's booked earlier than I thought; I tried to ring you, but you weren't answering. You look gorgeous, Hannah.'

He stood to kiss her cheek and as she breathed in a subtle spicy aftershave, all she could think was what a stunning man Zac Anderson was. He was wearing chinos and a black polo-necked jumper, topped with an expensive-looking black jacket. She felt her stomach do that wonderful flippy thing that only happens when faced with a man who has caught your eye, come into your life and you want to know better. The atmosphere in the room was suddenly ramped up, charged with expectation, sophistication, seduction. Zac bent towards her once more, kissing her open mouth, and she found herself responding. Must be the gin, she thought, dreamily and then, suddenly flustered, unsure, she pulled away.

'I was in the shower... and then I was drying my hair... I didn't hear anything... but the door... Zac, the door was locked. I *always* lock that door.' She glanced towards the heavy oak-panelled door.

'Not this time you didn't.'

'I'm sure I did.' Hannah felt herself waver: forgetting to lock the door was the only explanation. She *had* been in a hurry, needing to get in the shower before seeing Graham and Vivienne Maddison out of the hall, knowing she still had to go and check on Aditi's workmen and remind security there'd be workmen on the marble stairs most of the evening as well as ringing Lachlan to find out how his father was. She'd not managed either of the last two and, while she didn't really give two hoots about Aditi's *artisans* she knew she *must* ring Lachlan. Actually, *wanted* to ring Lachlan. She realised she was missing him – missing his lovely gentle brown eyes, his dependable sturdy six-foot-two height, his not minding her cold feet on his in bed at night. But also thinking that Zac would soon be waiting for her down at reception as they'd previously arranged. But now he was actually here, unexpectedly in her sitting room.

Zac put up two hands and shrugged, grinning. 'Come on, just make sure you lock it behind you this time. If we don't get a move on, we'll be late. Have you got a coat? It's cold out there.'

'I need to see Graham and Vivienne out...' Hannah started. 'And I must ring someone...'

'Oh, they've already left. Charlie, the security guy, was with them unlocking doors and seeing them out. Graham said to tell you they were off.'

'Right.'

The night, despite the year heading towards the spring solstice, was cold, frosty and clear, a huge full moon hanging languidly in front of them as they walked through the park towards Zac's rental car. Hannah realised she didn't quite know what to say to him – his sudden manifestation through what she was convinced had been a locked door had spooked her.

He finally broke the silence, looking up at the sky. 'The Northern American Indian tribes knew it as a Worm Moon.' He smiled, taking Hannah's hand in his own.

Hannah wasn't interested in North American sodding moons; much more interested in getting to the bottom of the mystery of her locked door. Which was *unlocked*. 'You know, Zac,' she finally said, 'that door *was* locked.' She stumbled slightly on her unaccustomed high heels and Zac put out a hand. 'I always lock it, and take out the key.'

'Do you?' He smiled down at her. 'Why?'

'Why do I lock the door? I think it's pretty obvious, living above the shop as it were. Anyone could just wander in.' She glanced at him meaningfully.

'No, why do you take out the key?'

'I once saw a film where the murderer slid a piece of paper under the door of this girl who lived alone. And then he pushed out the key through the keyhole onto the newspaper and then...'

'That old chestnut.' Zac started to laugh as he unlocked the car door. 'You'd have to have a pretty big gap under the door for that to work.'

'There's a *huge* gap under the apartment's front door,' Hannah said, not letting it go. 'Bill used to complain constantly about the draught coming through it.'

'The whole hall is pretty cold and draughty, isn't it? I'm surprised you live up there by yourself?'

'The west wing where the guests stay isn't a bit draughty,' Hannah retorted, stung at any criticism of her beloved Heatherly Hall. 'The conference centre, restaurant and guest rooms are cosy warm. Bill, my father, spent hundreds of thousands of pounds, once he'd made the decision to turn the place over to the paying public...'

'Oh? Where did he get the cash for that, then?'

Hannah paused, not quite sure of the answer to what she felt was a personal, if not impolite question. Was this the American way and she was being uptight and British? She, Rosa and Eva had been in their teens, busy with their own lives, when Bill made the decision to make Heatherly Hall into a public limited company and turn most of the place into a conference centre. The wedding venue came much later, and the subsequent opening of restaurant and hotel once the venue began to make money. 'I think,' she eventually started, 'he sold what artwork and antiques would fetch the most money as well as being given grants from the National Trust and other authorities wanting to maintain English ancestral homes. I believe there was a Monet, a couple of Picassos and a Lowry. Bill was glad to be rid of them – insuring them was a great drain on his resources.'

Zac didn't reply but, once they were in the car, belted up and turning out of the huge hall gates and heading down into the village of Westenbury and Clementine's restaurant, he glanced across at Hannah and smiled. 'So, you don't think it probable Bill knew exactly what happened to the Jet Set then? And secretly sold it to raise the cash he needed?'

'Sorry?' Hannah turned. 'Bill knew?'

'Oh, just a thought,' Zac said easily. 'I mean, turning a great pile like Heatherly Hall into a conference centre and then wedding venue must have cost millions, rather than thousands.'

Hannah fell silent. It had never occurred to her that her beloved Bill could have known all along where the missing jewels had ended up. But it actually made some sense: maybe on his father, Henry's, deathbed, the old man had told the young Bill that, as rumoured, he'd in fact taken and hidden the jewels himself, knowing that he just couldn't afford to give them away to Mrs Simpson. His plan being, when the furore of the theft of the Jet Set had died down, he'd then sell them on for the money so badly needed to keep the hall from falling even further into disrepair. Henry had died, Hannah knew, only a few years after the alleged theft, broken-hearted at losing his two eldest sons in the early years of the Second World War when Bill himself was just a small boy, the only surviving son of Henry, eleventh Marquess of Stratton.

'He never discussed it with you then?' Zac appeared unwilling to let it go.

'You seem very interested in the whole thing.' Hannah stared at his profile as they pulled in to the restaurant car park.

'I am.' Zac laughed, easily. 'I find it fascinating – I intend the Jet Set story to be a major part of the chapter on Heatherly Hall.'

'So, Zac,' Hannah started as Zac unbuckled his belt and opened his door, 'why were you wandering...?'

But Zac was already out of the car, waiting with outstretched hand for her to join him.

'Zac, why...?' Hannah was struggling to keep up with him on these damned heels, wishing desperately she'd eschewed the stilettoes for her usual trainers.

'Come on, we can chat once we're inside.'

And then they were inside, and Zac was charming the young front-of-house girl who was blushing furiously as he flirted companionably with her, complimenting her on her attention to detail as they were ushered to a table in The Orangery. And once seated, a white starched napkin snapped open like a starting pistol and placed on her lap, Hannah found herself enthralled at actually being in Clementine's for the first time ever. As well as mentally making note of the obviously well-trained, smooth-operating young waiting and bar staff, all in their black T-shirts, trousers and orange-logoed aprons, so that she quite forgot to ask why Zac had been seen up in the art retreat – which was usually locked – earlier in the evening.

'Hannah.' Zac took her hand over the starched white tablecloth. 'It's so lovely to be able to spend some time alone with you.' He smiled, levelling his dark blue eyes with hers, his hand warm in her own, and Hannah felt an almost explosive need to reach out her other hand and touch his face.

'You're very beautiful,' she heard herself saying and immediately regretted it. Shouldn't it be him saying that to her?

He laughed, showing incredibly white, straight teeth – an all-American smile – and stroked her hand with his thumb. It was a slow, sensual movement and he laughed again saying, 'I think it should be me saying that to you. And you are incredibly beautiful, Hannah.'

'Thank you.'

'As well as ambitious, confident and clever.' There was challenge in Zac's words.

Hmm, Hannah thought, the first one she'd take; she certainly wasn't taking the last two. She reached for the glass of champagne which appeared to have arrived in front of her. Hell, she needed that, she realised, downing it in one.

Zac laughed, sipping at his own drink.

'It's been a long day,' she apologised, smiling, the champagne bursting in glorious bubbles on her tongue before slipping down warmly to her insides and ending up somewhere below, making her feel incredibly confident and clever after all. As well as lustful, uninhibited and wanting to kiss the face off this beautiful man.

Zac poured her another glass of bubbly and, not having eaten all day apart from one tiny morsel of Greg's heavenly scallop taster, as well as forgetting that she and alcohol were not best bedfellows, especially after the triple gin she'd recently knocked back, Hannah upended her glass and knew the world was a wonderful place to be in. This gorgeous man sitting across from her was wonderful. She herself was wonderful: wasn't she a marquess's daughter? Chair of the management committee at Heatherly Hall? Hadn't she clinched the wedding of the year – nay the decade – the century even?

'You're smiling.' Zac laughed, pouring yet more champagne. 'I think all the responsibility you have taken on has been making you unhappy, lately? Not your usual self? I think *this* is the real you and you've let others put too much on you. Maybe your two sisters should take on a little more?'

Hannah nodded in agreement, feeling a little tearful. Yes, what *were* they doing to help move Heatherly Hall forward? OK, she conceded, somewhat grudgingly, Eva had done a great job with the art retreat, but that was a labour of love for her. *And* she'd ended up with the very gorgeous Andrea in the process. Eva always seemed to fall on her feet, succeed at whatever she attempted, have men fall in love with her and, although she'd gone through a rough time separating from Rayan, at the end of the day that had been her choosing too, surely? She'd got what she wanted – to be free and single again after more than fifteen years of marriage.

Whereas she, Hannah, was a bit of a disaster zone. She smiled at a memory and then, remembering it in full, actually started giggling and found she couldn't stop. 'Sorry, sorry,' she hiccupped, 'just remembering last summer when I put Napoleon in with the sows.'

'Napoleon?'

Zac was so interested, Hannah thought, so happy to listen to her. 'I thought the old boar... boar, not *bore*...' That set Hannah off again, and it took her a while to continue. She finished her drink and started again: 'I thought he was past it. Anyway, we ended up... *I* ended up... with sixty or so piglets I said I'd take responsibility for when all the farmhands were cross with me.' Bloody Lachlan and that even bloodier Ger had been *really* cross with her. How dare they?

'And then...' She giggled again, but was interrupted by the young waitress.

'Are you ready to order?' The girl was gorgeous, with a high blonde ponytail that swished silkily as she hovered with her iPad. She was indeed like a polished little show pony.

'I bet you can turn on a sixpence,' Hannah chortled, patting her arm. 'Now,' she went on, lowering her voice in the girl's direction and making a great show of confidentiality, '*I'm* in charge up at Heatherly Hall – you know the place? – and I'm always on the lookout for waiting staff like yourself. Hmm?' The girl turned pink, smiling self-consciously. 'We have a fabulous – absolutely amazing wedding coming up...' here Hannah winked, tapping her nose '...but I'll give you my card...' Hannah reached for her bag, searching through its contents. 'Here we are...' Hannah thrust a hand once more into the bag, before handing the girl, who was now quite scarlet, a rectangular pantyliner packet.

'Shall I order for us, Hannah?' Zac grinned, replacing the pantyliner discreetly back in her bag.

'Please do,' Hannah said in her best grown-up voice and, realising she was aping Julia Roberts in *Pretty Woman* in the posh restaurant with Richard Gere, started to titter once more.

Zac quickly made some decisions on the menu and Hannah reached for a breadstick, crunching loudly as she chomped on it, bit by bit.

'So, Hannah...' Zac smiled, taking the hand that wasn't holding the breadstick in his own warm one. 'Tell me what *you* think happened to the missing Jet Set?'

'Oh, *that* again.' Hannah exhaled somewhat crossly and, in the process, scattered masticated breadstick crumbs in Zac's direction. 'Oops, sorry.' She leaned over to remove a couple from Zac's beautiful black jacket. 'Sorry.' She giggled once more. 'Looks like you've got dandruff now.' She moved further in to Zac and whispered conspiratorially, 'I reckon it's still up at the hall.'

'Oh?' Zac's eyes never left her own. 'Did Bill tell you that?'

'Bill?' For a split second she couldn't quite work out who Bill was. In fact, her head was feeling exceedingly woolly. And then, remembering her beloved father, whom she'd adored so much, felt tears well. She brushed them away with her napkin, wiping her nose on its starched surface. 'I remember Bill telling us all about it when we were kids and again, when we were in our teens. He reckoned the jewels were still somewhere around, and that if anyone had ever tried to sell the famous central diamond – the Sah-I-Noor – it would have been flagged up immediately.' Hannah, shook her head, amazed that she'd managed to get out such a long sentence when her mouth felt as though it were stuffed with cotton wool. She reached for her glass of water.

'Or broken up and now a part of a whole load of other jewellery? Like the Brink's-Mat Gold?' Zac's blue-eyed stare was intense, and Hannah began to feel distinctly under pressure, claustrophobic even.

'Whose mat?' Hannah had no idea what he was talking about. 'Who's Brinks? Actually, Zac,' she said, suddenly feeling a bit cross with him, remembering her earlier beef with him, 'what the hell were you doing up in the art retreat earlier this evening?'

'The art retreat?' Zac held up two hands. 'Oh, is that a problem? I didn't think you or your sisters would mind me continuing my research?' Zac smiled winningly, taking her hand once more.

'Well, actually...' Hannah went no further as the waitress placed a bowl of something cold, liquid and unrecognisable in front of her.

'Enjoy your Gazpacho...' the girl started as the blood drained from Hannah's face and she stood, pushing back her chair until it toppled over and her mascara-stained napkin fell into the soup. 'Excuse me,' she snarled and set off, cannoning off tables, until she reached her target.

## 23

'So, you're able to keep your promise to someone else, then, Ben? Hmm?' Hannah, feeling as though she might burst with the unfairness of it all, poked her ex-lover rudely in the chest while ignoring the tall, exceptionally attractive – and very young – woman at Ben Pennington's side.

'Hello, Hannah, how are you?' Ben bent to kiss her cheek. 'Been drinking again, I see?'

'You always promised you'd bring *me* to Clementine's,' Hannah exploded, wobbling slightly on her heels and hanging on to the edge of the chrome and glass bar where the two newcomers were now standing, obviously waiting to be shown to their table.

'But you threw me out before I got the chance, Hannah,' Ben said easily. 'Packed my bags and chucked them out into the herb garden, as I remember. Anyway, you appear to be here now. That Scottish Highlands' fellow brought you, has he?' Ben peered round Hannah, looking down the restaurant in the direction she'd come, searching out Lachlan.

'You do know he's married?' Hannah spat, now turning to the woman at his side. She was more than gorgeous, she was absolutely stunning, her caramel-streaked hair piled up messily on her head, her exquisite almond-shaped brown eyes huge in her sun-kissed face.

'I am aware of that.' The woman smiled. 'But then, so am I.' She held up her left hand, demonstrating the huge five-stone diamond ring and plain gold wedding band.

'My God, you're as bad as each other.' Hannah stared incredulously at the woman, and then gave a little laugh that turned into a sob. 'And your husband knows, does he?'

'You'll have to ask him,' she replied, her voice calm, but with distinct undertones of pity. 'He's standing right next to you.'

Hannah turned round, expecting to see some cuckolded man behind her. When there was no one except Ben, Hannah's heart plummeted. 'You're married?' she asked, staring at Ben. 'You married someone else,' she now yelled loudly, 'when you never asked *me?*'

'Are you alright? Can I see you back to your table?' Clementine Ahern, the owner of the restaurant had appeared at Hannah's side, her voice conciliatory. 'Let me help you? It's Hannah, isn't it? From Heatherly Hall?' Clementine placed a gentle hand on Hannah's arm, turning her away from Ben Pennington and his new wife and back towards Zac who was now on his feet and coming to join them. Other diners were turning, staring, or deliberately avoiding looking at Hannah's tear-streaked face, at her cream-coloured dress sporting a trail of orange Gazpacho, some tutting they hadn't waited months for a table, and were about to pay a fortune for the privilege, just to find themselves in the middle of a fracas one might expect in McDonald's or Pizza Hut down in Midhope town centre.

'Would you like to sit in the lounge area for a little while?' Clementine asked. 'We can save your table until you're feeling a little better?'

'I'm sorry, I'm so very, very sorry,' Hannah sobbed both to Clementine and Zac and then, turning to the rest of the diners who were pretending not to be taking it all in, apologised once more. 'I'm so sorry to spoil your dinners.' She started heading for the entrance, utterly mortified at what she'd just done. 'I want to go home. You stay, Zac, I'll drive myself home.'

Hannah attempted to walk, head held high, in a straight line, but fell off her heels, stumbling into an elderly woman seated to her left and who glared, mouthing, 'Really...' as Hannah attempted to right herself.

'She can't drive,' Clementine was now saying to Zac.

'Of course, she can't.' Zac smiled at Clementine. 'It's OK, she didn't drive here; I'll take her home. You've my contact details – Zac Anderson – I'll be in touch to pay the bill.'

Zac took Hannah's arm none too gently, bundling her into his car and leaning over her to fasten her seatbelt.

'I'm so sorry,' Hannah said once more, tears rolling down her cheeks.

'Let's just get you home,' Zac said, pulling out of the car park rather too quickly and immediately heading in the direction of Heatherly Hall.

Neither of them said a word as they drove the five miles or so out of the village and finally through the gates of the hall, manned and opened by Charlie, from his office. His Dobermann barked a couple of warning shots through the car's open window and then slunk dispiritedly back into the office, before lying down and falling asleep once more.

Zac parked the car and helped Hannah out, placing a supporting arm around her shoulder and escorting her towards the stairs of the private east wing. 'Keys, Hannah?'

Hannah, now in a mortified state of shock, one shoe to hand, scrabbled in her bag with the other before handing her bunch of keys to Zac. And then, desperate to make amends, utterly ashamed of how she'd ruined her date with this lovely man, flung her arms round his neck, pressing her lips to his own.

Zac hesitated, but only for a few seconds before kissing her back. 'You taste of champagne and smell of Gazpacho,' he whispered into her hair, moving her so that her back was against the cold stone wall, his hand reaching for her breast swaddled in the softness of the cream cashmere, 'but I've been wanting to do just this ever since I first saw you.'

Hannah closed her eyes, willing herself to feel something, wanting to find oblivion in another's arms, but something wasn't right: he wasn't Ben.

But more importantly, so, so much more importantly, he wasn't Lachlan. Lovely Lachlan, steady, lovely Lachlan with his soft warm brown eyes. Who knew what she was like, but loved her anyway. Who never suggested she have more than one glass of wine, knowing as he did, that any more and she was tipped over into another world. A scary world where she appeared to have little control.

'Oh, Hannah,' Zac breathed, nudging his hardness against her leg, 'we need to go upstairs.'

'I'm sorry, I'm going up alone,' she said determinedly, the cold March evening air sobering her up more than any black coffee ever could.

'Oh, now that's a shame.' Zac dangled the bunch of keys over her head, teasing, reaching down to kiss her once more.

'My keys please,' she said, one hand reaching for the bunch, the other holding him away from her.

'Hannah, I've never once forced myself where I'm not wanted, believe me. But you and I… Come on, Hannah…' Zac reached out a hand to her shoulder, attempting to push her back once more against the cold stone of the wall.

'Give me the keys,' Hannah hissed, pushing him off.

'Give her the keys,' another voice shot out from somewhere to her right.

'Lachlan? Oh, you're back? How's your dad?'

'I'll make sure she gets upstairs,' Lachlan said icily, taking the keys from Zac's hand. 'I'm sure Hannah will be in touch in the morning. But meanwhile, I think it probably best if you leave.'

Zac raised his two hands in supplication. 'Of course,' he said smoothly, stroking Hannah's hair before bending to kiss her cheek, proprietorially. 'I'll leave her in your capable hands.'

'Lachlan?' Another voice, female this time, came across the

parkland. 'What the hell are you playing at? We've still another five ewes to see to.' Ger paused, pulling her woollen hat down over her red curls, winding her scarf tightly around her neck against the biting cold, whilst simultaneously shaking her head in the direction of the other three, once she'd taken in the situation. 'Evening, Hannah. You been out having a good time? With our American researcher friend, here?' She threw a disdainful look at the pair of them before heading back to the quad bike. 'You'll have to walk up to the meadow, Lachlan. I'll see you there.' And with that, she roared off without another word.

Zac threw an army-type salute towards Lachlan before turning on his heel and heading back towards his car.

Without speaking to her, or even looking in her direction, Lachlan unlocked the side door of the east wing, and headed for the stairs, all the way up the three flights, Hannah trailing after him. He came to the apartment door, unlocked and opened it and waited for her to walk past him.

'Lachlan?' Hannah turned, tried to take his arm, noticing the hand was still bound in bandage weeks after his accident with the wire fence, desperate for him to break into a smile and admonish her for her behaviour.

'Hannah, I'm going to make you a strong coffee, find you some paracetamol and a bucket. You need to get to bed and sleep this off. If you're feeling sick, don't actually lie down; sit up on pillows in bed.' He turned towards the kitchen area. 'And don't go to bed in your clothes. Get undressed for heaven's sake.'

'Lachlan, I'm sorry. I'm so sorry.'

'What are you sorry for, Hannah?'

'Not realising how much...'

'How much what?'

'You know.'

'No, Hannah, I don't know. And to be quite honest, I'm not at all interested in your sorrow.'

'Lachlan... I...'

'Hannah, I don't want to know,' Lachlan snapped. 'Now, I've

got ewes to see to. I'm going to have to get Daisy out of bed if we run into trouble.'

'Let me come. Let me come and help,' Hannah pleaded, looking round for her jeans and wellingtons, but stumbling over her discarded heels as she did so.

'Get up, Hannah,' Lachlan demanded, but nevertheless giving her a helping hand. 'You'd be absolutely no use whatsoever with the lambing.' He headed for the door, without looking back.

'Lachlan, I was going to ring you this evening. How's your dad? Is he better?'

Lachlan turned, grief etched on every inch of his face. 'He died. I'll be heading back there for the funeral next week.'

'Lachlan, I'm sorry, I'm so very sorry. I know how much you loved your father. But you shouldn't have come back so quickly. Surely you needed to be there with your family?'

'You're not even aware how little family I have left, are you, Hannah?' He paused without looking back. 'Make sure you lock the door behind me and remove the key. You don't know who's wandering around the place.'

And with that, he left, closing the door quietly behind him.

# 24

'What the hell is *she* doing here, Rosa?' Joe, obviously tired and stressed after ten days or so in Sweden, Denmark and then Germany, had put down the kettle he was just about to fill at the sink. 'She's out there in the garden with Chiara. Did you know she was here? What were you thinking, letting her in the garden, letting her have access to my daughter?'

· *Our* daughter, Rosa thought, but didn't say the words. 'Carys is staying here,' Rosa said quietly, reaching for Joe's arm but he shrugged it off angrily. 'I said she could stay here with us – with Chiara – in one of the spare bedrooms rather than across at The Jolly Sailor.'

'What!' Joe's fury reverberated round the vicarage kitchen like a pistol shot. 'You said what? Are you fucking mad?'

'No, Joe,' and this time Rosa raised her own voice. 'I am *not* effing mad. I've had over a week of Chiara trying every which way to get out and cross that main road to get to The Jolly Sailor to see her mum.'

'Why didn't you lock the door?'

'Chiara is quite capable of unlocking a door, Joe.'

'Not if you'd hidden the key.' Joe briefly shifted the vigilance of his ex-wife and daughter back to Rosa but then, as Carys pushed Chiara on the swing Rosa had erected once Joe and Chiara had moved in with her, turned back to the window. 'I can't believe you didn't tell me you'd done this, when I rang to speak to you and Chiara every night.'

'If I had, you'd have come back, and I knew you *had* to be there.'

'But Carys could have run off back to bloody Australia with her.'

'How could she? Chiara's passport is in the safe in my study with our own. And if she did take her…' Rosa paused '…*without* your agreement, border control both here and in Australia would be alerted immediately.'

'When's she going back?' Joe's voice was harsh, frightened.

'To The Jolly Sailor or Sydney?'

'Sydney, obviously, but if I had my way, I'd boot her straight back across the street to the pub this minute. I just can't believe you've let her into the house. Actually had her staying with us.'

'Joe.' Rosa took his hand and they both continued to watch the other two from the kitchen window. 'Do you want Chiara to be the happiest she can be?'

'Stupid question,' Joe snapped.

Rosa tried once more. 'If you don't let her be with her mum, Joe, she'll be miserable, resentful of both of us but, I think, probably mostly of me.'

'You're her mum.'

'That's not true and you know it. She's been here just six months with me.'

'You sound as if you *want* her to go.' Joe turned and faced Rosa. 'Is that it? You just don't want her here?'

'I don't know how you can say that.' Rosa found she was weeping. 'I don't know how you can even *think* it. Chiara is the child I've never had. Probably never *will have*.' Tears were streaming down her face now and she reached for the tissue up her sleeve. 'But I'm NOT her mum, Joe. Carys *is*, and she has every right to her daughter; to have Chiara with her and live with her.'

'She's not having her. I'm not letting her go.' Joe wiped away his own tears and Rosa took his hand once more.

'And an English court would possibly be on your side, Joe, although, more and more, the wishes of the child are taken into consideration, I believe. If you end up taking Chiara through a family court, she would say she wants to be with her mummy. As well as her big brother and her new baby sister. I suppose there's a chance, if a decision was made in your favour, they'd make Chiara a ward of court or whatever it is they do, so that she couldn't be taken from this country without the consent of the order. But I tell you now, Joe, you'll have one exceptionally unhappy little girl left behind with us.' Rosa didn't speak for a while, just stared out of the window as both Carys and Chiara, unaware they were being watched, continued to play, Carys chasing her round the lawn until, hysterical with giggles, Chiara fell, bumping her head on the metal post of the swing.

Joe was on the point of dashing out of the door to help, but Rosa stopped him, watching as Carys ran to pick her up, dust her down and then, once she appeared none the worse for her tumble, kissed her forehead and proceeded to take Chiara's hand, while rubbing at the small of her own back with her other.

'I think maybe your original idea of taking yourself and Chiara out to Sydney to live, so you and Carys could have shared custody, wasn't a bad one,' Rosa finally said, her tone despairing.

'But then I wouldn't have had you,' Joe said bleakly. 'I can't lose you again. Rosa, I don't know what to do.'

'Joe, be honest with me, tell me the truth. When you were married to Carys, when you were all together in London, was Carys a good mother? You see, when *I* knew her in London, when she was working for me, and mum just to Rhys, I never got any impression she was anything but a loving, caring mother to him. OK, she kept both her working and home life very separate, totally compartmentalised, and I only ever met Rhys the once – that was Carys determined to show she was a professional – but on the couple of weekends she came away with me, Hannah and Eva, her dad and stepmother always came over from Wales to be with Rhys. In fact, as well as the nanny who was with Carys for years, one or other, or both, of her parents were regularly at the house in Fulham. Just because she was a single mother, having to work, doesn't make her a bad parent. So, come on, was she a good mother when you were married to her? Does she deserve to lose her daughter?'

'She left me for another man. Left her children so she could go away.'

'That wasn't the question.' When Joe still refused to answer, Rosa tried another tack. 'Did you love her?'

'You know I didn't.'

'And Carys knew it as well, I would imagine. Living with a man who doesn't love you, who doesn't want you in his house, in his bed, in his life, can't be easy.'

'I kept to my side of the bargain. She was pregnant. We got married.'

'Can't be very nice living with a man who is only there to fulfil a bargain, Joe. Because of his daughter.'

'There was only ever you, Rosa. You *know* I married Carys because she was having my child and I'd ruined what I had with *you*. Thrown it in the fucking bin because of one drunken night I'll regret to my dying day…'

'Chiara was the result,' Rosa reminded him gently.

'…and I thought it the best thing to do at the time.'

'And if you hadn't, if you'd reneged on your responsibility, then more than likely Carys would have eventually ended up with someone else and quite possibly you'd never have had much to do with Chiara at all. Might never have seen your daughter, had anything to do with her upbringing.'

'I don't know what to do,' Joe said again, and his tears were falling freely now.

'So, answer my question, Joe. Was Carys a good mother to both Chiara and Rhys? And look, I know she eventually went off with Spencer Carter, but she was obviously looking for someone who *did* love her. Who *did* want her. Someone who she knew wasn't with her for all the wrong reasons.'

'Nothing to do with him being a billionaire then, you don't think?' Joe scoffed.

'Of course she's with him because he's wealthy. *I* know that. And I also know she's manipulative; can be self-obsessed. What I don't know, Joe, and only you can tell me this – was Carys a good mother to Chiara? To Rhys?'

Joe nodded, unable to speak. He nodded again, then finally whispered, 'The best.'


'Not now, Virginia. Please.' Hannah didn't even look up from the mug of tea she was desperately trying to keep down as her big sister strode into the Heatherly Hall office, obviously on a mission. Any movement of Hannah's head brought on the pernicious waves of nausea and self-loathing that had sat on her shoulders since waking in the early hours to the awful reality of the previous evening, as well as the splitting headache she could only liken to the continual eruption of Krakatoa.

When Hannah did eventually look up, the little smile, almost smug, playing on Virginia's face, spoke volumes. And Hannah knew she wouldn't be able to just sit and listen to the other's latest rhetoric without the need to throw up. Virginia, somewhat surprisingly, didn't say a word but simply moved around the office, adjusting the frame of a picture here; tutting at myriad rings left by Hannah's copious cups of coffee there; picking up papers and moving a bright red, recently gelled fingernail down their contents.

'Virginia…'

'It's Ginny.'

'Virginia,' Hannah repeated, debating whether to simply remove herself from the office and her big sister's presence and head back to the loo. Or even to bed. 'Virginia, I've a lot on.'

'I'm surprised you can take anything on after *last night*.' Virginia emphasised the last two words, triumphant glee in her voice.

'Last night?' Hannah's already leaden heart dropped further.

'Oh, it was the talk of Hilary's Bums…'

Hilary's Bums? Hannah shook her woolly head slightly. Yoga had doubled the church warden's arse as well as giving it the power of speech? Well, she, Hannah wouldn't be doing any more of *those* sessions, thank you very much, if that was the outcome. One backside – and a silent one at that – was more than enough to deal with.

'…and Tums class.'

Hannah felt herself wilt like overboiled spinach. The whole village knew? She, the managing director of Heatherly Hall, was now no better than a drunken fishwife?

'Like a drunken fishwife, I hear,' Virginia echoed Hannah's thoughts exactly.

'I think the term *fishwife*, when referring to a woman, is now classed as misogynistic,' Hannah started, but was soon overruled.

'Oh, utter tosh, I don't adhere to any of this woke rubbish.' And then, realising this admission didn't quite fit with the reincarnation of Ginny Forester-Astley, Virginia went on, 'Well not all of it, anyway. I mean, if a man wants to lose his, you know, his… wotsit and become transvestite…'

'Transgender?' Hannah corrected tiredly, putting her aching head into her hands.

'Or if Timothy decides he wants to wear my brassiere, then…'

'Virginia…' Hannah interrupted.

'Yes…' Virginia was on a roll, her tone now accusatory '… utterly appalling behaviour, Hannah. How could you? Defaming the good name of my family?'

'Virginia,' Hannah sighed once more, from the depths of her hands, 'the Astleys have *never* had a good name. You yourself always called Bill *a philandering waste of space. His* father, Henry Astley, more than likely set up the scam of the century over this damned Jet Set which, if it ever did exist, was probably stolen property from the get-go, nicked by George Astley – your great-grandfather – from Colonial India. And, if you go way back in history, the Astleys were probably warmongering rapists and pillagers.' (Was *pillagers* an actual word and, anyway, did the Astley ancestors go back as far as the Vikings? Probably not, but it was a good story and might wipe that smirk off Virginia's carefully made-up face.)

'Well, anyway, Hannah,' Virginia interrupted, apparently not appreciating the descent into notoriety her ancestors appeared to be heading towards, 'you obviously need someone to put *you* on the straight and narrow, as well as bring some sort of organisation into this place. We have a major wedding here in a few days' time and, I have to say…'

'Do you? Do you really *have* to say?' Hannah buried her head once more.

'I'm here to help. *I'm* now a major part of Heatherly Hall and, with my excellent organisational skills, that you, Hannah, so obviously lack…' Virginia picked up a tottering pile of papers with a little laugh and moue of disdain '…then I…'

'Virginia, don't *touch* those,' Hannah snapped, wincing as pain shot through her head (how many brain cells, if any, did she have left? Considering her shockingly abhorrent behaviour in Clementine's last night, had she actually had any to *start with*?) 'They're in the order I'm dealing with them this morning.'

'You need a proper filing system, Hannah.'

'What I need, Virginia, is to be left alone to do my work. The Livingston wedding is in *exactly* three days; the Agatha Christie evening in four.'

'Yes, and *I'm exactly* the person to take over… to help,' Virginia amended. 'So, why don't you and that Tara woman allow me on board? I'll soon have you all shipshape and Bristol fashion.'

Hannah finally raised her head. Surely Virginia hadn't really said *shipshape and Bristol fashion*? And *on board*? What did she think this was? The QE2?

'Virginia, I mean it; I don't need help at the moment. Actually,' she said, suddenly remembering, 'what you could do, is go over to the restaurant and check that all the cutlery and silver for the wedding has been cleaned and ready to go. If not, you could make a start on that? Joanna in housekeeping will show you where the Silvo and cloths are kept. We're closing the conference centre and restaurant, as well as Tea and Cake and gardens to the public from tomorrow, as we start setting up for the wedding.' She turned back to the computer, checking and rechecking her list.

'Silvo and cloths?' Virginia almost hissed. 'I don't *think* so; I've just spent a fortune on this manicure.'

'Take it or leave it. When you start working for a family firm you have to begin at the bottom. Be thankful I've not had you cleaning the lavs.' Hannah turned to look at Virginia, who appeared to be scanning the top of the desk with her large, baby blue eyes.

'Post not arrived yet? Ah here it is.' Virginia passed a thick, creamy, official-looking envelope towards Hannah. 'I suppose I should really be making sure this goes into Eva's hands.'

'What is it?' Hannah sighed once more, reaching for her bottled water.

'A notice to inform you that my brother, Jonny Astley, and I are contesting our father's will in our favour.'

'You said.'

'Well, this is *it. The letter*.' Virginia shook the envelope somewhat irritably in Hannah's face. 'There are, Hannah, generally two bases for contesting a will; either the will itself is invalid, or it fails to make "reasonable financial provision" for a family member or someone who was financially maintained before their death.'

'Right. If you say so.'

'The *Family Law Reform Act 1987*,' Virginia parroted (and Hannah recalled her big sister's skill at regurgitating huge tranches of the Bible when Rev Cecil'd been at the helm in Rosa's church) 'gives the same inheritance rights to illegitimate children as to legitimate children, whose parent or other blood relative dies intestate.'

Virginia paused for effect and Hannah raised an eyebrow. 'And?'

'*And* as our natural father did *not* die intestate, but made a will without provision for Jonny and me, we are still able to make a claim under the *Inheritance – Provision for Family and Dependents – Act of 1975...*'

'Fine, fine, up to you, Virginia, but I'll tell you once again, there was only a small amount of cash left to Rosa, Hannah and myself. There's the wine cellar of course and some personal effects of Bill's, but everything else was ploughed back into the estate; for the good of the estate.'

'I want my share of the 51 per cent shares in this place you three inherited,' Virginia insisted. 'It's only right that Eva should relinquish her hold on them and give them to *me*.'

'Well, if you want to make a whole load of solicitors very rich, then go ahead with this. Up to you. Meanwhile, the silver?'

'The silver?' Virginia's eyes were saucers of greedy anticipation. 'I'll get a share of the hall's silver?'

'The cleaning of it, Virginia. In the restaurant? With the Silvo?'

'What are *you* going to do?' Virginia asked sulkily, obviously put out that she hadn't managed to rile Hannah with the contents of the letter.

'I'm going, Virginia, to see if I can put right a great wrong.' Hannah stood, running a hand through her hair.

'Oh? Apologising to Zac Anderson for your behaviour last night? I can't believe you ended up fighting with your ex while being taken out for dinner by Zac. I spent some time with him last night.'

'Oh? Last night?' Hannah found she was only half interested.

'After he had to sort you out. Yes, Jonny and Billy-Jo invited me up here to dine last night.'

'With Tim?'

'Timothy?' For a split second it appeared her big sister had forgotten the man she was married to. 'No, no, it was his monthly model train meeting over in Cleckheaton. Anyway, I have to say, Hannah, Jonny and BJ...'

'BJ?' Hannah could only think Blow Job. Which, feeling, as she did this morning, as if her mouth was stuffed with pigeon feathers, was not a good thought.

'Oh,' Virginia trilled, 'just my little pet name for Billy-Jo. We're such pals. Anyway, they weren't overly happy with the rooms you've given them here. I mean, for heaven's sake, he *is* the Marquess of Heatherly Hall. And poor Zac – he was only wanting to pick your brains about the history of this place, you know, and then you go and embarrass him. I do hope you haven't upset him so that he's going to leave before we put on the play?' Virginia pouted. 'He's such a good actor – absolutely brilliant playing the part of Edward VIII for us. You'd never know he was an American: his upper-class English accent is superb. And he's so *handsome*.' She giggled girlishly. 'I believe he's a little in love with me, you know. Timothy is terribly jealous.' Virginia preened, examining her nails, awaiting Hannah's reaction.

Zac? Apologise to Zac? Well, yes, Hannah thought as she headed for the stairs and the estate manager's office, she supposed she should. But Zac Anderson, she realised, was way, way, way down her list of apologees.

Her pulse racing at the very thought of facing him, Hannah made her way across to the cabin that constituted the estate manager's office where, if he wasn't out on the estate or farmland, Lachlan could usually be found. The office was locked and, standing on tiptoe to peer through the window, she soon saw the place was deserted. Tutting crossly – she so needed to see him, to try and explain – she headed down to his flat in the old coach house, gathering armfuls of daffodils as some sort of peace offering as she walked. But again, there was so sign of him.

Hannah guessed Lachlan must be up in the long meadows adjacent to the many acres of Stratton woodland, seeing to the ewes and, not wanting to prostrate herself at his feet with Ger looking on, decided she'd drive down to Clementine's instead and apologise for her shocking behaviour to Clementine Ahern, before calling into the vicarage to see Rosa.

She possibly shouldn't be driving, Hannah realised, looking at her watch. But she had to get out, needed fresh air, needed to be away from Virginia's demands. And it was a good fourteen hours since downing almost the whole of that bottle of champagne, and she no longer felt under its influence. The after-effects certainly, but not the alcohol itself. All she felt was utter mortification and self-loathing at how she'd behaved towards Lachlan. Lovely Lachlan, who'd been there for her these past eight months: made her laugh, cooked her delicious pasta, rubbed her cold feet and found her warm woollen gloves when they were perennially lost. Who'd stopped her from drinking too much when she knew she shouldn't. Who'd loved her unconditionally.

And Ben Pennington? What was all that about? It wasn't that she still lusted after him; in fact, despite him sporting an obvious (honeymoon?) tan, she remembered thinking, just before she launched, that his blue eyes were cold, that his mouth appeared thin and mean, his voice sneery. No warmth there, whatsoever. Once she'd woken from her drunken sleep in the early hours of the morning, she'd lain there going over and over and over like an old 45 single (Richard still had his ancient collection) on repeat, just what she'd done, and why she'd done it.

Last night, in Clementine's, she'd felt the same jealousy, recognised the same worthlessness in herself, as when Eva'd won all the awards, was always top of the class, was the one all the other girls wanted to be friends with. As when everyone wanted to sit next to Rosa, to have her on their team; Rosa, who was loved by everyone just for being lovely, kind, funny and uncomplicated. She, Hannah, was the middle triplet: not one thing or the other, not super-bright like Rosa and Eva, nor utterly gorgeous like both her sisters. Last night, seeing Ben in Clementine's, where he'd promised to take her, but never actually had; where he'd been just standing, married to *someone else* – someone quite stunning – she finally accepted he'd never been that serious about her. That if she hadn't thrown him out, he'd have soon been on his way anyway.

And all those feelings of worthlessness, of being unloved, of not being anywhere as good as Eva and Rosa that she'd had, growing up, and which she thought she'd put behind her, had come flooding back.

She was a lost cause.

Hannah put the car into gear and set off towards the village.

# 25

## Heatherly Hall, Westenbury, Yorkshire

### Wednesday October 14th 1936, 7.30pm

Jeanie Haigh stopped in her tracks, looking back at the façade of the hall, now in absolute darkness. Not total, she realised: light, subdued, behind the heavy wooden kitchen shutters, was morphing into the dark October evening, illuminating the position of the basement kitchens from which she'd emerged ten minutes earlier.

Heart racing, blood thundering in her ears as adrenalin surged, Jeanie quickly turned back across the path she'd just walked, and ran towards the hall. She still didn't have to do it, she told herself. Could tell Mrs Walters – and anyone else still in the hall – she'd left her hat and her ears were cold. She opened and let herself back in through the side kitchen door, her tiny frame slipping seamlessly round the narrow gap she allowed herself, before closing it behind her.

'Mrs Walters?' she whispered. 'A've come back for me hat.'

Unbelievably loud snores rent the air from the cook sitting in her chair by the warm stove. Hell, they were even louder than her dad's after he'd had a few down at The Railway pub on a Sunday dinnertime. Jeanie stood, every sense on alert: her nose taking in the chicken and vegetable soup she'd spent that afternoon making: her eyes and ears quickly assuring her Mrs Walters would be comatose until the others – staff as well as his lord and ladyship – came back from their various forays, demanding drinks and late-night snacks.

And then she was off. Closing the kitchen door behind her without so much as a click, Jeanie slipped off her boots and, on stockinged feet, boots in hand, flew up the darkness of the stone stairs she'd taken earlier that morning. It felt like she was flying as she arrived in the shadows of the Great Hall and, like some sort of gazelle escaping a lion, sped up the marble steps and then soared up the red-carpeted stairs to Lady Stratton's bedroom.

She wasn't frightened now – she was a revolutionary doing what was right for the cause. For the working classes. For Mrs Pankhurst and Mrs Stopes.

For Frank.

With her hands still encased in their black woollen gloves, Jeanie reached for the brass knob on the bedroom door, turning it to the right. Nothing. Panic surged. She turned the handle to the left. Surely no door ever opened by turning its handle to the left? Nothing.

Jeanie looked to her right and silently moved to the adjacent door which must, surely, open into the sitting room adjoining Lady Stratton's bedroom? She reached for the identical brass knob and turned it to the right, expecting the same negative entry. But the door opened gracefully, certainly silently, on the new cream silk carpet and Jeanie was back in the room she'd left hours earlier. The cream-painted door to her ladyship's bedroom was slightly ajar and Jeanie slid round it with ease. The blood in her ears was now deafening and she wondered if she was actually dying, on her way to hell and eternity. Or was she in some sort of nightmare? She was going to wake up, relieved, any minute, and she'd be back in the lumpy but familiar double bed she shared with her older sister, Mags.

The dream was going on apparently.

Jeanie moved silently to the beautifully made early Victorian doll's house, bending down as she'd seen Lady Stratton do that morning through the slightly open bedroom door as, giggling conspiratorially with Mrs Casterton, her ladyship had deftly taped the drawer key to the corniced ceiling of a downstairs room with medicated sticking plaster. Tiny, exquisitely crafted tables and chairs tumbled towards Jeanie as her gloved hand reached clumsily to the ceiling. Nothing. Hyperventilating now, Jeanie managed to right the tiny pieces, moving her hand into the next room. A miniature grand piano fell onto the floor beside her knee and, again, Jeanie replaced it, and then her fingers found the soft material of the sticking plaster with its cold metal treasure beneath. Jeanie carefully peeled back the large piece of plaster, removed the key and went straight over to the walnut chest of drawers.

She inserted the heavy key.

The Goddess of Revolutionary Women was watching over her as her next actions segued seamlessly into place.

She turned the key and the drawer slid, almost dreamily, towards her.

She reached for the black leather box, deftly removed the necklace and its accompanying earrings – they were surprisingly heavy – dropped them into her left boot, replaced the leather box in exactly the position she'd found it, relocked the drawer and moved back to the doll's house. Kneeling, her breath now coming in short, painful gasps, Jeanie realigned the key behind the dangling material of the suspended sticking plaster before pressing hard over every bit of its surface to cover and hide the metal once more.

Jeanie exited the bedroom, then the sitting room and, on those same Bovidae feet, flew down the soft red-carpeted stairs, down the cold marble stairs, through the green baize door at the corner of the Great Hall, before descending the stone steps to the kitchen.

Mrs Walters was still utterly comatose.

Jeanie let herself out of the kitchen side door, stopping only to remove the actual necklace with its incredibly large central diamond – now seeming to glint accusingly up at her like some evil eye. She replaced it in the empty boot, pulled both boots on to her feet before running, painfully, across the fields and down to her house on Railway Terrace.

# 26

*The day before the wedding*

Hannah woke with a start, totally terrified, her heart racing, while she seemed to be gasping for breath. She fought her way out of the duvet to look at her phone.

Not even 5am. The dawn chorus was revving up, the myriad blackbirds, robins and wrens that nested in the parkland and surrounding woodland were eager to meet and start the new day despite the rain and cloud beyond her window, and the lack of daytime light.

Hell, the day before the wedding. Hannah felt nothing but utter panic. She couldn't do this; she was an absolute fake. An imposter. No better at being at the helm of Heatherly Hall and in charge of this wedding than she'd been as a youth worker.

She lay back on her pillows and attempted the deep breaths she'd been advised to take on some mindfulness website she'd googled. She started well, but then the breaths revved up and she found herself hyperventilating as she remembered all she had to do. But, more importantly, knowing she'd utterly messed up her relationship with Lachlan. She'd not seen him since the terrible evening when he and Ger had found her up against the stone wall with Zac Anderson. She'd rung him, messaged him, WhatsApped and emailed him constantly, but there'd been nothing in return. There were two well-worn paths that her boots had made across the parkland – one to the estate manager's office, the other down to Lachlan's staff flat where she'd knocked on his door, over and over again, embarrassing herself when other members of staff had come to their own doors to see what all the commotion was about.

She stopped trying to breathe correctly and, instead, picked up her phone again, hoping against hope there'd be a message from him, just a little something that would tell her he was ready to reach out a hand of forgiveness.

Nothing.

Knowing there was little chance she'd be able to get back to sleep, she padded over to the shower, turned it to cold and, shrieking and swearing, submitted herself to the bracing onslaught. Feeling a little more like she could face the day – this final day before the wedding when she still had so much to do – she quickly dressed in her black suit and white shirt, made strong coffee and set up her laptop on the kitchen table.

Two minutes later, she'd abandoned it, found paper and biro and was writing a letter – not an email or text – but an actual pen and paper letter to Lachlan, telling him she'd been happier with him these last eight months than ever before in her life. Could he at least see his way to giving her a chance? A chance to do what? To explain she'd, once again, been seduced by a smooth-talking man with a beautiful face and prove that, because he, Lachlan, was so lovely and had made a point of wanting to be with *her*, Hannah Quinn, the triplet in the middle, it must surely mean she wasn't, after all, as worthless as she thought?

Tearing up the letter and throwing it towards the kitchen bin with a snort of self-derision, Hannah glanced at the time: 6.30am.

Time to go to work.


'Oh, Hannah, look at Rosa.' Eva beckoned her sister over to the office window. 'What on earth is she doing coming out without her coat in this weather?'

Rosa was walking slowly across the park, seemingly unaware of the biting cold and sleety rain that was falling onto her thin vicar surplice, jeans and bare head.

'I'm going down to get her.'

'Take the umbrella,' Hannah advised, turning back to the computer. There was still so much to do and, despite Eva appearing calm and measured, as well as Tara reassuring her everything was on track, Hannah was still feeling something akin to despair. Were she and Heatherly Hall about to become a laughing stock, relegated to the bottom of the premier division for wedding planning, unable to climb back out of its murky depths, if her, Tara and Felicity's plans didn't pan out as they so desperately hoped?

Members of the press who'd been granted passes had started arriving, taking up parking spaces and demanding coffee and snacks in Tea and Cake, which had been put at their disposal. There was already a backlog of journalists and security staff spilling out of the door and into the rain, and tempers were fraying.

*HeyHo* magazine, having won and bought sole rights to the event (reputedly for a couple of million pounds) was already in situ, setting up scaffolding, lights, cameras and backdrops, and both Drew Livingston's and Aditi Sharma's security teams were now frisking and checking the huge numbers of people involved in ensuring the wedding's smooth operation, as they came and went through the main gates.

There was easy access into the parkland around the back of the hall from the fields and woodland out towards the Pennines, and Jefferson Garcia had, with a military precision seen only in Northern Ireland during the eighties, set up four six-hour guard duty shifts along the hall's perimeter. Charlie and Jason, the hall's own security team, had been demoted to issuing lanyards, as well as a litany of dire warnings if any aspects of security were to be breached. Any unauthorised freelance photographer gaining access to the wedding, and consequently selling pictures to a rival competitor, would be hounded through the courts and sued for huge amounts. Brutus, Charlie's Dobermann, was looking particularly pissed off at the unexpected hive of activity, creeping off to his bed, tail between his legs, whenever he thought no one was looking.

By the time Eva had run down the steps with the umbrella, Rosa was being frisked for the second time. 'Oh, for heaven's sake,' Eva shouted to the mountain of a woman towering above Rosa as she patted her down, 'this is my *sister*. She's the *vicar* who's marrying them tomorrow.'

The security guard sniffed. 'Anyone could put on a dog collar and say she's the one marrying them.' The guard bent to feel down the inside of Rosa's legs.

'That's definitely the village vicar,' Charlie shouted, hurrying forward with a lanyard. 'She christened my nephew last week.'

'OK, OK,' the guard said irritably. 'Just make sure you wear your pass at all times. Where's yours?' she demanded, turning now on Eva.

'Here,' Eva tutted, pulling it from inside her zipped-up jacket.

'On the outside. All the time, if you don't mind.'

'That's Ms Malik,' Charlie said almost reverentially. 'She owns the place.'

'I don't care if she's Queen Camilla and wearing a motherfucking crown.' The beefy woman sniffed again. 'No pass, no entry. Even if she does own the joint.' She took a good look at Eva. 'Actually, you look a bit like Kate Middleton. Are you related? My mom sure loves you royalty lot. If I could maybe get a picture later...?'

'Rosa,' Eva interrupted, ignoring both the guard and the rain running from the brolly and down her neck, 'where's your coat, for heaven's sake? Oh, Rosa, you're crying? What is it?' Eva placed an arm round Rosa's shoulders, hurrying her into the building. Once inside, she faced her. 'Rosa?'

'Joe's going to fly to Sydney with Carys.'

'What?' Eva spat furiously. 'He's going off with Carys again?'

'No, no, no.' Rosa sobbed. 'We've just *got* to let Chiara be with Carys and Rhys in Australia...' Huge sobs rent the air as Rosa struggled, but appeared unable, to compose herself.

'No, no, Rosa, you must NOT allow it.'

Rosa shook her head. 'It's not about me and Joe.'

'Of course it is.'

'No, it's about what Chiara wants. And she wants to be with her mum, and her brother and her new baby sister. I truly believe, after I've been talking to Carys for the last few days, that she was a good mother to her kids. She deserves to have her little girl with her.'

'But Joe?'

'Joe has finally accepted it, but says he wants to be the one to take her over there. It's a hell of a long journey if they do it all in one – twenty-four hours I think – and with Carys being pregnant...'

'And utterly unreliable,' Eva snapped furiously. 'Rosa, this isn't fair. You can't let Chiara go. You're her stepmum. You love her.'

'Carys is her *mum*. Chiara wants to go. It's either let her leave or it's all dragged through the courts and it will go on for ever. And Chiara will become more unhappy and resentful with us and I'll become the wicked stepmother.' Here Rosa sobbed more. 'And I couldn't bear that. Joe's only proviso is that he accompanies her there. And then, we look into the legality of shared custody. You know, Chiara comes to us in her long summer vacation.'

'Oh yes, that's going to happen, isn't it? Carys isn't going to bring her back, like an effing library book every year, is she? No way is that woman going to jump on a plane, deposit Chiara here with you and then return home and do it all again six weeks later. With a new baby to boot? And, Rosa, Australian kids' long six-weeks school holiday is in December. Christmas? You think Carys is going to let you and Joe have her every Christmas? No way, José.'

Eva's words only provoked more weeping from Rosa. As Eva

took her sister in her arms, a somewhat irritable voice interrupted their conversation.

'Excuse me.' Aditi Sharma had appeared behind them. 'I'm looking for the person who is actually going to be *marrying me* tomorrow.' She gave the red-eyed, wet rag that was the village vicar a hard stare. 'Is this yourself? Is there some sort of problem? I mean, you'll really need to smarten yourself up. What will you be wearing? There are photographers, videos, *HeyHo* magazine, you do realise?'

'Everything will be fine, Ms Sharma.' Eva smiled, torn between soothing the bride-to-be and her distraught sister. 'Rosa has just had a bit of a shock…'

'Well, I hope it's not going to affect her performance tomorrow? There have been times *I've* not been in the mood, when *I* might be somewhat tearful, hormonal maybe? You know? Just before I show up for filming? But a true professional puts her personal issues behind her and gets on with the job. Are you having a period? Is that it? Hmm?'

'Everything will be absolutely fine, tomorrow, Ms Sharma,' Eva repeated, smiling, but wanting to slap the woman. Hormonal for heaven's sake? How dare she?

'Well, I do hope so. Now, I believe you want to interrogate me at some point, Reverend? As to my reasons for marrying Mr Livingston?' She smirked. 'I think you only have to look at those thighs of his for your answer.' Aditi glanced across at Eva, holding her gaze. 'Would you not agree, Ms Malik?'

Eva found herself blushing furiously. Hell, had the woman seen her admiring Drew Livingston? Knew that those denim-clad long legs with their hard, muscled thighs, his tattooed arms (what was the matter with her? She loathed tattoos) and his longish black curly hair had been accompanying her in her night-time fantasies ever since he'd come to find her up in the art retreat the other week?

'So, why don't we reconvene, later this morning?' Aditi gave the pair of them an on/off smile. 'Meanwhile, I need to see about the chandelier. Where will I find Ms Quinn? Or one of her team?'

'The chandelier?' Eva stared.

'The chandelier,' Aditi said firmly. 'In the Great Hall. The professionals should be here by now. Up here, I believe?' She set off gracefully up the stairs, the other two, admiring her beautiful taut backside in the skimpy white jeans, following on.

'*The Professionals?*' Eva whispered back to Rosa who'd finally managed to stop crying, apart from an occasional hiccup. 'Does she mean Bodie and Doyle? Always fancied Martin Shaw when Granny Glenys used to insist on us watching that programme over and over again with her up in the care home. After a lifetime married to the Rev Cecil, I think she was in a better place ensconced with Martin Shaw, rather than in the vicarage, kowtowing to that miserable old devil.'

Rosa smiled through her tears. 'When Granny wasn't glued to her DVDs of *Dallas*.'

'In here?' Aditi knocked perfunctorily on the office door and, without waiting for an answer, swept in, Rosa and Eva following behind in a wake of expensive perfume.

'Ah, Ms Quinn, are they here? Have they started?'

Startled, Hannah jumped up from her seat. 'Is who here?' Was this something else she'd missed? Hannah looked down at her list and then across at Aditi, hoping for a clue.

'The chandelier?'

'The chandelier?'

'Ms Quinn, when my artisans were here last week renovating the marble steps in the Great Hall, they noticed how badly in need of a clean your chandelier is. I refuse to have my guests under a filthy light fitting. My team is going to sort it.'

'Oh, no, really. That would be a huge job; no one has ever been able to get it clean.' Hannah's face was pale. 'You're not going to have that done by tomorrow.'

'It will be done,' Aditi insisted. 'I've brought in my professionals who know exactly what to do. They will either get scaffolding up to it, or lower it to the floor.'

'It's terribly old. I don't think…' Hannah started.

'Bloody hell,' Eva whispered, in an attempt to cheer up Rosa. 'Remember *Only Fools and Horses* and the chandelier episode?' Eva started to laugh, found she couldn't stop, and eventually Rosa, despite herself, joined in.

Hannah glared at the pair of them.

'Something funny?' Aditi asked, turning.

'Oh, sorry, you'd have to be a Brit to understand. And watch sitcoms…'

'I can assure you I'm not, and I don't. Now, before I go over there to supervise my chandelier restorers, I'd like feedback from *your* team with a totally up to date, hourly itinerary for tomorrow. I'd like to see the exact spot my big bird will be landing. Is the elephant here yet?'

Big birds? Elephants? Hannah stared desperately towards Rosa and Eva for explanation of this new menagerie.

'I've arranged that the helicopter will arrive and land at 1400 hours although, I'm sure, Ms Sharma, you'll want to exercise the bride's prerogative of being late?' Eva was polite and to the point.

'And the elephant?'

'The elephant?' Eva and Hannah exchanged glances, while Rosa didn't even appear to be listening.

'The elephant for Drew's arrival at the ceremony?'

The elephant. Where the hell were they going to get an elephant at this late hour? Bad enough trying to get a washing machine repairer, a plumber or a dentist, (she could help with *that*, Eva thought desperately) but an effing elephant?

'All under control.' Eva smiled, reaching a finger to her nose, already a good millimetre longer. How far away was Chester Zoo? Did they do elephants by the day? By the hour even, like Avis did cars? And did they deliver like Deliveroo? Eva had a sudden vision of an elephant stuffed into the back of a Deliveroo cyclist's backbox.

'Are the other two around? If not, please call them. I have a lot to get on with.' Aditi raised an eyebrow at Hannah who, with a look of terror in Eva's direction, reached for her phone to summon Tara and Felicity.

'Rosa and I are just going over to check that the conference centre is ready to go, and the tables and chairs have *baubles, bangles, bright shiny beads tra la la la la...*' Eva burst into desperate song '...*and bo-o-ws*, ha ha – and your two chefs have arrived, Ms Sharma, settled in and been given the full run of the kitchens.' Eva grabbed Rosa's arm, pushing her none too gently towards the door.

'Rosa, where am I going to get a bloody elephant at this late hour?' Eva was racing up towards Hannah's apartment, Rosa running behind trying to keep up. 'OK. Keep calm, Eva,' Eva was muttering to herself. 'You've handled worse than this, Eva: remember that bloke who had a seizure as you were pulling out his back wisdom tooth and your fingers were trapped in his mouth and you had to call 999? Now, coffee first, Eva, strong to get your brain cells working, then laptop, yellow pages...' She unlocked the apartment front door and headed straight for the kettle.

'But did you agree to it?' Rosa, who was quite breathless after running up the two flights of stairs, was pulling mugs from the dishwasher.

'I thought they were joking. Having us on. I just laughed and said leave it with me, I can soon get to see a man about an elephant... or some rubbish like that. I never for one minute thought they were serious. Shit, shit, shit, shit, shit.'

'Surely hiring elephants isn't allowed?' Rosa frowned. 'The RSPCA must have animal cruelty laws?'

Eva was already dialling the number for Chester Zoo.

'Ah, morning, do you hire out elephants by the day? Actually, probably half a day will suffice.'

'Not April 1st till next week, love.'

'No, no, don't go. Hang on. I'm serious. We have an exceptionally important celebrity wedding here at Heatherly Hall in West Yorkshire, and an elephant has been promised...'

'Elephants are highly intelligent, socially complex animals who live in matriarchal herds, protect one another, forage for fresh vegetation, play, bathe in rivers, and share responsibilities for raising the babies in the herd...'

'I don't want *a herd*. Or a *baby*. Just a nice, well-mannered, average common or garden elephant...'

'...and their ability to feel pain – as well as sorrow, joy, and happiness – rivals our own. Domestic elephants live under the constant threat of physical punishment and are deprived of everything that is natural and important to them...'

'...Well, *you* need reporting then if you're constantly threatening them and depriving them of their elephant rights,' Eva retorted crossly. 'Look,' she went on, running a hand through her hair, 'I didn't ring for a David Attenborough-type Panorama lecture... No, no don't go. Please, is there anything you can do to help?'

But the woman at the other end had put down the phone.

'There's the annual Easter circus in the village,' Rosa said doubtfully. 'Apparently, since 2019, wild animals are no longer allowed to be exhibited or made to perform, but this circus has one remaining old elephant, kept as a sort of pet, I suppose. They bring him every year – let him roam on the village green; the villagers look forward to seeing him. There was a great write-up in the *Midhope Examiner* only last night, explaining that a circus is allowed to keep any remaining wild animals as long as they don't perform. *The Examiner* had obviously got wind that animal activists were out in force on the village green.'

'There are *animal activists* in Westenbury village?' Eva stared.

'Well, it was just Hilary Makepiece and her kids, to be fair. You know, with a home-made banner each.'

'Hilary's married to the village butcher, Rosa,' Eva scoffed.

'Not many animal rights in Darren Makepiece's butcher's shop, I wouldn't imagine.'

'To be honest, I think she was just after a bit of free advertising for her yoga classes. You know: *Down with animal cruelty. Up with peace, love and yoga.* Anyway, according to the article, Jumbo – had to be called that, didn't he? – is a most contented old boy.' Rosa paused. 'And, apparently, the clowns are a genuinely happy bunch too, if anyone was thinking of protesting against cruelty to clowns. Although in the photos they didn't look too jolly: you know, downward-turned mouths...' Rosa broke off, her eyes welling with tears once more. 'I've bought three tickets for me, Joe and Chiara.'

Eva patted Rosa's hand. 'I reckon the old pet elephant might appreciate a day off from the circus to be a guest at a wedding. I'll pay whatever they want – put it on Aditi's bill. Right, let's check everything's good to go over at the conference centre and see if the chefs have arrived. Then you need to do your God Spot with the blushing bride, and I'm off to charm an elephant keeper.'

# 27

As Rosa made her way through the rain and across the parkland to Heatherly Hall's tiny private chapel where, the following day, she would oversee the nuptials of Drew Livingston and Aditi Sharma, she recalled the last time she'd officiated in this four-hundred-year-old place of worship. So much had happened since Bill Astley had died, just eighteen months earlier, when she'd led the service – strictly humanist without reference to any deity in compliance with Bill's wishes – but this was the first time she'd been back in the beautiful little chapel where, down the centuries, a long line of Marquesses of Stratton had gathered to give thanks (hopefully for their abundance of material gifts) with their respective families.

She walked across the wet grass and through the crowds of planners and personnel (who, dependent on where they'd got to on their itineraries, were wearing airs of boredom, frustration, anger or downright terror) and she tried very hard to talk to God. Tried really hard not to ask what the hell he was playing at in those grey miserable clouds up above her head. OK, she wasn't in Ukraine; she hadn't lost her home and family in the terrible earthquake in Turkey just weeks earlier; and, to be fair, Joe had been returned to her, safe, sound and still loving her after the eight years without him. But how could The Almighty, after her being on his side for so long, now turn round and take Chiara from her and Joe?

Alright, alright, she continued to argue with herself, tripping over a whole spaghetti of electric cables belonging to God knows who (perhaps he did know), Chiara was still in her life, would always *be* in her life, even if she, Rosa, was no longer going to be anything more than a memory at the other side of the world for the little girl she adored.

Rosa knew she should have backed out of officiating this wedding; no one, on this, the most important day of their life, wanted to be facing a miserable old bat with unwashed hair and red eyes, liable to break down in tears at any moment. Rosa hesitated, dithering as to what to do. There'd be, she argued, a whole raft of local wedding celebrants who'd jump at the opportunity to step in at the eleventh hour to oversee the wedding of Drew Livingston.

Mind you, she'd really liked Drew. Had found him, after just the hour she'd spent with him over a cup of tea and a bun, and despite his wild rock star image, to be pleasant and, best of all, a man of integrity. She wasn't so sure about Aditi Sharma, though. Hadn't liked the woman at all. Hormonal? Having a period? Yes, Rosa *was* bloody hormonal with all these IV drugs and hormones she'd started and then given up on, knowing she and Joe couldn't give their full attention now to making babies. Rosa stopped, dithered some more, looking wistfully towards the main gates, and escape.

*You promised, Rosa*, she censured herself and, turning once more, carried on walking towards the chapel.

'Really, Ms Sharma,' Hannah was pleading an hour later as the pair of them stood side by side on the newly renovated marble steps of the Great Hall, looking upwards. 'I feel we'd be opening a whole can of worms were we to bring down the chandelier for cleaning. It's very old, so very fragile I would imagine. It's never been brought down for cleaning as far as I know.'

'I think you've made your point, Ms Quinn.'

'Oh, so you agree?' Hannah exhaled in relief. 'We shouldn't be attempting to lower it?'

'No, Hannah.' Aditi Sharma's tone was condescending rather than friendly. 'I can see that the chandelier has never been cleaned. It's absolutely filthy.'

'Well, to be fair, Ms Sharma, getting a squirt of Pledge up there on a weekly basis is, I'm sure you can see, virtually impossible.'

'That's why it needs to come down.' Aditi offered a little cat-like smile that didn't quite reach her eyes and Hannah knew she was losing the battle. '*I* shall be leading the Bharatnatyam and Kathak dancing here in this hall, Hannah, and the *last thing* I need is to be put out of step by a *filthy* light fitting. I tell you now, the Beckhams are particularly unimpressed with *dirt*.'

'But…'

'Ms Quinn, would you not take another long look at this stairway?' Aditi stepped backwards, fluttering a graceful, bangled arm at the refurbished marble, and Hannah did as she was told. 'You're not telling me that these beautiful old steps are not vastly improved after my artisans spent the night on them.'

'Spent the night on them? Oh, sorry, yes, I see what you mean. But…'

'Exactly. Now, I'm going to shoo you away…' Aditi proceeded to flutter her arms in Hannah's direction as though attempting to disperse a whole swarm of irritating flies, '…because you *obviously* have so much still to do, and my team here and I can then get on with this in peace. On second thoughts, I concede that bringing the chandelier down for cleaning will be impossible. Therefore, *I* shall go up to it myself. I have no fear of heights – indeed, in my most famous film, I was a circus trapeze artist and I did all my own stunts myself, high above the ground.' Aditi put up a beringed hand. 'No! That is my final word. The men will put up the scaffolding and I will climb up to it with my cleaning materials and my team will take photographs of me up there to show just how *brave* and *capable* I am. As well as how determined I am to have everything just so for this, the most important day of my life when I marry the man I adore. When it is *your* turn to fall in love, Ms Quinn, when love comes knocking on *your* door, you too will find yourself prepared to do anything for that one special person. Now, we're ready to go.'

She turned to the four men in white overalls who'd been waiting patiently with a whole pile of indoor folding scaffolding. 'Naveen, Vijay, Kishan, Rudra, if you please?'

'Oh, bugger it,' Hannah said under her breath. 'I hope the whole fucking thing comes down on your spoilt, fucking head.' She turned back and smiled sweetly in Aditi's direction, but the latter was obviously determined to have the last word.

'Oh, and by the way, there's some old woman looking for you.'

'Some old woman?'

'She said she'd be across at that little café of yours having a drink, and to tell you to go across there as soon as you can.'

Hannah knew exactly who'd be waiting for her in Tea and Cake.

Alice.

Dame Alice Parkes, internationally famous and celebrated artist.

As well as being the triplets' natural mother.

Despite knowing she'd be obliged to buy her several gins, Hannah smiled as she hurried over to Tea and Cake. How funny that Aditi Sharma, demanding the presence of Alice as her wedding gift to Drew, had had absolutely no idea who *the old woman* was. Hannah felt the score even up a notch.

'Hello, darling.' Alice greeted Hannah with a languid paint-stained wave of her hand, her customary kaftan-style dress unbuttoned to reveal tanned but rather hairy legs. 'Where are the other two?'

'The other two?' Hannah knew exactly to whom Alice was referring, but she wasn't going to make it easy for their birth mother, who'd handed the three of them over to her sister, Susan, at birth, apparently without batting an eyelid.

'You know, the dentist and the vicar?'

'For heaven's sake, Alice.'

'Darling, I'm just winding you up.' Alice gave a bark of laughter, which set off a bout of coughing. 'Behaving as you expect me to.' She stroked the young waiter's bottom as he leaned over the next table to serve a towering plate of ham sandwiches. Gone were the dainty platters of afternoon tea with scones and cream usually served at this time of day and, in their place were the sandwiches, hearty slices of quiche and large mugs of strong Yorkshire tea requested by the marquee erectors who'd broken off temporarily for a break and refuel.

'Oy, can you keep your hands off my staff, Alice?' Hannah said crossly. 'You'd be arrested if you were a bloke manhandling bottoms like that. Sorry, Dylan,' she apologised to the lad who appeared unsure whether to laugh, preen or complain.

'So, where are the bride and groom?' Alice asked, taking out a vape. 'Are they on site yet?'

'Put that away, Alice.'

'Not a dedicated shisha bar then?' Alice took a couple of crafty pulls on the vape but then, somewhat grudgingly, did as she was told. 'You need to keep up with the times, darling. Mind you, when did Westenbury ever do that? So, the groom? Can't say I'm overly bothered about meeting the bride.'

'Alice, you've been invited to this wedding because the groom, apparently, is a big art lover and connoisseur...'

'Good, that's what I like to hear.'

'...and not for the sole purpose of getting into his pants.'

'Oh, but darling, who wouldn't want to? Drew Livingston? I bet he's right up *Eva's* street.'

Ignoring her, Hannah went on, 'You do know Yves Dufort was invited as well?'

'Really?' Any reference to Eva's natural father, the Parisian artist with whom Alice had had sex before leaving Paris in a hurry, only to then sleep with Bill Astley, did have a tendency to put Alice into a bit of a sulk. She peered across at Hannah from under her long, greying fringe. 'And?'

'He's not been well, apparently. Said he'd have loved to join you here, but is unable to. Whether it's true or an excuse not to come over, I don't really know. Eva's had a couple of phone calls with him, and it appears he's not that well.'

'Never drank enough.' Alice cackled. 'That was always Dufort's problem. So, what am I supposed to be doing on the big day? And, more importantly, where am I sleeping the next few nights? I assume there's a lovely room waiting for me in this great pile?'

'You are an invited guest, like any other.' Hannah glanced across at the lanyard already round Alice's neck, though hidden under a swathe of colourful scarves. 'All you need to do is mingle and talk to the guests, but especially to Drew Livingston. You've been brought in as a gift for Drew from Aditi.'

'Brought in? Sounds like the washing when it rains. So, I'll be paid then?'

'I believe so. I think Eva's sorting all that. Although, Alice, I think the invitation to be present at the occasion's more than enough.'

'Oh, I don't know about that.' Alice pulled a face. 'I'd at least like my transport costs covered. The taxi from Leeds Bradford airport was almost eighty quid.'

'And I suppose you flew first class?'

'Is there any other way? Now, I'm a little tired after all this travelling. Do you think you could show me to my room?'

'Ah, well now, you have a choice: with Susan and Richard down at their place, or with Rosa down at the vicarage.'

'I don't *think* so.' Alice was most put out. 'I swore, once I left that vicarage where as you know the Rev Cecil ruled the roost with a rod of iron, I'd never go back. There must be plenty of vacant rooms here?'

Hannah shook her head. 'Full to bursting. All taken for the guests, as well as the bride and groom who are staying in the presidential suite.'

'Presidential suite?' Alice snorted. 'Since when did *a president* stay here?'

Hannah blushed slightly. 'The best suite of rooms anyway, that we reserve for the happy couple. Jonny and Billy-Jo have taken up residence in a suite as well. They seem to have put down roots.'

'Well, they are the Marquess and Marchioness of Stratton. Why wouldn't they? I believe you've a spare bedroom in that upstairs apartment of yours? That will have to do. Now...' and here Alice started to chortle '...what's this about that niece of mine – Violet? Veronica...?'

'Virginia. You know it's Virginia,' Hannah snapped, looking at her watch.

'...Virginia coming out of the woodwork as Bill's fourth daughter? Goody two-shoes Susan, the favourite daughter who could do no wrong, wasn't so good after all, then? Just wait till I see that sister of mine.' Alice yawned widely and noisily, still laughing. 'Could do with a kip, darling. Will have to keep my fantasies about that heavenly rocker as just that for the moment. Now, if I could have your key, and you could arrange for some of those sandwiches...' Alice nodded towards the next table '... and a nice bottle of red to be sent up, then I'll be out of your hair for the time being.'

'Ms Sharma?' Hannah had led Dame Alice back across the parkland where they'd both (to Hannah's mounting irritation, but Alice's apparent delight and immediate compliance) been frisked yet again, this time by a rather lovely young security man, and were now back in the Great Hall.

'Goodness.' Alice, for once, was lost for words. 'Is all this cleaning really necessary? Bill would never have condoned this, you know.'

'Apparently.' Hannah followed Alice's gaze upwards where two of the team of four white-overalled men were completing the task of building a makeshift scaffolding to reach the Great Hall's chandelier.

'Well, I've seen some erections in my day...' Alice started. Quickly taking her arm, Hannah led her towards Aditi Sharma who was standing below the chandelier, arms folded, a grim expression on her beautiful face.

'Ms Sharma?' Hannah repeated and Aditi turned, frowning when she saw who was at Alice's side, the phrase *some old woman* implicit in her glare.

'Yes? What is it now, Ms Quinn? Autograph hunter, is it?' She gave Alice a cursory glance before glaring at Hannah.

'Ms Sharma.' Hannah smiled, loving every minute of the introduction. 'I'd like you to meet Dame Alice Parkes, internationally feted artist and guest at your wedding tomorrow.'

'Oh? Oh! Dame Alice? Dame Alice Parkes? How *wonderful* to meet you. Thank you so much for agreeing to be with us.' Aditi took hold of the other's hands in her own. 'This is an absolute honour, Dame Alice.' She turned to Hannah. 'I do hope you're looking after Dame Alice, Ms Quinn? Accommodating her with all she needs?'

'Well, darling,' Alice sniffed, 'seeing as I'm Hannah here's *mother*, I do hope *you're* accommodating my daughter with all that *she needs*? Is all this... this paraphernalia...' Alice nodded skywards '...really necessary? It's the last thing she should be being stressed about before this big wedding of yours...' She broke off as her antennae twitched and she turned towards the man standing in the shadows. 'And is this the groom?' Alice smiled winningly in his direction and then frowned. 'I thought your hair was a lot longer? You appear to have left your wild boy, rocker persona behind...?'

'Zac? What are *you* doing here?' Hannah felt irritation turn to anger. 'I'm sure you can see we're up to our ears in wedding preparations? This really isn't the time – or place – to be researching your damned book.' Hannah took in the lanyard around his neck. 'And how did you get *that*? Security is strictly allowing only those involved in the wedding to come into the hall today and tomorrow.'

'Oh, Hannah, I didn't think you'd mind.' Zac smiled, walking towards her before stroking her arm. 'Charlie knows me now and was happy to hand over a pass. If it's a problem...' Zac put up two hands in surrender '...of course, I'll be on my way.' He looked at his watch. 'I've actually an appointment with the Hon Nicholas Howard and his wife, Victoria, up at Castle Howard later on.'

'Who is this person?' Aditi snapped. 'And he has a camera? Ms Quinn, I suggest you call security to take the camera from him and escort him from the premises.'

'Mr Anderson is a visiting professor from the University of Maine, Miss Sharma. I'm so sorry he's been able to make his way past security today but, I can assure you, he's only interested in the history of English ancestral homes.'

'Really, I'm on my way.' Zac bent to kiss Hannah's cheek, smiled at Alice and, with a nod of apology in Aditi's direction, began to make his way out.

'Leave your pass, Mr Anderson,' Hannah called, her tone and manner leaving Zac in no doubt that this was an order and not a request. 'You'll be able to come back to the hall for the Agatha Christie do, the day after the wedding.'

'Goodness, Hannah, *he's* rather lovely.' Alice watched as Zac took off the lanyard and placed it on a chair before, with the same (bloody daft, Hannah now thought irritably) salute of goodbye he'd previously offered herself and Lachlan, he removed himself from the hall.

Lachlan. With a thump of her heart, Hannah remembered she still hadn't been able to make contact with him since he'd pulled Zac off her the other evening.

'I've got to go,' she said. 'Key's here, Alice. Make yourself at home. Water's hot if you want a shower.' And, turning to Aditi, who now had a face like thunder, said, 'Many apologies for the historian being here, Ms Sharma. I'll have a word with security right now. It won't happen again.'

## 28

Hannah set off at speed, wanting to confront Zac, wanting to know what he was up to, but he appeared to have disappeared into the ether.

'Charlie?' Hannah found the security man sitting up against his hut, pulling lethargically on his cigarette with one hand and Brutus's ears with the other.

'Sorry, Ms Quinn.' He scrambled to his feet before quickly dropping and stamping on the tab end, crushing it into the grass where it joined the remnants of myriad others. 'Sorry. It's just that I seem to have been made redundant. I...'

'It's fine.' Hannah shook her head. 'Listen, Charlie, did you give Zac Anderson a security pass, this morning?'

'Who?'

'The American?'

'There's a whole *load* of Yanks over here.'

'It's not the damned Second World War, Charlie,' Hannah snapped. 'The American? Tall, dark...'

'...and handsome?' Charlie finished, grinning. 'The guy who's been doing all the research on the place?'

'Yes.'

Charlie frowned. 'Yes, I think so. He said, you'd know about it.'

'Well, I didn't. If he wants to come in again, ask me first, would you?'

'Oh?' Charlie's eyes lit up at the thought of a bit of gossip to relieve the boredom of issuing lanyards. 'Is there a problem then?'

'No. Did you see him leave just now?'

'No, but then again, you know...' Charlie made to move himself out from his hiding place behind the security hut.

'What about Lachlan? Mr Buchanan?'

'What about him? I need to ask your permission first before I let *him* in?' Charlie laughed. 'I thought he was estate manager?'

Hannah tutted. 'Of course he is. Have you seen him this morning?'

Charlie stopped talking, sniffing the air as if that would give him the answer regarding Lachlan's whereabouts. Or maybe he just needed to blow his nose. 'D'you know, Ms Quinn, I don't reckon I've seen him for days. Ages actually. His dad died, you know.'

'Yes, I did know... oh hang on...' Hannah set off at a trot across the park to where the strapping security woman who'd got her beefy hands twice on Rosa earlier, was now attempting to frisk an extremely irate Geraldine McBain.

'Will you get your fucking hands off of me!' Ger was in a high dudgeon, her Scottish accent on full alert. 'I *work* here. But...' seeing Hannah, yelled, 'for how much longer, is anyone's sodding guess.'

'Geraldine, have you seen Lachlan?'

'Why should *I* have seen Lachlan?' Ger snapped, zipping up her huge backpack and flinging it back over her shoulders with all the expertise of a coal merchant handling a sack of coal.

'Well,' Hannah said, as if speaking to a recalcitrant child, 'because he's your boss? Because you work with him?'

'He's not been here for days, Hannah. I've delivered all the ewes myself, apart from when I've had to get Graham Maddison in.'

'He's gone?' Hannah's heart missed a beat. 'Where?'

'Back to Balmoral.'

'But why?'

'Why? Och, you stupid bitch. Listen, ye might be my boss, but ye need telling. Lachlan's grieving his father, but comes back down here to help you and your sisters with this ridiculous bloody wedding ye just *had* to take on. And what happens? He finds ye practically having sex against the wall with that American pillock. And don't think it was just you that American was after. He's been sniffing round all of us… But *you* fell for his charms, didn't you? Ye'ad Lachlan all to yourself, but it wasn't enough: ye just had to sample the unknown treats in the wee sweetie shop.'

Hannah swallowed. 'So, Lachlan's gone? For good?'

'Listen, *Ms Quinn*, that man adored ye. And ye fucked up, good and proper.'

'I wasn't having sex against the wall,' Hannah managed to get out.

'No, ye were just about to get him upstairs where ye'd be more comfortable. And Lachlan saw it all. *I* saw it all.'

'Has he gone for good? Taken his things?' Hannah's pulse raced. *Please don't let him have gone.*

Ger glared some more at Hannah and then, relenting, shook her head. 'He's gone back up to sort the funeral. Said he'd be back in time to help ye with this Agatha Christie farce.'

'Not the actual wedding?'

'Don't push it, Hannah. Ye've enough people here to sort this wedding…' She trailed off as a large, battered purple lorry was allowed through the gates, making its way slowly round the back of the hall and towards the petting zoo nearly a quarter of a mile further on.

'And,' Ger hissed, furiously, 'if ye think I'm mucking out anything that comes out of *that*, yer aff yer heid.' She gave Hannah one last look of utter disdain before setting off at pace towards the far meadow and the last of the still-pregnant ewes.

*

With only Ger's flea in her ear for company, Hannah set off at a run behind the purple lorry, wishing she'd at least gone back up to the flat for her trainers. Panting now, she bent over in an effort to relieve the stitch in her side.

'Lachlan's gone, Eva.' Hannah was finding it very hard to keep the wobble from her voice.

'Gone? Gone where?' Eva looked down through the open nearside window of the lorry. She looked to be a very long way up, and Hannah started to shout.

'Back to Balmoral... He's left...'

'No need to shout, Hans, you'll frighten Jumbo. Hang on, how do I open this?' She turned to speak to the driver who suddenly appeared at Hannah's side on the ground, reaching up to give Eva a hand down. 'Paddy, this is my sister, Hannah Quinn.'

'Pleased to meet yer, Miss Quinn.' Paddy's accent was pure Southern Irish. 'Wid a name like Quinn, yer mest be one of the chosen few yerself?' He grinned. 'Right, one elephant I believe yer after?'

'But why've you brought him now?' Hannah asked in panic. 'We don't need him until tomorrow afternoon.'

'He has to settle into a place.' Paddy frowned. 'We'll need to bed him down for the night; keep him calm like.'

'Does he have a tendency to be, you know, *not calm*?'

'Ach, only if he's not a happy boy. I've brought him now; we'll settle him in an' then he'll be right as sunshine for this big wedding o' yours tomorrer.'

'Settle him in where?' Hannah turned to Eva. 'Where are we going to put him?'

'Ask Ger, she'll sort it. Give her a ring.'

'Ger is the last person to help. As far as I know, she's writing her resignation letter as she's delivering the last of the lambs.'

'Oh, God, Hannah, that's all we need. You really must have

pissed off both Lachlan and Ger big time. I tell you now, *I'm* not mucking this great animal out.'

'That's just what Ger said.'

'It's fine, it's fine.' Paddy grinned. 'Find me a nice big patch o' grass and let me settle him in. I 'ave to think about his animal rights, don't want him unhappy. Hang on a minute, girls.' Paddy reached for the lock and handle on the back door of the truck, raising the shuttered door to reveal a very large grey elephant.

'Is he Indian or African?' Hannah asked, stepping back in alarm at the size of the animal who was gazing down at her with tiny but intelligent eyes. 'I never know the difference.'

'Cover yer ears, me darlin',' Paddy crooned and Hannah immediately put up a hand to each side of her face.

'Not you, you eejit.' He laughed. 'Yer'll be away an' insulting yer man, calling him African. He won't take kindly to that, will yer, me darlin'?'

Hannah stepped further back as Paddy pulled down a ramp and led the elephant by a long rope onto the grass.

'Blimey O'Reilly.' Daisy Maddison had appeared at Eva's side.

'Oh, another one from home.' Paddy grinned. 'Ah, tis yerself, Miss Daisy. How's yer daddy?'

'Hi, Paddy.' Daisy grinned. 'How's it going?'

'You two know each other?' Hannah stared.

'Dad's on call every Easter when the circus arrives. My sister and I used to love going with him to see the animals, to check they were all OK.'

'Ah, yer daddy's a good man, Daisy. The very best.'

'I'm so pleased wild animals are banned from performing. It was too long coming. You've still got the ponies and the dogs, Dad said?' Daisy raised an eyebrow. 'I'm not convinced domestic animals should be performing either.'

'Oh, but they're a happy lot.' Paddy smiled. 'They're our family and we couldn't be finding them new homes. There's just the two ponies and the five dogs. Once they go,' he added sadly, 'and Jumbo here goes, well then it's time for me to go too.'

Daisy walked over to Jumbo, taking a couple of treats from her pocket, soothing and talking to the elephant as he ate. 'Good that you've brought him up here this afternoon, Paddy. Get him used to the area.'

'Got his outfit washed, ironed, ready and waiting.'

'His outfit?'

'He's been guest of honour at quite a few Hindu weddings.'

'Don't tell Alice that,' Eva grinned to Hannah. She reckons *she's* going to be the most important person at the do.'

'He loves the attention.' Paddy smiled. 'Now, if you can just show *me* a bunk for the night...?'

'Anything in the staff quarters?' Eva asked, in an aside to Hannah. 'If Lachlan's gone...?'

'Don't say that.' Hannah's face crumpled.

'I need to be near my boy,' Paddy insisted. 'Not off at the other side o' the park.' He grinned. 'Don't worry, I've slept in the wagon afore now.' He thumped the purple paintwork with affection. 'I'll peg the lad out near me, and I've got his fruit, hay and pellets in here.' Paddy banged the side of the truck once again. 'He'll think he's on his holidays.'

'Packed his trunk?' Hannah nodded vaguely, her mind only on Lachlan.

'Water?' Daisy snapped. 'Have you water for him? I'm not sure about this, Hannah. Dad, who is down as the lead vet for the circus – and that's a legal requirement – will need to know Jumbo is totally happy here, and looked after.'

'Yer daddy was round the day after we arrived, Daisy. Everything was fine. You ask him. And, there's several barrels-full o' water in the truck,' Paddy assured them. '*And* I'll take him down to your lake for a bit of a bath afore I get him dressed in his finery tomorrer.'

'You'll frighten the Crazy Ladies.' Eva grinned.

'Crazy Ladies?'

'A bunch of mad wild swimmers. They've been coming for years: Bill gave them permission to swim down there early in the morning. You know, before the visitors arrive.' Eva laughed. 'They'll think they're in the Ganges if they bump into Jumbo. I keep thinking I'll join them one of these days.'

'Not over the next couple of days they won't.' Hannah shook her head. 'They won't get past security.'

Paddy stroked Jumbo's trunk lovingly. 'Now, if you can just see your way to a bottle of the good stuff for meself, ladies...?'

'OK, that's all sorted.' Eva came up from the office, threw her phone onto the coffee table, and, closing her eyes, lay back on the sofa. 'Mum and Dad are going to stay with Laila and Nora for the night and take them over to Rayan's after school tomorrow for the next couple of days.' She sighed. 'I really feel I'm abandoning them. You know? Not a good mother at all. What if they want to go and live with Rayan and Yasmin full-time?' There was panic in her voice. 'Hell, it's almost ten, Hannah. I need to go to bed.'

'How about a glass of wine?' Hannah asked, from the kitchen.

'I thought you'd given up, after the other night's little fiasco?'

'It's just a small one.'

'I'm off to bed. Oh, bloody hell, I forgot, Alice is in the spare room, isn't she? What's she been *doing* all day?'

'She actually spent most of the afternoon and evening up in the art retreat. She just can't help herself when she sees canvas and paint. Have to say, I didn't quite understand what it was she was working on.' Hannah came and sat next to Eva, glass to hand. 'It's only a small one,' she tutted when she saw Eva's look of disapproval.

'That's because you're not an artist.' Eva opened one eye.

'What is?'

'That you don't see the meaning of what an artist is trying to portray.'

'Oh, give me a nice watercolour of a chocolate-box cottage any day. Something I can understand. So, you're going to have to bunk down with me tonight.' Hannah drained her glass.

'Alice fast asleep, is she?'

'She downed a bottle of wine.'

'Hannah...'

'I know what you're going to say.'

'Look, Alice has always drunk too much...'

'And I'm following in her footsteps?' Hannah snapped. '*You* inherit all her artistic talent and *I* just get her drink problem?'

'And is it a problem?' Both eyes were now open and holding Hannah's own.

'I just need a drink occasionally. And particularly over the next few days. Once this wedding and Jet Set farce are over, I'll...'

'You'll what?' Eva interrupted. 'Lachlan knew you were not handling the booze well. He had a word with me and Rosa.'

'He had absolutely no right to talk about me like that. How dare he talk to you two about me? He was supposed to *love* me. I bet he's been having a thing with Ger all this time. You know, their rooms next to each other...? I'll bet anything...'

'Oh, cut it out, Hannah. That's you putting your guilt over that pillock Zac Anderson on to Lachlan; it's the wine talking.'

'Nothing happened with me and Zac, Eva. I promise you. I'm frightened Lachlan's not going to come back.' Hannah made to move towards her empty wine glass but, one look from Eva, and she placed it back on the table.

'Well, you did mess him about, Hannah. I saw Ger later this afternoon – not too happy about Jumbo being allowed to roam on her territory – and she said Lachlan's assured her he'll be back the day after next, in time for the Agatha Christie evening.'

'He's not done anything to assure *me*. Refusing to have any contact with *me*. And I'm frightened everything's going to go tits up tomorrow.'

'I don't blame him for keeping out of your way. And, I *hate* that expression.' Eva frowned. 'I find it really vulgar. Hannah, both Tara and Felicity have got everything down to the fine detail. They've only just left and they're going to be back here by 5am. They both wanted to stay the night, but more chance of getting a bed in Bethlehem...'

'Always the llamas' stable.' Hannah chortled, and Eva joined in. She stood, stretching and yawning. 'Come on, put that wine down, make us both some Horlicks and then bed. Oh and no snoring or nicking all the duvet.'

## 29

*The wedding day, 5am*

'Hannah! Your phone!' Eva waved a hand around the duvet, looking for the offending article. 'For God's sake, where is it? It's the middle of the night.'

Hannah shot out of the bed she'd been sharing with Eva, the pair of them having spent the last few hours irritably kicking out at the other's heavy breathing, fighting for and losing possession of the duvet and, in Hannah's case, having several conversations with someone about miserable-looking clowns, dead daffodils and not enough effing canapés to go round.

'What? Where? Shit.' Hannah ran to the bedroom window, phone to ear, looking down on the parkland where a new dawn was trying its best to overcome the grey strata of the late March misty morning. 'I can't see him. It's dark down there. And very grey!'

'Can't see who? What is it? What time is it?' Eva joined Hannah at the window, trying to work out what her sister was looking for.

'On my way!' Hannah tossed the phone onto the unmade bed. 'That was Tara – she's just arrived. The bloody elephant's on the loose.' Hannah grabbed jeans and sweater, pulling them haphazardly over her Harry Potter pyjamas, before scrabbling to find trainers under the bed. 'Come on, Eva.'

Outside, in the dawn light, Tara and Felicity were standing holding hands, well back behind the wall at the edge of the hall's herb garden, but keeping a wary eye on Jumbo who appeared oblivious to their presence.

'Get Paddy!' Hannah shouted. 'Have you seen him? Where's bloody security when we need them? Hell, he's eating all the chives and garlic.'

'Garlic breath. Great, just what we need at a wedding.' Eva set off at a run, her pyjama bottoms (Rayan's he'd left behind) trailing over Hannah's too-big wellies she'd grabbed when unable to find any of her own footwear.

The grass was wet and, as she headed at speed towards Paddy's purple lorry, Felicity's plaintive imploring of: 'Don't leave us with this wild beast, Eva,' trailed behind her, merging somewhat incongruously with the much more melodic strain of the dawn chorus.

'Oh?' She came to a standstill, bending over to fight a stitch, as a man appeared out of the murky mist that was intent on hovering over the lake at the bottom of the parkland.

'Eva?' Drew Livingston stopped in his tracks, but then made his way towards her. 'What on earth's the matter?'

'What are *you* doing here?' Eva gasped, seemingly unable to take in the air her lungs so desperately needed, as well as the presence of the world-famous rocker now manifested in front of her.

'Well, as far as I remember, it's my wedding day.' For a moment he looked bewildered. 'I haven't got the wrong day, have I? It is Thursday? To be honest, I've been in the States so it could be any bloody day here.'

'But you're supposed to be arriving on an elephant.'

'Am I?' Drew started to laugh. 'That another of Aditi's little surprises?'

'It was one hell of a surprise to *us* yesterday. But we've got Jumbo ready and waiting for you. Well, no,' she gasped, one hand to her chest, 'that's a lie. He's actually scaring the bejesus out of all three wedding planners in the hall's cottage garden.' She stood up straight, exhaling. 'Drew, it's five in the morning. What are *you doing* roaming the place?' She had a sudden thought. 'You're not searching for the Jet Set, are you?'

'Jet Set?' Drew frowned. 'Look, I know Aditi and her team have invited the cream of Bollywood and the world of rock, but, calling them the Jet Set...?' He ran a tired hand through his long black curls. 'I flew into Manchester from the States last night and, since I was wide awake, I decided it best if I don't go to bed. Jet lag and all that. Came straight here. Blake, my PA, has everything ready for me – and I just decided to walk. It's so incredibly quiet and peaceful here after New York and Chicago. God, I'd love to paint all this.' He moved an arm across the vista of lake and woodland. 'Right, pineapples.'

'Pineapples?'

'I'm sure I read somewhere that elephants adore pineapples. Look, you run to the kitchens – I know the chefs are here, and already up and running – grab a couple of pineapples and I'll go and bash on the elephant keeper's door. That him down there?' Drew pointed to where the roof of the battered purple lorry was just emerging, like some great mythological beast, out of the mist. He smiled down at Eva and then kissed her cheek. 'Sorry, sorry, shouldn't be doing that on my wedding day.'

'It's fine, it's fine,' Eva managed to squeak before, red-faced and wanting nothing more than to kiss the face off the man, turned on Hannah's wellies and rerouted across to the conference centre in the west wing.

'Hello-o,' she shouted, across the stainless-steel work surfaces already loaded with food and ingredients. 'Greg?'

Silence, apart from her own words echoing back to her across the vast vaulted area of kitchen. She scanned the surfaces for anything resembling a pineapple. And then came a little cry, a little pitiful call for help. What the hell was going on now? Eva moved quickly in the direction of the sound, conscious she was trailing grass and mud across the immaculately clean tiled floor.

'The bastard.' A pathetic moan drifted up from the end of the work surface and, as Eva ran over, saw a pair of pink Crocs at the end of blue checked trousers sticking out towards her.

'What's the matter? What's happened?' Eva bent down to the little chef who was nursing what would eventually become a black eye. 'Mr Rao?'

Safe Rao moaned and whimpered some more. 'I don't do this. I don't work with the bastard. He been drinking...'

'What, at five in the morning?' Eva stared.

'He no good, alcoholic bastard. Celebrity chef? My backside! He go, scarpered because he know I get polis after him. It assault: GBH.'

'He's gone? He *can't go*.' Eva felt nothing but panic. This would tip Hannah right over the top, and more than likely into joining the – allegedly – drunk Jasper Solomon. 'Is he coming back?'

'Not if he want to live.' Safe brandished a huge serrated-edged kitchen knife he'd secreted in his chef's whites. 'He drive off. I ring police and they'll have him for drink driving. He already banned from driving twice. He finished as celebrity chef.' Safe pulled the knife across his own throat. 'He go to prison and be buggered,' he added gleefully before wincing in pain as, with a trembling hand, he felt at his eye.

'Where's Greg?'

'Greg?'

'The hall's chef. The one who gave a demonstration of some of the hall's dishes the other week?' Eva was gabbling now.

Safe shrugged. 'I go lie down. I cannot create when I so upset.' He promptly burst into tears, nursing his head in his arms.

'Please, Mr Rao, you need to get up, get that eye seen to and then start work on the wedding breakfast. Please...'

Oh, great stuff. And the bloody elephant was still on the loose.

Spotting a veritable mound of beautiful fresh pineapples at the other side of the kitchen, she set off for them before shouting over her shoulder: 'Man up, Mr Rao. I want you up and running: chopping, whisking and preparing, by the time I get back.'

'And you are?' the chef asked sulkily.

'I *own* this hall,' Eva said loftily, turning up the sleeves of Rayan's oversized pyjamas which were giving the impression of her having some rare genetic syndrome. Not strictly true of course, this *owning the hall* proclamation, but needs must in pulling rank when your chef was in the middle of a major hissy fit and there were a hundred guests of note expecting to be fed in just twelve hours' time.

Grabbing four pineapples, and placing them in a makeshift sweatshirt pouch, she set off once again. Jesus, she hadn't done as much running as this since the weekly Westenbury Comprehensive games afternoon. And never with four scratchy pineapples secreted in her sweatshirt pouch like some sort of confused kangaroo. To be fair, she'd rarely run at school, bunking off and heading for the hills with her gang of like-minded deserters and a pack of Silk Cut, leaving Hannah, who always wanted to come with her – and Rosa, who most certainly never did – behind in the changing rooms.

'Oh good, you've got something to tempt him.' Hannah, Tara and Felicity offered up a collective shout of congratulations.

'What do I do now?' Eva asked.

'Well, just try and lure him out of the garden and back down to Paddy's lorry,' Tara suggested. 'Shouldn't be too difficult.'

'Here,' Eva shouted from the safety of the wall while brandishing two pineapples like Carmen Miranda, '*you* do it then.'

'I'm allergic to horses.'

'He's a sodding *elephant*.'

'Exactly. I'll probably be *more* allergic.'

Jumbo's olfactory senses were obviously as good as his – alleged – memory senses and with his trunk outstretched, gave a (quite remarkable, for such an old man of advancing years) trumpet of greed before setting off at speed towards Eva.

'Shit.' Eva felt the adrenalin surge. Fight or flight? Flight was looking exceptionally the best option here.

'Stand your ground, Eva,' Felicity called from behind the wall.

'*You* stand your sodding ground,' Eva yelled back. 'And, Hannah, *you* need to get down to the kitchens – both wedding chefs have gone AWOL.'

'What?' The operatic chorus behind the wall wailed as one. Then rallied. 'Right, kitchens,' Tara shouted, backing out from her place of safety. 'Come on.'

'Don't leave me,' Eva yelled as a grey trunk snaked towards the pineapple. 'Fuck,' she whispered. 'Here, Jumbo, Jumbo, good boy.' The elephant regarded Eva kindly before very politely curling the tip of his trunk around the fruit she offered up and putting the pineapple piecemeal into his mouth. He chewed contemplatively for a good minute before lowering his great grey head expectantly towards Eva once more. 'Right.' Eva exhaled. 'No point in just standing here feeding you fruit salad, Jumbo lad.' She set off slowly towards the purple lorry some distance down the park, the elephant at her side, his trunk, like some terrifying snake, never far away from her pouch of fruit. She stopped and rewarded the elephant with a second and then third pineapple before exhaling in relief as she saw Drew Livingston walking quickly towards her, Paddy the elephant keeper following in his wake.

'Oh, God, Eva. You OK?' Drew started running and then, seeing this might upset Jumbo, set himself at walking pace once more.

'Ah, Jumbo, me darling, what d'you think you're doing, going off like this?' Paddy, still in the previous day's clothes but appearing bright and cheerful, made his way towards Eva and the elephant.

'What d'you think *you're* effing doing?' Eva hissed, her terror at being left in charge of his elephant, turning to fury. 'I could report you for this, Paddy: RSPCA and all that. Have Jumbo taken off you and put into foster care.'

'Sure, and he's a quiet old boy. Wouldn't hurt a fly. Oh, pineapples? The very thing. Although, they do have a tendency to give the lad a bit of the old belly ache.' And on cue, as though confirming this, Jumbo emitted a thunderous and protracted breaking of wind. 'There now, so, how about you having a little practice on riding him, sir?'

Drew looked terrified. 'I'll kill Aditi. And how the hell do I get up there?'

'Well.' Paddy grinned. 'There's this way...' He whispered something in Jumbo's ear, offered him a treat from his pocket and the elephant lifted a bent leg, offering it up as a stepping stool, which had Paddy immediately up on his back, soothing and chatting to the animal. 'Or...' Paddy whispered soft, encouraging words and Jumbo immediately lay down in front of the other two. 'Come on, I'll give you two a lift where you want to be, then I'm going to give Jumbo his breakfast, a bath and start dressing him in his finery.'

'No way am I going up on that.' Eva stepped backwards.

'Come on, Eva, I need to practise my entry, apparently.' Drew put out a tentative hand to the elephant and, with the other, took Eva's hand, holding it there. 'He's actually rather sweet.'

'Sweet? Listen, I've got to get across to the kitchens...' She stopped. No point in telling the groom there appeared to be a distinct dearth of chefs to prepare his wedding breakfast. 'Oh, God! OK, if I really have to.'

Paddy slid down to the ground and helped first Drew and then Eva on to the elephant's back. 'Put your hands round your man's waist...' he commanded, taking hold of the rope round the elephant's bridle. 'You know, Jumbo loves this. He loves it all.'

Eva placed her pyjama-clad arms tentatively round Drew

Livingston's waist, but Drew took her hands firmly, holding them tightly in his own. Jumbo lumbered to his feet and, rolling slightly, Eva wondered if she was going to be seasick, but as the elephant moved off, following Paddy towards the conference centre, she began to relax and enjoy the experience. Particularly having her arms around the world's most famous rocker, her nose pressed into his soft warm sweater.

'And don't you worry, sir.' Paddy smiled up at the pair of them. 'When it comes to this afternoon, there's a proper seat with a canopy for your arrival at the wedding.'

'Are you sure that doesn't hurt him?' Drew asked. 'I'm happy to arrive like this if you'd rather. This is jolly comfortable.'

'I don't think Aditi would approve,' Eva said. 'The red and gold of the canopy match your outfit apparently.'

'My outfit?' Drew turned slightly. 'I'm wearing a cream tux, and that's final. I don't mind a ride on the elephant here, in fact, I might go down with Paddy and give Jumbo his breakfast, but I'm not getting dolled up like a Hindu god for anyone...' He broke off, his thumbs caressing Eva's hands below the cotton fabric of Rayan's old pyjama top and it went through Eva's mind how ridiculously incongruous that she was wearing her ex-husband's PJs while wrapped around one of the most iconic men on the planet. She knew she was behaving like a schoolgirl with a crush, but also knew she was loving every minute of the attention the superstar was bestowing upon her.

'Eva? I...' Drew broke off, bringing Eva's hand to his mouth where he kissed it softly. 'I... Oh... I'm sorry...'

'Paddy,' Eva called down quickly, her face scarlet. 'Can I get off? We're here. I need to get off.'

When she was safely back on the ground and well out of the horribly dangerous compulsion to press every bit of herself into Drew Livingston's warm body, she shouted back up at him. 'I'm going to get someone to take you up to the art retreat later on this morning. I'll arrange for you to have coffee with Dame

Alice Parkes – I know she'll be happy to chat with you about her artwork.'

And, unable to meet Drew's eyes, to let him see just what she was feeling, she scampered off (as much as one *can* scamper in oversized PJs and wellies) to the hall's kitchens.

# 30

*The wedding day, 6.30am*

She couldn't carry on to the wedding venue in her pyjamas and smelling of elephant.

And with her head and heart full of Drew Livingston.

Spotting Charlie already at his post (he'd be making a fortune in overtime) Eva trotted off in his direction, shouting: 'Charlie, I need to get back into the apartment; I don't have my key. Can you let me in?'

'Where's your pass?' Charlie shouted back, walking towards her, Brutus trailing at his heels.

'Oh, don't you start,' Eva snapped. 'Just let me in.'

'I've strict instructions, Ms Malik…'

'Yes, and I've a strict timetable, Charlie, so just get yourself up to the flat and let me in.'

Twenty minutes later, she was showered, dressed in the formal business suit expected of her and running back towards the wedding venue. Although still only 6.30am, the park and beyond was already resembling Piccadilly Circus at rush hour, every window in the hall and conference centre illuminated, while whole crowds of officials, all seemingly with coffee to hand, were intent on ensuring the wedding celebrations of Drew Livingston and Aditi Sharma went off without a hitch.

Without a hitch? Eva thought grimly. There was going to be one hell of a hitch if there was no one to prepare the wedding breakfast. And if Drew was refusing to wear the outfit Aditi was demanding of her soon-to-be husband. Oh, and now it appeared the police were here, the car and officers being stopped and inspected before being allowed to drive up to, and park outside, the conference centre. All they needed now was the fire brigade and ambulance service to join in the fray.

'Sorry,' Eva, pleaded, running up to the car as the two police officers – young and looking as if they couldn't arrest the skin from a rice pudding – alighted, 'but would you mind awfully driving round to the back of the kitchens? The last thing we need is the press getting hold of this.' Eva glanced back towards the main gates where a bevy of uninvited press, as well as fans who'd apparently been camping out all night to see the arrival of the famous couple and their guests, were already gathered.

Eva directed the police car, and waited for them to follow her through the staff entrance, the pair of PCs obviously enthralled at unexpectedly finding themselves a part of this whole extravaganza.

'I heard Beyoncé was flying in...' the first officer was saying to the other.

'The Beatles, apparently – well what's left of them. My gran will be *so* jealous when I tell her...'

'Right,' Eva snapped, 'can you make this as quick as you can? We need Mr Rao to start cooking ASAP. If you follow me?'

Eva led the two youngsters through to where Hannah, Tara and Felicity were trying to cajole the tiny celebrity chef into giving instructions to his staff who were standing nervously waiting.

'I can't do it,' he was moaning. 'My head is pounding: the vicious attack on my person by that jumped-up no-good bastard has brought on one of my migraines. I have flashing lights; I can't stand – I can't even *see* out of this eye.' He sat down suddenly once more, moaning and putting his head into his hands before bursting into a fresh bout of sobbing.

'Mr Rao, we need a statement from you,' the woman police officer was saying. 'We need to know what happened? And we need to get you to A and E to have that eye seen to.'

'Did you get him?' Safe asked, raising his head. 'Jasper Solomon? I know his registration. It JS23. You get him and do him for drunk driving – it will be third time. And then you get him for attempt murder.'

'Mr Rao,' Tara's voice was soothing. 'We need Mr Solomon back *here*. Now.' She turned to the police officers, pleading, 'Do you think you could arrest him tomorrow?'

'That no good,' Safe hissed. 'He not be over limit tomorrow… And if he turn up back here, I not work with him. I *kill* him!' He brought out the huge kitchen knife, brandishing it in the others' direction.

'Mr Rao,' the young male officer now spoke. 'You have a bladed article on your person, and in a public place.'

'It's a knife,' Hannah said in exasperation.

'Exactly,' the two police officers replied in unison.

'He's a bloody chef,' Hannah and Eva hissed as one.

'And he's making threats to kill,' the male PC went on. 'Serious stuff.'

'Can you not pretend you didn't hear?' Felicity asked hopefully.

'What's up?' The gathered kitchen and serving staff, increasing by the minute as they started to arrive for work at their allotted time, turned as Greg, the hall's chef, arrived with his two sous chefs, all immaculate in their kitchen whites. 'What's up?' he asked again.

'We appear to not have our celebrity chefs, Greg.' Hannah exhaled, placing her head in her hands. 'This is a total nightmare.'

'What's up?' Daisy Maddison echoed, joining the gathered crowd.

'Daisy, it's your turn *tomorrow*,' Hannah snapped. 'What are *you* doing here?'

'Been helping Ger with the last of the lambing. Seeing as how Lachlan's *not here*,' she added accusingly, right back at Hannah. 'Saw the police car and wondered what was going on.'

'It's all under control, Daisy,' Hannah said wearily. 'We'll see you tomorrow.'

'Doesn't look to be,' Daisy sniffed.

'Well, unless you're a trained chef…'

'Me? Can't even make a decent scrambled egg,' Daisy said cheerfully. 'But I know a woman who is, and can.'

'Is and can what?' Eva joined in.

'Is a trained chef – the very best – and can help you here.' She turned to Greg. 'You can take over most of this, can't you, Greg? How about if I ring Clem to assist?'

'Clem?' Hannah, Tara, Eva and Felicity turned to Daisy.

'Clementine Ahern down at Clementine's,' Daisy said. 'I used to waitress for her a few years ago. I bet she'd come up if she knew the situation.'

'Clementine Ahern?' Hannah frowned, remembering the coolly efficient way the owner of the famous restaurant down in the village had dealt with her when she, Hannah, was lambasting Ben Pennington in front of all her restaurant guests. 'Oh, no, no,' Hannah objected, utterly embarrassed. 'Why would she?'

''Cos she's a mate of mine? Because I patched up her old dog, George, last month when he was knocked over? Because she's lovely? And, because, Hannah, you appear to have no other option. We know Greg is brilliant – he started with Clem when he was sixteen, didn't you, Greg…?' Greg nodded his red-faced smile. 'But even *he* can't be supervising the preparation of all *this*.'

\*

*3pm*

'I think it's going to be all alright, Eva.' Hannah met her sister as Eva was making her way back to the wedding venue after checking all was well with Jumbo once more. 'I want to marry Clementine. She's just wonderful.'

'I think you'll find she's already married,' Eva said dryly, 'to that rather gorgeous BBC correspondent Rafe Ahern. And then, relenting, gave Hannah's arm a quick squeeze. 'You've not had a thing to eat, have you? Hannah, you must look after yourself.' Eva moved nearer to her sister. 'You've not been drinking, have you?'

'Drinking?' Hannah glared. 'No, I've not even had a coffee yet.'

'Right,' Eva grabbed Hannah's arm, turning and propelling her back into the kitchen she'd just exited. 'Coffee.' She ordered. 'I need one, as well as something to eat.'

'I'm too nervous to eat,' Hannah objected. She turned again. 'I've got to see if everything's ready to go across at the chapel.'

'Rosa's already up there. She arrived an hour ago and is just going through it all with Felicity. Tara is checking, for the umpteenth time, that the attendants and security up on the top fields know exactly what to do with the guests who're arriving by helicopter. There's going to be at least twenty of the things. So, come on, a five-minute break and get some food inside you.'

'You look as if you could do with this, Hannah.' Clementine Ahern, in full chef whites, handed over a big mug of tea and a bacon sandwich. 'Best thing to steady nerves.'

'Not coffee?' Eva asked, knowing she, herself, craved another cup, but accepting, instead, a mug of tea.

'Makes you too jittery.' Clementine smiled. 'Believe me, I've been there.'

'But,' Hannah said, through a huge mouthful of sandwich, while gazing round at the hive of activity in the kitchen, 'you seem so relaxed and calm here.'

'I've learned, over the years, to try and stay calm and just get on with it.' Clem laughed. 'Had to do that when Bill nicked Greg from me. He's an absolute gem, that boy. Look after him,' she advised. 'Now, we're all on target: both Solomon's and Rao's assistant chefs have taken me through the menus and where everything is and I've delegated accordingly. It will all be fine, Hannah.'

'Look, Clementine, I really did mean to come in to the restaurant and, you know, apologise for my appalling behaviour the other evening. I did actually set off, and then got waylaid. Anyway, you need to know...'

'Hannah, it's fine.' Clementine patted her arm and smiled. 'We've all been there, all done something we regret.'

'Yes, but...'

'Really, let's just concentrate on getting this show on the road. It's going to be fine. Honestly.'

### 3.30pm

'You got your *yawn of yellow*.' Eva smiled across at Hannah while the pair of them stood watching the arrival of the groom as Jumbo moved slowly and deliberately across the park and towards them. 'The daffs couldn't have been more splendiferous if you'd come out last night and painted them with a bucket of yellow paint.'

'You're being unusually poetic.' Hannah tutted but, looking round at the beautiful parkland with its yellow carpet in different shades of lemon, to ochre, to school-bus yellow, she felt she could sit and script a few Wordsworth-worthy lines herself.

'To be honest, I don't know whether to laugh or cry,' Eva whispered as they watched Paddy proudly leading Jumbo by a red-tasselled silk rope towards the Heatherly Hall chapel at the far side of the grounds, stopping every now and again as instructed by the *HeyHo* photographers.

'Do NOT go and get the giggles now,' Hannah warned. 'You know, like you did at Grandpa Cecil's funeral.'

'It's just watching Paddy, all dressed up in his red and gold outfit to match Jumbo's fabulous colours, and then looking up at Drew who looks more like James Bond than a Hindu prince in that cream tux. He'd have been better arriving in an Aston Martin DB5 than on an elephant.' Eva didn't think she'd ever seen the rock star looking more gorgeous; more downright glamorous.

'And the wanting to cry?' Hannah interrupted her thoughts, taking a sideways glance towards Eva, eyebrows raised.

'Oh, I suppose I'm missing my girls when I don't see them for a couple of days. And Andrea as well.'

'You've not heard from him then?'

'Oh, I've *heard* from him. We've spoken several times on the phone, but it's just been, you know: How are you? How are the sculptures going? Are you remembering to eat? That's the problem with being involved with an artist – and I should have known and accepted that, having Alice as a mother – the art *always* comes first. I guess I'll always come second in Andrea's life.'

'And is that OK?' Hannah looked directly at Eva.

'What, my not being Andrea's main priority? I don't know, Hannah, I really don't.' Eva screwed up her eyes, trying not to cry. 'He's been back in Milan weeks now, and I'm trying to remember what he looks like, what he smells like, the feel of his hair in my fingers...'

'Blimey, you are being poetic.' Hannah laughed. 'What you mean is, you can't remember what he's like in bed?'

'Oh, I can certainly remember that...' She broke off as Paddy and Jumbo, carrying Drew, neared and Eva didn't know whether to wave as though the king was passing by, give him the thumbs up or just smile across at him. In the end, she did the latter.

Drew Livingston's eyes never left her own as he was carried towards her and Eva felt her heart race and her face flush.

'And you think you'd have been any better off with a rock star?' Hannah waved at Drew and Paddy and the accompanying entourage, looking knowingly at Eva as she did so. 'If you wanted steady security rather than glamour and uncertainty, you should have stuck with Rayan. You can't get steadier than a dentist. Especially when he has a drill in his hand.'

'Says the girl who doesn't know what she wants from a relationship,' Eva snapped, embarrassed that Hannah was obviously aware of what she'd thought was her ongoing *secret* lust for Drew Livingston.

'You thought I didn't know?' Hannah grinned, echoing Eva's thoughts. 'About your continuing passion for the lovely groom? And,' she went on, 'I *do* know what I want from a relationship. I want Lachlan. Eva, I miss him so much. I've been such a bloody idiot.'

'I'm not going to argue with that,' Eva said. Paddy and Jumbo had drawn level with the pair of them and, grinning from ear to ear, Paddy raised a hand and shouted, 'Top o' the mornin' to you both!'

'Please don't tell me he just said that,' Hannah snapped, a rictus of a smile on her face. 'It's supposed to be a Hindu-inspired wedding, not one from the Irish boglands.'

'D'you know, I don't reckon Paddy's from Ireland at all. One of the hall's cleaners reckons she was at junior school with him in Batley.'

They both started giggling. 'Come on, we need to get over to the helipad…'

'The *helipad?*' Eva gave Hannah such a look she wanted to laugh more.

'A'reet then, that bit o' grass up yonder where t'bride should be landing any minute now.'

\*

*4pm*

Hannah, standing in the porch of the tiny chapel, offered up an audible sigh of relief towards Tara, Eva and Felicity. Capacity being limited, Aditi had agreed to just a select few family and close friends attending the actual ceremony, with the rest of the guests invited for drinks, the seated wedding breakfast and party afterwards.

Looking ravishing in the traditional embroidered and ornately designed lehnga, Aditi had eschewed the tradition of wearing red, instead choosing to be married in ivory, cream and gold. Mehndi decorations covered her entire body, from her feet and fingers to her head and shoulders and Hannah didn't think she'd ever seen a more stunning bride. And at least Drew, in his cream tux, was colour co-ordinating his bride's outfit.

Aditi hadn't been overly forthcoming about her family, explaining her father had died when she was very young, and that she was estranged from her mother and brothers who hadn't been happy with her chasing the dream of becoming a Bollywood star and running away to Mumbai when she was just eighteen. She wanted, she'd told Hannah and Tara, her wedding to reflect both Indian and British cultures and traditions and, while she was happy for the ceremony to be performed by Rosa, following the Christian values by which Drew himself had been brought up, she did want to introduce into the ceremony the Indian tradition of the *Pokwanu*. Instead of her family, Aditi had arranged that three of her women friends should formally welcome Drew and his guests.

One of these best girls, tiny and shimmering in the same ivory and gold as the bride, reached up to Drew, standing on tiptoes to apply a *tilak* to his forehead before escorting him down the tiny aisle of the Heatherly Hall chapel to await Aditi in the traditional manner.

And then it was Rosa's turn, greeting the couple with a smile and a few words of welcome before taking them through the simple ceremony both Aditi and Drew had requested; hearing their vows and proclaiming them man and wife.

Eva, standing at the back of the chapel with the others, closed her eyes momentarily, knowing that there now would never be – could never be – any fanning of the flames of that tiny spark she knew had been there between herself and Drew Livingston.

*You daft person*, she censured herself, *you totally and utterly ridiculous person*. What had she been expecting? Drew to turn round at the last minute, shout he couldn't *possibly* marry Aditi when the woman he really loved was standing at the back of the chapel? That would have gone down like a lead balloon with Rosa. And with Hannah. Eva smiled to herself. Not to mention poor old Aditi.

'You're smiling, Eva?' Tara touched her hand. 'Wishing it was you?'

'Me?' Eva gave a bark of forced laughter. 'I've just untangled myself from one husband. Don't think I'm ready for another just yet. Do you?'

'Right. Rosa's done her bit.' Tara laughed back. 'Come on. Our turn now; let's get over there and make sure everything's going to be fantastic. Time to party!'

## 31

*The day after the wedding, 11am*

'Thank you, dear God, thank you for getting us through yesterday without too much going wrong.' Hannah leaned back in her chair in Tea and Cake, draining her cup of coffee and dabbing at toast crumbs from the plate in front of her. 'I'm not sure I can *ever* put myself through anything as big as yesterday, *ever* again.'

'You will.' Tara grinned. 'Now you've done it once, you'll be hungry for more. The usual little weddings will seem small fry after what we achieved here yesterday. Personally, I'm already gunning for the next big one. Because, after this, you know, there'll be a rush of big, posh weddings: the phone's already been ringing all week according to Liz in the office. We need a meeting next week to look at those. And, as far as I can see, we're going to have to take on more staff: Felicity's going to need another part-time assistant over in the wedding venue while you and I look after the rest of the hall.'

'It's all the clearing up afterwards.' Hannah glanced out of the café window where, once the last guests had been ferried away either by car or helicopter, the construction teams, electricians, marquee people, gangs of cleaners, gardeners, security and other workers had sprung into action, working throughout the night and into the morning to bring the hall back to its original state.

'Rosa?' Hannah half stood as she saw Rosa hovering by the entrance. 'We're over here. Come and have a coffee.'

Rosa walked across and sat down with the other two and Hannah took her hand. 'You OK, Rosie Posie?'

'I think so.' Rosa appeared not to want to talk in front of Tara and, as Eva joined them, Tara, getting the message, stood. 'Right, it's almost midday. I'm away to the wedding venue and kitchens to check on how the clearing up's going on over there. Greg's back in charge of the Agatha Christie refreshments this evening. I'll see where he's up to and leave you three to it.'

'I'm going to send Clementine the biggest bouquet of flowers known to woman,' Hannah said. 'As well as paying her a bonus once she sends in her bill for yesterday.'

'Good idea.' Eva nodded. 'Right, coffee and buns all round?' She waved at the four waitresses who were clearing tables after the café had served a steady stream of bacon, egg and sausage sandwiches to the workers still on site. 'When you've a minute, Jill? Three coffees and any cakes you have left?'

'You'll be lucky.' The waitress grinned. 'We've been descended on like a swarm of locusts all morning.'

'Great work all of you,' Hannah called. 'Many thanks.'

'So, Rosa,' Hannah and Eva turned back to their sister. 'What's happening with Carys?'

'She's hired a car and driven over to Wales to see her parents before she flies back. She wanted to take Chiara with her – she is their granddaughter after all – but Joe said no, particularly as Ted and Gwynneth are spending a month in Sydney with Chiara and Rhys when the new baby's born. So, you know, they'll be with Chiara then.' Rosa took a deep breath and a big gulp of the cappuccino that had arrived at her side. 'School finishes for the Easter holiday next Friday and Joe's sorting everything out for the pair of them to fly out to Sydney with Carys a few days after that.'

'Oh, Rosa, no.' Hannah and Eva took a hand each. 'I still think

Joe's absolutely mad letting her go with Carys,' Eva snapped crossly.

'I think the whole situation *has* turned Joe slightly insane,' Rosa sniffed, wiping a tear. 'He's in a bit of a state. And I'm *not* going to cry anymore,' she added, looking at the Eccles cake in front of her and attempting a bite, but replacing it, uneaten, on the plate. 'If you'd seen how ecstatic Chiara's been, now she's with her mum again, you just couldn't deny her the right to be with Carys. You know, she's always been a slightly timid, anxious little thing, always with a bit of an air of sadness about her. That's all gone now she's got her mum back, and knowing she'll soon be living with her big brother again as well.'

'But totally devastating for you and Joe.' Hannah stroked Rosa's hand.

'We've been discussing emigrating to Sydney ourselves.'

'Oh, Rosa, no.' Hannah and Eva stared.

'Well, if you go, *I'm* coming with you,' Hannah said stoutly.

'Oh yes? And take your precious Heatherly Hall with you, brick by brick?' Rosa managed a smile as she gazed out of the window at the hall's beautiful, mellow façade.

'Well, you're not going without *us*.' Eva shook her head. 'So, probably not a good time to ask, but what's happening with your, you know, your *frozen eggs*?' Eva lowered her voice not wanting the still-busy café to overhear.

'Oh, we've just *had* to put it all on hold. I rang the clinic and they said to stop all the hormone treatment for the time being and to start again once Joe's back and we're both in a better place. 'Not that I can ever imagine what that better place is.' Rosa looked at the pair of them. 'Anyway, stress is the last thing you need when you're going for IVF.' Rosa drained her coffee. 'It just wouldn't have worked if we'd gone ahead with creating the embryos and trying to implant them. The little things would have said: "Oh no, we don't want *this* miserable pair for parents" and… you know… they'd have…' Rosa was sobbing freely now '…they'd have gone back to… you know… to heaven…'

'Rosa, don't worry about helping out with tonight's Agatha Christie evening,' Hannah said, taking her hand once more. 'You need to rest.'

'No, I *don't*.' Rosa attempted a smile, wiping her eyes. 'I need something to take my mind off it all. 'I'll stay and help now for a couple of hours and then I'll pick Chiara up from school. Joe and I are going to bring her up this evening to watch the play and join in with the treasure hunt.'

'That's cheating.' Hannah smiled. 'You *know* where the eBay Jet Set's going to be hidden.'

'I don't actually,' Rosa said. 'We have as much chance as… Oh…' She broke off as Drew Livingston appeared at their table. 'Goodness, I thought you'd have left by now, Drew?' She looked round for Aditi and the entourage that normally accompanied the pair wherever they went.

'Hello, Rosa, Hannah…' Drew sat and turned to face Eva, holding her gaze for a lot longer than was probably necessary and Eva felt her pulse race, knew she was blushing. 'The thing is, we're not flying out to India until Sunday. There's a whole load more celebrations planned over there, apparently.' He sighed, looking round to order coffee. 'This whole wedding thing has been more tiring than a fifteen-day gig across the States. And seems there's things to come that I didn't even know about.' He smiled. 'I just hope there's more elephants – I seem to have acquired a bit of a thing for them.'

'Right.' Hannah pulled a face, uncertain how to answer.

'Dame Alice and I got on so well yesterday – thank you, she really was the guest of honour.'

'Not Jumbo then?' Hannah laughed.

'Him as well. Anyway, Alice and I are going to work together on a canvas up in your art retreat for the rest of the day. If that's OK with all of you?'

'If Alice has agreed to that, grab her while you can.' Eva smiled. 'She's not usually so, so... *accommodating*.'

'She's not *usually* got a very sexy gorgeous rock star as her pupil.' Rosa grinned and then, realising what she'd said, went slightly pink. 'So,' she went on hurriedly, 'what's Aditi going to be doing on this, her first day as a married woman? She doesn't mind you abandoning her?'

Drew smiled. 'Not at all. Says she wants to hike over those hills of yours.'

'Aditi does?' The other three stared. 'She'll need walking boots.'

'Apparently. Says she wants fresh air and solitude after all the stress of the wedding.'

'Right.' The girls exchanged glances.

'And then,' Drew went on, 'she told me to tell you she'd like to put in a guest appearance at some do you're putting on here this evening?'

'The Jet Set farce?' Hannah, Eva and Rosa exchanged even more looks of disbelief.

'It's a village thing.' Hannah frowned. 'You know a very local, amateurish am-dram to celebrate the centenary of one of Agatha Christie's novels. Everyone's getting dressed up.'

'Right.' Drew shrugged. 'I've no idea. She just came out with it over breakfast. Have to say, you three, we couldn't have asked for a better suite of rooms or breakfast. That chef of yours is something else. I think Aditi's planning to pinch him.'

'I do hope not, we've had our fill of GBH in the hall's kitchens.' Nerves at being so close to this man was making Eva talk gibberish, and she blushed once more.

Drew laughed. 'She's always had this thing about one day having a personal chef join her little entourage, to travel around with her and cook up her favourite dishes once she's off set.'

'Sorry,' Hannah said seriously. 'She can't have Greg. Greg's going *nowhere*.'

'So, we'll stay another night if that's OK with you, Hannah?

And then we'll be out of your hair and get down to London and the flat to pack more stuff before heading to Heathrow on Sunday?' Drew's eyes lit up as he stood to leave. 'But right now, I'm off for my lesson with Dame Alice.'

'Just watch her,' Rosa teased. 'She has a thing for younger men.'

'And me a newly married man?' Drew didn't smile and Eva caught him looking at her intently before he pushed back his chair and, with a wave, walked off.

# 32

*6pm*

Hannah found she was biting what was left of her nails once more. She'd assumed, once the whole planning and finale of the Livingston wedding was over, she'd be able to relax, have a day off, catch up with some much-needed sleep. But all she wanted was for Lachlan to reappear. She'd rung and messaged him so many times but, apart from one curt text telling her he was busy with the arrangements for his father's funeral, and he'd be back at some point, he appeared to not want to engage further with her.

Hadn't Ger said he'd planned to be back, not for the wedding, but in order to help out with the Jet Set evening? And yet, here they were, with just an hour to kick-off and there was no sign of him. What if he wasn't going to come back? What if he'd crashed his car on the way back south? What if he'd fallen in love with Bridget again, back in Balmoral? She knew all about Bridget from Balmoral! How could she bear it, when it was all her own stupid fault?

As usual.

She had managed to have a two-hour nap after lunch, catching up on the huge amount of sleep she'd recently missed, and had woken feeling slightly more optimistic about herself and her life. Anticipating Lachlan's return, she'd showered, washed her hair and was about to climb into the rather slinky red dress he'd bought her for Christmas, but now, wearing the dress, remembering it was Lachlan who'd bought it for her, she just felt something akin to despair at his not being here with her. She took a couple of deep breaths, knowing a glass of wine would help neutralise the panic, when she remembered. Hell, she should be in 1930s dress. Abandoning the little red number, she crossed the bedroom, rifling through the drawers until she found the silky black vintage dress she'd bought for a flappers' fancy dress do years ago. It smelt a bit musty, and she was probably going to be ten years out of date fashion-wise, but the intention was there. She pinned up her long dark hair, tied a black scarf round her forehead, added a bright red feather from a display of dried flowers and, after clipping on long black dangly earrings, went to check out her reflection in the mirror. Shoes? Heels? She couldn't bear the thought of another evening tottering around the place in heeled court shoes, and reached for her pair of big black Doc Martens. Once she was ready to mingle with the audience after the play, she'd nip back up to the apartment and swap them for the red heels that would go so well with the red feather; for the moment, she didn't care *what* she looked like, it would just have to do – it was only the locals, not London Fashion Week.

Hannah added red lipstick to match the rather jaunty feather and went to pour herself a glass of wine; just one would be fine and, realising the time, downed it quickly before making her way along the corridor and down the red-carpeted steps before descending the newly refurbished marble staircase to the Great Hall. Looking at her watch, she hurriedly went to find Daisy and the rest of the Westenbury Players who were in various stages of dress in one of the spacious storerooms off the Great Hall.

'Break a leg,' she shouted gaily as she closed the door behind her. 'Everyone ready? Do we all know our lines?'

'Darling, of course. We're professionals.' Vivienne Maddison, looking wonderfully glamorous as Winifred Astley, raised an eyebrow as well as the cigarette holder in her hand. 'And I think you've forgotten to change your footwear, darling.' Vivienne threw a pained expression in the direction of Hannah's Doc Martens.

'Oops, silly me,' Hannah chortled, otherwise ignoring the jibe. 'Well, *you're* all looking wonderful: very authentic, very Agatha Christie-ish.'

'We've had a visitor, Hannah.' Virginia, playing the part of Wallis Simpson, adjusted her own, rather strange-looking hat and preened before glancing down at Hannah's feet and adding, 'Do you really think those great boots of yours appropriate for Heatherly Hall management?'

'Oh?' Hannah asked, ignoring her sister's last comment.

'Well, Aditi and I became *such* pals yesterday – she said she really didn't know how she'd have got through the entire day without my assistance, particularly after I introduced her to the Marquess of Stratton and BJ – that she's just been down with some bottles of champagne and glasses for us all. How kind is that? She is *such* an artist, *such* an utter professional...' Virginia looked pointedly at Hannah's footwear once more. 'Now, Hannah,' she went on, appearing to consider for a moment, her head on one side like a little bird. 'Would there have been Bhangra dancing in 1936 do you think? We could have her on at half-time.'

'Half-time?' Hannah stared at her big sister. 'How long is this farce going on?'

'Well, after the play and before the treasure hunt, perhaps? Just before refreshments are served? I did rather get the impression Aditi would like to perform again the dance she did last night for our wedding guests.'

*Our* wedding guests? Hannah felt irritation mount. 'Virginia, why on earth would Aditi Sharma want to perform Bhangra again? For the locals? Don't be ridiculous.'

'Because, Hannah,' a lilting voice came from behind her, 'I am *so* full of joy and happiness after my wedding yesterday, I just want to carry on dancing. I would be honoured to give something back to you and Heatherly Hall, as well as to dear Ginny here, for being my right-hand woman yesterday.'

'I'm not convinced Indian dancing quite fits in with our theme of 1930s' Agatha Christie novels.' Turning towards the Bollywood star, as everyone else assembled in the storeroom had already done, Daisy now made her way over to Hannah, Virginia and Aditi.

'And you are?' Aditi turned gracefully on her embroidered satin pumps to face Daisy, a welcoming smile on her beautifully made-up face. She proffered a hennaed and jewelled hand in Daisy's direction.

'Erm, Daisy. Daisy Maddison. Village vet. And, tonight, Matthew, I'm going to be Lady Stratton's younger sister, Margaux Casterton.' The usually sanguine Daisy appeared uncharacteristically flustered in the presence of such Bollywood royalty and, catching Daisy's startled expression as well as the reference to Matthew Kelly, the game-show host, Hannah started to giggle.

'Matthew?' For a split second, Aditi narrowed her eyes and then she smiled graciously. 'I'm *sure* you must know, Daisy,' Aditi purred, 'that for the very first time ever, Agatha Christie Limited, which looks after the author's estate, has franchised her stories to an Indian filmmaker? He's planning a film based on a novel by your Queen of Crime.' Aditi placed a long manicured red nail to her lips. 'That's all I can tell you at the moment, but you can see the connection now?'

'Well, yes, thank you, Ms Sharma, if you say so.' Daisy almost curtsied in the star's direction.

'I really don't think...' Hannah started.

'Let the lass dance at half-time, if she wants to, Hannah.' Denis Butterworth, the verger, dressed as the Heatherly Hall butler, walked with his tray towards the others. 'It'd be grand.

A real treat, love. I've seen some of the stuff you do, on telly. It meks for a right good show.'

'That is *so* kind.' Aditi smiled, one seductive hand on Denis's black-tuxedoed arm.

'Fine, fine,' Hannah said, wanting to get the evening started and over with as soon as possible. 'I've no objection if the players themselves haven't?'

'We haven't,' they chorused as one, and Hannah realised they were already well stuck into the gifted champagne.

'The Great Hall's really filling up.' Eva, her dark hair rolled up in an authentic, late 1930s style, and dressed in a purple tea dress she'd hired from the local fancy dress agency, popped her head round the storeroom door. She frowned and then started to laugh as she took in Hannah's 1920s flapper dress atop her 2020s great black biker boots. 'Sartorially elegant, Hans,' Eva grinned and then said, 'Right, what can I do? Can I help anyone? I've left the girls out in the audience with Rosa and Joe. Mum and Dad are here too – Alice is sitting with them.'

Hannah moved over to the door to peer round it. 'Blimey, did they even know she was here?'

'Of course. But it's the first time they've seen her since the big reveal about Virginia. Mum and Alice are already at daggers drawn: Alice appears to have downed her fair share of gin and is chortling away, having a wonderful time getting at Mum about Virginia being Bill's biological daughter and not Dad's. Mum looks like she's sucked a lemon, says she feels a stroke coming on, and Dad's sitting between the pair of them trying to keep the peace... Oh...?' Eva turned as she saw Aditi pirouetting and coiling her beautifully graceful hands seductively towards Denis Butterworth whose eyes were out on stalks, his fat little tummy bouncing suggestively in response. 'What the hell's *she* doing here?' She started to laugh. 'Denis looks as if he's died and gone to heaven.'

'Ask Virginia,' Hannah snapped. 'Nothing to do with me. Right.' She turned back to the players who, with several glasses of fizz inside them, were tapping their feet along to the music Aditi was now moving to through the expensive Bluetooth speakers she'd brought along with her. 'It's time, everyone. Come on.'

'Hang on, where's Edward VIII?' Daisy asked, frowning as she looked round.

'Abdicated a long time ago, love.' Denis grinned, his hips gyrating against the rhythm of the beat.

'Right, our Denis, that's enough of that.' Sandra Butterworth shot a look in the verger's direction. 'If you've that much energy, there's plenty of weeds in the churchyard you can work it off on, in the morning.'

'Zac? Anyone?' Daisy continued to scan the room.

'He's not on until halfway through, Daisy,' Graham Maddison called, his eyes seemingly unable to leave Aditi's hypnotically gyrating bottom.

'He's here, somewhere,' Vivienne answered. 'I saw him earlier. He said he was off to the loo.'

'Nerves probably.' Sandra nodded knowingly. 'I could do with spending a penny again, myself.' She glanced hopefully at the door before whispering, 'Where's the nearest little girls' room? And you, Denis, you don't want to be caught short: you know what you're like with *your* little problem.' She glared at him as he continued to bop, a sheen of sweat on his pansticked face.

'Audience is getting a bit restless,' Eva warned, glancing at her watch before popping her head back round the door to survey the waiting assembled villagers. 'Full house out there. I think I'd better check Greg and his team are ready with the refreshments in, what…? Three-quarters of an hour or so?'

'But where's Zac?' Daisy was becoming anxious. 'Have *you* seen him, Hannah?' She turned, almost accusingly, in the other's direction. 'Have you *been with him* today?'

'*Been with him?*' Hannah scowled across at Daisy. 'What's that supposed to mean? What are you implying…?'

'Come on,' Vivienne, interrupted, taking charge. 'Zac's not on for a good thirty minutes or so. Let's get started.'

'I'll go and look for him,' Hannah snapped crossly, still glaring at Daisy. 'I'll tell him he needs to be down here, ready to go on in twenty minutes.' She set off through the stockroom door, quite taken aback by the size of the audience seated in the round on all four sides of the Great Hall. She stopped for a good minute, scanning those assembled to see if, by some miracle, Lachlan might be amongst them.

He wasn't.

She moved quickly and quietly towards the newly renovated marble staircase, glancing across and up towards the hall's showpiece chandelier hanging majestically from its mooring on the mezzanine floor at the very far end of the hall, well away from the audience below. She ascended the steep flight of marble, taking in the long corridor, scanning its length for any sign of Zac Anderson before turning and heading towards the red-carpeted stairs that led to her own apartment. She quickly turned the handle of her door, reassured that it was still locked, before running upwards once more to the art retreat. Locked also.

Where the hell was he?

The slightly tinny-sounding rendition of Christopher Gunning's 'Hercule Poirot: The Belgian Detective' that Daisy, Graham and Vivienne had chosen to introduce *The Jet Set of Heatherly Hall* production had now started to play, its jaunty yet haunting notes rising upwards through the three floors as she ran along the length of each vast and dimly lit carpeted corridor in search of Zac.

'Oh?' Hannah stopped suddenly as a figure, dressed in black and camouflaged in the dark, hove into view at the very far end of the mezzanine floor. Keeping to the shadows, Hannah inched her way forwards, glad she herself was wearing black.

Any idea that this was possibly Lachlan aping the iconic

Milk Tray Man, intent on leaving her a box of chocolates in forgiveness, was rudely demolished when the figure uttered a furious litany of, 'Fuck it! Fuck it! Fucking well fuck it...' reeling in the line on his fishing rod from his position above the newly cleaned and sparkling chandelier.

His *fishing rod*? Hannah mouthed a couple of choice expletives of her own, screwing up her eyes and straining to see as the black-balaclava-wearing figure released the line once more. A good five minutes passed, her heart pounding, the blood beating a rhythmic tattoo in her ears, but she didn't miss the triumphant hiss of 'Yessss!' as the figure slowly and methodically reached for the end of the reeled-in line.

'You beauty. You fucking little beauty.' The figure lifted the object to his lips, kissing it reverentially before carefully taking it from what appeared to be some sort of large metallic hook. He slipped it into an open bum bag around his waist, zipping it closed and pulling the black balaclava upwards and off his face and head, exhaling loudly as he did so.

'What the fuck do you think you're doing?' Without any further thought, Hannah raced down the length of the corridor towards Zac Anderson.

'Leave it, Hannah.' Zac was already starting his exit.

'Leave it? Leave what? What are you *doing*?' Hannah grabbed at the bum bag around Zac's waist. 'What are you taking from *my* hall? Something for your *research*?' She held on tightly, clawing at and managing to unzip the black bag, but the next moment a heavy black boot caught her in the ribs and she went down with an 'oof' of shock and pain as Zac turned to make his exit.

Some superhuman strength, born of utter fury, had Hannah reach out from the floor for his leg. He kicked out once more but she grabbed the fabric of his black trousers with both hands, using it to lever herself up slightly and, without thinking, sank her teeth into the bare flesh of his calf muscle as he fell to the floor beside her.

'You fucking bitch,' he snarled, bending towards her and, with an open hand, cracked her across the head before attempting to stand once more. But, as he did so, Hannah grabbed at the bag around his waist, hanging on with a strength and determination she knew she would never again, in all of her life, replicate.

She suddenly knew what was in the bag and this man wasn't having it.

Zac lost his footing slightly but quickly stood, dragging her along the floor as she held on to the bag around his waist, kicking out repeatedly with his booted foot at Hannah's head and face, but unable to make his getaway as she held on like some sort of maniacal limpet.

His balls. His testicles: Hannah knew she had to get him in the balls. Hadn't she sat through enough cases of feral kids when she was a youth worker to know that, when arrested by the police, they weren't averse to making a bid for freedom by kneeing officers in the genitals?

As Zac Anderson bent his knees once more in an attempt at prising Hannah's tenacious grasp from the bag, she launched, pulling back her right arm and, with a curled fist, slammed it into his testicles with all her might. He tottered back slightly and she saw her chance. She kicked out at his groin with her own Doc-Marten-booted foot and, as he bent over, gasping and retching in pain, she managed to get to her feet and finish the job with one final hard boot to his balls.

Her head spinning, her right eye already closing where Zac had landed a kick, she thrust a hand into the unzipped bag around his waist, grabbing at the heavy, diamond-studded Jet Set in its interior and, limping in pain, set off.

But Zac was as determined as she was.

She was back at the mezzanine floor, looking over and into the depths of the magnificent Heatherly Hall chandelier from which Zac Anderson had seemingly retrieved the long-lost Jet Set necklace. She leaned down, wheezing painfully, unable to draw any breath into her lungs, looking across at the model-sized

Westenbury Players and audience two floors below. Gathering the last remaining strength in her poor battered body, she fell to her knees, flinging the necklace with all her might towards the players and audience, just as Zac Anderson, seeing what she'd done, slammed a final kick into her ribs, before lurching off into the shadows.

## 33

'Mummy, what's that?' Eight-year-old Laila Malik turned away from Daisy who was playing Lady Stratton's sister and holding forth on the utter stupidity of the Marquess of Stratton commissioning a piece of jewellery for that quite dreadful Wallis Simpson.

'Mummy, I need a wee.' Four-year-old Nora, seeing her mother's attention was no longer on the play, shook Eva's arm none too gently, but Eva shushed her, turning to Rosa on her other side.

'Can you hear someone shouting?' Eva frowned.

'Part of the play.' Rosa nodded. 'Shh.'

'Yes, but what's that? Something's just landed over there?'

'All part of the play,' Rosa said again. 'It must be. It's good. Isn't it? Daisy's brilliant… Oh look, there's Zac now… I thought he was supposed to be Edward VIII…? He's not dressed very much like…'

'What the hell's he doing?' All eyes were now turned away from the actors on the stage in the round, to the figure dressed in black, hunched and limping towards the back of the hall.

'Looks more like Richard III than Edward VIII.' Joe Rosavina was laughing. 'I didn't realise this thing was a comedy.'

'Joe, shush,' Eva ordered, rising from her seat slightly. 'Listen…'

Daisy, Vivienne and Graham Maddison, realising something was going on that hadn't been rehearsed, came to a standstill, turning and looking over the heads of the audience to where Zac was now feverishly on his hands and knees while Sandra Butterworth (dressed in a too-short black maid's outfit that didn't quite disguise her overly large behind) carried on determinedly and somewhat woodenly with her lines: 'Your coffee, m'lady. Shall I pour it here or would you prefer it in the drawing room?'

And then a loud: 'No... No... don't let him get it...' interrupted the silence as a disembodied voice drifted downwards from somewhere above. 'No...' followed by several moans and then sobs.

'Mummy, I'm frightened.'

Nora took hold of her big sister's hand who patted it sagely, whispering, 'I think it's a bit like a Shakespeare play, Nora. I think there must be a ghost up there. Mrs Beaumont, my teacher, told us all about *Macbeth*.'

'Don't like ghosts, Mummy. I want to go home. Want to see Daddy.'

'They're only acting.' Laila smiled condescendingly. 'You're too little to understand.'

'Where's Hannah...?' Eva was standing now, looking upwards and across to the mezzanine floor at the far end of the hall. 'That's Hannah, I know it is... What's *she* doing...?'

All heads turned now to Eva who was out of her seat and running towards the back of the hall, some of the audience standing to see what was happening as the ghostly voice from above continued to moan, Nora now joining in, screaming loudly: 'Mummy, Mummy, it's the ghost... don't...'

Eva belted towards Aditi Sharma amidst loud whispers and exclamations from the audience, which was now on its collective feet, gawping in excitement as the famous star dropped to her knees, joining the man dressed all in black on the floor.

'Isn't that Aditi Sharma...?'

'It's that Bollywood star...'

'She got married here yesterday, you know...'

'Why's she still here?'

'I hope Drew Livingston's still here... always had a thing about *him*...'

Eva came to a standstill, uncertain what to do next but, as moans continued to drift down from above, she turned back to the seat in the audience she'd just vacated, yelling furiously: 'Joe, Dad, get upstairs to the mezzanine corridor. Hannah's up there – I can hear her.'

'Get back,' Aditi Sharma snarled as Eva turned towards the pair on the floor once more. 'Just get back.'

And then, out of the corner of her eye, Eva saw it: a black looped string with a huge sparkling centre – the famous diamond only slightly dimmed from its almost one hundred years of captivity in the Heatherly Hall chandelier – caught neatly on the bracket of one of the Italian-inspired brass wall sconces that had illuminated the back of the Great Hall since the installation of electric lighting at the turn of the previous century.

Aditi Sharma's feverish gaze shifted from the dusty floor and, following Eva's almost hypnotic stare at the light fitting, the star jumped to her feet, gracefully pirouetting in Eva's direction before launching herself unsuccessfully at the Jet Set dangling above her.

'What on earth are you *doing*, Aditi?' Drew Livingston, who had just made his way from the presidential suite where he'd been catching up on some much-needed sleep, strode through the mesmerised audience to his new wife.

With a regal gesture of a graceful hennaed hand, Aditi pointed upwards to the out-of-reach necklace above her head before turning to the captive audience and proclaiming, in a pronounced theatrical voice: 'On behalf of the Indian Government, I claim ownership of the Sah-I-Noor diamond, stolen – yes *stolen* – from its rightful owners in Andhra Pradesh in India by George Astley, ninth Marquess of Stratton. We will, of course, make sure it is returned to where it belongs when my husband and I travel to India in the next few days...'

'That's a right tale an' 'alf if ever I heard one.' Sandra Butterworth, adjusting her white lacy maid's cap (she reminded Eva of someone she'd once seen in the Readers' Wives section of a men's mag) snorted disparagingly across at Aditi. 'And what about *him*...' Sandra pointed an accusatory finger in the direction of Zac Anderson '...where does *he* fit into your little plan, Lady?'

'I *beg* your pardon?' Aditi wheeled round to face the verger's wife, her eyes narrowed.

'I've *seen* you: seen the pair of you. Up to no good. Thought you were safe having a bit of rumpy-pumpy in the church graveyard across from the pub, didn't you? To be honest, love, I thought it were Kadira from The Balti House in the village. You know, getting her own back on that husband of hers who's always at it with anyone he can get his hands on. And, like a good Christian, I were only too happy to turn the other cheek; let Kadira have a bit of happiness. It were only when I saw you tonight in that back room, intent on seducing our Denis with your dancing and your... your flaunting yourself at him, it were only then I recognised you, and realised who you were.'

'Don't listen to her, Drew.' Aditi turned and put a hand on Drew's arm. 'She's a bigoted, racist, nosy old village woman who has mistaken me for someone else. Trying to make trouble because of my heritage – and because I was dancing with her husband, and she didn't like it.'

'That diamond belongs to *me*.' Zac Anderson managed to pick himself up from the floor, wincing, and holding on to his groin area whilst doing so, testament to the kicks Hannah had managed to bestow just ten minutes earlier.

'You?' Eva laughed scornfully in his direction and the audience turned as one.

'Me. I have a right to it. Treasure trove. I found it.'

'Aye lad, and *I* now know exactly how *you* knew where it

was all along.' The audience, the actors centre stage and those acting out their own little drama underneath the chandelier, turned, craning necks to see who was speaking now. 'I've been doing my own bit of *research* after you tried to pump me for information down at The Jolly Sailor.' Roy Newsome pointed a finger. 'I know exactly who *you* are, son, and why you think you've a right to that diamond hanging up there.'

'I've had enough of this. Come *on*, Diti.' Zac Anderson snarled his response and, with a final spurt of superhuman strength, obviously fuelled by fury and desperation, he made a sudden dash and jumped for the Jet Set necklace, lifting it cleanly from its mooring on the wall light fitting before grabbing hold of Aditi Sharma's arm and manhandling her towards a side door.

'But what about *me*?' A plaintive wail, this time from the small huddle of remaining actors waiting to go on stage, rent the air and the audience turned yet again. 'You said you loved *me*, Zachary, and that we were going to be together...' A white-faced Virginia ran towards Zac and Aditi, attempting to grab at any part of Zac's anatomy or clothing that would prevent him leaving without her. 'My case is packed. I've got my passport like you said. Like we planned.'

'Virginia...' Eva put out a hand to arrest her big sister in her mission to get to Zac. 'Leave it. *Please*, Virginia. Stop it, now. *This minute.*'

Zac attempted to shake Virginia from his arm, pushing at her furiously until she tottered on her heels and fell to one side, catching and pulling at Zac's black hoodie as she did so, making him stumble slightly himself.

And then Zac and Aditi Sharma were off, racing across the floor of the Great Hall towards the exit as the audience and actors stood, apparently frozen to the spot, unable to stop them. Just as he and Aditi managed to open and get through the door, a large, auburn-haired man in an outdoor coat pushed through from the other side, launching himself at Zac Anderson, rugby-tackling the American to the floor, reaching for and seizing the

Jet Set necklace held in the other's hand, before Zac took off and disappeared, Aditi racing after him.

'Lachlan!' Eva shouted in relief. 'You took your bloody time!'

An elderly woman sniffed somewhat disparagingly in the direction of her husband as they joined the rest of the stunned villagers trooping out of the Great Hall, and into the chilly March night.

'It *started* alright,' she opined. 'I mean, I was quite enjoying it all. But then it all went a bit, you know, *modern*, what with Sandra Butterworth's lines about rumpy pumpy in the graveyard. Not very respectful to the Royal family, was it, Barry? You know, having Edward VIII dressed in a black hoodie and jeans and limping about in a graveyard? The queen, God bless her, wouldn't have been at all impressed if she was still here. Mind you, I blame Covid and Brexit. It's Paddington Bear and marmalade sandwiches one minute, Bollywood actresses the next. And why *did* that Aditi woman suddenly get in on the act? They didn't have Bollywood back in 1936, did they?' The woman shook her head. 'I got a bit lost after that.'

'Oh, I thought it was very good, Kath.' Barry nodded sagely as he pulled on his cap. 'Very *avant-garde*. Mind you, I could do with a pint now. Got any money on you?'

# 34

*Two days after the wedding, 9am*

'Where's Lachlan?' Hannah, groggy from just a few hours' sleep and a surfeit of painkillers, attempted to sit up, wincing as she tried to look round, hoping against hope that he'd be there, waiting for her to wake up.

He wasn't.

'Eva? Where is he?'

'Lie back down, Hannah,' Eva scolded. 'You have to stay put in that bed.'

'But have you seen him?' Hannah almost pleaded. 'What happened to him once I was carted off to A and E?'

'I don't know where he is, Hannah,' Eva soothed. 'Ger will probably know. Once he'd managed to grab the necklace out of Zac's hand, Zac was so wild he kicked out at Lachlan like he had done with you and then, when Jude Mansell and Graham Maddison came racing down through the audience to help Lachlan, Zac ran off, pulling Aditi with him before, apparently, both of them driving off at speed. The police are coming round later to talk to you. You'll be able to have him for GBH.'

'And attempted theft?'

'Don't know about that. Zac was going on about treasure trove. You know, finders keepers sort of thing.'

'And where's the necklace now?'

'In the safe. I don't know if the police will want to take it.'

'Why would they?'

'Well, we don't really know *who* the damned thing belongs to.'

'Heatherly Hall, obviously.'

'Not *really* as obvious as that, Hannah.' Eva's eyes widened. 'And, presumably, the matching Jet Set earrings are still in the chandelier. We need to think of a way of getting those out before every jewel thief from here to wherever tries to get their hands on them.'

'So has Zac kidnapped Aditi then? You know, taken her with him as a sort of hostage?'

They both looked up as Rosa brought in a tray of coffee. 'From what *I* saw, Hannah, Aditi was more than willing to go off with him. No coercion there whatsoever. She's been having an affair with Zac, according to Sandra Butterworth.'

'What?' Hannah stared at Rosa through her one good eye. 'She was marrying Drew, but having a thing with Zac too? Hell, that was quick work on Zac's part. He was trying to get *me* into bed...'

'Yes, and you were going along with that, Hannah. Don't play the innocent...'

'Alright, alright, Eva. Don't go on at me, I've got a raging headache.'

'But, Hannah, you need to know...'

'What? What? Is it about Lachlan?'

'Virginia.'

'What about Virginia? What's she done now?'

'Virginia was about to run off with him!'

'With Lachlan?' Beneath the black, ochre and purple bruised skin, Hannah went pale.

'No, you daft thing.' Eva began to laugh. 'With Zac. With *Zac!* Can you imagine? Apparently, she'd a bag packed and her passport ready to leave with him after the play. Tara and I had to cope with a totally hysterical *Ginny* after Zac ran off. Alice loved every single minute of it! Lapped it all up, chortling like a drain. Unfortunately, local gossip being what it is, Timothy'll get to hear of his wife's own personal little drama being acted out in front of half the village. Poor old Barty and Bethany will be teased to hell and back at school.'

'Where *is* Alice?' Hannah asked. 'Has *she* seen Lachlan?'

'She got that new young waiter, Dylan, from Tea and Cake to drive her to the airport early this morning. She's hosting some exhibition in Paris this evening.'

'She didn't say goodbye.' Hannah frowned.

'Have you *ever* known Alice say: "Thank you and goodbye"? She flits like a butterfly to the next social occasion without a single thought for the one she's leaving.'

Hannah lay back on her pillows trying to take it all in. 'So, Zac and Aditi? I don't get it. Were they *both* after the Jet Set then? Aditi, because she wants it returned to its rightful owners in India, and Zac because he's a sort of bounty hunter? Did they meet here, have a fling and decide to combine their efforts to find it into one?'

'I reckon the only place Aditi wanted the Jet Set ending up was her own pocket.' Eva raised an eyebrow. '*I* don't get it. As the number-one female Bollywood actor, she must be absolutely loaded. Why get involved with trying to nick a piece of jewellery—?' She broke off as a knock came at the outer door to the apartment and Hannah attempted to sit up once again, looking round hopefully. 'Is that Lachlan?'

It wasn't.

'Hello, you three, may I come in?' Drew Livingston's head appeared around the door of the apartment.

'Come in, Drew. We're all in the bedroom.' Rosa half stood, but Drew had already made his way over while Hannah, disappointed at the newcomer not being Lachlan, was now remonstrating with Eva that she was absolutely fine and needed to get up; she had work to do.

'No, you don't, Hans.' Rosa pushed her sister none too

gently back onto the mound of starched pillows. 'For a start, it's Saturday...'

'What's that got to do with anything? More visitors at the weekend on a Saturday. More help needed all over the place. Hello, Drew.' Hannah slid back down under the covers. 'I didn't realise you were still here.'

'Well, I was on the point of checking out, but you know...?' He trailed off, his face drawn, a two-day stubble managing to make the rocker look more sexy than simply tired and unkempt. But he also appeared terribly unsure, lost even, as well he might.

'I'm so, so sorry about Aditi,' Rosa said, standing up and walking over to Drew. She hugged him, unable not to. 'You must be feeling absolutely *dreadful?* Is there anything we can do? Come and sit down, Drew. I'll make you some coffee.'

'Well, not what I expected anyway: you know, married for all of one day and now heading for the divorce courts.' Drew gave a somewhat hollow bark of laughter, but remained standing, apparently at a loss as to what to do or say next.

'Had you no idea what was going on?' Hannah sat up once more, wishing she'd at least got some lippy to hand.

'Nope.' Drew sighed. 'Although certain things are beginning to make sense now. I guess I was just too busy with work to see what she was up to. But, never mind about me. How are *you* feeling, Hannah? That's one hell of a black eye.'

'I'm fine...'

'No, you are *not* fine,' Eva snapped. 'Two cracked ribs, your entire stomach and legs covered in bruises where the bastard kicked you, cuts and swelling to your hands and that dreadful closed-up black eye. Don't even think of getting out of bed,' she warned as Hannah poked a tentative leg from the duvet. 'Rosa and I have made the decision to close the hall over the weekend.'

'What?' Hannah made another attempt to get out of bed. 'No, you can't do that.'

'Too late, managerial decision,' Eva said firmly. 'And, it's time for more painkillers.' Eva concentrated her gaze on Hannah rather than meeting Drew's eye, afraid to give too much away as to how she was feeling about this man.

'So,' Rosa went on, 'you say things are beginning to make sense, Drew? In what way?'

'Well, to be fair, our relationship was probably never a match made in heaven. We'd only been together two months or so before Aditi proposed.'

'*She* proposed?'

Eva and Rosa both stared, but Hannah said, 'And why not? Good for her.'

'I was flattered – I mean you don't get more gorgeous than Aditi Sharma – and she caught me at a time in my life when I was beginning to despair of ever finding... you know...' Drew appeared embarrassed '...that *special* one we all hope we'll end up with. Anyway, I'm the first to admit, I've had my share of women, carousing and drink; you know, *the lot* and, despite all that – or maybe, who knows, *because* of that – I reckoned I'd missed the boat in the romance stakes. After twenty years or so of constant travelling, of performing all over the world, of the... you know...'

'Sex and drugs and rock and roll?' Rosa patted his hand. 'Which can all get a bit too much eventually?'

Drew laughed. 'And you'd know about that, would you, Reverend?'

'Well.' Rosa smiled. 'To some degree.'

'Don't tell me.' Drew laughed even more. 'You were in The Communards along with Reverend Richard Coles?'

'My sister, Rosa,' Hannah started proudly, but wincing as she turned in Drew's direction, 'started and ran a major financial company in London. You may have heard of Rosa Quinn Investments?'

Drew stared, eyeing Rosa up and down. 'I have actually. I think my financial advisers worked with your team at one point?'

'Possibly.' Rosa smiled.

'And the drugs?'

'I was addicted to uppers,' Rosa said. 'Needed them to keep on top of all I had to do. Not a world I ever want to go back to.' She shivered slightly at the very thought.

'Really?' Drew stared across at Rosa, nodding empathetically. 'So, you understand what I was searching for then? A cottage in the country, maybe near the sea, away from the rat race I'd made for myself? I wanted to be in love, Rosa, wanted to find someone who would love me for myself, for *me* – Andrew Livingston from humble beginnings in Northallerton – not Drew Livingston, the rocker I'd created and become, with all the wealth and trappings that go with being that person.'

'So, why not some ordinary girl from up north, then?' Eva blushed as she said the words. 'How come you ended up with Aditi who most certainly didn't fit the profile you were after?'

'I fell in love, I suppose. Or was it the idea of being *in love* I was after? I soon realised it wasn't really what I wanted. Probably knew this was a very bad move, a totally wrong decision.'

'So, why didn't you break it off?' Eva asked almost crossly.

'Have you never been in a situation where you're on a roundabout and can't get off? Someone keeps pushing it round and round and, even though you're feeling sick, you stick with it because you don't know what else to do? You're incapable of jumping off, and it's probably just easier to stay on board?' Drew raised an eye in Eva's direction. 'Never gone down one road when you know, in your heart, it's not where you should be heading?'

'Going to dental school, I guess?' Eva frowned. 'When I should have followed my heart and gone to art school instead.'

'Yes, but you were only eighteen at the time, Eva,' Hannah interrupted. 'Easily swayed by Mum and Dad. Drew here should have known better at his age, hooking up with a Bollywood star who'd set her cap at him for whatever reason.'

'Hannah!' Rosa and Eva turned and glared in Hannah's direction.

'Well, that's rich coming from you,' Eva snapped. 'You've suddenly become Heatherly Hall's resident agony aunt?'

'Actually,' Hannah said thoughtfully, her one good eye gleaming, 'I think that would be a jolly good idea. You know, we could...'

'Enough already.' Eva shook her head crossly, pushing Hannah back onto the pillows.

'Hannah's right.' Drew smiled. 'I should have got out when I realised it wasn't right. Particularly when I was given the opportunity to do just that when the Scottish castle wedding place fell through.'

'Right.' Eva appeared slightly flustered. 'You do know, it didn't "fall through" as such?' Eva air-quoted the words.

'Oh?' Drew's eyes narrowed.

'So, when your wedding arrangements at Falkness Castle, with just seven or eight weeks to go, suddenly *fell through*, Aditi told you – and us – that the castle had reneged on the deal to have James McDonald Ballantine at the reception to sketch the guests, and that's why she'd fallen out with them?'

'That's right.'

'Not true. I've been trying to get to the bottom of what was going on with Aditi; what she was up to. I rang Scotland and asked, just this morning. Ballantine was booked and raring to go apparently.'

'He was?'

'Aditi needed to give you a reason for throwing in the towel with Falkness Castle in order to bring the wedding here to Heatherly Hall.' Eva paused, trying to gauge Drew's reaction. 'Anyway, once the whole furore was over last night, and Mum and Dad had driven Hannah up to A and E, and Joe had taken the girls for a sleepover down at the vicarage, Rosa and I had a long chat with Roy Newsome.'

'Who?' Drew frowned.

'Local bloke. Lived in the village all his life. He's the one who really got us started on finding out more about the whole Jet Set mystery…' Eva trailed off as her phone rang.

'Oh, just talking about the man.' She smiled. 'He's here now? Will you bring him up, Molly?' She turned to the others. 'I asked Roy last night if he'd come back this morning for a chat. When you, Hannah, would hopefully be back from the hospital. He's on his way up from reception now.'

'I'll leave you,' Drew said, standing.

'No, really, Drew. You're more than welcome to stay.' Eva knew she didn't want Drew Livingston to leave. Wanted to hold on to him for just that bit longer, before he disappeared from their lives for ever. 'I think Roy's about to shed a bit more light on what's been going on. Have you got any goodies, Hannah, or shall I send down to Tea and Cake?'

'I *did* know quite a bit more than I was letting on,' Roy Newsome admitted, once he was sitting, mug of strong tea and a chocolate muffin to hand. 'You know, when you three girls came for that chat in The Jolly Sailor back in January? I'd been sworn to secrecy years back, by my dad, Frank, about what he knew. I realise it sounds bloody dramatic, but he told me all about it when he didn't have long to live. He was a man of integrity, was my dad, and once I'd promised, that was it. I like to think some of his ethical honesty was passed down to me. But now, with what happened last night, I think it's about time to have the truth out in the open.'

'You told us there was a young girl, Jeanie, who worked here in the kitchens?' Eva said, encouragingly. 'You thought she might have had something to do with the Jet Set going missing?'

'Aye, I did tell you that. Probably told you girls too much at the time.'

'Well, you didn't really, Roy.' Rosa smiled across at him. 'You actually clammed up once we started talking about Jeanie.'

'You're right, I did. Didn't think it fair to give the lass a bad name, even though it was nearly a hundred years ago.'

'So, what happened?' Drew was as fascinated as Rosa, Hannah and Eva.

'Well, according to my dad, he'd been to the pictures down in the village with Jeanie. He was courting her, although I don't know how serious he was about her. Apparently, he told Jeanie funds were needed for the cause...'

'The cause?' Drew interrupted.

'Aye, my dad had not only been down to London, demonstrating against Oswald Mosley's Fascist lot... the Battle of Cable Street it was called...'

Drew nodded. 'Learned about that in A-level History.'

'...but a week later he walked some of the way with the Jarrow Marchers when they passed through Barnsley. My dad told me he was so fired up after getting involved with both demonstrations, that he'd totally taken on board what Harry Pollitt, General Secretary of the CPGB was urging all its members to do.'

'Which was?' The three girls and Drew leaned forwards.

'To *find a way, by whatever means*, of showing solidarity with their marching comrades as the Jarrow lot continued on with their journey to London.' Roy raised an eyebrow. 'That daft lass, Jeanie, took my dad literally.'

'She took the Jet Set? Goodness.' Rosa brought both hands to her face. 'Poor girl. Poor impulsive girl.'

'So, according to my dad, he'd no real idea *how* she did it. I've never understood why the jewels weren't under lock and key.'

'In a safe even? Surely?' Hannah put in, her one good eye opened wide.

'We'll probably never know how she got hold of them. But, according to my dad, she'd run like the clappers from the hall with the jewels in her boots.'

'Her boots? That must have been bloody painful, seeing the size of that diamond last night.' Eva stared at Roy.

'So, Jeanie ran down to his house at the end of Scar

Terrace – he still lived there with my grandma and grandad. She was in a right state, he said. He came out to her in the garden and she told him what she'd done. Done it for him and the cause. For the revolution. The daft lass. Anyhow, my dad said he was so shocked, so terrified, he couldn't think straight. And then, he took her by the arm and dragged her back across the fields and through the woods and back up to the hall. Told her if she was found out, she'd spend the rest of her life in prison. At the end of the day, she'd stolen jewels intended for the King of England.'

'Blimey.' Roy's narrative had shocked the girls almost into silence. 'Off with her head, if it had been Henry VIII's jewels, anyway?' Hannah pulled a scary face.

'Possibly.' Roy smiled and nodded. 'So, my dad waited for her in the pitch-black, lying down in the long grass in the surrounding fields as she let herself back into the hall. She was going to say she'd left her hat or something, if anyone asked her what she was doing back there; tell them it was her sister Maggie's hat if anyone asked, and her sister wanted to go out in it. Some such tale or other they concocted between them on the way up.'

'And?' The others leaned forwards once more.

'How the hell did it end up in the chandelier?'

'You'll have to ask that American. He knew it were there.'

'Zac? But how could *he* know?' Hannah shook her head.

'When he booked himself into The Jolly Sailor and started chatting to me, he knew about me.' Roy grinned. 'He knew about me, alright. Didn't trust him as far as I could throw him.'

'Oh?'

'Pretended he didn't, of course. But he somehow knew Frank was my dad and, when I questioned him, he said someone had told him about my dad being at the Battle of Cable Street. Said he was researching people who'd actually been there for a book he was writing.'

'Well, that *is* true, Roy,' Hannah said. 'He *is* an historical researcher. He's a professor from Maine University, over here on sabbatical, researching the history of British historic houses.'

'No, he's not.' All eyes swivelled to Eva. 'Couldn't sleep last night, worrying about you, Hans, and what had gone on. Once we got you into bed, I tried to bunk down on the sofa. I managed a couple of hours, but then I did some googling. No Professor Zachary Anderson at Maine University. I went through everything, including lists of academic and research staff. If Maine wasn't five hours behind us, and it hadn't been a Friday evening, I'd have been ringing the university. And I *will* do that on Monday.'

'Roy,' Rosa now asked, 'you shouted across at him last night. Said you knew what he was doing here? What he was up to?'

'Aye, I did. So, your Professor Zac Anderson from Maine is, I'd almost guarantee, Jason Harrison, whose family were originally from round here.'

'How on earth do you know that?'

Roy laughed. 'I know it's probably hard to imagine now, but I was Detective Inspector Newsome down in Midhope in my day. It was my job to find out what people were up to. Of course, it's a hell of a lot easier these days, what with computers and the like, but I try to keep my hand in…'

'But…'

'And, for my sins,' Roy went on, now in full flow, 'I'm chair of the Midhope Family History Society. Keeps my detective skills honed trying to find people's long-lost ancestry and working out family trees. Fascinating stuff. Anyhow, it wasn't too difficult to find out what had happened to Maggie Haigh all those years ago.'

'Maggie?' Eva shook her head, puzzled. 'I thought she was called Jeanie?'

'Jeanie was the daft lass who worked at the hall, who,

according to my dad, stole the Jet Set, but I reckon one other person knew about it and she knew *exactly* what Jeanie had actually done with the jewels after my dad made her go back and put them back the best way she could.'

'Hang on, Roy,' Hannah said. 'I'm getting a bit lost here.'

'Sorry, I'm jumping ahead of meself now.' Roy took a big bite from his muffin, chewing methodically while the others silently urged him on. 'So, as I said, my dad ran back up with her to the hall. She was in one hell of a state, absolutely beside herself with terror. He saw her slip round the kitchen door and disappear.' Roy paused for a good few seconds. 'And he *never* saw her again after that.'

'What? *Never?*' All four, hanging on to Roy's narrative, spoke as one.

'No.' Roy shook his head. 'My dad waited and waited and waited. Waited until almost ten o'clock. He saw the family and servants coming and going, the family starting to return in the cars, but Jeanie never reappeared.'

'What happened to her? Had they caught her trying to put the Jet Set back?' Rosa's eyes were out on stalks.

Roy shook his head. 'My dad – and he could only surmise what actually happened – thinks Jeanie must have been in such a state of utter panic that she came back out of the hall through a different door. Maybe she couldn't go through the kitchen; maybe there was someone there? He reckons that while he was lying down in the wet grass, waiting for her, she missed him, thought he'd left her to fend for herself, and ran back down to her house alone. Anyroad, the next thing he knew was when the whole village woke up to the news: Jeanie Haigh had been found dead on the railway line, taken out by the Manchester to Leeds Express at six o'clock the next morning.'

'Oh, the poor, poor girl. Had she jumped under it?' Rosa was almost in tears.

'Possibly. As I say, my dad said she was in such a state, *anything* could have happened. He reckons that, given where she was killed, she was taking a short cut across the tracks towards his house on Scar Terrace. Desperate to see him, probably, before she went back up to the hall, terrified, to work. Remember, this was the morning of the king and Mrs Simpson's visit to Heatherly Hall. She'd have had to be there early for kitchen duty and, she knew, once they discovered the Jet Set had gone, the whole of Heatherly Hall would be in uproar, the place swarming with police.'

'But your dad didn't really know what happened to her?'

'No, not really, only because of what then happened at the funeral. Maggie Haigh, absolutely heartbroken as you can imagine at the tragic death of her little sister, totally launched at my dad after the burial.' Roy nodded his head towards Rosa. 'Got him to one side in the churchyard – aye, Jeanie's down in your churchyard, Rosa – and accused him of killing Jeanie. Said if it hadn't been for my dad with his bloody Russian Revolutionary ideas, Jeanie would never *ever* have taken the Jet Set. Maggie and Jeanie shared a bedroom, apparently, and Dad reckoned Jeanie must have told Maggie *exactly* what she'd done with the Jet Set to get them off her hands – to get rid of them when she was unable to put them back where she'd taken them from. We *now* know, after last night, she must have dropped them into the chandelier. Maggie told my dad she was going to the police; she'd tell them it was all my dad's fault, that it was him who'd put her up to it.'

'And did she?' Drew was still as riveted as the others. 'Go to the police?'

Roy shook his head. 'That would have implicated her sister. Can you imagine the utter shame Jeanie's family would have had to bear? Not only round here, but splashed over every national newspaper? That their daughter had stolen Wallis Simpson's jewels? Not long after that, apparently, Maggie left Westenbury: went into service in Manchester, Dad said. And, as far as he knew, after becoming a WAAF during the war, met up with some GI, married him and went to live in Canada.'

'But how on earth did *Zac Anderson* know they were in the chandelier?' Hannah asked.

'Because,' Roy replied in some triumph, 'Jason Harrison – aka Zac Anderson – is the grandson of Maggie Haigh, originally from Westenbury, and hence the great-nephew of poor old Jeanie Haigh.'

# 35

Promising Hannah she'd find and send Lachlan up to the apartment, Eva made to accompany Roy Newsome back down to reception.

'I'll come down with you as well.' Drew attempted a smile. 'I could do with stretching my legs before I drive back to London.'

The three of them walked down in silence to reception where Roy signed himself out and, Molly, one of the receptionists, accompanied him back to the main gates and his car.

'Seems strange, no visitors here today,' Eva said. 'Saturdays are normally so busy, but we made the decision, after all that's happened, to remain closed all weekend. I guess the press will be down in droves soon. Security have been told not to answer any questions, as well as not let anyone in.'

'Will you walk with me, Eva?' Drew asked. 'I'd like to be down by the lakeside once more. The hours I spent down there with Paddy and Jumbo were so... so *good*.'

Eva smiled at that. 'How are you feeling?'

'Tired, emotionally shattered, utterly embarrassed.'

'Embarrassed?' Eva glanced across at him as they walked.

'To have been taken in by a beautiful face. To have been marrying someone I really didn't know that well. She didn't love me, Eva. She loved what I have. What she thought she'd gain materially – monetarily – by becoming my wife.'

'But why? A woman as successful as Aditi must have her own fortune?'

'All gone.'

'Sorry?' Eva stopped and stared.

'This morning, for whatever reason, Vikram chose to tell me the truth.'

'Aditi's PA? I thought he'd have left? Gone with Aditi?' Eva frowned. 'And the truth?'

'Apparently, Aditi owes a fortune. She's *earned* a fortune over the last few years and, apparently, lost it again. Fancy cars, private jets, apartment on Central Avenue; top five-star hotels wherever she went; Hermès handbags: you name it, she's bought it. And, at the same time, acquired a nice little addiction to gambling.'

'Gambling?' Eva stopped once more. 'Are you sure?'

'Casinos are Aditi's go-to pleasure. It's where I met her – *Resorts World Casino* in New York. I was there for a bit of fun; she was there to feed her addiction.'

'Are you sure about all this?' Eva said again.

'Vikram's so fed up with her – apparently, he's not been paid for months – he's singing like a canary. Wouldn't put it past him to be already talking to the Sunday tabloids.'

'I can't believe this.'

'Eva, gambling isn't just the prerogative of down-and-out men throwing the last of their giro at the bookies, or stressed mums hoping the lottery ticket they've just bought will be enough to take them off to a better life.'

'But why would a beautiful, talented woman like Aditi throw all her money away like that?'

'Why does an alcoholic continue to drink even though they know it's killing them? Why does a heroin addict do anything for one last hit? Why did I continue to snort coke when…'

'You were addicted to drugs?'

'I *was*. I'm totally clean now and have been for many years. I was able to recognise Aditi's love of the roulette tables, but had absolutely no idea the extent of her addiction. I should have done. Totally proves I didn't know her. You know, that I was marrying a dream?' Drew paused. 'Vikram seemed to think Aditi knew this Zac Anderson bloke as well.'

'Well, I think *that's* yesterday's news,' Eva tutted. 'She was obviously seduced by him, like both my sisters and probably half the staff here at the hall were as well.'

'No, no.' Drew shook his head. 'I don't mean she got to know him here at the hall. Vikram, once he saw them together last night, knew he'd seen him somewhere before. Six months or so ago.'

'Oh? You reckon Aditi knew Zac Anderson before she planned to have the wedding here?'

Drew nodded. 'He's an actor apparently – albeit a two-bit one – and always hustling for parts.'

'A *professional* actor?' Eva stared. 'As opposed to Daisy – and obviously Virginia – roping him in to play Edward VIII for the Westenbury Players?' Eva gave a bark of laughter. 'No wonder Virginia kept banging on about Zac being "such an utter professional".'

Drew gave a wry smile. 'The United States is one of the biggest markets of Indian movies outside India. Some of the top Hindi movie stars have created a mass following in America. Aditi loved it over there – hence the apartment on Central Park Avenue. Anyway, according to Vikram, he knew he'd seen Aditi and Zac together in the States, long before Zac turned up here at the hall.'

'Right. They planned all this then?'

'Aditi would have known about the Sah-I-Noor diamond, as do the majority of Indians. It's a bit like, I guess, the Greeks knowing about the Elgin Marbles.'

'So, you think Aditi was trying to return the Sah-I-Noor

to the Indian Government? You know, like she said to the audience?'

Drew laughed mirthlessly. 'I don't think for one minute there was any altruism in Aditi's plan to recover the diamonds. No, I think Aditi was probably having an affair with Zac. That's perhaps how it started. And then, together they hatched a plan to return the diamonds to their own pockets, not the Indian Government's. Zac must have been told by his grandmother, Maggie, before she died years ago, just where Jeanie had thrown the necklace. Meeting Aditi would have spurred him on to do something about it – you know, find out if the family story, handed down over the generations, held any truth. A wedding here at the hall, with them both hoping that the diamonds were still in the chandelier after all these years, was a great cover.'

'And, when Aditi was intent on refurbishing the marble steps and cleaning the chandelier, supposedly for your wedding guests, it was with the aim of spending as much time as possible in the Great Hall to see if the Jet Set was still in situ?' Eva paused. 'And then, her climbing up there confirmed the jewels were there but, presumably, she was unable at that point to retrieve them without help from Zac? Obviously didn't want her helpers to know what she was up to?'

Drew nodded. 'Obviously.'

'I'm so sorry, Drew.' Eva stroked his arm, feeling overwhelmingly sorry for the man.

'Guess I was a bit of a pawn in their game.' Drew smiled ruefully. 'That's why I said I feel so embarrassed.'

'But what on earth was Aditi thinking she could *do* with the diamond? She'd never have been able to get it out of the country in her suitcase?'

'When you're an addict, you'll look for any lifeline to fuel your next hit. She probably hadn't thought that far ahead. And, you know, Zac would have worked it all out: there are certainly ways and means of smuggling diamonds from the UK.

Possibly via Holland? Who knows? I doubt Aditi would have ended up with much of a share if that charlatan had actually managed to pull off the theft. As I see it now, Aditi had met me, saw me as the answer to her financial problems, but then had a second lifeline when Zac, with whom she was already involved, came up with the plan to shift our wedding to Heatherly Hall.'

'More of an Agatha Christie mystery than we ever imagined then.' Eva smiled, looking across the lake where a flock of mallards was rising gracefully and symmetrically from the water. She breathed in the chilly spring air, taking in the subtle earthy scents of newly stirring soil, of grass stems and garlic from wakening roots blended with the tantalising fragrance of the park's first mowing after its winter sleep.

'You are so lucky living here, Eva.' Drew turned, looking down at her with such intensity, Eva felt herself grow pink and had to look away. 'Now that… you know… I'm not… you know…' He took her arm, and she knew he was going to kiss her. And, she also knew, she didn't want him to.

'I don't actually *live here*…' she started, suddenly unsure. Hadn't she been having little fantasies about Drew Livingston? Hoping that he'd…? What? Fancy her too? Fall in love with her? Eva turned towards the man in front of her and knew that's all it had ever been: just that – a fantasy.

'I'm so sorry, Drew, the thing is—' She broke off once more as she heard her name being called. Not once, but several times.

They both turned as a figure walked determinedly towards them. Eva shaded her eyes against the spring sunshine, unable to make out who was intent on making their way across the park, shouting her name.

Her first thought was Rayan: oh, please don't say something had happened to Laila or Nora? No, not Rayan. Eva squinted against the bright light. Joe, then? Was there a problem with Rosa? Oh, Lachlan perhaps? Good, she'd found him, or rather he'd found her – she needed to direct him back up to Hannah's apartment before Hannah got herself out of bed and...

Eva felt her pulse race and then she was off, running towards the man, leaving behind the little fantasy she'd woven with Drew Livingston, which was just that: a daft, schoolgirl crush on an ageing, not overly happy rocker.

'Andrea!' Eva flung herself into Andrea Zaitsev's waiting arms. 'You're back?'

'I no longer stay away from you, Eva. You refuse to come to me in Milan. I have to find my way back to you. I not without you a second longer. I make decision in early hours of yesterday, and I come straight back home to you.' Each sentence, in Andrea's broken English, was accompanied by a soft kiss to Eva's closed eyes, to each cheek, to her nose and finally to her open mouth, silencing the words she was attempting to utter.

'But is all your work completed over in Italy?' Eva finally managed to get out.

Andrea shook his head. 'No. But I am getting there. I leave it all for a while and come back to you because I don't concentrate without you. I am able to do next stage back here in workshop. Three or four months' work here. And then, then Eva, you come back with me? I don't do this without you...'

'But my girls, Andrea?'

'I love your girls. We sort all that. We have summer in Milan with your lovely girls. You come and see Italy? And then, I come back here for winter. Winter in Yorkshire again!' He shivered dramatically. 'It fine if *you* with me...' He broke off, looking past her. 'Eva, there is man standing by the lake. Looking as if he not know what to do with himself... *Col Cavolo*...' Andrea stopped speaking once more, staring intently at Drew, who, indeed, did look as if he didn't know where to put himself. 'He look just like Drew Livingston, my music hero...'

'It *is* Drew Livingston.' Eva smiled. 'Long story why he's here, but come on, I'll introduce you to him.'

Eva led the way and, as she reached Drew, stood on tiptoe to kiss his cheek. 'Good luck,' she whispered. 'If things had been different...'

'Another time, another place,' Drew said softly into Eva's hair, briefly touching her hand, which said it all. And then, managing a smile, he turned to Andrea. 'I don't believe we've met? I'm just leaving.'

'You're welcome back here any time,' Eva said, knowing that she meant it, but also knowing Drew would now probably never return. 'Any time you need to retreat from the world, to paint or stroll with elephants through the park, we're here for you.'

Eva watched as Drew walked, a solitary figure, returning to the hall to fetch his things and check himself out. She turned back to Andrea. 'Andrea, I thought you weren't coming back.'

'Why would I not come back to you, *cara*?' Andrea stared at her in disbelief.

'But I've probably had four texts from you in, what, nearly two months?'

'If I text you, if I message you, I lose the concentration I need for my work. I hear your voice, see your messages and then it gone, pow! I don't concentrate for rest of day and spend work time just thinking of you. Of being with you.'

'Oh, God, another artist.' Eva smiled. 'I should know what you lot are like, having Alice Parkes for a mother.'

'But *she* leave you for ever. She give you away. Eva, I no more *give you away* than give up my art. I rip out my 'eart for you.'

'Art or heart?' Eva began to laugh. 'Get over yourself, Andrea.'

'Eva, I'm serious. I love you.'

And as Eva looked into those startling blue eyes, as she ran her fingers through his black curls and he bent to kiss her once more, she knew he did. He really, really did.

'And now, Eva, we jump back on my bike...'

'Are you not feeling a bit, you know, saddle sore after twenty-four hours on that bike?'

'Just a little perhaps.' Andrea bent his knees, squatting experimentally and wincing slightly as he did so. 'The thought of you keep me going, all the way through Switzerland and France when I thought I'd stop for rest. And now, I take you home to bed and make love to you for the rest of day. And all night too.'

Eva started to laugh, suddenly feeling more at peace than she had for months. Italians: they were so full of it. 'Yes please.' She laughed. 'Oh, yes, yes please.'

# 36

*1pm*

'Ger, where's Lachlan? Have you seen him?' Hannah closed her eyes slightly, wincing as the pain in her cracked and bruised ribs threatened to have her on her knees at Geraldine's apartment door.

'Bloody hell, Hannah.' For once, Ger appeared lost for words.

'Lachlan? Is he here with you? Or out on the estate? Have you seen him?'

'I didn't realise you were in *such* a bad state – what the hell are you doing out of bed?' Ger took Hannah's arm and, because she couldn't do anything else, Hannah allowed the other woman to lead the way into the tiny sitting room. The TV was on, and Hannah saw Ger was in the middle of watching some Scotland v England rugby match. 'We're about to trounce you Sassenachs,' Ger gloated and then, taking in Hannah's white face, hastily shifted a pile of agricultural books from the sofa before propelling her none too gently into the vacated space.

'I do hope you're going to press charges,' Ger said, pouring a tot of whisky from the bottle on the sideboard and handing it to Hannah.

'I'm on rather a lot of painkillers,' Hannah said, shaking her head. 'And, I've given up alcohol.'

Ger raised an eye. 'Oh?'

Ignoring the look of disbelief on the other woman's face,

Hannah asked again, 'Lachlan, Geraldine? I've knocked on his door, messaged, WhatsApped and rung his mobile, but he's not answering.'

'Well, he won't, Hannah.' Ger's tone was sympathetic, rather than the usual caustic riposte.

'Won't or can't?'

'Both, I would imagine.' Ger glanced at her watch. 'He should be arriving back in Balmoral about now – he set off at 6am this morning.'

'What?' Hannah stared. 'But he only just arrived back here last night.'

'Good job he did as well, or that pair of jewel thieves would have run off with the infamous necklace, I hear?'

'You weren't there then?'

Ger snorted disdainfully. 'Me? Och, I've better things to do than sit on my backside watching a bunch of amateurs prancing around in wigs and panstick thinking they're God's gift to the acting profession.'

'So you didn't actually *see* Lachlan bring Zac Anderson to the floor to retrieve the Jet Set then?'

Ger shook her head. 'He told me all about it when he turned up back here after it had all died down. He has a black eye to match your own and I had to patch him back up a bit. That hand of his isn't totally better yet, you know,' she went on, accusingly. 'And rugby-tackling that wanker Zac Anderson to the floor has done nothing to help it.'

'No, I can imagine.' Hannah wasn't quite sure what she could say to make the situation – which Ger appeared to be making out was her fault – any better.

'I made him food and we shared a bottle of wine and then I took him to bed.'

'You did *what?*' Hannah's eyes turned on Ger in fury.

'His own bed, Hannah. His own bed. And without me in it.' Ger threw her a look. 'He was utterly bushed. He'd set off at 4am yesterday to get here.'

'To get here? But he didn't arrive, as far as I know, until around 7.30pm last night?'

'He didn't. Apparently, he'd promised he'd be back yesterday for your Jet Set farce – couldn't make the wedding because it was his father's actual funeral on Thursday – and Lachlan...' here Ger looked directly at Hannah '...Lachlan is a man of integrity, and when he's promised he'll do something, he makes sure he does it.'

'But what on earth took him so long?'

'Atrocious Friday traffic on the M6. There was an accident, apparently, which closed the motorway and he was stuck on it for hours. And then, as he neared Penrith, he had a blowout. Took another four hours to be carted off the motorway by the RAC and find a suitable tyre for that old Land Rover of his.'

'Why the hell didn't he just turn round and go back?'

'That's what *I* said,' Ger sniffed. 'But you know Lachlan: a man of his word.'

Hannah felt her head begin to pound and tears start. She felt so weepy and droopy and utterly sad. 'Ger, is he coming back?'

Geraldine looked at Hannah directly. 'No, I don't think he is.'

'Did *he* say that?' Hannah found she was actually crying now. 'Has he packed up his things? His books and clothes. His bagpipes? Has he taken MacDuff?'

'Of course he's taken MacDuff.' Ger shot Hannah a look of derision. 'Have you ever known Lachlan go anywhere without his dog?'

'I need to get a key,' Hannah said almost feverishly. 'Need to see if he's packed up his things. Why didn't he say goodbye? What was the rush to get back today?'

'There's a service of remembrance being held at his father's kirk later this afternoon.'

'His kirk?'

Ger tutted. 'His father's *church*. There was no way Lachlan was not going to be there for that.'

'I cannot believe Lachlan drove back down here just for one day, knowing he'd have to drive straight back the next.'

'I've the key,' Ger said, standing. 'To his apartment. He left it with me this morning before he set off.'

Hannah's heart sank. 'He'd only do that if he wasn't coming back,' she said, closing her eyes.

'Hannah, you can't blame him,' Ger said crossly. 'You messed him around, flirting and dallying with that other pillock right in front of him. And of course, he heard about your little set-to in Clementine's with that other wanker you were involved with. That's two men you were showing more interest in than Lachlan himself. Plus, you know, your little drink problem...?'

'I don't have a drink problem,' Hannah almost gasped.

'Oh, I think you do. Lachlan feels deeply, Hannah. And when Bridget went back to her husband last year, he came south hoping to get away from it all. I reckon he's headed back north now, to remove himself from hurt once more.'

'The key, Ger? Please?'

'Come on,' Ger said, her tone slightly kinder. She moved to give Hannah a hand up from the sofa before turning to the chest of drawers behind her and fishing in the top one for the key.

Together they went to the adjacent apartment, Ger offering an arm whenever Hannah appeared to falter. Ger turned the key, and Hannah knew immediately he'd packed up and gone. Everything was neat and tidy, the bookshelves bare, the sink left clean with a yellow dishcloth, neatly folded, on the taps; the bed stripped of linen. The wardrobe, when she opened it, was empty except for the rack of assorted coat hangers that seemed to sneer accusingly in her direction. The tiny bathroom, when she made herself go in there, was clean but devoid of towels, toothbrush, shampoo or shaving paraphernalia.

'Did he tell you he wasn't coming back?' Hannah pleaded. 'He must have said *something*.'

'Not his style.' Ger shook her head. 'Just takes himself out of a situation he no longer wants to be in, without any fuss.'

'Right,' Hannah said. 'Give me the key – I'm locking up. And then I'm going.'

'Do you need some help back? You've a lot of stairs to get up.'

'No,' Hannah said determinedly. 'I'm going to Scotland. Balmoral, isn't it?'

'Oh, don't be so bloody ridiculous, Hannah,' Geraldine snapped crossly. 'I'd say you were mad chasing after him if you *didn't* have cracked ribs, but seeing you *have*, as well as being half out of it on codeine, you are utterly bonkers even thinking about it. You can't drive in this condition.'

'I'll get the train.'

'Oh? And there is one, is there? To Balmoral?'

'I've no idea, but I'll get there somehow.'

'Seven hours it'll take you, changing at York, Edinburgh and Perth. You'll have to go to Aviemore and then get a bus or a taxi across to Balmoral – and I bet Uber hasn't ventured that far north yet.' Ger raised an eyebrow, looking across at Hannah with an accompanying pitying shake of her lustrous red hair.

'I can *do* that. I need to see him, need to tell him I've messed up.'

'He already knows that.' Ger shook her head impatiently and then folded her arms, looking Hannah up and down, obviously considering. She didn't speak for a good thirty seconds and then tutted. 'Listen, Hannah, I know you think I've got the hots for Lachlan and that I'm trying to dissuade you from going up there because of my own feelings for him. I love Lachlan, but only because he's a very special person. Probably my best mate.'

*When he should have been mine*, Hannah thought bleakly, utterly depressed now.

'Anyway, he's over ten years older than me. And…' she paused '…listen, you might as well know, there's only ever been *one* person in this place I've fancied.'

'*You* fell for Zac Anderson as well?' Hannah stared.

'What? That tosser? Oh, for heaven's sake!' Ger glared across at Hannah who, as she locked up Lachlan's empty apartment, and desperate to sit down, was beginning to feel totally out of the loop.

'Drew Livingston then?'

'I can see what your sister saw in him, but no.'

'Ger, I really can't be doing a *Starter for Ten* right now.' Hannah limped towards the outer door. 'I'm going to pack an overnight case and get a taxi to take me to the station.'

'And you know Lachlan's address, do you? Know where he is?'

'It'll be in the HR office. Not a problem. A taxi will get me to his place once I get to…? Where was it? Aviemore?'

'No, ye're *not* doing this. I'm not letting ye. Eva and Rosa would never forgive me if ah didn't stop ye.' Ger's accent was becoming more marked in direct proportion to the irritation she was obviously feeling with Hannah.

'I'm your boss.'

Ger gave a little snort of derision. (She was an expert in derisory snorts, Hannah realised.) 'Fire me then. I've had enough of this place. It was bearable with Lachlan next door, but now he's gone… and also…'

'Also what?'

'It doesn't matter.' Ger's glare was combative. 'Oh, for fuck's sake,' she breathed. 'I was going home to Glasgow for a few days *next weekend*, but I'll just have to bring it forward. Come on, let me get a few things together, ring my parents to tell them I'm on my way and then I'll take you back over and get what you need. And then we'll head off.' She tutted crossly once more in Hannah's direction. 'I can't believe I'm doing this…'

'It's a six-or-seven-hour drive,' Ger warned once she helped Hannah into the snazzy little red MX5, adjusting the seatbelt whilst having regard for her boss's ribs. 'Not much less than the train.'

'Drop me off down at Midhope station then, and I'll *get* the train.' Hannah felt so tired she just wanted to sleep for ever; felt she just couldn't do with being bossed about by Ger McBain a second longer.

'Oh, don't start that all over again,' Ger ordered. 'Right,' she went on, handing Hannah a bottle of water, 'before we set off, dose yourself up to the eyeballs, plug yourself into some gentle music or a podcast or something, and sleep.'

'What are you? My mother now...?'

Without another word, Ger pressed a button and Hannah's seat shot back almost horizontal and within minutes, once they'd driven through the park and out of the gates, Hannah was asleep.

She slept for the first couple of hours until they passed Penrith, and then nodded off again until Ger pulled into a service station at Carlisle where she woke, stiff and with her mouth parched, desperate for a drink. Ger simply passed her the water and then indicated they should get out and use the loo while she stretched her legs before continuing northwards. She bought them both coffee and a sandwich, which Hannah was unable to eat, giving hers to Ger who demolished the lot. They sat for five minutes, the only conversation being Hannah insisting that whatever the petrol and refreshments were costing Ger, she must send her the bill once they were back in Yorkshire.

By 6.30pm, despite the lengthening hours of daylight as they motored north, night-time was falling. ('You'll lose an hour's sleep tonight,' Ger warned, 'clocks go forward at midnight.') But Hannah watched as towns she'd only ever heard of in history books or on the news – Lockerbie, Beattock, Bannockburn and Dunblane – came and went as the car ate up the miles.

Ger, an exceptionally fast but competent driver (didn't she do everything competently?) took the A9 heading for Braemar.

'Not too long now,' Ger advised at last.

'But what are *you* going to do?'

'How d'ye mean?' Ger's accent again appeared more heavily pronounced now she was back on home territory.

'Well, where will you stay tonight? With Lachlan?'

'Och no. I'll drop ye off and then head back down to Glasgow.'

'You can't do that.' Hannah was genuinely horrified, run through with guilt at putting Ger to such trouble.

'Another hundred miles or so back down the motorway and I'll be in the pub for last orders by ten.'

'Right. What if Lachlan's not here?' Hannah felt sick. 'What if he refuses to see me?'

'He knows you're coming.'

'He does?' Hannah twisted round to stare at Ger's profile, grimacing with pain as she did so.

Ger simply nodded. 'You don't think I'd be driving all this way if there was a chance he'd buggered off for a wee mini-break, do you?' She turned and actually laughed at the thought.

'Ger, why are you doing this?'

'Because if I hadn't, you'd have been bloody daft enough to get the train instead. Knowing British Rail, you wouldn't have got here until tomorrow. And, *knowing you*, you'd have probably got lost. And I'm doing it for Lachlan.'

'OK.'

There was silence for another ten minutes until Hannah finally asked: 'So, come on then, Ger, who is it at Heatherly Hall you've fancied all this time, if not Lachlan?'

'I thought you'd have had some insight... mind you, not convinced insightfulness is your best characteristic...'

'Thanks for that.'

'Still no idea?' Ger turned, looking long and hard at Hannah and Hannah wished she'd keep her eyes on the road.

As the penny finally dropped, and Hannah felt her pulse race and her cheeks redden under Ger's amused scrutiny, she whispered, 'What? Me?'

'You?' Ger started to laugh. 'No, I do *not* fancy you. You're far too flaky.'

'Oh, thank goodness for that.' Hannah breathed a sigh of relief. 'For a minute I thought you were trying to tell me you're gay.'

'I am.' Ger was thoroughly enjoying Hannah's obvious discomfiture. 'And, I've had a total thing about *Eva* since the minute I set eyes on her.'

*Bloody hell*, Hannah thought, somewhat irrationally, *Eva wins the round again*.

'So probably time for me to move on. Saw her with the Italian stud this morning. What a waste of a strong, beautiful woman.' Ger laughed as she pulled into the yard of a row of cottages and killed the engine.

## 37

'Hello, Lachlan.' If Hannah had been feeling pretty awful for the past twenty-four hours or so, it now appeared nothing compared to being confronted by a grim-faced Lachlan at the door of his father's cottage.

'You'd better come in.' He moved past her, allowing her entry but, instead of greeting her with a kiss, a smile, with a touch of the arm even, he carried on walking down the path to where Ger was lifting out Hannah's case from the tiny boot, where he stopped, kissing Ger on the cheek and engaging in what appeared to be a somewhat heated conversation.

Hannah dithered, uncertain what to do, so, instead of moving inside from the unlit doorstep as directed, she simply stood and waited, bending painfully to stroke MacDuff's ears who was sat obediently at her side. Five minutes later, Ger roared off, scattering stones and mud, and Lachlan walked back up the path.

'I'm really not sure why you're here, Hannah.' Lachlan stared down at her, taking in the closed black eye, the purple and ochre bruises that appeared to be perniciously taking over her whole face.

'Don't look at me,' Hannah pleaded and, attempting levity, added, 'To be fair, your face isn't a good deal better than mine.' And then, when he didn't respond, but simply walked over to the sink with the kettle, she added, 'Thank you.'

'For what?'

'For saving the Jet Set necklace. He'd have got away with it if you hadn't launched at him and managed to wrest it out of his hands before he ran off. Eva said you were absolutely wonderful.'

Ignoring her, Lachlan filled the kettle, spooned coffee into a cafetière and then simply stood with his back to her, gazing out through the window into the black night and the farmland within it.

'Lachlan, I'm sorry,' Hannah started. 'I'm so, so sorry for hurting you.'

'You need to sit down,' Lachlan said gruffly. 'Before you fall down.'

As Lachlan poured water, took milk from the fridge, and unhooked two large cups from a mug tree on the side, Hannah sat on one of the pair of battered chairs facing the open fire. MacDuff, after the excitement of newcomers, sighed loudly, positioned himself in front of the fire and on Hannah's feet, and promptly fell asleep.

'So, why *are* you here?' Lachlan asked, handing her the mug, which seemed terribly heavy in her bruised and cut fingers. 'Your hands as well?' Lachlan took the mug from her, placing it on a side table.

'And two cracked ribs.' Hating herself for it, Hannah went for the sympathy vote.

'And you *still* wanted to go with the bastard?'

'How do you mean?' Hannah stared up at him in confusion.

'After he'd beaten you up? What the fuck *is* the matter with you, Hannah?'

'I don't know what you mean,' Hannah repeated. 'I was upstairs on the mezzanine floor, totally winded and unable to move until Dad and Joe came up and got me. Why on earth would I want to go *anywhere* with him?'

'I heard the verger's wife telling someone that you'd thrown yourself at him just before I got there: that as he tried to make off with the Jet Set, you grabbed hold of him in front of the whole audience, telling him your bag was packed and your passport ready and that you loved him.'

'*What?*' Hannah wondered if she were going mad and shook her head in confusion. 'I did *what?*'

'If he hadn't shaken you off, you'd have gone with him, wouldn't you? And, now that he's disappeared with that Bollywood actress, you somehow managed to get Ger to drive you all this way up here to have another crack at *me!*'

Hannah closed her one good eye, feeling sick. And then she stood, slightly wobbly, but stood nevertheless. 'If you think I'm capable of chasing after some man who I'd not only thrown out of my life weeks before, but who beat me up as I tried to get the jewels he'd just stolen out of his bag…' Hannah shook her head. 'I'll leave you in peace, Lachlan.' With her head held as high as was humanly possible, she made for the front door. Grabbing her little overnight case, but ignoring MacDuff, who was trotting patiently beside her, she walked out into the black velvet night, not caring where she was going, but needing to remove herself from someone who could think so utterly, utterly badly of her.

Two strong arms reached for her, preventing her from passing through the little garden gate that led to the yard and she instinctively lashed out at Lachlan, elbowing him in fury. 'Don't you *dare* touch me. Get *off* me. Now.'

'Where the hell do you think you're going?' Lachlan was just as angry.

'There must be a pub or B and B in this godforsaken place. I'll find it and get the train home tomorrow. Oh, and just for your information, I *never* slept with Zac Anderson, despite you thinking I must have done. And as for begging him to take me with him…? Get *off me*, Lachlan,' she hissed once more as he put out a hand when her case, like the worst kind of supermarket trolley, was intent on heading in the opposite direction. 'You're absolutely right, I shouldn't have come.' Breathing heavily, fuelled by sadness and anger, she turned one final time to him.

'Just what did you hear Sandra Butterworth say?'

'Sandra Butterworth?'

'The verger's wife,' Hannah snapped.

'She said: "That ridiculous sister of the vicar's has obviously been having an affair with the American, and what an utter show she's just made of herself! Begging him to take her with him; telling him her case was packed and her passport ready."'

'Virginia.'

'What about Virginia?'

'Zac Anderson had been having a thing with Virginia, and she was obviously ready to leave Timothy, Bethany and Barty for the bastard.'

'A thing with *Virginia?*' Lachlan stared in disbelief. 'As well as with you?' Lachlan glared at her once more.

'I didn't have any *thing* with him,' Hannah protested tiredly. 'I was stupid, fell for his patter, for his seduction technique…'

'So you *were* seduced by him?'

'Lachlan…' Hannah looked him directly in the face '…the sum total of that "thing" was two, maybe three kisses, and yes, to my shame, at least one instigated by me, not him; a dinner at Clementine's where he poured too much champagne down me and I ended up making an utter fool of myself shouting at my ex…'

'Hannah, you only shout at an ex when you still feel something for them.'

'Or when you've had too much to drink and all the distaste for that affair comes to the surface once more…'

'If you say so.'

'As Ger told me straight, on the way here: I'm *flaky.* I'm sorry to have wasted your time, Lachlan; I'm more than sorry you've been forced to leave Heatherly Hall because of me, and you'll never know how much I regret, how utterly *sorry* I am to have messed up the one good thing in my life.' Hannah found she was crying, seriously now, and she turned, reaching blindly for the handle of her case once more, trundling it with some difficulty through the garden gate.

'You need a new case,' Lachlan said, attempting to prise it from the bottom of the gate where it had lodged itself.

'I need a new *personality*,' Hannah sniffed, taking the case from him. 'Lachlan, I know you won't believe me, but I love you. I've messed up the single really good thing in my life because... because that's what I appear to do with good things for some reason.' She shook her head almost in despair. 'But, listen, Heatherly Hall needs you as well. The whole estate has never looked so good, or been as productive with you in charge of it. Please come back. And I *promise* you, if you do, I'll keep out of your way. I won't try to tell you I love you, won't gaze at you across the boardroom table at meetings...'

'So, Virginia you say?' Lachlan interrupted.

'Hmm.'

Lachlan started to laugh and it was one of genuine humour. 'That *bampot* sister of yours was taken in by the bastard as well?'

'Stupidity appears to run in the family...' Hannah broke off, staring into space, suddenly understanding. 'Virginia! Of course! Zac Anderson *did* let himself into my apartment. Told me the door was unlocked when I bet *anything* he'd persuaded Virginia to let him borrow her set of keys for the hall. She'd demanded her own set once she was trying to establish herself as *Lady Ginny Forester-Astley*, and Eva and I agreed to let her have a set like we both have, in order to shut her up a bit. He'd have flattered her and, I bet anything, asked to borrow the keys: told her he was researching the history of Heatherly and far easier if he could move around with his own set. He probably had them duplicated the next day.' She exhaled, closing her eyes at the realisation.

'Hannah, I'm not coming back.'

'Right... right... OK...' Hannah felt her heart plummet. How could she bear to lose him? 'Lachlan, please...'

'I'm *not* coming back...'

'Right.'

'...if you're not prepared to gaze at me over the boardroom table any longer.'

'Right...' She felt something akin to hope stir and she glanced sideways up at him through her one good eye.

'It's the only thing that kept me going through those interminable board meetings you insist on, when all I wanted was to be out in the fresh air, out on the estate, with MacDuff.'

'You knew I was looking at you? Eyeing you up?'

'Of course.'

'Even at the beginning, when I couldn't stand you? When you were sarcastic and bossy and horrible to me?'

'Even then.'

'You knew I fancied you from the start?'

'You didn't even know it yourself.' Lachlan started to laugh.

'Bit full of yourself, Lachlan Buchanan.' Hannah glared up at him.

'C'mon in, now, hen.' Lachlan reached a hand to Hannah's face, stroking the bruises gently. 'Ye'r gaun nowhere the night.'

'If I knew what you were saying...?' Hannah started, but Lachlan reached down, kissed her on the mouth, took her case in one hand, her own bruised hand in the other and led her back up the unlit path to the cottage.

# 38

## April

In the second week of April, the vicarage lawn and flower beds were shrouded in a veil of early morning mist, while the mighty yews and oaks, not to be intimidated, appeared determined to poke their heads through the gauzy sheet covering their trunks and lower branches. Denis Butterworth had been working in the garden all week, helping Rosa to cut back a plethora of unwanted suckers growing round the base of the trees and shrubs, as well as clearing out-of-control nettles and brambles. Even when the verger was quoting his gardening god, Monty Don with: '*You have to be coldly realistic, Vicar, and look your garden in the eye*', Rosa had resisted the cutting back of too much of the overgrown plants, knowing it to be home to so much wildlife.

Rosa moved away from the window, glanced across at the kitchen clock and went to fill the kettle, expecting Eva to pop in for a quick coffee after taking her girls to school as she so often did these days. Rosa knew it wasn't coffee Eva was after but, now that Joe was in Sydney, having flown out with Carys and Chiara the previous week, she and Hannah had dropped in daily, checking she was alright, was eating, was sleeping, wasn't spending the day in her pyjamas, crying at losing her stepdaughter.

It was good of Eva to be so solicitous, especially as she had Andrea Zaitsev back in her life and in her bed. Rosa was so glad he'd returned: she really liked Andrea, and you only had to see him with Eva to know how much in love they were with each other.

After calling in at the vicarage, Eva, Rosa knew, would be heading on up to the hall where she wouldn't be able to resist popping in to the workshop in the grounds where Andrea would be hard at work at one of his sculptures, no doubt swearing in Russian or Italian at his current creation before wrapping himself around Eva once more, refusing to let her go and then blaming her for putting him off his stride. Rosa smiled at the picture. Then Eva would be off up to the art retreat, sorting out art materials, visiting tutors and guest lists for the coming week.

Hannah would no doubt have already been up and at work for the past couple of hours, constantly making sure Heatherly Hall was being the best it could possibly be. Rosa had been at the weekly board meeting the previous morning – the first since the Livingston wedding and Agatha Christie evening – where the committee had sat through Hannah and Tara's reports and been given feedback of the two events. And then later, going through other matters on the agenda, Hannah had disagreed with something Lachlan had objected to and gazed across the boardroom table at him for what seemed much longer than necessary. 'Overruled, Mr Buchanan,' Hannah had said pompously, but Rosa had seen the love for Lachlan in her sister's eyes, as well as that for Hannah returned in Lachlan's gaze.

'Is that kettle on, Rosie Rosavina?' Eva's voice broke into her thoughts as the vicarage front door banged shut. 'I'm desperate for caffeine. You OK?' she asked, scrutinising Rosa's pale face as she'd done every morning since Joe and Carys had left for Australia. 'Missing Joe? And Chiara, of course?' She went to hug Rosa, patting her back as one would a small child. 'Joe'll be back next week. Why don't you treat him to Clementine's and, you know, psych yourselves up for this new appointment in the clinic in Wimbledon…?'

The door banged once more. 'Ah ha!' Hannah grinned, pulling

off her jacket. 'Thought you'd have an Extraordinary General Meeting without me, did you, the pair of you? Good job I saw you sneaking in here, Eva.'

'I wasn't *sneaking* anywhere, you moron,' Eva said mildly. 'What's up?' she asked, turning to the newcomer. 'Not like you to be down in the village before nine? Had enough of Lachlan back in your bed already?'

'I'll afford that the contempt it deserves,' Hannah said. 'I actually had the first appointment with your new dentist across at Malik and Malik.' She bared her teeth in the others' direction and ran a tongue across them. 'Had a good inspection and clean. Shame to spoil it with coffee and Rosa's delicious flapjacks.' She glanced hopefully in the direction of the cake tin.

Eva waved the letter Rosa had just handed to her, towards Hannah. 'Rosa's got another appointment at the clinic.'

'In Wimbledon?' Hannah's eyes widened. 'The egg clinic? Well, that's good, isn't it?'

'Suppose.' Rosa shrugged. 'But, you know, what if it doesn't work? What if I find out, after nine years, they're all duds.'

'Don't call your precious eggs names.' Hannah was visibly upset. 'Duds? That's awful, Rosa.'

'Sorry, I just don't feel I can get excited about it all anymore. I've gone off the boil now, and I'm sure, losing Chiara, Joe will feel the same.'

'Try not to think that you and he have *lost* Chiara,' Hannah ventured. 'You can go and visit her every year. Maybe at Christmas? Mind you, I suppose vicars should be in their church at Christmas...?' She trailed off. 'And I don't suppose Joe will be looking forward to sitting in cold baths again – you know, to cool his wotsits in preparation for the sperm donation.' Hannah smiled sympathetically towards Rosa. '*That* can't be very relaxing, can it?'

'Can you try and be a bit more positive for Rosa, Hans?' Eva glared.

'Hannah's right, Eva. Probably the last thing on his mind, you know, attempting to make a new child when you've taken, and left, your little girl, at the other side of the world.' Rosa's eyes filled with tears. 'I can't stop crying,' she admitted. 'My stomach is constantly tied up in knots and I can't get off the loo – I'm beginning to dread Sunday service and funerals in case I have to dash out. I actually threw up this morning,' she confided, 'and now, with this new appointment...' Rosa took the letter from Hannah '...where I'll have to face the fact that it might all be too late and I'll never have a baby... I feel so sick...' She thrust the letter on to the table and rushed to the downstairs lavatory.

'Oh, didn't Hannah want coffee?' Rosa asked, coming back into the kitchen ten minutes later looking less washed out, but feeling no better. 'I was only having her on when I said there was no cake in the tin.'

'She's just popped into the village for the paper,' Eva replied.

'Why?' Rosa frowned. 'She has it delivered up at the hall. She has all the papers delivered to the conference centre. Doesn't she?'

The vicarage door banged open and shut once more.

'I thought you had papers delivered...?' Rosa started but broke off as both Eva and Hannah, standing together for some obvious sort of moral support, looked decidedly shifty.

'Oh, heavens,' Rosa said, sitting down. 'What? What's the matter? What do the pair of you know, that I obviously don't?'

'Not *know*...' Eva hesitated '...just *think*...'

'Think? Think *what*?' Rosa was feeling irritated with the pair of them. Wished they'd both go so she could get on with her work, get back out in the garden to start planting spring seedlings. She had so much to do, but she was feeling so strange. God, she did hope she wasn't going down with the virus that had had Sandra Butterworth in bed for the last few days. Rosa ran a tired hand through her hair and glared at her sisters. 'Well?'

'Go on.' Eva nudged Hannah.

'You.' Hannah nudged her back. 'It was *your idea*. I just carried out your instructions.'

'*What?*' Rosa asked, shaking her head.

Hannah took out a paper bag from her tote and thrust it in Rosa's direction. 'Eva thinks you might be… could be…'

'Oh, for heaven's sake, Hans,' Eva interrupted. 'Rosa, you look and sound *just* like I did when I was pregnant with the girls. Washed out, irritable, throwing up. And your tits are huge.'

'Should you say *tits* to a vicar?' Hannah attempted levity now that they'd done the deed.

'Pregnant?' Rosa shook her head once more. 'I'm *not* pregnant. I can't *get* pregnant the usual way. You *know that*, Eva.'

'How do you know? You're having periods again, aren't you?'

'Not very often. I might end up with one every six months and then nothing.'

'So, when was your last one?' Eva demanded.

'Oh, Eva, I can do without this.' Rosa glared at Eva. '*I* don't know; months and months ago, I think.'

'Exactly. How are your boobs?'

'Same as they've ever been. On my chest, in front of me.' Rosa put up a hand to her breasts underneath her trendy navy clerical shirt, but kept them there. 'Actually,' she said, 'they do feel bigger.'

'Sore?'

Rosa felt at her breasts once more and nodded. 'Very. Like before a period. Hopefully I'm due another one. That's why I'm feeling so bloody irritable with the pair of you.'

'Right, off you go.' Hannah took back the box and, after much pulling and swearing at the cellophane, retrieved the pregnancy test stick and handed it to Rosa. 'Go on, we're here for you. Best to do it while we're with you.'

'I'm *not* pregnant, Hannah,' Rosa snapped, but took the stick. 'Where do I pee, Eva?'

'On the stick would be good.' Eva smiled. 'Go on.' She pushed Rosa gently back in the direction of the lavatory.

*

When she reappeared in the kitchen, Rosa found Hannah and Eva holding hands in a way they hadn't done since they were kids and crossing the road in the village with Susan. She handed the stick to them.

'Well?' Eva demanded, squeezing Hannah's hand, which was still sore from Zac Anderson's handiwork until Hannah winced and said '*ooofff*' but kept it there anyway.

'I don't *know*. I haven't *looked*.'

Eva, as eldest and bolshiest of the Quinn triplets, took charge.

'OK,' she eventually breathed, allowing a slow smile to spread across her face. 'We're having *a baby*. You did it, Rosa, you did it, all by yourself.'

# Epilogue

*August*

On a beautiful summer Sunday afternoon at the end of August, the Quinn triplets – Eva, Hannah and Rosa – welcomed the High Commissioner of India to the United Kingdom to a tea party on the lawn in front of Heatherly Hall where, watched by invited guests and family, as well as the media, the girls formally returned the Sah-I-Noor diamond to the Indian Government.

Over a quintessentially English afternoon tea – tiny sandwiches, scones bulging with homemade strawberry jam and clotted cream as well as cakes and pastries awash with pillows of whipped cream – Hannah turned to her sisters.

'Do you really think we should have *done* this?' she asked for perhaps the hundredth time since the management committee had made the decision to return the precious gem back to its rightful owners. 'I mean, just think what we could have done with all that dosh if we'd flogged it: the whole conference centre refurbished and a *gym*... we could have extended and built a fabulous gym... a swimming pool...'

'Hannah, we've been through all this.' Rosa laughed. 'You *know* it was the right thing to do.'

'I *don't* know. Did I end up with cracked ribs and a black eye, saving it from that pillock Zac Anderson, just to *give it away*? George Astley won it fair and square; surely if he won the diamond in a game of cards, it was his? And now ours? Well, the hall's anyway.'

'From what we've heard of the ninth Marquess of Stratton, and the way he squirrelled the diamond away in a vault in London for decades, the diamond probably *wasn't* won totally fairly. Who knows?' Eva upended her glass of champagne. 'Lachlan,' she called, over her shoulder, 'come and join me in a glass of fizz? I hate drinking alone, and now that Hannah's gone teetotal and Rosa won't be touching the stuff for at least another four months, I need someone to keep me company.'

Rosa, laughing at Eva's attempts to beguile Lachlan into joining her, turned, her face lighting up even more as Joe walked towards her, bringing her a cup of tea.

'You alright?' Joe asked Rosa. 'Do you want to sit down?'

Rosa shook her head, placing a protective hand on the neat little bump making an appearance through her pink clerical shirt, as Joe looked down at her with concern. And with love.

'You sure you're OK, Rosa?' he asked again and, when she nodded in the affirmative, feeling happier and surer of herself than she had for months, Joe simply took her hand in his and dropped a kiss on her dark-haired head.

'Anyway, don't forget,' Eva was now saying, 'we've still got the diamonds in the Jet Set *earrings*. Those didn't originate in India, so I think we can claim *those* as our own. They might fetch quite a bit, and you could put that towards an annual cleaning of the chandelier, Hannah?' She started to laugh at Hannah's face.

'Jonny and BJ are after them,' Hannah said gloomily.

'As is *Ginny*, more than likely.' Rosa grinned.

'Seeing as Virginia is still trying to keep her head down and mend her marriage to Timothy, as well as make peace with the parish committee and the WI and all the other groups she's part of, I don't think she'll be sticking her neck out and claiming what she feels is her inheritance just at the moment.'

'Give her time.' Lachlan moved from where he'd been talking to Daisy and Jude, walking over to join the others and ruffling

Hannah's hair while grinning down at her. 'Poor old *Ginny*'s had the stuffing knocked out of her at the moment and, especially as she hasn't got Jonny and Billy-Jo as back up, she'll be wearing her hair shirt for some time to come.'

'But she'll be back, no doubt.' Hannah, who could never sulk for long, placed both arms round Lachlan, burying her nose into his middle, loving the feel of him, the smell of him, knowing she'd almost lost him but he was hers again, once more.

'Right,' Andrea Zaitsev said, joining the others with a glass in his hand. 'A drink, I think, to send Jet Set diamond on her way back home…' He smiled as glasses and cups were raised. 'And another for new bambino on *her* way…' Andrea turned to Rosa and Joe. 'But also, to lovely Eva who is keeping me here at Heatherly Hall because I just cannot be without her.'

'The Quinn triplets.' Lachlan raised a glass. 'The gorgeous Girls of Heatherly Hall.'

# Acknowledgements

The idea for *A Wedding at Heatherly Hall* – I'd originally intended naming it The Jet Set of Heatherly Hall – came to me on a visit to an exhibition of Stonehenge at the British Library in London. One exhibit was labelled "The Jet Set" and, intrigued, wondering if way back in early history, druids were into bling and off to Saint Tropez, I read further. This Jet Set was an ancient necklace and earrings made from the famous Whitby jet and, standing there, I knew there was a third story to be written in my Vicar of Westenbury trilogy.

Thanks, as always, to my lovely agent, Anne Williams at KHLA Literary Agency, for her unstinting help, advice, friendship and loyalty.

A big thank you to all the members of the editorial team at Aria, Head of Zeus, who have helped to make all my books the best they can possibly be.

And of course, to all you wonderful readers who read my books and write such lovely things about them, a huge, heartfelt Thank You.

# About the Author

JULIE HOUSTON lives in Huddersfield, West Yorkshire and is the author of thirteen Women's Contemporary novels. She is married, with two adult children who've flown both the nest and their roots to live in London, leaving her with a very aged, but incredibly sprightly, Cockapoo. She still teaches junior aged children when the phone rings asking for cover, and sits as a magistrate in both adult and youth courts. She runs and swims because she's been told it's good for her, but would really prefer a glass of wine, a sun lounger and a jolly good book. You can contact Julie via the contact page, on Twitter or on Facebook.

X: @juliehouston2
Facebook.com/JulieHoustonauthor